CHASING
SUNSETS

CHASING SUNSETS

a cedar key novel

EVA MARIE EVERSON

Revell

a division of Baker Publishing Group
Grand Rapids, Michigan

Published by Revell
a division of Baker Publishing Group
P.O. Box 6287, Grand Rapids, MI 49516-6287
www.revellbooks.com

Printed in the United States of America

Library of Congress Cataloging-in-Publication Data
Everson, Eva Marie.
      Chasing sunsets : a Cedar Key novel / Eva Marie Everson.
          p.   cm.
      ISBN 978-0-8007-3436-7 (pbk.)
      1. Divorced mothers—Fiction. 2. Self-actualization (Psychology)—Fiction.
   3. Islands—Florida—Fiction. I. Title.
   PS3605.V47C47 2011
   813'.6—dc22   2011003209

Eva Marie Everson is represented by Wheelhouse Literary Group, www.Wheelhouse LiteraryGroup.com.

11   12   13   14   15   16   17   7   6   5   4   3   2   1

To those who have loved, lost, and loved again.

Acknowledgments

Years ago, while looking for a place to "get away and write," my author-friend Janice Elsheimer and I headed toward the west coast of Florida. We'd heard of a place called Cedar Key. A haven, we were told, for writers. I fell in love with it immediately. The stories of past glory and present beauty called out to me. And so I begin my "thank you" list with Janice. Thank you so much for daring to go the first time and for returning with me again and again.

Thank you, Kristy, for trusting me with pieces of your story and a glimpse into the world of a single mother. This isn't your story—it's the story of so many. But you inspired me to write it.

Thank you, Ramona, for reading the first pages and telling me if it "hooked" or not. Thank you, Gayle and Rene, for your willingness to read as I wrote . . . and rewrote . . . and rewrote again. Thank you, Rene, for your honesty in saying, "I don't like it," which forced me to start over, work harder, and make it happen for Kimberly and Steven . . . and the reader. Thank you to my wonderful novel group (Larry, Linda, Shellie—who read the entire manuscript!—Loyd, Craig, and

Edwina). Thank you to Christian Writers Guild Word Weavers Orlando. You be awesome! Thank you, Linda Morgan, for your medical expertise. Thank you to ACFW (American Christian Fiction Writers) for having all the answers when all I have is questions; to Nicole and Emanuel Rivera for the lovely song interpretation; and to the best freelance editorial voice I have, my daughter Jessica. And a special thanks goes to Patt Dunmire, who read when I couldn't read another word.

Thank you to the folks in Cedar Key who gave so much of their time so I could interview them. For anyone who is so inclined to now take a trip to paradise, there really is a Kona Joe's, a Dilly Dally Gally, a Tony's with its World Champion Chowder, a Coconuts, a Cook's Café, and Cedar Key Market. Some of the people are figments of my imagination, others are flesh and blood. So, thank you to Edie and Kona Joe, to Anne Graham Miller, extraordinary photographer, to Andy Bair (of the Island Hotel) who talked with me for such a long time about history and ghosts, to the good folks at Park Place who put up with me on my visits.

Of course, thank you to the team at Baker/Revell. Extraordinary editors Vicki Crumpton and Kristin Kornoelje rock!! And who could possibly rock more than my agent, Jonathan Clements? No one!

Thank you to my fans who continue to think I write good stories. I love you and appreciate you, every one!

Finally, to those who stand beside me and around me, supporting me always and in all ways: my sweet Savior—my first love—Jesus, my honey-hubby Dennis, and all those who have come from that love, one way or another.

Prologue

Last night I dreamed of Cedar Key. In my dream, I returned to the vacation home of my childhood by way of State Road 24 and our family's dark blue '79 Cadillac Fleetwood Brougham station wagon.

My father drove.

The year was 1982. I know, because in the dream, I was twelve.

My mother—looking remarkably like Princess Diana since she'd had her hair cut and highlighted as the trend demanded—sat on the passenger side of the front bench seat. From where I sat, I had a perfect side view of her. Her head lolled against the headrest; she kept her eyes closed behind large white-framed shades. After a moment, my eyes drifted from her face. I counted the odd-shaped freckles that danced across her tanned shoulders, exposed by a strapless floral sundress. Every so often she took in a deep breath and sighed; even in that, I thought her to be the most magnificent creature.

Mom was pregnant with my baby sister Ami, though no one knew it at the time. In my dream I knew it, in that ethereal way one has of knowing those kinds of things.

My sister Jayme-Leigh, whose nose was stuck so far into a book it was a wonder she didn't just fall right in, rode between our youngest sister, Heather, and me. At the backseat passenger's window, Heather's face turned upward toward the afternoon sun to ward off car sickness. She held tight to her Cabbage Patch doll. Her lips were moving in perfect time to the lyrics of the Lionel Ritchie tune playing on the radio; anything to keep from throwing up. I tried to make out the song, but in my dream it was oddly distorted.

Such is the way of dreams.

"We're nearly there, girls," Dad said, as he always did when we neared the road leading to our waterfront property.

Mom's eyes opened on cue. She pulled her shades down to the tip of her pixie nose, turned toward the three of us, and said, "All right, pets. Let's get our stuff together. No need scrambling when we get there." She shifted to face the front again, and when her eyes locked with mine, she winked. "Did you bring your camera?" she asked.

I nodded.

Soon enough the car rolled up to the house, which was elevated by cypress boards and veiled behind the dripping moss of a dozen ancient live oaks. Dad slid the gearshift to park. Four doors opened simultaneously, and we tumbled out. Within seconds I could taste sweat on my upper lip, could feel it beading in my armpits. Mom went to the back of the car, gently dictating orders of who was to carry what to the house, while Dad, keys rattling between his fingers, took heavy steps toward the front door.

Heather was the first to ask when we could go swimming. Mom, as she always did, reminded us that suitcases had to be unpacked and groceries put away. We hurried—my sisters and me—as fast as we could at twelve, eleven, and eight, our feet barely skimming the gleaming pine floors as we scampered for our shared bedroom. Suitcases were emptied, closets and drawers were filled, swimsuits were donned, and then, like horses being set free from the barn, we barreled down the narrow z-shaped outdoor staircase. I quickly spied Dad sitting in one of the Adirondack chairs on the cement platform near the water's edge and raced to reach him first. Hearing my arrival, he turned his handsome face—cast in shades of bronze by the sun, which had begun to dip toward the marshy horizon—and smiled. "There's nothing like this, Kimberly-Boo," he said, using the name by which he'd called me my whole life. "Not a place in the world like Cedar Key."

I squared my shoulders. "How do I look, Dad?" I asked. "Do you like my new bathing suit? Mom bought it for me at Burdines."

Before he could answer, Jayme-Leigh and Heather were with us, both breathing hard. "Why do you always have to do that?" Jayme-Leigh asked me. "You always have to get to Dad first. Like he's some race you're trying to win."

"I do not," I said.

"You do," she insisted just as Dad said, "Girls, are we going to the city park or are we going to stand here and argue?" The city park was Cedar Key's public beach area.

Heather slipped her hand into Dad's and squinted up at him, her white-blonde ringlets already damp from perspiration. Magically, we were then standing in the Gulf of Mexico, sun shimmering atop its water like crushed diamonds on glass. Seagulls flew overhead, cawing to each other, and Dad sat in a lawn chair along the shoreline. He now wore bathing trunks without a shirt. Bronze skin and chest hair glistened under suntan oil.

"Dad!" I called out. "Come in the water with me!"

He answered with a chuckle then pointed to the medical journal he'd been reading. "You play," he said. "I've got some reading to do."

"I'm going to stand on my hands underwater," I said, undeterred. "Watch me, okay?" I physically prepared myself for the balancing act by putting my feet together and arching my spine. "Dad? Okay?"

Just then the sound of a boat's motor interrupted my persistence. I turned toward the roar. It was Mr. Granger—Steven's dad—returning to the nearby dock with another group of tourists on board. Thirteen-year-old Steven stood next to his father. He wore frayed cutoff jeans and a light blue tee with Granger Tours written in large letters displayed in an arc across his chest.

Seeing me, he waved.

I waved back, a little too anxiously, though maybe not for a twelve-year-old. In doing so, my foot slipped from the grainy Gulf floor beneath . . .

. . . and in the early morning hours, in the master bedroom of my Glenmuir Mediterranean-style home, I fell out of bed.

1

The Juvenile and Family Courthouse is cold, no matter the time of year. And it always smells the same, like heartache and justice, wood polish and sweat, leather and lace. The effect it has on me, from the moment I turn down the long stretch of road leading to the white brick building, never changes. My stomach clenches, then flips. I break into a cold sweat. My head spins.

Today was no different. I pulled my four-year-old white Honda CR-V into the parking area, my eyes scanning for an empty space and, at the same time, my ex-husband's sparkling new Jaguar XJL. Supercharged and gun-metal gray. I was unsure as to whether I hoped he would be there before me or not, but when his car was nowhere in sight, I felt instant relief.

I parked under the shade of a blooming pink crepe myrtle, turned off the car, took a deep breath, and sighed. "God be with me," I said out loud. I gave my watch a quick glance. It was nearly 1:30 in the afternoon; our hearing was set for 2:00.

Set for 2:00, but experience told me we could be sitting there for several uncomfortable hours before our case was called. I reached over the console for the short stack of manila folders I brought with me, each one meticulously labeled.

DIVORCE PAPERS

CHILD SUPPORT

CORRESPONDENCE/CHARLIE AND KIDS

CORRESPONDENCE/CHARLIE AND ME

EVIDENCE OBTAINED BY C. JEFFERSON

A tapping at my window startled me, and I jumped. I turned toward the noise as I pressed my hand against my chest. "Heather!" I let out a breath. "You nearly scared me to death."

My younger sister stood bent over at the waist, her pretty face just inches from mine, separated only by the window glass. She smiled, even as her brow furrowed. "Are you okay?"

I opened the car door. "I am now." I returned the smile as I swung my legs toward the asphalt. "You're here."

"Where else would I be?" She wrapped me in one of her delicious hugs as soon as I stood. "You're my big sister and you need someone to be here with you. So, here I am."

I hugged back then pulled away. "I can always count on you."

Unlike my relationship with Jayme-Leigh, Heather and I shared a bond like that of twins. We understood each other's needs, sometimes even before we knew them ourselves. And, other than always being right about everything, she was so easy to get along with. Her laughter came effortlessly, her close-set blue eyes sparkling. Always.

Sometimes a tad too much. I closed my car door. "What are the kids up to?" I opened the back door to retrieve the matching jacket to the flared floral skirt I'd chosen for the hearing.

"Swim practice. It never ends, even when school is out." She tossed her head. Her white-blonde curls, which refused to be tamed, even when clipped at the back of her head, shimmered in the harsh Florida sunlight. "But don't worry about the time; now that Toni and Tyler are old enough to drive, my role as Mommy is dwindling."

We walked toward the courthouse. "What does that mean?" I asked.

Heather shrugged. "Nothing." I thought I detected a choking in her voice. "Just that with the twins at seventeen and Lenny at fifteen, there's not much they need from me these days."

"Other than cooking their meals, washing their clothes, picking up after them, making sure they're home by curfew . . . other than that?"

Heather looped her arm with mine. "You'll know soon enough, Kimberly-Boo," she said. "Chase is fourteen already, and with Cody being—what?—eleven, pretty soon the three of you will be ships passing in the night."

We ascended the courthouse steps as I said, "But doesn't this give you more time with Andre?"

My sister snorted, an annoying habit she's had her whole life. "He's always so busy putting in those long hours at the drugstore . . . at least that's where he says he is."

My brother-in-law Andre has worked as a pharmacist for CVS "since it was Eckerd," as he puts it. While I was sure it was true his hours were demanding, I was equally as positive some of his time spent away from home was to avoid a sometimes overly clinging wife. "I'm sure he is exactly where he says he is," I said just as we reached the double glass doors, which I opened for us.

15

Heather stepped in ahead of me. Viewing her from the back—and her dressed in a floral sundress, odd-shaped freckles splayed across her shoulders—I was reminded of the dream I'd had the night before. I felt an emptiness fall from the middle of my throat to my stomach, missing Mom again more than I thought possible.

Of all us girls—Jayme-Leigh, Heather, Ami, and me—Heather looked the most like Mom. We all had Mom's square jaw, china-doll lips, and blonde hair. Ami had more of Dad's oval face and dark features. In recent years, Jayme-Leigh had taken to dying her hair auburn because—she said recently during a family dinner—as a pediatrician, she was taken more seriously.

That comment caused me to frown. After all, I'm not only blonde, I'm an educated schoolteacher.

"So what does that make me?" Heather had asked across the great length of my mother's dining room table with our father at the head and our stepmother sitting properly at the other end. Quiet and reserved, Anise closed her eyes and shook her head so slightly I wondered if anyone other than me even noticed it.

Baited for a fight, Jayme-Leigh merely blinked and raised her brow. "Exactly what you are, Heather. A homemaker. And before you start something, I'm not belittling your role within your family." She looked over at Andre, whose broccoli-filled fork was suspended between his plate and his O-shaped mouth. "I'm sure Andre and the kids would be lost without you."

"Why is it," Heather now said as she dropped her purse onto the belt of the security scanner, "that I always feel the family is trying to convince me of Andre's undying loyalty or my children's need for me?" At the direction of the pretty but stoic-faced police officer on the other side of the metal detector, she walked forward.

I gave a smile to the officer standing at the head of the x-ray scanner as I dropped my purse, my jacket, and my files onto the conveyor belt. "How are you today?" I asked him.

"Good," he said, not smiling. "And you?"

"Good, thank you." I gave a glance to the officer sitting at the monitor. He looked to be all of twenty-one. Dedicated, his eyes never left the screen.

I followed my sister's steps through the metal detector. It went off.

"Step back through, ma'am," the officer on the other side of the metal detector said. Her face continued to reflect her no-nonsense attitude.

My shoulders drooped, but I dutifully went back through. The officer at the head of the belt said, "It may be your shoes."

I looked down at the black linen strapped wedge sandals I'd worn in hopes of looking a little less like a teacher and a little more like a *serious* mother. Whatever that meant. I slipped off the shoes, placed them in a small tray on the conveyor belt, and stepped back through. This time I didn't set off any alarms.

Minutes later, Heather and I sat side by side on a hard bench near Hearing Room 102S. From our position, which I had purposefully chosen, we had a perfect view of the front door. My body temperature had already started to drop; I eased my arms into my jacket just as the front door swung open, letting in a blast of hot air and blinding sunshine . . . and Charlie. All six-foot-three of him.

"Well, there he is," Heather said under her breath. "Mr. Suave and Sophisticated himself."

I watched numbly as he casually dipped his tanned hands

into the pockets of his khaki chinos. Ralph Lauren, I'd wager. He swore by Ralph Lauren. He drew out the contents and placed them in a bowl on the conveyor belt. His wallet and brown leather belt followed. All the while he conversed with the same officer I'd briefly chatted with earlier. To look at them, one would have thought them old chums. Yet I knew the chances were slim they'd ever seen each other outside of this courthouse.

Charlie stepped through the metal detector but not before sharing a chuckle with both the officer at the head of the conveyor and the one viewing the monitor. Even the stoic-faced officer on the other side seemed to be in on the little joke.

I absentmindedly chewed on my bottom lip. Beside me, Heather was adding her two cents, but I couldn't make out a single word she said.

The metal detector sounded in alarm.

Charlie smiled, only one side of his mouth going up as he looked down at the officer who I could see was smiling up at him.

"My gosh, he's a charmer," Heather said.

This I heard. Like I needed to.

"I know."

"Even gray hair looks good on him."

"More silver than gray."

"What did he do, have one of those tans you paint on?"

I started to laugh, then muffled it. Charlie returned through the detector, removed a large gold link bracelet previously hidden by a starched long-sleeved white shirt. This time the alarm didn't go off.

"Who wears long sleeves in this heat?" Heather said.

I looked at my arms cloaked by my jacket. "He knows

how cold it can get in here." I glanced at her bare shoulders. "You'll be freezing before you leave here."

She shook her head. "I'm never cold. I think I'm going through the change already."

I didn't comment. I couldn't. I could only stare at the man I'd once pledged my life and undying love to. He slid his belt through the loops of his pants, adjusted the waist along his narrow hips.

Oh, Lord . . . why does he still have to look so good to me?

"Would you stop staring at him?" Heather chided. "You act like a timid sophomore ogling the senior quarterback."

I pulled my eyes away from Charlie and to my sister. She was right. I was acting like a schoolgirl. "I could shoot him for looking so good," I said.

"How much weight would you say he's lost?" Her eyes followed him as he walked to the other side of the narrow waiting area.

"Twenty-three pounds exactly." I looked at Heather, who had turned her attention to me. "I know because he told Cody, who made it a big point to tell me."

Heather pulled her eyes away from mine and back to Charlie. "Not to say that he couldn't have stood to lose a few pounds. Your good cooking had fattened him up. Nothing wrong with that . . ." Her voice trailed in the mix of courthouse chatter. "I thought you told me you didn't need an attorney for this."

"We don't," I said. "We're just seeing a general magistrate."

"Then who is Charlie talking with? Isn't that his attorney?"

I swung my head around to face the other side of the room. Sure enough, Charlie's ruthless attorney stood next to him with his wheeled catalogue case at his feet. "Alex Jansen," I whispered. I looked at Heather. "My attorney said this was going to be easy. All I had to do was express to the G.M. what the children have told me, show some of Charlie's emails between him and the kids and him and me, present the evidence of the private detective I hired, and ask that his visitation this summer come with stipulations."

"Stipulations? Personally, I'd ask that the court never let him see them again."

My mouth gaped. "I'm not trying to keep him from his children, Heather," I said. "I'm simply asking the court to remind him that he should keep his partying to the times when the kids aren't with him. He's setting a bad example of adulthood. One we promised we'd never set for the boys." Of course, we'd promised a whole lot of other things Charlie had conveniently forgotten.

Heather opened her mouth in rebuttal, then closed it. Her attention shifted to the doors again. "What is *she* doing here?" she said when she found her voice.

I looked over. Anise was stepping up to the security conveyor.

"She volunteered," I said, keeping my eyes on the forty-nine-year-old gentle beauty who'd captured our father's heart. Their marriage had done as much to shake the core of our family as our mother's passing only a few months before their nuptials. "I couldn't hurt her feelings and say no."

"I could have." Heather's shoulders squared, and she pressed them against the wall behind her.

When Anise spotted us, she smiled, then cut her eyes over to where Charlie stood watching her. Almost imperceptibly, she held up a finger as if to ask us to wait one minute, then stepped to our right, walking toward Charlie and Mr. Jansen.

Heather sighed so loudly I expected the front doors to blow open from the inside out.

"Shhhh," I said.

"What does she think she's doing?"

The question was rhetorical. Anise was not the kind of person to draw lines in the sand. Family was family, no matter what. Charlie, in Anise's way of thinking, was the father of two of her step-grandchildren.

Her *grand*children. Neither Chase nor Cody remembered my mother, their biological grandmother. Anise had bestowed as much love on my sons as she did everyone she came into contact with. While Heather would never fully forgive Dad for his hasty marriage to Anise, I couldn't fault him. Her gentleness was, in many ways, an exact replica of Mom's. And, while Mom had been a stunning beauty, Anise's loveliness was earthy.

I watched now as Anise reached Charlie. He cupped his hands around her upper arms; she rested hers under his elbows. They exchanged the briefest of hugs, a kiss on the cheek, then drew back. I watched as they spoke . . . as Alex Jansen looked on, concern flashing across the sharp features of his face. But then Anise turned to Alex, extended her hand in introduction, and I smiled in spite of myself as the shadow from his face lifted. He, too, now smiled easily. His shoulders fell in defenselessness.

Heather continued to grunt.

"Heather, hush." I looked at her. "I don't need any problems here." I could sense more than see Anise coming toward me, so I turned to greet her with a smile I knew she'd return. She moved like a ballet dancer, feet shod in flat slippers, the hem of her full olive green linen skirt flowing along her calves. She wore a long-sleeved, pin-striped cotton blouse barely visible behind an oversized shawl. A gold collar pin winked in the filtered sunlight.

When she reached us, I stood. Heather remained seated.

Anise hugged me in the same manner as she had Charlie. She whispered, "You look marvelous. Strong and sure of yourself."

I stepped back as Anise peered around me. "Heather," she said. "Hello."

"Hi, Anise." At that Heather stood. "I have to find the little girls' room." She looked around as if she actually needed to go. "Any idea where it is?"

I sighed. "It's exactly where it was the last time you were here, Heather," I said. I nodded toward Charlie. "It's that door just past where Charlie and Mr. Jansen are standing."

Heather swiveled toward me as she took her first steps. "I guess I'll have to make nice talk with Charlie." Her dramatic flare was almost comical.

When she was no longer in earshot, Anise said, "I've blown it with her again."

I returned to my seat, and she took Heather's place. "Don't worry about her."

"I've tried so hard to be her friend but . . ." Anise raised her delicate hands, then dropped them back into her lap. They lay cupped together as though one supported the other.

"I know." It was all I knew to say. At forty-nine—only eight years older than me, and twelve years older than Heather—she certainly *could* have been one of our peers. While I do admit to having been shocked by Dad's sudden marriage, I wanted him happy. While two emotions conflicted within me, I eventually allowed the latter to win. Heather had not. Jayme-Leigh remained much too wrapped up in her own life to share any opinions. Although, I reasoned, her pediatric practice *was* in Dad's office. She had more reason to stay neutral than the rest of us. Ami, the baby, was in her mid-teens when Mom died. Anise became the healing balm she needed, filling every gap Mom left behind. Back then, Ami was showing extraordinary talent as a ballet dancer. Anise—though not nearly as gifted—had spent the better part of her childhood in a dance studio. This gave them a common ground on which to build a lasting foundation.

The heavy double doors leading to the courtroom opened. A commanding bailiff stood in the gap, clipboard in hand. "Klein," he bellowed. "Anyone here for Klein? We're ready to get started." Then he looked around at the mass of others waiting for their legal fate as a handful of people walked slowly toward the courtroom. "Be with the rest of you shortly. Just sit tight."

I blew a pent-up breath from the deepest part of my lungs. My chest actually hurt.

"Are you all right?" Anise's hand came to rest on mine. "You're trembling."

"Yeah," I answered. "It's just that . . ." I looked at my hands and then to Anise. "Yesterday I received papers that Charlie is countersuing me."

Anise's face showed concern. "For what?"

"Spring break."

"You mean, them not going to his place?"

I nodded as I pressed my lips together. "If Charlie asks for that time back, that will mean him getting the kids five weeks instead of four." I closed my eyes and tried to imagine. My sons. Away from me for thirty-five long days. Twenty-eight days was bad enough.

Anise patted my shoulder. "Don't worry about it. Just tell the truth about what happened."

But I couldn't help myself. Unwillingly, I allowed my eyes to trail the length of the room, along the pattern of the marble floor, to Charlie's polished shoes. I raised my eyes up the height of him, focusing briefly on the narrowing of his hips and waist, knowing with a wife's familiarity the once-before and now-again rock hard abs beneath the crisp white shirt. When my eyes found his face, I jumped. He was looking directly at me.

But his eyes held not one of the emotions of the kind and loving man I'd married. These were the cold, distant eyes of the man I had divorced.

2

It was nearly 4:00 before our name was called.

"Tucker," the bailiff bellowed.

I sucked in my breath as I always did in these moments, then reached for my files and purse I'd placed on the bench beside me. *Father, be with me*, I prayed. *But no matter what happens, I trust you.*

We walked into what had become a familiar place. The red carpet, the maple furniture. The high ceilings, the stark white walls. The blinds at the windows, blocking the outside sunshine. The general magistrate's "bench" where large books and stacks of papers and files were scattered in disarray. The polished but worn spectator benches behind the petitioner and respondent's tables, which were separated by a podium.

It had become almost too familiar.

Two judicial assistants and two police officers were in place, waiting to begin. Being the first to enter, I walked to the far table, placed my files on it, and looked for the general magistrate. I had asked for G.M. Lane. She always played fair in her courtroom by keeping calm control over cases—family cases and those involving children being the worse for rages or outbursts of violence—and she was a mother. The other times I'd had to come before her—both concerning Charlie's failure to pay his child support in a timely fashion—she had cautioned us about our attitudes toward each other. She reminded us that we were *both* parents to our wonderful sons. She told me how lucky I was to receive any child support at all, then warned Charlie about playing the "oops-I-forgot" game.

"I won't play those games with you, Mr. Tucker," she had said, expressing her ruling in a thick Caribbean brogue. Her honey brown skin looked radiant under the fluorescent lighting, and the rows of braids shimmied as she spoke.

I looked forward to seeing her again. Just knowing she was sitting in front of us would calm me, I knew.

Charlie was taking his place, and his attorney beside him. I looked over my shoulder to see Anise and Heather sitting together but not close. Anise's eyes were closed, and I knew she was praying. My stepmother lived her faith quietly, but there had never been any doubt of its strength within her.

A side door opened—the door leading to the general magistrate's office—and I turned my attention to the front with a smile. But instead of the expected G.M. Lane, G.M. McPherson stepped out.

I bit my bottom lip and sucked it into my mouth. This was not good.

I looked over at Charlie, who gloated as he peered back at me. He knew as well as I did that McPherson always sided with the fathers.

One of the young judicial assistants, dressed Florida casual, stood as the general magistrate sat, robes billowing around his paunchy frame. "Stand for the oath, please," she said.

Charlie and I stood.

"Please raise your right hand . . ." She waited as we complied. "Do you solemnly swear or affirm that the testimony you shall give will be the truth, the whole truth, and nothing but the truth, so help you God?"

The words were spoken rapidly, but we knew what they were. What they meant.

"I do," I said, hearing Charlie say the same beside me.

"Go ahead and be seated, please," Mr. McPherson said. "I'm sure you are both aware that Ms. Lane was to be on the bench this afternoon. She's been called away on a family emergency, and I have been asked to sit in on her cases." He smiled—a Cheshire cat grin cutting into fleshy cheeks—while I groaned inwardly. "I hope you don't mind."

"Not at all, sir," Charlie said.

I remained silent. *I trust you, Lord.*

Mr. McPherson looked down at the papers before him. "This is a case of Kimberly Claybourne Tucker versus Charles Samuel Tucker, case number one-zero-zero-zero-fourteen-sixty-seven." He looked up. "Mr. Jansen, are you here to represent Mr. Tucker?"

"I'm here if he needs me, sir."

His eyes shifted to me. "And you are without representation, Ms. Tucker?"

"I . . ." I cleared my throat. "I was told I wouldn't need representation."

My voice scarcely sounded like my own.

His eyes widened. "All right, then." Another look at the paperwork before him and he continued, "This matter of contempt was filed by the petitioner, Ms. Tucker, on May 13th . . ." I tried to hear the words, each one, and to not focus on Charlie sitting so close to me, smelling like expensive department store cologne, looking better than he had in years. Why did this man, who'd hurt me so bad, have such an effect on me? Still.

Stop it, Kim.

I blinked, determined. ". . . notice was sent to Mr. Tucker . . ." The words of the general magistrate jarred me back into the courtroom. I blinked toward Mr. McPherson, who looked at Charlie. ". . . and he is present." He shuffled the papers of our file together, clasped his hands, and continued. "The parties have been sworn. Ms. Tucker, you may proceed."

I glimpsed at the files I'd placed on my table. "Your honor," I said, "the defendant and I divorced a little over a year ago. Since that time I have had to come back to this courtroom three times because Cha—Mr. Tucker got behind on the ordered child support."

"Your honor," Mr. Jansen said. I turned to see him shift in his seat. "The issue of child support is not why we are here this afternoon and is not relevant."

"He's right, Ms. Tucker. Unless you brought that issue up in the contempt forms, you'll have to stay away from that topic."

I felt my cheeks flame. "Yes, sir." I cleared my throat. "The reason I'm here today is that my husband is awarded four weeks of the children's summer break, beginning May 31st of this year. In our divorce papers—which I have here—we were ordered that if we—Charlie *or* I—started dating other people, we would not do anything in front of the children that would be deemed improper." I extended a copy of our divorce settlement to the bailiff, who in turn handed it to Mr. McPherson.

"All right," he said. I was silent as he took a moment to study the paperwork. "Continue."

"Recently," I continued, pulling a paper from the file

marked E<small>VIDENCE</small> O<small>BTAINED BY</small> C. J<small>EFFERSON</small>, "our oldest son came home from a weekend visit, telling me—"

"Hearsay," Mr. Jansen barked.

"Don't tell me what someone else has said, Ms. Tucker," Mr. McPherson warned.

My shoulders slumped. "What if I have proof?"

"What kind of proof?"

I slipped the folder C<small>ORRESPONDENCE</small>/C<small>HARLIE AND</small> K<small>IDS</small> out from under the file marked C<small>ORRESPONDENCE</small>/C<small>HARLIE</small> <small>AND</small> M<small>E</small>. "I have an email between Chase—our son—and his father."

"Your honor," Mr. Jansen said. "I'd like to see that, please."

Mr. McPherson looked at Mr. Jansen so fast, his jowls quivered. "When I'm done, Mr. Jansen."

I handed the copy of Chase and Charlie's correspondence to the bailiff.

"As you can see, our son emailed his father voicing his concern about his father's extracurricular activities while he and his brother are with their dad. He told his father he was uncomfortable seeing his father with one girl during one weekend visit and another girl the next."

I heard Charlie snort.

How dare he?

"He also voiced his concern that his father often goes out during their weekend visits, leaving the boys with his parents—their grandparents—and that he doesn't return until the early hours the next day."

Mr. Jansen, who had been passed the email, interrupted. "Your honor . . ."

"Hold on, Mr. Jansen. When you are talking—if you are talking—I won't allow her to disrupt you." He looked at me again. "Go ahead, please."

I pulled another piece of paper from my files. "This is an email from my ex-husband to Chase, expressing his concern that our son feels that he can dictate to him what he can or cannot do as an adult."

"I can appreciate that," the general magistrate said.

I paused, then reached into a new file as the bailiff returned the correspondence between Charlie and Chase. "This is an email to Mr. Tucker from me," I said, "in which I tell him that Chase had come to me about the emails he and his father had exchanged. In this email"—the bailiff took the paper from my extended hand—"I remind Charlie—Mr. Tucker—that our divorce agreement states we are not to do anything in front of the children—"

"Yes, yes," Mr. McPherson cut in. "You mentioned this. Ms. Tucker, tell me, what do you deem improper? Because from where I'm sitting, simply dating doesn't seem improper."

It was a question I had not expected. "Well . . . I . . . I think that when the boys—Chase and Cody—are with their father, he can forgo his little . . . escapades."

Charlie moved beside me. "Oh, come on . . ."

I turned in time to see Mr. Jansen place a hand on Charlie's arm. Client looked at attorney, who shook his head, demanding compliance.

Mr. McPherson said, "Mr. Jansen . . ."

"It's okay, sir. My client apologizes."

Mr. McPherson turned his attention back to me. "Is that what you are here to ask, Ms. Tucker?" He held up one of the papers I'd handed to his bailiff. "I have a very vague order here in a divorce decree. What is an escapade to one is nothing more than a date to another. Do you see the problem I have with this?"

I straightened my back. "Yes, your honor, but don't you think some things are obvious?"

"Like what, Ms. Tucker? The boys are going to their grand-parents' while your ex-husband is out on a date. Is there anything I need to know about your ex-in-laws? Are they dangerous criminals?"

Charlie's parents were Ozzie and Harriett. Ward and June. Jim and Margaret. Good Christian people—owners of a landscape design nursery—who had worked hard to rear a decent family and who didn't deserve anything negative even being hinted about them. I'd not previously discussed any of this with them. I felt that—with Charlie being their son—their allegiance would naturally fall to him.

"Of course not," I said.

Mr. McPherson turned to Charlie. "Mr. Tucker, are you bringing women into your home, exposing your sons to any type of sexual conduct or misconduct?"

I looked at Charlie, who was looking straight at me. Without batting an eyelash he said, "Of course not." He returned his gaze to the G.M. "Your honor, I love my sons." He swallowed. "You mentioned my folks. They're good people. They've worked hard to build a family business and to rear three sons who work equally as hard. They taught us Christian values, and I want to pass those along to my boys just as they did to my brothers and me."

I furrowed my brow then opened the final file on my table. Facing Mr. McPherson, I said, "Sir, not to take away from his parents—who are fine people—but I have hired a private investigator who reports that Mr. Tucker goes out a lot, drinking in different bars, leaving with different women . . ." I opened my mouth to continue but nothing more came out.

"Ms. Tucker," the G.M. said, "could it be that you still have feelings for your ex-husband and what this is really about is that while you don't want him, you don't want anyone else to, either?"

Again, I fell silent, stunned. Tears stung my eyes. I tried to focus on Charlie, then Mr. McPherson, and then Charlie again. "No, sir," I said, keeping my voice steady. "Any feelings . . . any *love* . . . I ever had for Charlie died when he told me he was having an affair." I swallowed again. "The day I begged for counseling and he asked for a divorce."

3

"Ms. Tucker," Mr. McPherson droned, "allow me to stop you and tell you what I think."

I immediately became silent.

"What I think we have here is jealousy in its pure and simple form."

I opened my mouth to protest, but the G.M. raised his hand to stop me. "Don't say anything else, Ms. Tucker. I have the floor now." He looked at the papers before him again and then back at me and Charlie. "The two of you are adults—at least I presume you are—and you are the loving parents—which is obvious—of two fine boys. Ms. Tucker, your husband asked for a divorce, which you clearly did not want." He tapped the papers. "But it seems you didn't get your way on that. So now you want control over your ex-husband's whereabouts. What he does and who he does it with. Should I presume you haven't dated since the divorce?"

My face grew hot. I blinked and willed myself not to cry. Date? Who had time to date with a full-time teaching job, two active sons, a large home to keep up, family who demanded so much time. If weekdays were about work and the boys, weekends were about the house, family, and church. Besides, every male I knew was a pal of Charlie's; none of them were about to ask me out. "No, I haven't dated anyone," I answered.

"Well . . . I think your boys will be just fine with their father during his visitation with them." He looked at Charlie. "But, Mr. Tucker, I should warn you; these boys are obviously old enough to spill the beans on you and old enough to be molded by what you do. Remember that you do have influence over the character they'll develop in this life. Make your time with them about them, okay?"

"Yes, sir."

"You understand what I'm getting at?"

"Absolutely, sir." Charlie's voice didn't quiver at all. I dared to look at him again. His jaw was firmly set.

"Your honor," Mr. Jansen interrupted, "we'd like to bring up the matter of the countersuit."

The general magistrate looked from Mr. Jansen to his bailiff, who reached over the expanse of the desk and pointed. Mr. McPherson's eyes followed the bailiff's finger, then he picked up a fresh sheet of paper. "What is this about?" He sounded exasperated; I hoped that would be to my benefit.

"If I may," Charlie began, "my ex-wife managed to keep the boys from me during this past spring break vacation. I'm asking that the week I lost be tacked on to my time with my sons during summer break."

Mr. McPherson looked at me. "What do you have to say about this?"

I placed my hands on the table and leaned forward. "Our sons told their father they didn't want to go with him for the week. They had an opportunity to go with my father and stepmother to Cedar Key—they have a house there—and when they asked their dad, he okayed it."

"Mr. Tucker?"

"That's not entirely true, your honor. The boys talked to me about it, but I never said it was okay. If they told their mother that, then I guess I'll have to have a little talk with my sons."

"Charlie," I blurted.

"Ms. Tucker . . ."

From behind me I heard Anise's gentle shushing, like a mother calming her child.

I quieted my mouth and my heart as best I could.

"Mr. Tucker, what happened after you realized your sons would not be joining you for the week?"

Charlie leaned forward and rested his forearms against the table before him. "I called my ex-wife a number of times . . ."

I opened my mouth to protest but refrained.

"I drove past the house, but I didn't see my wife's car. I even tried to call Chase on his cell phone, but it always went straight to voice mail. Of course, once I found out that he was in Cedar Key it made sense. Cell service isn't always good there."

"Your honor, my ex-husband most assuredly *did* tell our sons that they could go. Our sons are not liars, and I resent the implication that they are."

"Ms. Tucker, I think we both know that children will tell tall tales to get what they want."

"Not my sons."

"Spoken like a true mother. Now, what about Mr. Tucker's implication that he tried to call you?"

"If he did, my phone never rang. Well, I mean my phone rang, but I have caller ID, and I didn't see any evidence of him calling the house."

"I called your cell," Charlie said.

35

I looked at him and then back to the general magistrate. "Or my cell phone."

"It was always off. You can't say your phone registers calls when it's off. Your phone is just like mine, remember? And I know mine doesn't."

"Then why didn't you leave a message? Or call the house?"

"Ms. Tucker . . ."

"I'm sorry, sir. This is the kind of thing he is notorious for doing."

Charlie chuckled quietly beside me. "Notorious . . ."

"Mr. Tucker, keep your comments to yourself, please."

I turned back to see Charlie's reaction. Mr. Jansen's look warned Charlie to be quiet. Charlie nodded.

"Now, Mr. Tucker, what do you say to this?"

Charlie raised his hands, then dropped them. "I'm sorry, your honor. I didn't leave a message because I was married to my wife for sixteen years—my ex-wife, excuse me—and I know her." He looked at me, then quietly added, "Probably better than she knows herself. She turns off her phone so she can say there was no communication thereby keeping herself innocent in all this."

I shook my head. I knew this tactic and I knew it well. He attempted to show the G.M. his tender side. That he loved me. Or had loved me very much at one time. As I had loved him.

"As for the house, like I said, I drove by and didn't see her car in the driveway so I assumed she was with the boys and her parents."

"My car . . ." I started to say to Charlie, then turned to the front. "My car was in the garage, your honor."

"Mr. Tucker?"

Again Charlie raised his hands and dropped them. "We always parked in the driveway."

"Before the divorce, yes. After, no. With Mr. Tucker's stuff gone—which took up every square foot of space in the garage—I am now able to park in the garage."

"All right," Mr. McPherson said. "I'm ready to rule on this. Mr. Tucker, would you like to make up the time you lost?"

"I would, sir."

"All right, then. Ms. Tucker, I am ruling on behalf of Mr. Tucker on this issue."

I felt my heart sink to my stomach, my legs turn to rubber.

"Mr. Tucker, when does your summer visitation begin?"

"Next Monday, your honor."

"Then let the record show we are extending his four weeks to five beginning next Monday, May 31st, and concluding . . ." He looked at his assistant.

"Five weeks is Monday the 5th of July."

Mr. McPherson looked at Charlie. "Bring them home on Sunday evening, typically?"

"Yes, sir, 6:00. But that's the fourth and a holiday."

"Then we'll make it Monday the 5th at 6:00. And Mr. Tucker, I do not want to hear that you spent these weeks with women while your boys spent time with your parents. Spend the time with your sons, you hear me? This time is precious, and believe me, it'll be over soon enough."

"Yes, sir."

"Ms. Tucker, I take it you won't try anything to keep him from his sons."

I started to protest. I'd not done that . . . *ever*. But to say so would only be spouting words into the air. I merely shook my head.

"Court is dismissed then. You are free to leave."

Forty minutes after my being sworn in, Heather, Anise, and I stood by Anise's car—a glacier pearl Nissan Murano—staring at one another as though in shock. I pretended not to notice when Charlie and Mr. Jansen walked across the parking lot, Charlie strutting like a peacock to his car, which he'd parked right next to mine. I kept my eyes focused on a crepe myrtle, though peripherally I could see all I needed to. I heard the chirp-chirp of the car's alarm system being deactivated and the car door click open.

"Tell my sons I'll call them later tonight," he called out.

I turned my face from the sound of his voice, my chin to my shoulder. "Oh, God," I whispered to the asphalt below my feet. "How could this have happened?"

Heather cleared her throat, and I looked at her just in time to hear Charlie's car purring to life. "What?" I asked, the word barely making it past the knot in my throat.

She looked down at her watch. "I hate to commiserate and run, but I've *got* to get back home before the kids do and . . ."

I looked at her hands. They trembled.

I nodded. "I understand. Thank you for being here." My voice cracked over my last words.

My sister wrapped her arms around me and squeezed. "It's going to be all right, you hear me? We'll spend the entire five weeks pampering ourselves. We'll go shopping and we'll lunch together. We'll lay out by my pool every day and we'll get manis and pedis once a week." She drew back, cupped my face in her still shaking fingers, and said, "And for one whole week we'll go to the beach. My treat." Then she blushed. "Well, mine and Andre's."

I nodded. Bless her for this, even though I knew it would never happen. Not all of it anyway.

"Okay, then." She leaned over and kissed the side of my mouth. "I love you. You know that, right?"

I nodded again. Then she turned, said a brisk "good-bye" to Anise, and was on her way.

I collapsed against the Murano. "What am I going to do?" I asked as the sobs overtook me.

Anise immediately took the place Heather had occupied earlier. In the arms of my sister I felt loved, but in Anise's I felt safe. "You will begin by coming to the house for dinner tonight."

I shook my head. "I can't, Anise. I can't."

Anise took me by my shoulders and shook them ever so gently. "Yes, you can. Your father insists upon it." The way she said "insists" made it sound more a command than a kind invitation.

"When did he say that?" I asked between tears.

"Earlier today. He said that no matter what happened today, he wanted you and the boys to come to dinner." She kissed the side of my head. "And so you shall." She linked her arm with mine then escorted me to my car. "Where are the boys?"

"Home, I presume. Unless they went to a friend's to play." My chest heaved several times. "Oh, Anise, how am I going to tell them?"

We'd reached the car then, and she pressed me against it as if to let go would be the worst possible thing to do. "Tell them what, Kimberly? That they'll be spending time with their father this summer?" Her gray eyes stared firmly into mine. "Charlie may not be thinking clearly, but he won't hurt them. Not physically, anyway. You talk with them before they go and be sure to speak with them after. Any emotional damage you'll just have to deal with. That sounds awful, but it's the way of it." She sighed. "Kim, you've raised them well. They're good boys. You'll see. They'll be fine." She smiled. "Besides, give Charlie enough rope, and he'll hang himself."

I blinked the final tears away from my eyes. "What do you mean?"

"I mean, if he is as much of a playboy as I suspect he is, then he'll soon grow tired of two boys underfoot."

I gave a half-smile. "True."

"I think the judge in there was pretty direct in his order that he spend five whole weeks with Chase and Cody. Now, who do you think will be more anxious for them to come home? You or him?"

And with that, I giggled, though my heart was shattering into a million fragmented pieces.

4

One thing I would say on Charlie's behalf: he'd given me remarkable sons. They were very much the image of their father, in stature and in coloring, though Cody's hair was streaked with blond, like mine. Over the years family members had teased, saying, "If you hadn't carried them, we'd be surprised to hear they were yours at all."

But they were mine. They were my heart. My reason for getting up in the morning, for going to work every day, for coming home at night. They were my reason for breathing, especially since their father had left our—at one time—perfect family.

Thinking of them, and thinking back over the sixteen years of my marriage, I wondered—I wondered *again*—what I had done wrong. Where I'd failed as a wife to Charlie.

It had all been so idyllic. We'd met at the Christmas party of a mutual friend my junior year of college. At six-three, Charlie towered over nearly everyone else in the festive and warm room. I'd noticed him immediately, and he was equally drawn to me. Or so it seemed at the time. We wondered how we could have not met each other until then, but thanked God that he'd brought us to each other when he did. During that Christmas break we were nearly inseparable. No matter where we went, our dates were spent talking. Talking about everything. I shared things that were from the deepest parts of myself. He did the same. By the time I'd returned to college, we'd met each other's families and decided to be exclusive.

At Easter, Charlie—already employed by his family business—snuck a simple one-carat diamond ring into one of the plastic eggs in the basket my mother had sentimentally placed at the foot of my bed while I slept. The next morning, Charlie joined us for breakfast before services so he'd be with me as I explored the treasures snuggled in the Easter grass. He grinned as he pointed to first one egg and then another. "What's in that one, Miss Boo?" he'd ask, using the name that always earned him a smile. "What about this one?" until finally he pointed to the egg holding the ring.

With the opening of a plastic egg, we were engaged. And then, that year when the church was decorated spectacularly for Christmas, my father escorted me down the long aisle of the First United Methodist Church where, with me in a gown fit for a princess and the two of us surrounded by family and friends, we'd pledged our lives, our love, and our loyalty, each to the other. For a lifetime.

Or so I thought.

My sons were waiting at the door leading from the garage and into the house. Their faces were expectant . . . and handsome. Our golden retriever, Max, stood between them. I opened the car door and climbed out, deciding to leave the files where they were for the time being.

"Well?" Chase said.

I forced a smile as I walked toward them. "Let's go inside, okay?"

Cody looked pensive. "Does that mean you lost?"

As if my heart could break more than it already had, it fractured one more time. I placed my hands on their shoulders and turned them toward the inside of the house. "All I want to do right now is get out of these shoes. We'll talk in my room. Deal?"

Both boys hung their heads as we rounded the corner of the hallway leading to the in-law suite and then came into the foyer. Our footsteps and Max's pawsteps echoed on the polished oak flooring and up to the high ceiling. With me between my sons, we took the stairs one at a time. "What did you two get into while I was gone?"

"I went to Jared's for a while." I looked at my son. At fourteen, Chase was beginning to show signs of manhood. Fuzz on his chin and over his lips. A deepening in his voice. Hair in the pit of his arms.

"And what about you, Cody?" I ruffled the soft, straight hair that crowned his head like a halo.

He shrugged. "Read mostly."

"Good book?"

"Yeah."

"Do you want to tell me about it?"

"Not really," he answered with a shrug.

We stepped from the curving staircase and sank into the plush carpet leading to the bedrooms and the room Charlie once used as a home office. An entire year and a few months since he left and I'd done nothing more than close its door. Anise insisted we turn it into a room where the boys could gather with their friends—especially as they got older, she said—but I wasn't sure I wanted a bunch of teenagers that close to our bedroom.

My bedroom. The master suite I'd once shared in passion with my husband. *Ex*-husband.

My sons followed me into the room I'd redecorated after Charlie's departure. Before, it had been a reflection of our lives together. Now, it was a picture of my attempt at independence. I sold the mahogany bedroom set Charlie picked out for us and replaced it with a contemporary taupe upholstered platform bed with matching dark-wood retro furniture. I pulled up the carpet and had hardwood floors laid. The only accessories were milk glass; the only framed artwork for the walls was 16-by-20 framed black-and-whites of my sons—taken by my mother at the house in Cedar Key when Chase was a toddler and Cody a newborn.

Those pictures would stay with me forever; they were her last gift to me.

My sons ran to the bed and plopped on top of it while Max found his place at the foot of the bed. He curled around himself once before plopping to the floor with a sigh. "I'll be right back," I said, then slipped into the dressing room. Minutes later I was wrapped in an ankle-length cotton robe tied off at the waist. I joined the boys in the middle of the bed and tucked my feet up under me.

"Okay," I said with a sigh. "Cody, there's no winning or losing with this."

"What does that mean?" he asked.

"It means that you boys will spend five weeks with your father this summer—"

"Five?" Chase was quick to realize an extra week had been added. "How did *that* happen?"

I wasn't about to tell my sons that their father lied in court, that the extra week was because of the spring break fiasco. If they found out, it would be from Charlie. "Well, I told the judge everything we've talked about . . . about how Dad dates when you'd rather he be hanging out with you guys," I answered. "And the judge—who is very smart—told your dad to behave and to enjoy his time with you." I closed my eyes. They burned from the stress of the day. "I'm sure," I said, opening them again, "your father has learned his lesson and will be more attentive to you from now on."

"Like before?" Cody asked. "When we all lived here as a family?"

"Yes," I said. I leaned over and kissed his soft cheek. "Like before."

Chase's shoulders slumped. "We'll never be a family . . . it'll never be like it was before."

I sat up straight. "That's not true, Chase. Your dad will always be your father. And I will always be your mother. And you and Cody will always be brothers. That makes us a family."

Cody's bottom lip trembled. "But what if Dad marries one of those girls he's always going out with? What if they have babies?"

I cupped his chin in my hand. "Don't worry, sweetheart." Quite honestly, it was all I knew to say. The idea of Charlie remarrying never occurred to me.

Chase, who was more man than boy, it seemed, slid off the bed and faced me. "So, what's the plan?"

"Well," I said, joining him. I extended my hand to Cody. "First, Mom is going to take a bath."

"Get that courtroom smell off ya?" my youngest asked.

I touched the tip of his nose with my finger. "Yes. In the meantime, you boys go wash up. We're going to Pop's and Nana's for dinner."

"Cool," Cody exclaimed.

Chase crossed his arms. "Mom, you know what I mean. When do we have to go to Dad's?"

"You *get* to go to your father's on Monday. You'll be back the 5th of July."

I watched his face as he calculated the days. Resigned, he said, "Let's go, Code."

"'Kay." Cody's shoulders slumped as he trudged toward my bedroom door. He was halfway to his room by the time Chase reached the hallway.

"Chase?" I called after him.

He turned, placed his hand on the door frame, and said, "Yeah, Mom?"

I walked the distance separating us. "Listen. The judge said that Dad isn't supposed to spend his five weeks with other women, leaving you guys with your grandparents. In other words, Dad has to be present and active in these five weeks. I figure he'll have you at work with him during the days, but the nights belong to you and Cody, you hear me?"

He nodded.

"I want you to promise me that you'll call me every chance you get. Let me know everything is going as it should, okay?"

Chase smiled as though he'd been chosen top man for a secret mission. "Got it, Mom."

The knot in my throat grew a little larger. "I love you, son."

With that, he slipped his arms around my waist—my son, who is as tall as me—and whispered, "I love you too."

Anise's meals were healthy. Fresh vegetables—deliciously prepared with proper seasoning—were practically the centerpiece of the dinner table. In the years since she married Dad, I'd never seen anything but poultry and fish on the meat platter.

And never fried.

For some reason, despite being typical boys, my sons loved eating Anise's food. If I prepared the same dishes, they would balk, but in Anise's kitchen a freshly snapped string bean was like shoestring fries. So, as soon as we arrived, they bounded toward the kitchen to see what needed to be done in final preparation.

I, on the other hand, went to my father's den, where I knew he'd be, where he'd always gone after a long day of taking care of everyone else's children. For the hour between his arriving home and the dinner meal, Dad stayed secluded in the masculine warmth of his own cave. Mom used to say he was decompressing. Heather joked that he was decomposing. I just counted the minutes until he emerged so I could feel his arms around me, his masculine strength blending with the feminine love Mom brought into every room she ever graced with her presence.

I tapped on the rich wood of the six-paneled door as I swallowed hard. "Dad?"

My father's baritone voice called out, "Come in."

I cracked the door open and peeked in. Dad sat in his favorite easy chair, legs stretched out with his stocking feet crossed at the ankles and resting on the ottoman. His reading glasses were perched on his nose. A medical journal was spread loosely by the fingertips of his hands. The years had barely touched him. Even now, with the evening sunlight streaming in from the window beside him, he looked more sixty than seventy.

He gave me his best "I heard all about it" look. I tucked my chin to my chest and slipped inside, closed the door, and leaned against it.

"Hey, Boo," he said. "Come sit."

I looked up to see him push the ottoman an inch or two forward before placing his feet on the floor.

I did as I was told.

"Anise told me what happened."

I kept my eyes on my hands. "It was brutal, Dad."

"She also said Charlie lied to the judge."

I looked up at my father. "I don't want the boys to know."

Dad leaned forward, rested his elbows on his knees. "Not telling them is the right thing to do."

I felt a couple of tears slip down my cheeks. "What I don't understand is why Charlie is so angry with me. What did I do wrong? I was a good wife. A good mother." *As perfect as you've always expected me to be. As I've always expected of myself.*

"I'm sure you were, Kimberly."

My tears fell faster. Dad pulled a handkerchief out of the back pocket of his pants and said, "There, now . . ."

"Dad." I took the handkerchief and wiped my nose. "Can you tell me something?"

My dad's soft blue eyes looked like sapphires in the room's light.

"Why do they do it, Dad? Why do men stray?"

The natural tan of his skin flushed. "Kim . . ."

"I'm not saying you would know from experience. But men talk, don't they? Like they do in high school? And these days, middle school? You know, locker room gossip."

Dad smiled at me. "I'm not sure men *gossip*, Kim. Exaggerate, yes. Gossip, no."

I wiped my nose again. "You know what I mean," I said with a half smile.

Dad cracked his knuckles, first on one hand, then the other. His shoulders were hunched, making his face look rounder, his cheeks rosier. "Boo, if you were my son, I'd answer you one way. A little more locker room talk, since you brought that up. But you are my daughter, and I'm just not sure how to answer this question. I can't imagine anything you did to cause Charlie to stray much less to give up on your marriage." He shook his head. "Your mother—God rest her soul—and I didn't always see eye-to-eye, and sometimes we fought like enemies rather than lovers, but I could have never walked out on our marriage." He looked away. His eyes shifted back and forth as though he were pondering something. When he looked back at me, he added, "Not for any reason."

I glanced out the window. When the house had been built, two years after my parents' marriage, Dad's den window provided an angular view of the street we lived on. Within a month, he'd planted a long row of sago palms that kept the view tropical without blocking the sunlight. Now, with an afternoon storm threatening to come as it always did this time of year, I watched their fronds shimmy in the warm breeze.

"I know you're thinking about a lot," Dad said. "And I want to add one more thing."

I turned back to him. "What's that?"

He stood, walked over to the antique rolltop desk against the opposite wall, and pulled open a drawer. When he returned to the chair he dangled a key from between his index and middle finger.

Not just any key, a house key.

Not just any house, the one on Florida's west coast.

"What's this?" I asked, knowing the answer full well.

"I want you to go to Cedar Key while the boys are with Charlie."

I stood. "What? Go to Cedar . . . why would I go to Cedar Key?"

49

A tap on the door brought Dad to his feet and me to swirl around to face Anise as she stuck her head in. "Dinner is almost . . . oh. I see you've told her already."

She walked in, leaving the door ajar, and crossed the room to my father. Like butter over hot toast, she slipped her arms around his waist, bringing her body close to his. He kissed her temple and said, "I only got as far as telling her I'd like for her to go."

I stepped away from the two of them and over to the bookcase where my father's priceless collection of first editions was displayed in alphabetical order, according to author. "You'd like me to go? But why? I haven't been to the house in years. Not since . . ." I couldn't finish it. Couldn't say it.

"Your mother died."

I nodded.

The kids had gone with their grandparents, but not me. There was too much of Mom there. Too many memories. Too many of her photographs.

The one thing Mom and I shared—that none of her other daughters were interested in—was photography. When she was a child, it had been the connection between her and her father, a professional photographer. The *only* thing they had in common, she told me. Mom made sure that was not the case with us.

When I was eight years old, she'd slipped a Kodak 110 in my Christmas stocking along with a package of cube-shaped flashbulbs. While the relationship between the camera and me was somewhat disastrous (I kept cutting off the very thing I was trying to photograph), Mom said I had "the eye for photography." By the time I was twelve, I was shooting with a basic .35mm, and by age fifteen I had a case full of lenses, filters, and a bulk loader for rolling my own film. While my friends participated in a variety of sports, I stood on the sidelines and photographed them. I became the official photographer for any and all high school events, which made me feel satisfied, as though I'd participated in them. Volunteering to photograph my senior prom allowed me to say no to any guy who asked me to be his date. Mom finally demanded that I at least allow my cousin—who was a year younger than me—to escort me because "no young lady should ever go to a dance unescorted."

It was their effort. Not to make sure I went to the prom with a date but that I continue to move forward after that past summer in Cedar Key.

And Steven.

"Dad," I said, breathless. "I'm just not sure I . . ."

Dad crossed his arms as Anise's arm fell from around his waist. She said, "I'll stall dinner."

She left the room.

"Tell me something, Boo." His voice was firm but kind. "What's keeping you from the beach house? You always loved it there when you were a kid."

I shook my head. "When I was a kid, yes. But really, Dad. I'm a grown woman now. What in the world would I do there all by myself, day in and day out? It's not like I'm a teenager killing time with Rosa or Heather."

Or Steven.

"Good point, but what do you plan to do in Glenmuir? What do you have planned for the long weeks the boys are with their father?"

"Well . . ." I said, pacing a few steps along the bookcase. "I thought I'd read."

"You can read in Cedar Key."

"And I thought I'd work on my lesson plans for next year."

"You can do that in Cedar Key too."

"Heather and I have talked about doing some girl things . . . you know, like manis and pedis and shopping trips."

My father raised a brow.

"Dad, why is it so important to you that I go to the coast?"

Dad looked at his feet and sighed. "Do you remember Eliana?"

"Of course I do." I smiled at the thought of the house-keeper and her raven-haired daughter. "Remember when Rosa and I pretended we were sisters as though there wasn't a difference to be found?"

Dad's eyes met mine. "There wasn't. I always taught you girls never to look down on anyone because of their station in life."

"And we haven't. Well, maybe not all of us . . ."

Dad grimaced. "Jayme-Leigh. If that girl weren't so smart and such a good doctor, I'd swear she wasn't mine." He chuckled as though only to himself.

I smiled at him. "So, back to Eliana."

"She passed away recently."

"Oh, Dad. I didn't know . . ."

"Rosa called. Her mother still went to the property every week to clean it—did you know that?"

"No."

"I've paid her year-round whether we were there or not. A house has a way of getting dusty and moldy when its owner isn't around."

I forced a smile. "So then? Why do you want me to leave mine?"

"I need to hire someone else now. I want you to take care of it for me."

I blinked. "But you and Anise go for part of the summer. Why not do it then?"

52

"There are some things I need to take care of here before I can go."

"What kind of things?"

"Work related, Kimberly. Not for you to worry about."

"If they are work related, why not let Jayme-Leigh take care of them?"

He shook his head. "These are things I have to handle, Kim." He placed his hands on his hips. "Look, sweetheart. I need you to do this for me, okay?" He sighed. "I've always been able to rely on you, haven't I?"

"Of course but . . ." I put my fists on my hips. "This really has nothing to do with Eliana, does it? It has more to do with getting me to Cedar Key. Away from here."

"Let's face it, Boo. Remember last year when the boys spent part of their summer with Charlie? You were like a caged animal. You drove us all a little crazy and yourself even more."

That much was true.

"And it's only going to be worse this year," he said.

"And you think that by doing this little thing for you—finding a replacement for Eliana—I won't worry about my sons?"

Dad shook his head. "Oh no. You'll still worry, but . . ." He winked at me. "Have you forgotten the magic of Cedar Key?"

I took several deep breaths, thought about the question, and answered it honestly within my own heart before answering my father. "Yes, Dad. I have." I looked at my sandaled feet, wiggled my toes. "But I haven't forgotten that summer. Have you?"

"No, Boo. I haven't forgotten. But maybe it's time to build some new memories." When I didn't answer, he added, "If the house goes too long without someone to keep it up, no telling what it'll look like by the time Anise and I get there in July." He sighed for added drama.

"It won't be *that* bad." We stared at each other until my resolve broke. "Okay, Dad. I'll go to Cedar Key; I'll find a replacement for Eliana. But then I'm coming straight home."

Dad chuckled as he wrapped an arm around my shoulder and steered me toward the door and dinner. "Promise me one thing, Boo."

"What's that?"

"That if you *want* to stay, you will."

I stopped long enough to kiss his cheek. "I promise, Dad. But I won't want to stay, so don't be disappointed."

Dad smiled. "We'll see. Like I said, there's magic along the marshes of Cedar Key. You just need to be reminded."

5

On the way home I told the boys we'd spend the next day doing anything they wanted. I'd barely gotten the words out of my mouth before they yelled, "Wet 'n Wild!"

I groaned. "Wouldn't you guys rather stay home? Sleep late? Go to the pool and read a good book?"

"Oh, come on, Mom," Chase said from the backseat. "You know you love Wet 'n Wild. You love anything that has to do with water."

I smiled. "It's true."

I was reminded of my father's request that I go to Cedar Key, and for a moment, I thought of the marshes, the beach, the stretch of the Gulf. Maybe it wouldn't be so bad . . .

"All right. Wet 'n Wild it is. We'll get there when it opens and leave when it shuts down. How does that sound?"

Happiness rushed from the backseat.

I spent the next day splashing and laughing with my children. When the day was over and our bodies were thoroughly sun-kissed, we headed home. The sun had nearly set, slathering the gray at the end of the day in hues of pinks and blues. I thought again of Cedar Key and its spectacular sunsets.

Of how residents and visitors gathered to watch nature's end-of-the-day show. Something deep within me—a feeling I'd long ago forgotten—stirred.

When we arrived home and I'd shut off the engine of the car, "Fun Mom" became "Just Mom."

"Okay, young men of mine. Upstairs to shower."

"We know, Mom," they both said.

"We're not two anymore, you know," Chase said.

My sons. When did they think they'd grown up? "Uh-huh. Okay, then. Who's up for popcorn and a movie after your showers?"

Chase and Cody scampered toward the back door, each one carrying part of our day's gear. I gathered what was left and followed them. Max met me at the top of the stairs, tail wagging, eyes expectant. I reached down to pet him. "Who left you in the house?" I asked as though he could answer. I looked toward the boys' rooms and called out, "Whoever is not in the shower, Max needs to go outside." Max immediately bounded down the stairs to wait for his savior.

Upstairs in my room I started the shower. The phone rang as I peeled my bathing suit from the stink of my skin. I was content to ignore it, but a minute or so later I heard a loud knock on the bathroom's closed door. "Mom!"

"Yes, Cody." I reached for a towel, wrapped it around me, and opened the door just wide enough to peek out.

"Dad is on the phone for you."

Expectancy was in his eyes, a look I never quite got used to. As if, with every call, there lay the possibility of reconciliation. Perhaps, I imagined his mind wondering, if they talk long enough, and the conversation is friendly enough . . . perhaps . . .

"Did you tell him I was about to get in the shower?"

My son's face went blank. "No."

I smiled in hopes of easing any negative feelings I had about this moment. Charlie was the last person I wanted to speak with. "Well, did he say what he wanted?"

Again the eyes brightened. "No, but I told him we went to Wet 'n Wild today."

I nodded. "Okay, well . . . tell him that I am in the shower and I'll call him back."

Cody shook his head. "I can't. He said to tell you it's important. And he sounds really serious."

A sudden fear overtook me. What if one of his parents was sick? Or worse? "Tell him I'll be there in a minute." Cody nodded and started to back away. "Oh, and Cody . . ."

He looked at me, then blinked. "Yes, Mom?"

"Close the bedroom door on your way out."

"I know, Mom," he said.

I closed the bathroom door, turned off the shower, and dashed into the bedroom, where I picked up the bedside phone. I heard Cody on the extension, happily telling his father about the day and about how many times he'd ridden and conquered the Storm, one of the thrill rides the park offers.

Charlie replied with, "Buddy, that sounds great, and I promise we'll do that when you come for your visit, but I think I hear your mom on the other line."

I squared my shoulders. "Cody, you can hang up, sweetheart. Get your shower, okay?"

"Okay, Mom. Love you, Dad."

"I love you too, buddy."

My heart twisted. When I heard the click of Cody disconnecting his extension, I said, "What's wrong?"

"What do you mean?"

"Cody said it was important. Is it your parents? Has something happened to one of them?"

"Good grief, Kimberly. Calm down. I just want to talk to you about picking up the boys and—"

"What's so important about that? You get them on Monday. Just like last year; pick them up at 9:00 in the morning. They'll be ready."

"Whoa there, Miss Attitude."

"I don't have an attitude, Charlie."

There was a chuckle from the other end. Sarcasm dripped all over it. "I believe you do," he said.

"No. I don't."

"Is this the way it's gonna be?"

I was quiet before asking, "What are you talking about?"

"Are we going to act like this? Like children talking about our children?"

My body went rigid. "Don't you dare, Charlie. Don't you dare talk to me about acting like a child. Don't you . . ." The knot I'd grown accustomed to swelled in my throat. I kept my teeth clenched, both out of anger and to keep the boys from hearing me scream. "Don't you dare say I'm not acting like a parent when you . . . you know you lied in that courtroom, so don't you start with me." My last words twisted around the knot.

"Kimberly, stop it. It's just like the judge said. You're jealous. You want me. You can't have me. And someone else does."

"From what I understand, a whole lot of someone elses." I heard him snicker and I closed my eyes. "What. Do. You. Want."

"I want to pick up the boys tomorrow night rather than Monday morning."

"Why?"

58

"Because I work on Mondays, Kimberly. Not all of us get the summer off."

I could hear my heart hammering in my chest. "No."

"Give me one good reason why not."

"Because Sunday is mine. And, by the way, what do you plan to do with your sons while you are at work? Because, Charlie, if you tell me that one of your little bimbos is watching my children—"

"Stop it, Kim. Stop it now."

I knew that tone in Charlie's voice. I'd crossed a line. I hated myself for it, but I couldn't seem to stop the venom when Charlie was around. Still, for the sake of my sons . . . "What are you planning to do?" I asked again, this time keeping my voice calm.

"I'm taking them to work with me. I was working the business by Chase's age, and Cody is not that far behind him. I think it will be fun for them both. I've already talked to Mom and Dad about it, and they think it's a great idea." He took a moment, I knew, to let it all sink in. Hard as I tried, I could find no fault with anything he said. "Now before you try to drag my mother and father into a battle . . ."

The knot had grown so large I could scarcely speak at all. "I'm not," I whispered.

"Good. Now, back to my picking them up on Sunday evening."

"No," I repeated. "I want my last night with my sons."

Charlie shot an expletive into the phone. "They're not dying, Kimberly. I'm bringing them back in five weeks."

"Don't you talk to me like that, Charlie Tucker. Don't use words like that with me."

"Do you ever hear yourself, Kim? Don't do this. Do that. My way or no way."

I felt myself reeling. I stepped back, leaned against the mattress of the bed. "Is that it?" I asked. "Is that why you left? Because you think I have to have my way all the time?"

"For crying out loud. I'm not in the mood for this. I just want to pick up the boys, spend some time talking with them about what we'll be doing before work starts on Monday morning, have a little summer celebration like we used to. That was it. But if it's gonna be like this . . ."

Like we used to . . . before. Before the separation. Before the divorce. We'd made such a big deal about summer break. The boys picked the restaurant we'd eat at. Around a booth's table we'd talk about vacation plans, what we'd do for fun on weekends, game nights, and the challenges and laughter that came with it. Like we used to.

My heart was throbbing. "No," I said. "It's not going to be like this. What time do you want to pick them up on Sunday evening?"

"You're sure?" Charlie's voice sounded like that of a young boy. Like, oh-golly-gee Mrs. Cleaver.

No. I want one last night with my sons . . . I want my marriage back . . . I want to know why my husband found me so unlovable that he walked out on a good life and two fine boys . . . I want . . . "Yes. I'm sure."

"All right. I'll pick them up at . . . what time is best for you?"

Best for me . . . "Seven?"

"Seven it is. Tell the boys I love them."

"I will."

I started to hang up without saying good-bye when I heard "And Kim?"

I returned the phone to my ear. "Yeah."

"Thanks."

"Sure."

By 6:45 on Sunday evening, the boys were packed, their stuffed backpacks tossed by the front door, and they sat oh so casually watching some nonsense television in the family room.

I walked from the kitchen—where there was really nothing left to clean—and the door leading to where my sons sat. I crossed my arms and leaned against the door frame, taking in the sight of them, breathing in their scent. "Did you pack your toothbrushes?" I asked.

Chase looked up at me. "Mom, we have toothbrushes at Dad's."

"Oh. Right."

I walked back into the kitchen, made a cup of hot tea in the microwave, then returned to stand and stare again. Chase looked up at me, gave a crooked smile and winked.

So much like his father . . .

I smiled back. "Don't forget to call me, okay?"

"Okay, Mom."

My son. My nearly grown son, sitting straight back in an overstuffed chair, ankle resting on knee. The flip-flop hung from his foot, and every so often he jiggled it to bring it back to rights. They both wore dress shorts and polo shirts and their hair was haloed by the sunshine pouring through the window. So handsome. And in five weeks, they'd be older. Wiser, perhaps.

And I would have missed the transition.

A commercial interrupted the boys' show. Cody looked at me. "Are you really going to Cedar Key while we're gone?"

I nodded. "Looks that way."

"Man, I wish I could go. Don't you, Chase?"

Chase gave his brother a look that read "Proceed with

Caution." He leaned forward and said, "Well, we're going to Dad's, Code. We'll learn the business and spend some time with Grandma and Grandpa."

"Do you think Dad will pay us?" Cody asked his brother.

Chase and I both laughed. The question was so typical of Cody.

"Maybe," Chase said.

I heard a car pulling into the driveway. My head felt light, my body heavy. The dread I'd been waiting for finally fell on me. I hated these moments. This was more than a weekend visit where I could tell myself that at least I had time to shop, take naps, or go to the movies, which I rarely did. But at least I could tell myself I could if I wanted to.

This was five long weeks. Thirty-five days.

And all I could think as I watched my sons stand and walk toward me—toward the front door—was that I was not the one who left and yet I was the one who had to let her sons leave for an extended period of time.

Cody shot past me, but Chase stopped long enough to kiss my cheek. "We'll miss you."

The knot returned. I could only nod.

I heard the front door open, Cody exclaim, "Hey, Dad!"

"Hey, buddy!"

From my position I could watch or not, my choice. I chose not. But I could picture them hugging. Then I heard Chase say, "Hey."

"Hey, bud . . ." A pause. Then, "Got your backpacks ready, I see. Wanna put them in the car for me?" A scrambling at the door, followed by, "Wait up, boys. Tell your mother good-bye." Backpacks dropped to the floor.

I turned then, my cup of now cold tea still in my hand. Both boys walked to me, hugged me one at a time. We said

"I love you," and then they were out the door, lugging their summer necessities on their backs.

Charlie remained in the doorway. I looked at him, forcing my eyes not to leave his. He jiggled his keys, nodded once, then turned and walked out, leaving the door open behind him.

I waited until I heard car doors shut, the engine hum to life, and tires crunch over a fine layer of sand scattered atop the brick driveway. I pressed my back against the hard edge of the door frame. I slid down—inch by inch, hurt by hurt. By the time I came to rest on the floor, I had reasoned that as difficult as this separation was for me, it would be even more so for my sons.

And for them, I cried.

6

An hour later I was lying on top of my bed, wrapped in a cotton robe, my right hand clutched around a mug of warm milk while my left loosely held the television remote. For a half hour I flipped channels, never staying past the first two minutes of whatever show was on. A commercial was an automatic "flip."

I had just taken a sip of milk when my cell phone rang. I jumped, thinking it might be one of the boys.

It was Heather.

"How are you holding up?" she asked, as though my sons had both tragically died.

"It's only been an hour, Heather." My voice held a lilt so as not to just break down and cry some more. Still, this was Heather. My best friend. I could be honest with her. "I hate divorce, Heather. Hate it. Look what it's done to my children. Five weeks away from their mother."

"Awful."

"It'd be one thing if Charlie lived across the country. But, he doesn't. He lives across town. You'd think the judge would understand that being separated from a parent—especially a loving mother—for weeks on end is an emotional wound that's just not necessary." I fingered the wide sash of my robe. "I feel like I've lost an arm without them here. Knowing they're just down the hall . . . or the block. Or in the kitchen making a late-night snack."

"I'm sorry, Kim."

I shrugged. "It's not your fault." *It's Charlie's . . .*

"I talked to Dad today," she said as an obvious change of subject. "He says you're heading for Cedar Key tomorrow."

"No," I answered. "Not tomorrow. Tuesday."

"Oh, good! Then let's spend the day playing tomorrow."

"I can't. I have to get this house in order. I need to wash clothes. I don't want to come home to piles of laundry."

"How long are you staying?"

"I don't know. Days? A week maybe."

From the other end of the line I heard the clinking of ice against glass, the sound of my sister taking a sip of her drink. *Her first of the night? Her third?*

"What about Max?" she said then. "Want to leave him here?"

"No, I'll take him with me. Max loves the water; he'll have a good time there."

"And he'll be company for you."

Thank you, Heather . . . thank you for reminding me I am alone.

"Yeah."

"Ami's got an opening coming up in two weeks. I thought you and I could fly up to Atlanta for that. How does that sound?"

"Sounds good. Do you want to go ahead and book the tickets or shall I?"

"I will. Or, if you're up for the adventure, we can just drive." She giggled. "I'll let you know what I decided."

65

Another clinking of ice against glass. I wanted the call to end; I hated talking with Heather during this time of the day. "Heather, I'm tired. I'm going to get a good night's sleep so I can get it all done in the morning."

"All right. After I finish my Coke I'm going to wash dishes. Sounds like a fun night, doesn't it?"

Her Coke . . . "Nothing like it." A thought came to me and I said, "Heather, do you want to go get those manis and pedis tomorrow?"

"Meet me at the day spa at 1:00."

"I'll be there."

"Perfect. When you get back from Cedar Key, we'll go shopping for our trip to Atlanta."

Already a plan. I liked it. Spa days, shopping, traveling to Atlanta, the ballet. And, of course, Cedar Key. Somehow I'd get through these five weeks. "Sounds good."

We said our good-byes. Ten minutes later, I was sound asleep.

The television remained on.

By 10:00 Tuesday morning I had loaded the car with luggage filled with enough clothes and other necessities to keep me covered for two weeks—just in case things didn't go as well as I'd hoped—a cooler full of food that might go bad before I returned, and a large bag of dog food I'd purchased the day before.

"Come on, Max," I called into the house from the garage door.

Faithful Max strolled into the mud room, smiling. He paused momentarily, then—seeing the car's back door left open for him—darted past me. He positioned his seventy-seven pounds of muscle and golden fur onto the seat, then peered through the front windshield, looking anxious. *Where we going, Mom? Where we going?*

The drive to Cedar Key—though I had not made it in years—had not changed. The trip to the island had always been nearly as wonderful as the being there. When I was a child, the farther away from the city Dad drove, the happier I became. Life was good in Cedar Key. Mom relaxed more. Lethargic in a princess-amongst-the-pillows kind of way. Dad slipped easily into his role as her Prince Charming. They laughed a lot. Kissed a lot. Loved each other and their children with wild abandon. My sisters and I played with little conflict amongst ourselves. Rosa was there too. Always. She and her mother added a new dimension to our relationships with one another.

Dad and I always woke first. We'd meet in the kitchen. Dad would pour two mugs of coffee and one of hot cocoa. He'd tell me, "Grab a seat, Boo. I'll run this up to your mother and be right back."

I pictured Mom propped in bed, dressed in her pink cotton Eileen West nightgown, waiting for her prince to return. After Diana became Princess of Wales, I pictured Mom wearing one of the beautiful tiaras I'd seen the British beauty wearing in photographs and on television. If it was good enough for the future queen of England, it was good enough for my mother.

Picturing Mom was all I was allowed to do; we weren't allowed in the master bedroom until after Mom had gotten ready for the day. Dad cautioned us to be "extra special quiet" in the mornings so Mom could take her after-coffee nap. After becoming a mother, I wondered how my mother managed to have four children, play at the beach most all afternoon and late into the night, wake at eight to Dad's coffee, then slip under the covers to nap until ten or eleven o'clock. Even after Ami came along, it was more Jayme-Leigh who took care of the baby than Mom. A premonition, perhaps, of my sister's future as a pediatrician.

Children were one of the two passions Jayme-Leigh has always possessed. Not her own children, of course, but rather those belonging to others. Her relationship with Ami mirrored that of Heather's and mine. In a unique sort of way, our family of six lived divided by twos. Mom and Dad, Jayme-Leigh and Ami, Heather and me.

But in Cedar Key, we added Eliana and Rosa.

Eliana. A woman of Hispanic heritage who lived in a modest house near the cemetery and worked hard at keeping other people's houses beautiful. A woman with a quick laugh and eyes that twinkled when she spoke. A woman totally dedicated to my mother and father.

It was Eliana, I now realized as I turned onto SR 24—that long stretch of two-lane blacktop leading from civilization to the island of my young summers—who provided Mom the time to play with her husband and children and to sleep until nearly noon. It was Eliana who cooked and cleaned and made sure our clothes were washed and dried and pressed crisp. It was Eliana who stayed late after supper to load the dishwasher and wipe the counters, and it was Eliana who, early the next morning, unloaded the dishes and returned them to their proper places in the cabinets. So different from Nell, who came twice a week when we were at home. Nell helped Mom; Eliana was a mom.

And then there was Rosa, the little tagalong child dressed in our hand-me-downs, who played with the Claybourne children as though there were no differences between us. Rosa

. . . I wondered now where she might be living, what she was doing, and how life had turned out for her.

I watched the sun slide toward the horizon in the west. The foliage, thick on both sides of the road, allowed sunlight to wink between the quaking leaves of the soaring trees and the sleek green vines that wrapped around the trunks and branches and then slithered between them like snakes in the grass.

It was a tunnel that led to the marshlands of another world. Cedar Key.

I turned off the highway and onto the bumpy dirt road leading to the house. Green vines and trees had given way to miles of marshes, which then gave way to ancient live oaks. Their branches dripped with the silvery-gray strands of Spanish moss so thick they formed shimmering veils behind which the houses stood between the road and the water. As my father had done with his car on the weekends and summers of my youth, I turned my Honda along the short driveway leading to the house. I shoved the gearshift to park and sighed.

I had returned to Cedar Key.

"Come on, Max," I said.

If his panting was any indication, Max was more than happy to exit the backseat.

After liberating the dog, I grabbed my medium-sized suitcase from the trunk. Even though the suitcase had wheels, the ground was thick with sand and crushed shells, so I heaved it up then walked to the z-shaped cypress board stairs. I took the steps one at a time until I'd reached the front door, which was actually at the side of the house. Max was not far behind me.

"Ready to see our home?" I asked him. I dropped the suitcase between us, then added, "Well, for the next few days anyway." I fished the key my father had given me from the deep pocket of my capri pants, slid it into the keyhole, and flipped it to the right.

The door to our temporary home opened. Max bounded in as though he'd been coming here every summer of his seven years.

I turned to look out over the landscape as I inhaled the salty air. The blended fragrances of fish and grass sent memories rushing through me faster than I could reel them in. In that moment I knew more than I'd known up until then that there were things here—within this house and on this island—that I was not ready to meet. Recollections of my parents, my sisters, and of our lives as they dovetailed. Thoughts of my mother and me traipsing along the Gulf coastline, photographing scenes of wildlife and people and the places they lived and worked and played. Memories of Dad, young and tan, relaxing—albeit in the scorching sunlight.

I leaned against the door frame and turned fully toward the water, watching the sleek grasses bend with the breeze. An osprey's nest perched high above the ground was empty. A few yards away, gulls flapped their gray and white wings over the movement of blue and green below. They formed unique angles and they called me to the water's edge.

I whistled for Max, who quickly joined me on the landing. I closed the door and we bounded down the stairs then walked to the platform where, just a few nights before, I'd dreamed of my father sitting, waiting for me to join him before we went to the city park.

I sat in one of the Adirondack chairs—the same one Dad had rested in—crossed one leg over the other, leaned back, and closed my eyes. The sun warmed the left side of my face and my skin grew clammy under the afternoon's wet heat.

Without opening my eyes, I raked my hands through the length of my blonde hair, forcing the roots up. Sweat beaded along my scalp as I twisted the strands until they formed a makeshift bun. When a breeze brushed across the back of my neck, I leaned back again. At my feet, Max plopped down with a sigh.

For a moment I imagined my sons had made the trip with me and that they were, right now, upstairs unpacking their suitcases, shedding their travel clothes, and then shoving their long, tan legs into swimming trunks. Any minute they would come skipping down the stairs, their voices reaching me long before they did. They'd call my name, "Mom!" and then they would insist I get up and take them to the park *now*. Max would beat all of us to the car.

But a dream was all it was. All it could be.

Anise had turned the bedroom Dad and Mom had used into a guest room, then created a master bedroom out of the room my sisters and I had shared. No longer was the room dominated by a king-sized bed draped in white linen. The mounds of fluffy pillows my mother had rested herself upon were also gone. Mom's sense of Victorian-meets-beach had been wiped away. It now reflected Anise's back-to-nature touch.

The old master now had twin beds with headboards of ornate black wrought iron. The wall behind them was draped with flax-colored curtains, though no window was there. The matching bed quilts were scalloped and white and had detailed vermicelli stitches outlining coastal shapes. The pattern of the bed skirts was of large flax and white check, and the pillows matched them. The windows were hidden behind wood-grain plantation shutters, which I threw open wide as

71

soon as I entered the room. I stood for a while staring out at the sky, watching it turn deep shades of red and orange as the sun took its rest for the day. I leaned against the sill and tilted my head to the right to see large pink clouds forming above. Cotton-candy skies, Mom had always called evenings like these.

"Max," I said to the one who had just made himself quite comfortable on one of the beds, "tomorrow we'll go watch the sunset." I looked at him. His tongue was hanging from his mouth as he smiled at me. "Sometimes, I swear you know exactly what I'm talking about."

He barked.

I sat on the opposite bed from him. "You see, Max," I went on, "this island is so special that if you look one way in the morning, you can watch the sun come up. But if you look the other way in the evenings, you can watch it go down."

With that he bounded off the bed and out of the room.

7

Summer 1987

"Come on . . ."

"I can't."

"You mean you won't."

I shook my head. The blonde hair that fell straight on both sides of my face tickled my shoulders in the late afternoon sunlight. I stood a few feet from the Gulf's shoreline, brushed the wet sand from the tops of my slender tanned legs and then from my hands. "Obviously, you don't know my parents, Steven Granger. If my father caught me out at 6:00 in the morning watching the sunrise with you, he'd kill both of us."

Steven grinned, white teeth appearing whiter against the bronze skin of his face. "Then tell him. I've got nothing to be ashamed of." He winked. "Do you?"

I crossed my arms, felt the warmth of them against the bare skin of my midriff, and my cheeks flamed. "No," I said looking down. At my feet was the crumpled canary-yellow cover-up that matched the bikini I'd begged Mom for before we came to Cedar Key for summer vacation. Mom thought the bathing suit a little too risqué, but I insisted it was the style and that we'd not find anything different anywhere else. "Besides," I'd said, "it's just a suit, Mom. It's not like I have guys pawing me or anything."

But in my heart, I knew whom I bought it for and just whom I hoped would take notice. And so far, it had worked. Steven's eyes never left me when we were together . . . and he made sure we were together as much as possible. Even on days when he'd have done better to have worked with his dad.

Steven bent down to retrieve the cover-up, shook it loose of sand, and then handed it to me. The same sun that warmed me shimmered on the dark blond hair—cut in feathery soft layers—of the boy standing before me. "Need any help putting this on?"

I kept my eyes locked on his. "No, I do not," I said. Then, slipping the gauzy material over my head, I said, "I'm not a child that you have to dress, you know."

"I'd say."

I smiled at him before we turned to walk toward the grassy knoll rising above the beach where 2nd Street crossed in front of City Park. Behind us the voices of children and adults playing and laughing faded into the sound of gulls cawing. Steven and I were in a world of our own. We took slow steps, occasionally bumped shoulders, cast longing gazes, and then finally clasped our hands together. "So, what'll it be?" he asked. "Just say the word and I'll pick you up at your front door at 6:00. Otherwise, I'll meet you at the end of the lane from your house." He stopped walking, and I stopped with him. "Just promise me that tomorrow we'll be watching the sunrise together."

I looked at him long and hard. "Dad will say no."

"Tell your mom you want to take some pictures, then.

You've got your license, you can drive the car. I'll meet you where Dad docks his boat."

I felt myself smiling long before my lips broke apart in a wide grin. "Okay, then."

Steven looked elated. "Really? Are you serious?" And then he laughed. "I'll bring the coffee."

I wrinkled my nose. "Hot cocoa, please."

He pulled me to him, pressed his lips against mine for one salty sweet moment. "I'll bring whatever you want."

"What shall I bring?" I asked, picturing us, blanket spread out on his father's dock, legs dangling over the edge, feet grazing the water. A thermos of hot cocoa stood between us and napkins filled with . . . I didn't know what . . .

But Steven shook his head. "Nothing. I'll bring it all."

"Okay."

We started walking again, over to the gazebo and then back to where he'd parked the red '76 GMC 4-by-4 his father had allowed him to buy with the money he'd saved over the years of working on the boat. "How about tonight?" he asked. "Got plans for tonight?"

I couldn't help but giggle. After all the years I'd stared after him, Steven Granger finally knew I was alive. Really alive. And not just in the "kid sister" kind of way. Not as it had always been before when he treated me no differently than any other summer resident on the island.

Not that I hadn't worked hard to make sure it would happen too. After winter break on the island—the one where Steven hardly said hello to me—I joined one of the new women's workout clubs near home, lost some excess girl-to-woman pounds, and firmed up my stomach muscles. A month before we were scheduled to come to Cedar Key for the summer, I'd talked Mom into a shopping spree at Dillard's, which included the bathing suit and a stop at the Clinique counter where I was taught—at last—how to properly wear makeup. The salesgirl admitted it wouldn't take much to accent my positives, telling me I was a natural beauty. Still, I'd come away with eyes shadowed in smoky shades and lips pouting with shimmery lip gloss.

As usual upon arrival at our summer house, my sisters and I bounded up the stairs to get everything unpacked so we could get to the water as quickly as possible. And, as usual, I was the first to meet up with Dad by the shoreline. "Good gracious alive. Who is this young woman standing in front of me?" he asked, sizing me up and down.

"Dad . . ."

He stood from his chair, rubbed his chin in mock admiration and study, and said, "Now, I do believe my daughter, my little girl," he said winking, "who rode all the way from Orlando with us ran up those stairs a few minutes ago. But I do not remember this young woman riding with us in the car."

"Dad!"

His face grew stern then. "Seriously. What's with all this? Do you need all this makeup and . . . do those shoes actually match your swimsuit?"

I turned. If he were able to read my face—and I knew he could—he'd know that seeing Steven again was behind the transformation, and he'd have me in a gunnysack before I had a chance to protest. "I'll meet you at the car, Dad."

"Uh-huh," he called after me.

"I'm driving!" I yelled back.

"Only if I say so!"

"Dad!"

Now it was Steven who eyed me, albeit in a different way than my father had. "What about tonight?" I asked him.

"Do you think your dad would mind if we went to see the sunset together?"

"We'll be there anyway. Mom told me earlier that tonight will be a good one to catch some shots."

Steven squinted in the sunlight. "Well, that's all well and good . . . but can I pick you up and take you with me? Do you think they'd mind?"

We reached the truck. He opened the passenger door for me. A red towel was scrunched along the seat, placed there to protect the fabric. I straightened it, then hoisted myself up and in using the chrome running board. Steven closed the door behind me and ran around the front as I leaned my arm out of the opened window, hoping for a breeze. Even though he'd parked in the shade of the one bushy tree at City Park, inside the truck felt like two hundred degrees.

"I'll have it cooled down in a minute," he said as he bounded into the driver's seat. He started the engine, adjusted the air-conditioning, then fiddled with the gearshift on the floorboard between us. Looking from it to me, he said, "Scootch closer."

I happily complied.

Halfway to the house he asked, "So what time can I pick you up?"

"We usually eat about 7:00. How about 8:00?"

"Sounds good. That'll give us plenty of time before sunset."

"Why don't I bring some Cokes? I mean, after all, you're bringing the hot cocoa in the morning."

He smiled at me. "*If* your parents say it's okay."

I thought for a moment before answering. "It'll work out."

He shifted gears as he rounded the road from A Street to 3rd. Thick shrubs and palms lined the right side so densely it was impossible to see through. I stared out at the landscape, thinking. Devising a plan, as I seemed to be doing a lot of lately. I knew what needed to be done for it to all work out. The best time to talk to Mom. The right time that she'd agree to anything. Just as she had with the shopping spree.

The perfect time . . . "It'll all work out," I said again, then glanced at Steven, who looked at me and then to the road.

"If you say so, Boo."

A million butterflies took flight inside at the sound of the endearment spoken from his lips. So different than when Dad said the exact same name. "I say so," I said, then leaned back and closed my eyes, already dreaming of the life Steven and I would someday have together.

A life in Cedar Key.

8

I was awakened early the next morning by bamming at the door. I forced my eyes open; Max was already scrambling out of the room. "Max," I called out, then pushed the sheet from off my pajama-clad body. "Max!"

The bamming continued. Max added his two cents by barking like a mad dog.

"Max, get back," I said when I finally made it to the door. I gently pushed at the bulk of him with my foot.

He complied, forced or not.

"Who is it?" I asked through the barrier between me and whoever thought it was so important to wake me at—I looked at my watch—7:00 in the morning.

"Who are *you*? That's the question."

The voice sounded as though it belonged to an older woman. I cracked the door open and peered out. "May I help you?" I asked.

Sure enough, my early morning intruder was an older woman—in her late sixties if I had to guess—with silver hair cut in a pageboy. Her skin was tanned and leathery like that of women who'd spent too much of their days in the sun and not enough time listening to the warnings of the surgeon general. Her eyes, though kind, were distinctly authoritative. "May I ask who you are?" she asked again.

"Yes, you may," I answered. "I'm Kimberly Tucker."

"Well, you are in Dr. and Mrs. Claybourne's house, and I've not been notified that anyone was coming."

I blinked. "What?"

"Dr. Claybourne or Mrs. Claybourne always notifies me if anyone other than them is coming here for a visit. I got no such call."

"Who *are* you?" I asked.

The woman put her hands on her hips. "Are we back at that again? I asked you first."

I pressed my fingertips to my chest. "I am Kimberly *Claybourne* Tucker, Dr. Claybourne's daughter."

The woman stepped back. "No," she said. "Oh my goodness, but you sure are. Why I haven't seen you in . . . I don't remember when I last saw you."

I shook my head. Behind me, Max shuffled away, sensing, I suppose, that the "danger" was over and his role as protector was no longer necessary. "I still don't know who you are," I said.

"Why, honey," she said, her accent that of the natives, "I'm Madeline Lewis. Oh, just look at the expression on your face. You don't remember me. Of course you don't. I've worked down at the market since God laid sand on the Gulf beach. Your mama used to call me and tell me what she needed and I'd bring it to her. Remember?"

I did remember. Still, it didn't tell me why my father would use her to secure the beach house. I nodded. "Yes, I remember now. But, Mrs. Lewis, why are you checking on my father's house?"

"Miss Lewis, honey. Though the good Lord knows I wish there had've been a pretty gold ring around my finger . . ."

I thought, *You can have my old one* . . . but I remained silent.

"Your daddy started asking me some time ago—goodness, I guess it was shortly before your pretty mama died, back when she first came down so sick. I've been doing it ever since."

"Oh," I said. "Would you like to come in?" I stepped back, opening the door fully.

"Don't mind if I do," she said, then walked past me. Stale tobacco and used ashtrays wafted past me in her wake.

I closed the door. "Would you like coffee, Miss Lewis?" I asked.

"No, no. I just had my morning coffee down at the café."

We walked the three steps down into the family room, where sheets still covered the furniture and the blinds kept the room dark from the morning light. "I haven't really had time to do anything," I said, pulling a covering from the overstuffed loveseat and then directing Miss Lewis to it.

"First things first," she said. "And what I mean by that is: you call me Maddie, like everyone else, okay?"

I sat on the covered sofa across from her. "Maddie," I said. "Thank you."

"You're welcome."

I stood then, walked over to the windows, and jerked the drapes apart. The room came to life, and I squinted against the harshness of the light. When I turned, I was instantly dismayed and embarrassed by the thin layer of dust dancing in the air and lying across the few uncovered pieces of furniture. "Goodness, looks like my work really is cut out for me." I returned to my seat. "You may be able to help me,

Maddie. Dad sent me here to find someone to replace Eliana. At least that's his story and he's sticking to it."

"Ah," she said. "I'm sure there's a story in there somewhere." She sighed. "Eliana. God rest her soul." Then she paused before adding, "A replacement in what way?"

"Um . . . in the cleaning way," I answered. "Dad told me she was still keeping up with the house . . . but not since she died." I laughed at my statement. "Of course, not since she died." I leaned forward. "If you don't mind my asking, why didn't Eliana keep watch for visitors?"

Maddie leaned back and crossed her legs. She wore knee-cap shorts. Again I noticed how dark and wrinkled her skin was. "I don't claim to know why your daddy asked me to do what he asked me to do. I just did it. But, on the other point, here's what I'd do if I were you," she stated. "I'd post something down at the market. You know, a flyer with your phone number written several times across the bottom so that people can tear them off and call you."

"That sounds like a good idea," I said. "I have to go to the market later anyway for milk and things like that." I pulled my hair over one shoulder. "So then, I take it you don't know anyone off the top of your head."

"No," she said. She remained quiet for a moment, then added, "I suppose you know that her daughter Rosa works down at the realty office."

"I didn't know that, no," I said. "But I was hoping to get to see her."

Maddie's lip thinned. "Well," she said.

I wasn't sure where the conversation was heading. I said, "It looks like it's pretty hot out there already."

"This summer has been just miserable so far," she said. "The humidity is thick enough to kill ya."

"Fortunately, I won't be here long enough to suffer under it."

"You're married, I take it," she said. "You said your last name was Tucker now."

I looked down at my left hand, naked of any rings whatsoever but still marked by the thick band I'd worn. "Divorced," I answered. "Two boys—Chase and Cody—who are with their father right now." The familiar knot formed in my throat.

"And the rest of the family?" She coughed out a throaty laugh. "Your stepmother is the nicest thing but pretty closemouthed, so I don't ask too often. But I'd love to know how the rest of you are doing."

I laced my fingers. "Fine. Doing very well. Jayme-Leigh and Dad have a pediatric practice together. I'm sure Jayme-Leigh will have the whole thing soon enough."

"It's about time your daddy stopped working so hard. I tell him every time I see him, I say, 'Ross Claybourne, why don't you and Anise quit all this working all the time, sell the house in Orlando, and move to Cedar Key.'" She laughed again. "He always blames it on Anise, saying that she wouldn't want to sell her flower shop."

"No, I don't imagine she would."

"How about the rest of you?"

"Heather is married. Three kids. Ami is a member of the Atlanta Ballet Company."

"I remember how proud your mama was of her. Of her dancing."

"Yes."

Then she pointed a bony finger, its nail painted in shimmery fuchsia. "But you," she said. "She was especially proud of you."

"Me?" I laid my hand against my chest. "Why was she proud of me?"

Maddie laughed one more time. "Goodness, what wasn't she proud of. You played piano, you were a cheerleader, you were homecoming queen, your all-A grades, your photography . . . the list goes on and on."

Mom was proud of me. I looked around the room, my eyes resting momentarily on each piece of her framed work. "Mom's photography was the best, though," I said.

"Your mother told me one time, she said, 'Maddie, Kim is going to go far with her photography. She's got the eye for it.'" When I didn't answer, she added, "So, what are you doing with it?"

I shook my head. "I'm teaching full-time now. The boys, church, different things like that. I'm afraid I just don't have a lot of time . . ."

With that Maddie pushed herself forward. "Well, now, that's a real shame," she said.

After Maddie left, I made coffee, fed Max, then took a shower. I dressed in a simple pair of plaid bermudas with a matching red-wine tee. I slathered my skin with sunscreen, put on a little mascara and lip gloss, then slipped my feet into a pair of white sandals. Max was sleeping on the cotton rug in the guest bedroom so I was able to leave unnoticed and without guilt.

Little about downtown Cedar Key had changed since my last visit. Or, for that matter, since my childhood. Perhaps a shop here and there, but it was still the island time forgot and I had not.

Years ago my father purchased a book by John Muir, a man who, in the late 1800s, walked a thousand miles from his home in Indianapolis to the Gulf of Mexico. Quite a bit of his time had been spent in Cedar Key. Dad read his copy of the book until the pages fell from the binding and insisted we girls do the same. Afterward, he asked me, "Well, Boo. What did you learn?"

Wanting to make Dad proud, I stood as if I were about to give a book report crucial for an A and said, "I think that when we push ourselves to do something like walk a thousand miles, we find more than just people and towns and plants and water."

Dad's expression showed just how pleased I'd made him. "And what would that be, Boo?"

"I think we find ourselves . . ."

Now, with the car parked on 2nd Street, I stood staring at the crossroads of my past and present. And something that felt like my future, though I couldn't imagine how that might be.

My stomach rumbled; I realized I'd not eaten breakfast. Hot as it was—and it was sticky hot—I walked to a small diner, Cook's Café. There was nothing fancy about it, but it was air-conditioned and offered the aroma and presence of bacon and eggs and pancakes.

After breakfast I walked the block to Dock Street. In the marina, boats rested from their labor. In the Gulf beyond Dock Street, a few of their brothers and sisters were already hard at work or play. Tourists and locals milled in and out of the shops and cafés, chatting casually. Some rode around in rented golf carts.

As it had always been, nothing about Cedar Key conveyed effort—not even work, hard as it might be. To my left, water lapped lazily against the shoreline and the cement breakers. Gulls cawed as if to demand everyone stop what they were doing just to listen. The sun—nearly straight up—beat down as though it were on a mission.

I spotted a bench shaded by a shiny tin roof where A Street curved at the harbor. Wanting time to just sit and absorb, I walked past the tour boat docks—all three of them—and forced myself not to look at the one owned by Steven's father. Too many memories . . . most of them good.

Too good.

Each one leaving me remarkably sad and unsatisfied. How was it, I wondered, that the moments of our youth could affect the emotions of our adulthood?

When I made it to the bench, I sat and stared straight ahead. It was easy to do, to sit and watch the water. The boats. The couple leaning against the metal barrier between the sidewalk and the Gulf below. Too easy to pretend it was me, as it had once been. One half of a whole.

Past the couple and the edge of a restaurant that jutted out over the water, I spied the tip of Atsena Otie Key, the island that had been the original Cedar Key. I remembered the old history lessons Steven had given me, of how Atsena Otie— pronounced without the *t* in Atsena—had played its role in the Civil War and how the Eberhard Faber Pencil Company had built a lumber mill there in the late 1800s.

"Thirty years later," Steven said as we sat upon one of its beaches, "a ten-foot tidal wave hit the island and the mill was destroyed. Only a few houses survived enough to live in or repair, and those were floated over to 1st Street on Cedar Key." He pointed; I followed the long tan arm and callused hand and tender finger to the land on the other side of the water.

Just the night before, that very same arm had slipped around my shoulders, had drawn me close to its owner, and its owner had pressed his lips—soft and sweet—on mine. The kiss had intensified and, as is often the case with teenagers, had left us both frustrated and wanting so much more.

In my seventeen years, it had been my first such experience. Sitting there next to Steven, I only knew that I didn't want it to be my last.

9

Revving motorcycles and voices caused me to look over my left shoulder. Two un-helmeted bikers leaned into the curve, then drove past me. I followed them with my eyes, then looked over my shoulder once more. There were people standing near one of the docks, talking about their upcoming tour, wondering when the guide was going to arrive.

"We reserved for 11:00," a woman in the small group said.

"Then he should be here any minute."

I smiled, then looked back toward Atsena Otie. Here these people were, in a hurry to take a relaxing boat tour. No sooner thought than I heard a boat's motor. I looked again to see a boat with "Granger Tours" painted in dark green on the side. A man sat near the back, in the shade of the covering, navigating.

It wasn't Mr. Granger.

I lowered my eyes and wondered if Mr. Granger—a man my father's age—might have passed away. Perhaps someone had taken the business over, had kept it going. I stood, turning back to where I'd left my car on 2nd Street, which forced me to walk past the dock where the man welcomed the group on board. I squinted behind my shades, trying to make out who the man might be, but he wasn't even vaguely familiar.

Most likely a teenager Mr. Granger had trained to do the work Steven had done so many years ago . . . before he'd left for college.

Past the docks and the marina, I looked back a final time. While the group had all managed to get settled in the boat, the man remained standing on the dock. He looked at me then raised his hand in a friendly hello, and I returned it.

I continued to my car, feeling alive. *This is Cedar Key*, I thought. Casual, hot, and—above all—friendly.

I'd almost forgotten.

Max was more than a little happy to see me when I returned to the house. We played outside for a while, then returned inside, where I made the poster to take to the market. That done, I asked Max if he wanted to take a ride. He assured me he did.

The market stood on the corners of 3rd and D Streets. The small warehouse's blue façade front had double doors held wide open, three newspaper stands on their left, and a Coke machine plus two ice freezers on the right. A large window over the newspaper stands was plastered with various colorful advertisements; the side of the building boasted a mural of life on Cedar Key when Indians alone had lived here. On both sides was a variety of golf carts, cars, and bicycles.

I left Max in the car with the windows half down. "Stay put," I told him. He barked in obedience.

Inside, Maddie stood at the cash register. "Oh, you brought it, did you?" she asked, spying the white between my finger and thumb.

I held it a little higher and smiled. She walked to a bulletin board near the front door filled with other such papers, cou-pons, and a few old high school announcements held by tacks. Maddie popped several of them away with her thumbnail. The old papers floated to the floor and landed about her feet. I bent down to retrieve them as she said, "Hand me your flyer, Kimberly."

I did.

"There you go," Maddie said. "You'll be getting calls in no time."

"I hope so," I said.

"Meanwhile, if you need someone to give the place a good cleaning, I know someone who might do that."

I felt myself brighten. "You do?" If Maddie knew someone, I'd be home in a couple of days.

"One time only, though," she said as if she'd read my thoughts.

"Oh."

"But she might know someone . . ."

"Well, that's true." I sighed. "Okay, let me get a few things. I left Max in the car with the windows cracked, but it's still too hot out there."

"You do that. I'll call my friend and let you know some-thing."

I gave Maddie my cell number with appreciation for her help, got my groceries, and then returned to the register. Scanning the items, Maddie asked me, "Will you be going down to see the sunset tonight?"

"I've thought about it." I didn't have to ask where. I knew where the locals gathered; the place my mother and I used to go . . .

"You should. Days like today the sunsets are always so pretty."

"Will you be there?" I asked, helping by bagging my groceries.

"Sure will. I think my friend might be there too."

I looped my hands through the handles of the plastic bags. "That would be wonderful. I'll see you there."

I pulled the sheets off all the furniture in the house, going room by room, neatly folding the coverings and making a stack of them on the round wicker and glass dining room table. Max had gone exploring and promised to be back before supper. When I was done with my task, I sent a text to Chase, who texted right back. Yes, they were fine. Dad was behaving. So far. I told him I missed them both and to give Cody a hug for me. He said he would.

Max was not home in time for supper. I stood on the deck outside the door and called for him. When he didn't return, I went back inside, slipped my feet into a pair of flip-flops, and went out to search. It didn't take long to find him. He was next door, having made friends with the neighbor's cat.

"I'm afraid they don't know they're natural enemies," the lady of the house said to me from an open window. Her house, like Dad's, was raised. Two cars were parked under the flooring of the house, and a wooden staircase led to the front door.

I shielded my eyes with my hand and said, "No, I don't suppose they do."

"Hold on a sec there and I'll be right down."

I waited until the door opened. The woman stepping out onto the front deck was much older—probably in her late seventies—thin and humped at the shoulders. Her hair—silvery gray—was pulled straight back, braided, and then wrapped in a bun at the nape of her neck. It wasn't difficult to see how beautiful she had been as a young woman.

She wore slacks and a long-sleeved shirt with a light sweater, in spite of the heat. I felt bad that she should have to come all the way down the stairs, but she beat me to the bottom step before I was able to cover the distance.

"I take it you are Ross and Anise's daughter," she said.

She extended a hand and I took it. It was—of all things—cold; the skin was as delicate as an onion's. For a moment I thought not to correct her, but then said, "Actually, I'm Ross's daughter, Kimberly. My mother passed away in '99."

A glimpse of empathy crossed her wrinkled face and then vanished. "Darlin', I didn't realize."

"That's okay," I said.

"I love your daddy and your stepmother. They are two precious people."

I nodded, then added, "I'm sorry. I don't remember you."

"No. I moved here permanently about—oh, I don't know—five years ago. Used to come here for vacations and such. Then, just after my beloved passed on into glory, I decided to make Cedar Key my home."

It was my turn to express my sympathy. "I'm sorry to hear that. I mean, about your husband."

"You married, darlin'?"

"No. Divorced. Two boys."

Her eyes sparkled. "I had three of my own. Three boys, two girls. Lost one son and one of my girls . . . but the Lord is good."

I blinked, not knowing exactly what I should say. Finally, I said, "I didn't get your name."

The woman laughed then and said, "I didn't give it, now did I? I'm Patsy."

"Nice to meet you, Patsy."

She took my hand, this time, I knew, for support. "I tell you what. Since your dog and my cat are still visiting, why don't you come in and have a bite of some supper with me."

"I certainly wouldn't want—"

"Wouldn't want what, hon? To be a bother?"

"Surely you weren't expecting anyone . . ."

"Never." Her voice was laced with poignancy. "But there's always hope."

"I have Max's food poured in his dish."

We turned to look where my dog and her cat were rolling in the grass together. "Clearly he's starving," she quipped.

I continued to hold her hand as she led me toward the stairs.

"Did you already have your supper planned?"

"I honestly hadn't thought about it." We were at the door. I turned back to where Max and the cat were now looking up at their owners. "By the way, what's your cat's name?"

"Oreo," she said. "See that milk mustache?"

Oreo—who looked as if he had dressed for the black-white ball—yawned at us. "We apparently bore him to tears," I said.

"He's my buddy," she said, then patted my hand. "And he's faithful." Patsy opened the door to her home and shuffled in. "Like the Lord."

I followed behind her, saying nothing.

The home was decorated with simple beach-style furniture and the occasional antique piece, perhaps—I wondered— from her years of being a wife and mother. The only wall hangings were portraits of those I assumed to be family members, some born before Patsy and some after.

"I made a casserole," she said as I closed the door. "Do you like casserole?"

"I suppose it depends on what's in it."

Patsy chuckled, but she didn't answer. While she moved gingerly in the direction of what I assumed was the kitchen, I stepped over to an antique Bombay table decorated only by small framed photos. "Are these some of your family members?"

"I would assume so. Can't see displaying the faces of folks I don't know."

From anyone else, the words would have seemed sarcastic, but not from Patsy. Her words didn't bite, they nibbled. "You'll have to tell me who they are," I said. I picked up a three-by-five of a well-put-together couple with their two picture-perfect children sitting in front of them. They all wore blue denim jeans with pressed white shirts.

"That's my granddaughter," Patsy said as she came up beside me. She pointed to the young woman. "Lauren. And her husband Brandon. Their kids." She tapped the glass behind which two cherub faces smiled for the camera. "Their names will come to me sooner or later." She chuckled then shuffled back toward the kitchen.

"Where do they live?" I asked.

"California."

"That's a long way away." I followed behind her. "Can I help you with anything?"

Patsy's kitchen was decorated in peach and sea foam green. The window over the sink had neither valance nor blinds, and the late afternoon sunshine crept in. The view of the marshes was calming; the bright greens of midafternoon had changed to deep.

"Plates are up there in the cabinet. Why don't you set the table over in the corner there?"

A table big enough for two was pushed against a wall in the corner. I moved about in the room as though I knew it well, finding plates, napkins, and forks. Patsy had some sweet iced tea in the refrigerator; I poured two tumblers full and placed them on the table. A few minutes later we were eating tuna casserole in silence.

Finally I said, "So you had five children?"

"I did. Thirteen grandchildren, and a whole pile of great-grans." She cocked her head to one side. "It's something else, clearly it is . . . seeing one generation come in, then another, and another."

I smiled.

"What about you? Two, you said?"

"Two. Both boys. Chase and Cody."

"Do you work? Outside the home, I mean?"

"I'm a teacher."

"God bless you. I wouldn't want to be a teacher in this day and time."

"It's a challenge."

Patsy shoved another spoonful of tuna and noodles and green peas between moist lips. "I never worked outside of the home. Goodness knows inside kept me plenty busy."

"Do you get to see your family often?"

"Not often enough."

"Where are you from, Patsy?"

"South Carolina. You?"

"Orlando."

"I moved down here about five years ago, but I said that now, didn't I? Sold the old house and bought this house from the people who'd lived here for quite a number of years. Those are the neighbors you probably remember."

I nodded. "Probably."

"How long has your daddy owned the house next door?"

I took a sip of tea. "Since before I was born. The first time I can remember being here, I think I was . . . maybe five."

"Summers mostly?"

"And holidays. Some weekends. As we girls got older, it got harder to get away . . . what with so many school activities going on."

"I remember those days."

I looked at my watch. "Patsy, let me help you clean up. I want to make sure I get down to see the sunset tonight." I gathered together my plate, fork, and tumbler.

"We have some pretty ones, don't we?" Patsy remained seated.

"Would you like to go with me?" I asked from the sink. I turned on the water and rinsed my plate.

Patsy didn't answer right away. I looked over my shoulder. She appeared to be pondering the suggestion. Oddly, even though we'd just met, I kind of hoped she'd say that she'd like to go. Finally, she said, "You know, I think I will."

I smiled. "Wonderful." I returned to the table to clear away the rest of the dishes. "Patsy, what time do you think sunset will be?"

"Lately it's been around 9:00." Patsy drew herself up from the table, then held on to the side for a moment.

"Are you all right?"

Watery eyes met mine. "Fine. Just getting old."

I finished the dishes with Patsy beside me and then told her I'd be back to get her at 7:45. When I went outside, I found Max sitting at the foot of the stairs and Oreo nowhere in sight.

"Come on, Max," I said. "Let's get you fed."

Max panted as he looked up at me. I patted his golden head and said, "Looks like you and I have made two unlikely friends, eh?"

Max barked his agreement.

10

The aroma of cocoa mixed with the humidity already thick in the air. Night's clouds had taken flight; a remaining few stood guard over the bay. Close to the dock they were dark gray. Nearer to the horizon they were soft shades of white and gold. Directly above Dog Island was a deep stretch of dark blue centered with shades of pink.

The sun was rising.

Between Steven and me lay a paper plate filled with sticky buns, a covered Tupperware bowl of homemade granola, and two small containers of yogurt. Between sips of cocoa and kisses, we nibbled on the breakfast Steven's mother had prepared for us the night before.

"Here it comes," I whispered, raising my camera slowly as though it might startle the sun away.

"We still have a while to go," Steven said.

The sun could stay below the horizon forever as far as I was concerned. The longer it took it to rise, the longer I could sit on this dock with the boy I loved.

I shot the picture anyway along with two or three more. "Still, it's pretty, don't you think?"

"Beautiful," he said.

I looked at him. Instinctively I knew he wasn't talking about the vista before us. I shifted as close as the plate would allow, then leaned over for the hundredth kiss that morning alone. Maybe even the millionth. I'd stopped counting the night before when we'd held hands on the beach of Atsena Otie and watched the sunset, two young lovers completely alone.

"I could do this all day," I finally admitted.

"Not me. Dad said I've got to work today . . . said I've spent way too much time goofing off with—and I quote—that Claybourne girl."

I playfully shrugged a shoulder. "As long as you aren't goofing off with any other girl, I can live with that."

He smiled, then looked out over the water lying nearly motionless, rippled only by the one or two early morning fishing boats. Even the birds above and the fish below seemed to think it was too early still.

I raised my camera again. The lone white cloud had risen higher in the sky; the pink below it became more vivid. I took the shot then lowered the camera once more.

"What are you going to do with all the pictures you take?"

"I'm taking a photography class at school this coming year. There are also some contests I can enter." I smiled at him. "Why?"

"I dunno. Just wondered, I guess." He paused. "Do you think you'll do that for a living one day? Take pictures?"

I felt myself shiver in the heat of the morning. Steven had opened a door to talk about the future . . . would it include *ours*? "Maybe. Dad says I should become a photojournalist. Maybe go to work for *National Geographic*."

"You'd be away from home a lot, I imagine."

Again I shrugged. "I guess. I mean, that is . . . if I decide to go that route." I looked out over the water and swung my legs like scissors cutting through time. "What about you? What are you going to do? Work your dad's boat?"

His eyes opened wide. "Heavens no. I'm leaving for Florida State in the fall. I'm going to study business management . . . get off this island and get a real life."

I felt disappointment slide down my spine. "Where will you go? After college, I mean."

"I don't know. After four years of college there ought to be some door open to me. I'll look for the right doors and I'll walk through them."

"Is that it?"

Steven nodded. "I guess so. It's as far ahead as I can think right now anyway." He paused, then added, "Look."

I followed his gaze to the horizon, where the sun now hung low in the eastern sky, veiled in baby pink. Darker pink clouds shaped like a V spread wide above it, finally giving way to the white that had been there all along.

I raised my camera, took shot after shot, mindless—almost numb—to its beauty. A great blue heron flew into view. I captured it forever with its wings spread wide, gliding over the calm of the water in search of a place to land. The sun rose higher, turning neon pink and orange. The sky around it returned to gray-blue. Magically the orb before us changed its color again, from neon to blazing yellow surrounded by shimmering red. A wide line on the water, now dotted with waking herons, rippled under the reflection.

I finished one roll of film, then replaced it with another. I shot eight more photos then lowered my camera for good. All the while Steven had sat there, staring at the landscape before us, unaware—I felt—of the war going on inside me. The need to capture the moment versus the concern that I was only a summer fling to Steven.

When he was so much more than that to me.

"How do you think you did?" he finally asked.

"Good, I think."

"There's a photo lab on the mainland in Gainesville. Maybe we can take them there this evening . . . pick them up tomorrow?" He looked down at the plate, picked up a sticky bun, tore off a piece, and extended it toward my lips. I opened them, allowed him to feed me, then nibbled on his fingertips, which he drew back.

"Careful," he said, but elaborated no further.

He swung his legs and jumped to stand on the deck. I carefully packed my camera into its case, keeping my eyes away from his, then allowed him to help me stand. He glanced at his watch. "I gotta get you home and then get to work."

I nodded.

"Okay if I pick you up at 6:00? We'll grab a burger or something . . ."

"With fries?" I said, maybe a little too quickly. One thing I knew about Steven: he loved fries.

"You know me well." He winked. "Sound good?"

"I'm sure Mom will say it's okay."

Rosa was waiting outside when Steven brought me home. She leaned against one of the oaks, twirling her long dark hair around a finger. Seeing us, she straightened. I waved with all the enthusiasm of a girl spying her best friend. Rosa lifted her hand lazily, then let it fall.

"Thank goodness Rosa is here." I looked at Steven as the

truck slowed to a stop. "If I can't be with you, at least I have her and Heather to pal around with."

Steven's gaze appeared guarded. "What kind of stuff do you do with her?"

"Swim mostly. Otherwise we look at *Glamour* magazines and talk about hair and makeup. You know, girl stuff."

He leaned over and kissed me so quickly I almost missed the moment. "Just be careful."

I drew back. "What does that mean?"

"Nothing." He smiled then. "I really have to go."

I stole a final kiss, then bounded out of the car and over to Rosa. Together we watched the truck back out of the driveway, then turn sharply and head back for the main highway.

"So, where have you been?" Rosa asked. She leaned against the tree again, crossed her arms.

"Steven and I watched the sun rise." I raised my camera. "I think I got some good shots."

Rosa's smile was crooked. At fifteen she had already bloomed into an exotic island flower. I was certain there were not too many boys who hadn't tried to date her already. But Eliana—a widow with no husband to keep the proverbial shotgun prepared—had stood firm and stated emphatically that Rosa would not see any boy until she was sixteen. Even her escort for her quinceañera had been her cousin Luis from the mainland.

Secretly, I wondered though. Rosa was like a wild mustang that couldn't be saddled with the rules of her "overprotective mama."

"You went out with him last night too?"

I felt heat rush to my cheeks. "We did. Last night it was the sunset. Tonight . . . dinner."

"Dinner? Steven Granger is gonna buy you dinner?"

I kicked at the sand with my sandaled toes. "Well . . . burgers."

Rosa laughed. "Not me, *chica*. When I date, the boy is gonna take me to the fancy places in town or there will be no dating Rosa Rivera."

We walked over to the platform, where the Adirondack chairs gleamed white in the morning sunlight. "Do you have your eyes on anyone?" I asked.

Rosa laughed lightly. "Maybe." We sat. "But tell me more about you and Steven," she coaxed.

I crossed my legs, leaned my head back, and closed my eyes. "It's all good."

"Does he kiss you? I mean, other than that little pecking thing I saw in the truck there."

I looked at Rosa and nodded. "Oh yeah."

"What else do you do? Come on, now. You can tell me."

I laughed then. "No," I said. "Nothing like that. Just kissing."

"But you want to, no?"

"But I won't. I've made myself a promise to wait, and I'm going to wait."

Rosa looked up at the house. "Papa Bear would kill you if you didn't, I'd suspect."

I laughed again. "He'd kill us both if he even thought it was a possibility. But Dad knows where I stand on that issue. He knows I want to wait."

Rosa stood and looked down at me. "Then, *linda*, I suggest you be careful how you behave when you are with Steven."

"Meaning?"

Rosa reached over and tugged at the loose strands of my hair. "It means, if you don't want to fight the bull, stay out of the ring."

11

The first thing I noticed about Patsy when she opened the door was the small digital camera wrapped in her hand.

"Ready?" I asked.

"As I'll ever be," she answered.

During the drive to 1st and G streets, I asked her more about her family, most specifically if any of them lived nearby. "Not near enough," was all she said in answer.

"You said you're divorced. I imagine your sons are with their father now?"

I looked straight ahead. The sun was sinking fast and the sky was turning exquisite shades of red and orange. "Yes," I answered. "For five weeks this summer."

"Is this week one?"

I could only nod. "Patsy, do you live here full-time?" I asked for change of subject.

"Every day of the year as long as the Lord allows."

I jutted my chin outward. "Do you ever get tired of this vista?"

"Never." She raised her camera. "That's why I brought

this thing. One of my grans sent it to me. He's stationed over in Iraq, and he says my pictures keep him close to home."

"How nice of you to send him photographs, Patsy. I'm sure he enjoys your letters too."

"What letters?" Patsy almost huffed. "We keep in touch on Facebook. Of course, he can't tell me anything important like where he is and what he's doing, but at least I know he's all right."

"My oldest, Chase, is on Facebook. Cody is champing at the bit for an account, but I told him he has to wait until he's thirteen, like the rules say."

Patsy reached over and patted my knee. "You're a good mama."

It felt like the wind had been knocked out of me. "I just love my sons."

We turned off the main road and onto 3rd. "So then do you keep up on Facebook with what they are doing while they're with their father?"

"Uh . . . no. I don't have an account."

"What? Well, hon, let me get you set up later on, okay? You need to keep up with your boys. Especially these days."

I smiled at the older woman. "Will you?" I asked. "I honestly hadn't thought of getting an account to keep up with them."

Patsy looked out her window. "Land, will you look at that sunset. Downright romantic." She grinned at me. "Nothing personal, darlin', but I sure wish you were a man right now."

We laughed together as I turned off 3rd and onto G Street. By the time we reached 2nd and G, a few cars were parked along the Gulf side of the road so I slid into place behind the last. Patsy opened her door and slung her legs out. "Now, listen. I can't walk up to 1st, but you go on ahead. That's where all the locals like to gather. I'm just gonna sit right here and take my pictures."

I looked toward the place where I knew most of the people would be standing. I'd hoped to see Maddie and her friend there. "I hate to leave you here . . ."

"You're not leaving me," Patsy said. "I'm kicking you out."

I opened the door. "Can I leave my purse here then?"

"Of course." Patsy looked around as she said, "Where's your camera?"

My chest tightened. "I left it at home."

She turned back toward the Gulf. "I'll have to share some of mine with you then."

I nodded then stepped out of the car.

The air was thick. Heavy. The skin of my arms and legs became clammy. But the scene before me was beautiful. I watched as locals ambled from their homes across the street, many of them with a glass in their hands. They chatted with each other like old friends . . . and I was sure most of them were. This was the time of night when work had ceased. The calming of day. A time when, like the sun on the water, reflections could be made without fear.

The sun sunk lower toward a line of trees marking where Cedar Key attempted to wrap around itself. Low-lying clouds turned gold and hung like a net over the glistening water. Beneath them several gulls swooped as they called out. Though I wanted to walk on ahead in hopes of finding Maddie, I found myself unable to move, mesmerized by painted nature.

"I thought that was you."

Startled, I turned in the direction of the voice. A man stood shadowed only a few yards to my left. "I'm sorry?"

"Kimberly, right?"

I squinted. With the distance between us I could only make

104

out his build—tall and muscular—and the dark crop of his hair. He wore tan shorts, an untucked short-sleeved shirt, and Birkenstocks.

When I still said nothing, he added, "Kimberly-Boo?"

Struck with fear, I managed, "Who are you?"

He took a step forward. The scent of expensive cologne and Gulf water met me before he said, "You don't remember your old island buddy, I suppose."

My breath came ragged as my heart skipped. *Could it be?* "Steven?"

Another two steps and I could see his face. He'd changed over the years. Blond streaks had grown dark brown. The boyish features had given way to a man's. Then they'd been soft; now he seemed handsomely chiseled. The brow was naturally furrowed and eyes less carefree. But the impish grin hadn't been stolen by time. That alone remained. "One and the same."

"I . . ."

"Don't know what to say?"

"Quite frankly, no."

Now he stood directly before me. And when he smiled I saw the young man I'd fallen so giddily in love with as a teenage girl. "I thought I saw you today from Dad's boat. Wasn't that you walking near the marina? I waved . . ."

"That was you on the boat?"

"Yep. That was me. You waved back so I thought . . ."

I laughed lightly. "I thought you were some teenaged boy your father had hired for the summer."

Steven laughed too. "I am."

"So what are you doing here?" we asked in unison.

"You first . . ." he said.

"I'm here for Dad. The woman who took care of the house passed away."

105

"Eliana."

"Yes."

"The whole island mourned. She was a staple here, you know."

"She was like another mother to me . . . though I admit I hadn't seen or spoken to her in years."

Steven blinked. "Why not?"

I dipped a shoulder. "I . . . it's just been hard to be here since . . ."

"Your mom passed away?"

I turned back toward the sunset. The sun had gone to its nightly home, and the sky had become a brilliant shade of red. "This is really something, isn't it?"

Steven bent a little at the waist for a better look at me, then straightened. "Tourists sometimes come out here to watch the sunset, then walk or drive away the minute it disappears. What they don't know is that if they'd just wait about fifteen minutes, that's when the sky really puts on a show."

"I remember." Oh how I remembered. More than the colors of the sky I remembered the firework displays inside my own head when, under the canopy of the emblazoned sky, Steven used to wrap me in his arms and kiss me until my knees buckled.

But of course I didn't say that.

We were silent a moment until Steven spoke. "So, where's your camera? I can't remember a time I didn't see you without one slung around your neck."

I looked down at my feet and whispered a silent "thank you" to Heather that I'd gotten a pedicure. "I don't take pictures anymore."

More silence.

"How long are you here for?"

I looked back to the boy of my youth. The one who had taken one summer and turned it into an elusive dream . . . and my life into a nightmare. The boy turned man, who hardly deserved to know how his rejection had affected me. "Not long. I'm only here to find a replacement for Eliana."

"I don't think she's replaceable," he said with a smile, "but I'd venture a guess that if you went to see Rosa, she could help you."

"Rosa. Why do you say that?"

"She owns a real estate office here . . . she's Rosa Fuentes now." He chuckled. "I guess she figures Cedar Key isn't big but it's persistent." He dipped his head. "A lot like Rosa."

I turned fully toward him again and crossed my arms. "Owns it? I was told she worked there."

"Oh no. She owns it. Lock, stock, and barrel."

"So you think she could help me find someone? Because if she could, that would be terrific."

"She has a staff of women who clean some of the rental properties so I don't see why not." He pointed across the street with his thumb. "I'm renting one of her places until I can figure out what I'm doing."

"You don't live here?"

Even in the near-darkness I could see Steven pink. "Now I do. Until Dad either gets well or decides to sell the business. After that, I don't know . . ."

"Your father is sick?"

"Had a massive heart attack last fall."

"I'm sorry. I hadn't heard."

Steven raked his bottom lip with his teeth, made a hissing sound and then said, "So where do you live now?"

"Orlando still."

"Married?"

I couldn't help but laugh. "Why does it seem that is always the first question out of anyone's mouth?" I looked back at my pitiful toes and tightened the hold I had on myself. "No. I'm not. I was, but I'm not now."

"Me too."

I looked back at him, my senses sharpened. "I heard you got married . . ."

Steven looked out across the water. "Long story. Too long." Then, looking at me, he added, "But the good news is that I got one fantastic daughter out of it. Eliza. She's in college now, can you believe it?"

College? Mine were in middle school. "No, I can't."

"You? Do you have kids?"

"Two sons. Chase is fourteen and Cody is eleven."

"Ah . . . the best is yet to come."

"So I hear."

"It will be the time you'll wonder why you had them. Then, they'll become adults and you'll know."

For that I had nothing to say and, apparently, neither did he. He shoved his hands into his pockets and said, "Hey, would you like to come over? Have a cup of coffee or something cold to drink? I don't drink alcohol . . . but I have sodas . . . water . . ." He grinned.

I glanced toward where my car was parked. In the dusk, I could no longer make out my companion sitting there. "I have someone with me."

Steven blew out a breath. "Oh."

"No . . . not a man . . . I assume you mean a man . . . no. I have Patsy . . . uh. Goodness, I don't even know her last name."

"Patsy Milstrap? Older woman? Lives next to your dad's house?"

Apparently people living in Cedar Key still knew everyone who lived in Cedar Key. "Yes."

He grinned; I could almost see relief rush across his brow, and in spite of the years since we'd last kissed good-bye "until next time," I couldn't help but feel smug.

"Okay, then," he said.

"Well."

"Maybe I'll see you around the island."

"I don't intend to be here long."

We stared at each other, both blinking in silence.

"All right then," he said.

"Good-bye, Steven." I extended my hand.

His gripped mine easily, the palm torn between soft and callused. I wondered what he'd done before returning to his father's boat. "It was good to see you again, Kimberly."

My hand slipped from his. I shuffled past the man I'd once thought I couldn't live without, the boy whose name I'd written all over the inside front cover of every composition book of my senior year of high school. The man-child who had broken my heart as it had never been crushed before.

Until Charlie.

Then, when I was halfway between Steven and Patsy, I heard him call out, "Boo!"

I turned. He was jogging toward me. When he came to a stop, he placed his hands on his hips and said, "Listen, I know this is kind of short notice, but . . . would you like to have dinner with me tomorrow night?"

"Dinner?"

"Yeah. You know, we'll go to a restaurant . . . sit down . . . eat? It won't be McDonald's on the mainland"—he winked—"but it'll be good."

"So you mean . . . like a date?"

Steven blinked, then widened his eyes. "Well, you don't have to call it a date if you don't want to."

I pressed my hand against my chest, felt my heart hammering beneath. Traitor. "No, I mean . . . I just . . . it's just . . ." Surely my smile looked foolish. I laughed in an effort to cover up the anxiety. "I haven't been asked out on a date since I married Charlie."

His brow furrowed. "Not even since the divorce?"

"No."

"You've just divorced?"

I shook my head. "It's been over a year."

"Then Orlando is filled with fools."

My cheeks grew warm. "Thank you for that. But the truth is, Orlando is filled with Charlie's friends. None of them would dare ask me out. No one wants to cross Charlie Tucker."

His face softened with compassion. "Charlie Tucker is a fool too." He blinked. "I should know."

I smiled. "Thank you for that too."

"Tomorrow night then?"

I nodded. "That would be lovely."

"I'll pick you up at 7:00. We'll eat then come back here to watch the sunset again." He glanced toward the water. "It's never the same twice, you know."

"Yes," I said. "I remember."

I called Heather as soon as I got back to the house to tell her about seeing Steven after twenty-four years.

"You sound like a schoolgirl."

I sat cross-legged at the head of my bed. "Don't be silly. I'm just excited that I have an actual date. And one Charlie can't bully."

"Did he tell you what happened after the two of you had your summer of love? About him and his . . . wife?"

I gritted my teeth just as Max sauntered into the room then landed with a plop on the floor. "Max sends his best," I teased in an attempt to change the subject.

"So he did or he didn't?"

"No. Maybe I'll ask him about her tomorrow night." I jutted my chest for a semblance of bravado. "I'll throw in a question or two about his divorce too."

"That should make for interesting conversation." I could hear the frown on Heather's face.

"Change of subject . . . how is everything there?" I'd been listening—as I always did with Heather this time of day—for any slurring of her words, any clinking of ice against glass. So far, I'd heard none. Or, I thought, maybe I'm getting too used to the sound of it all.

"Andre worked late again tonight. No big shock there. Kids are busy as ever and certainly not in need of me hovering over them. I, on the other hand, have started a belly dancing class."

"A what?"

"For exercise. I just got home . . . Andre nearly flipped because dinner wasn't on the table. But I say a ham and cheese sandwich never hurt anyone."

"What time is the class?"

"Six to eight, twice a week."

I looked at the digital clock on the bedside table. It was nearly ten. "And you're just now getting home?"

"My new friend Leslie and I went out for a . . . a while afterward."

Went out for a drink, she meant to say. But, I reasoned, she didn't sound drunk . . . or even buzzed. "Oh."

"Have you talked to the boys?"

"Chase called Monday night, and since then it's just been texting. I'm going to text them as soon as you and I hang up and see if they're still up."

"Go text then. I'm going to go shimmy in front of Andre and see if I can gain his attention in the process."

The very idea made me grin. "You do that. I'll call tomorrow for details." I sat up straight. "Wait! No. No details."

"Yeah, yeah. You're the one who better call with details. I want to know why I had to hear you cry for a solid year after your summer—"

"Of love. Yes, I know. Bye, Heather."

"Bye, sis."

12

Chase returned my text wondering if they were still awake with: "Y, C&C r up."

I'd learned to read the shorthand. *Yes, Chase and Cody are up.*

Not wanting Charlie to hear the ring of the phone and possibly interrupt my time with my sons, I texted back: *Call me.*

Seconds later, I heard Cody's sweet voice. "Hi, Mom."

"Cody. How's it going?"

"It's going good. Dad has us working every day, and I'm pretty tired at night."

"What kind of work are you doing?" I stretched out on the bed just as Max groaned on the floor beside me. "Oh. Max says hey."

"Maxey . . ."

"I'll give him a kiss for you."

"Okay." He paused. He moved on to my question. "Just stuff around the business. Nothing big."

"Like what?"

"Mostly I'm kinda hanging out with Grandpa."

"I bet Grandpa loves that."

"I do too."

I wanted to know more, but Cody was too young and too loyal to spill the information I hoped for. "Where's Chase?"

"Right here. He's watching some show on the television Dad put in our room."

"A television in your room?" A breaking of my rule against too much media in the bedroom. But, I realized, that was my rule, not Charlie's. I'd wanted us to be a family when we were watching television, not everyone hidden away in their own rooms. Charlie, I thought, only wanted them out of his hair.

"Yeah. Cable and everything."

"Everything? What does that mean?"

A shuffling on the other end and then I heard, "Hey, Mom."

"Chase, what did Cody mean 'and everything'?"

Chase snickered a little. "Nothing. Just that we have a bunch of channels to keep us entertained and out of the way."

Cody's sweet voice spoke in the background. "That's not true, Chase."

"It is true, Code. You just can't see it."

"Chase," I said. "Talk to me. What's going on over there?"

"Nothing, really. Dad works all day and gives us enough to do to keep us busy. I like it, actually. I like the work. I can't see myself doing it the rest of my life, but I like it."

I sighed. In an odd sort of way, I wanted Chase to tell me that something sinful was happening so I could run into court and prove my case. Then again, I never wanted my sons exposed to any more than they'd already been exposed to by just being children caught in the middle of divorce. "I'm glad to hear that."

"Did you find someone to clean the house?"

"Not yet, but I have some leads." It dawned on me then that I hadn't seen Maddie or her friend at the sunset. Of course, cleaning it was one thing, keeping it up twice a month was another altogether.

"So you'll be home soon?"

"Should be."

"You don't sound too happy about it."

I sat up. "What do you mean?"

"Well, last time I talked to you, you said you wanted to find someone and get home as soon as possible. But just now you sounded . . . I don't know . . . kinda disappointed."

That's because your mother has a date . . .

"Being in Cedar Key is better than I remembered."

"I love Cedar Key. I don't know how you could've stayed away so long."

Shame, I thought. I'd fallen so stupidly in love as an impressionable seventeen-year-old to a boy who had so quickly forgotten me. "Me either," I answered. "Anyway, I'll say good night. I love you, Chase."

"Love you too, Mom."

A rustle on the other end of the line and then I heard Cody's voice. "I love you too, Mom."

"I love you, Code. Sleep tight."

"Don't let the bedbugs bite."

It rained during the night. Not a storm really, but enough that I heard the patter of raindrops on my window. When I let Max out the next morning, the grass was still wet and the air was now thick enough to slice.

After breakfast and a shower I put on a pair of tan cargo pants, a navy scoop-neck cotton blouse, and a pair of leather slide shoes. I ran a brush through the length of my blonde hair then secured it with a navy scrunchie in the center of the back of my head. For the sake of it, I swished the ponytail

115

a few times and felt the tickle of hair against the bare skin between my shoulders. I felt like a teenage girl again.

I left Max after telling him I would be back soon. "Mind the store, will ya?" I asked him. He panted at me, then curled up near the window where the sunlight fell on the floor.

While I thought it would be easy to find the realty office where Rosa worked, it wasn't. After enough time to find *anything* in Cedar Key, I parallel parked on the opposite side of Dock Street's shops and restaurants, just across from a gift shop called Dilly Dally Gally. The windows were decorated well enough to entice me to stop in the shop for the heck of it. But a quick glance from the dashboard clock to the storefront sign told me it hadn't opened yet.

When I got out of the car, my eyes automatically cut toward the Gulf waters and, in particular, to Steven's father's dock. The corner of my lips twitched when I saw that no one—and nothing—was there.

The aroma of hot brewing coffee mixed with the scent of salt and marsh turned my head in the opposite direction. A small café boasting a Big-Bird-yellow shingle and a red neon "open" sign in the window beckoned me. I stepped between the slow-moving traffic and opened the door to the heavenly scent of coffee beans, fried eggs, and warm bread. Several people sat in the café area to the left, a few of them reading the morning news. A table of four chatted about the antics of the evening before. One woman sat in the back, staring out the window toward Atsena Otie. A mug of coffee stood forgotten in the center of the soda shop table between her and the pane of glass.

"Good morning."

I turned my attention to the counter where, on the other side, a pretty woman just a few years older than me stood.

She wore her long blonde hair pulled tight in a ponytail, which hung from the loop of her white Kona Joe's baseball cap. Her smile was as bright as the white tee she wore under a multi-colored apron.

"Good morning," I said.

"Hungry?"

"No . . . well, the coffee smells marvelous."

"How about an iced mocha latte?"

With the increasing heat outside, to sit inside with such a suggestion was better than anything I could come up with. "Sounds perfect."

The woman set about preparing my coffee. "Vacationing?" she asked.

I opened the change purse I'd brought with me and pulled out a few dollars. "Not really. My father owns a house here, and I'm trying to find someone to clean it when no one is here."

The woman placed a plastic cup of iced coffee on the countertop between us and gave me the price, then said, "Eliana must have taken care of it before."

"Yes," I said, handing her wilted bills. "Keep the change." I took a sip through the straw and said, "Oh my."

The smile showed approval. "Good, huh?"

"Better than good."

"I'm Edie, by the way."

"Kimberly . . . Kim Claybourne Tucker."

"Dr. Claybourne's daughter?"

I nodded as I took another sip, then said, "Do you know where Rosa—Eliana's daughter—has her realty office?"

"Of course. It's between the Historical Society building and the Baptist Church on 2nd. Easy to miss if you aren't looking for it."

"And even if you are."

The sound of chimes behind me indicated others were entering the café. "I'll go have a seat," I said. "Thanks for the information."

I chose a table near the back window even though the sunlight blasting through caused it to be the warmest spot in the room. Overhead, ceiling fans were motionless. The woman who'd been looking out the window turned to look at me. "Hello," I said.

"Morning."

I sat. "Quite a few here."

"I come here every morning just to stare out at the water and the land. The fishermen. The gulls and the herons and the pelicans. Put them all together and they center me."

I smiled at her words, then turned toward a rack of photography gift cards standing near the door leading to the back deck of Adirondack chairs and footrests painted with pink flamingos over parrot-green slats. Over them, wind socks swayed and twirled in the Gulf breeze. I took another sip of coffee, then stood and walked over to the display. Each card held an artistic image of life in Cedar Key. I pulled out one, which was of a sailboat in front of the bows of two others docked at the marina in the glow of early morning sunlight, and studied it.

"That's from over at the marina," the woman said.

"Yes," I said with a nod.

I replaced the card and removed another one. "That one is from over there on Atsena Otie."

I turned and looked at the woman. She seemed so small. She wore white shorts—which seemed all the whiter by the tan of her thin legs—and a yellow sleeveless tee. Her short salt-and-pepper hair framed her face. Her eyes were green, greener still against the backdrop of the water. She wore an expression I well knew. "You took these, didn't you?" I asked.

"I did."

"They're great." I returned the card and turned the display to view others. "What do you shoot with?"

"Just a point and shoot. I don't have anything fancy."

"But you have an eye . . ."

"Always shoot toward the light, I say. Keep your eye on the light and everything else will fall into place."

I pulled a few cards then and said, "So you sell these?"

The woman nodded. "My name is Anne."

"Well, Anne . . . do I pay you or Edie?"

"Edie." She blinked then added, "What do you shoot with?"

"What?"

"Your camera."

"Oh, I don't have . . . how did you know?"

"You asked me what I shoot with. Only camera buffs and serious photographers use that terminology. Otherwise you would have just asked me what kind of camera I have. Even that would have been a giveaway. Most people don't know to ask."

I looked down at the short stack of cards now in my hand. "I haven't taken any photographs in a while." Then I looked up and smiled. "But these are impressive, Anne. Thank you."

I left after paying for the cards, returned to my car, and headed toward 2nd and E Streets. Edie was correct when she said that if I wasn't looking for the realty office, I wouldn't find it. It was safely tucked behind a white picket fence and a blanket of shrubbery. I parked the car, then walked up the steps of the expansive front porch.

A hot cross breeze blew from end to end, causing the clusters of white wicker front porch rockers to sway back and forth and the large baskets of hanging ferns to wave in the sunlight. Overhead, the narrow boards of the porch ceiling were sky blue and had fluffy cumulus clouds painted on them. It was the next best thing to being in the open.

The bronze placard to the right of the front door was as unassuming as the location. A plate with "Come On In" engraved on it was adhered to the white wooden door. I knocked anyway.

"Come on in!" the voice of a woman ordered.

I opened the door by way of an old brass knob. It squeaked in response.

A woman who appeared to be in her thirties sat on the other side of an L-shaped desk in a room that had, at one time, served as the living room of someone's home. Sixteen-by-twenty glossy photographs of Cedar Key landmarks were framed and hung on burnt orange walls trimmed with cream-colored baseboards and ornate crown molding. "Can I help you?"

I discreetly wiped at the sweat beading over my lips. "I'm looking for Rosa Fuentes."

"Do you have an appointment?" she asked.

The air seemed to go still around me. The scent of vanilla from a burning candle on a small table across the room and near the sitting area made me feel lightheaded and unsure of myself. "No," I said. "I'm an old friend."

"Your name?"

"Kimberly Tuck—Kimberly Claybourne."

The woman stood. I watched her as she walked out of the room, past open eight-panel glass French doors, which led into another room, and then disappeared around a corner to the right. I stood listless for a moment, then walked to the sitting area. I sat on the contemporary winter white sofa

splayed with an assortment of brightly colored throw pillows.
I felt the cushions envelop me, but I didn't sit back. I crossed
my ankles and kept my back straight. A moment later the
woman returned and said, "Rosa said to come on back."

I followed the point of the woman's coral-painted nail to
the direction she'd just come from. I went into a square hallway that opened up to four doors, all of which were closed. I
felt like a contestant on the television show I heard Dad talk
about—the one where people dressed up and had to choose
a door to get a prize. Door number one . . . door number
two . . .

"It's that door right there," the woman said from behind
me. "Right in front of you."

I stepped to the door and tapped with the knuckle of my
index finger.

"Please come in."

The voice was rich with Latin flavor.

I opened the door.

The room was painted the color of fresh cream, and the
carpet—thick and luxurious—was the same. The U-shaped
desk positioned near the floor to ceiling window was ultra-
contemporary cherry and glass. Everything about the room
from the wall hangings to the ficus at the left of the window
screamed success.

A petite dark-skinned beauty stood in the center of the
U. Her black hair was pulled back in a chignon; rebellious
wisps had managed to fight their way to hang loose about
an oval face. Her eyes were as black and penetrating as I'd
remembered and the lips just as pouty. The package as a
whole was dramatic to say the least.

"Rosa."

I expected my old friend would run around the desk and that

we would embrace in a long-overdue hug. Instead, she extended her hand for a shake and said, "Kimberly. It's been a long time."

I couldn't for the life of me remember her ever calling me by my full name. When she heard Dad call me "Boo" she would too. Otherwise she called me Kim and sometimes even "Boo-Boo." But never Kimberly.

I took her hand. It was cold and unfriendly.

"Have a seat," she said, indicating a chair on the other side of her desk. She returned to her executive's chair as she said, "Are you shopping for a vacation home?"

"No. I . . ." I cleared my throat. This was not going at all the way I'd expected since Steven had suggested Rosa's contacts. "How have you been, Rosa?"

She looked around the room and said, "Busy, as you can see. Cedar Key is back on the upswing in rentals and sales."

I expected her to ask about me. When she didn't I said, "I'm sorry about your mother."

I watched her swallow hard, press her lips together, and then look out the window. The sunlight revealed the shimmer of tears pooling in her eyes. She took a deep breath and turned back to me. "She was one of a kind."

"She was for sure."

She pursed her lips, then parted them and said, "How can I help you then?"

My shoulders sank between the blades. "I was told you may be able to help me find someone to replace your mother as a housekeeper for Dad and Anise."

"There will never be a replacement for my mother." Rosa's words were clipped and barely audible, but I made them out just fine.

"Well, no . . . that much is for sure. Still, Dad wants me to find someone to—"

"Why didn't he come then?"

"Dad had some pressing issues at the office and . . . to be honest, Rosa, he thought that if I came it would give me something to do while my sons are with their father for the summer."

Rosa's face softened. "You have sons?"

"Two. Chase and Cody."

Rosa reached for a polished silver frame on her desk and turned it toward me. Three handsome boys reflected their mother's stunning beauty. They looked like models. "I have three."

I noticed then the wide band over a massive engagement ring on her left hand. "You've done well, Rosa."

"I've worked myself nearly silly to get here." The ice in her voice had returned, and I was completely at a loss as to why.

"I saw Steven Granger last night. He said you may have a suggestion for someone to help with the house."

Rosa leaned back in her chair. "That must have been quite the reunion." Then she smiled, catlike. "He's still something else to look at, isn't he?"

I felt my face grow hot, and I blinked several times in an effort to gain my composure. "I guess. Rosa, I just need to find someone to clean the house on a regular basis so I can get back to Orlando."

She took a deep breath and exhaled slowly. "I'll see what I can come up with."

"I appreciate that."

"Have you done anything else to try to find someone? An ad in the *Cedar Key News* perhaps."

"The paper? I hadn't thought of that. I did put up a flyer down at the market."

"That's good."

"You know, the kind with the bottom cut for tearing off."

"Of course." Then she stood. "Well, perhaps between all that we can come up with something."

I was being dismissed. Just like that.

I stood too. "Thank you." I opened my change purse and pulled out a piece of paper I'd earlier folded and placed within it. "Here's my cell number. I look forward to hearing from you."

Rosa took the paper, placed it on her desk as though it were a piece of lint, and said, "Like I said, I'll see what I can come up with." She forced a smile. "Good to see you again, Kimberly."

"You too, Rosa," I said, then turned and left the office, feeling a little like I'd just left a freezer.

13

I checked on Patsy that afternoon before I went inside to get ready for my evening with Steven. She was "Facebooking" with one of her grandchildren. "Just let me know when you want me to get you set up," she told me.

I assured her I'd be asking soon.

At home, Max was more than a little happy to see me. He shot past me in a blur, his nails clipping the stairs as he bounded toward the yard. I watched as he found his spot and then ambled off toward Patsy's, presumably in search of Oreo.

I went inside then. I took a long tepid shower to cool me from the day's heat and humidity, then went to the closet and stared into it. I had no idea what to wear. Was Steven taking me someplace fancy and intimate or to one of the more casual tourist eateries? After determining that surely this was going to be more of an informal date, I chose a cotton scoop-neck summer dress covered in red, yellow, and green flowers. I pulled my hair back in a ponytail, took it down, then put it back up again.

Not being one to wear much in the way of makeup, I applied a tinted lotion to my face followed by a single stroke of mascara and a light coral lip gloss.

While I waited, I went into the living room and dialed Dad's cell phone number. He answered on the third ring.

"Hey, Dad."

"Hey, Boo. How's it going there?"

Right to business. I hadn't found anyone yet to replace Eliana, and I felt the slow dance of not measuring up swirl inside of me. "A couple of things look promising. I posted a notice down at the market, and last night I ran into someone, who suggested that I stop in and talk with Rosa. Did you know she owns a real estate business here?"

Dad was quiet for a moment before saying, "Yes, I know. I see Rosa every so often when I'm over there."

"Oh."

"What did Rosa say? Anything of interest?"

"Not really. In fact . . . well, never mind. I asked if she could help me find someone to clean the house. She seemed pretty noncommittal about it."

"I'm sure she's very busy."

"I guess."

"Anything else? Have you talked with the boys?"

I smiled. "Yes. They're doing fine."

"Good."

From where I sat, I saw Max running across the back lawn. "Dad," I said. "I met Patsy next door. Max and her cat have become fast friends."

Dad chuckled. "Ah, Patsy. She's a sport, isn't she?"

"She's something else. She's going to teach me Facebook so I can stay in better contact with Chase, and he can keep me up to date on Cody."

"Facebook . . . I don't know how hardworking adults have the time."

It was my turn to laugh. "Me either, Dad." I sighed. "Well, if I get a nibble, I'll let you know, okay?"

"Sounds good."

I ended our call and stretched. Thirsty, I decided to get a bottle of water from the wet bar pint-sized refrigerator. As I twisted the cap, I noticed the framed photograph next to the bar, one my mother had taken. It was of various-sized bar glasses, lined up and gleaming in either the early morning or the late afternoon sunlight. I leaned toward the 8-by-10 matted work and noticed for the first time that every glass held the telltale sign of a woman's lipstick. Each glass was turned so that the impression of lips faced the bottom right corner of the photo.

It was as if Mom had kissed the scene before she photographed it. "She was truly something else," I whispered.

Somewhere in the room I heard her voice: "Kim, you are simply amazing, sweetheart. Simply amazing. What made you think to tilt the camera like that . . ."

I shook my head just as a knock echoed through the room. *Steven.*

When I opened the door, I found Max sitting on his haunches at Steven's feet.

"Hi," he said. Steven wore black vintage wash jeans, a golden tan waffle tee, and Converse shoes.

"Hi."

He looked from me to Max and back to me. "This yours?" A dimple cut deep into his cheek, and I smiled.

"He's my buddy," I said, repeating the words Patsy had spoken to me of Oreo. "Max, this is Steven. Steven, Max."

Steven shifted to a squat with one knee resting on the deck

and the other supporting his elbow. He extended his hand, and Max placed his paw dutifully in it. "Nice to meet you, Max."

"Come in," I said. "I'll get my purse."

Max shot in and headed straight for the kitchen, where his food and water bowls waited for him. Steven closed the door and said, "I'm glad you didn't dress up. I forgot to tell you it would be casual."

I picked up my purse and twirled around as I put on my best "stunned" expression. "What? I don't look dressed up?"

Steven cocked his head to one side. "You know what I mean."

I nodded. "I do." I started for the door. "Shall we then?"

"We shall."

Steven took me to a rustic waterfront restaurant, Coconuts, which was upstairs over the billiards bar. He escorted me to a table for two next to the window, which overlooked the Gulf and an old fisherman's shack that appeared ready to collapse under the weight of any breeze, no matter how weak. "It's still here," I said.

"The locals call it the Honeymoon Cottage," Steven said.

"I remember."

"This is great seating. We'll have a nice view of the sunset if you decide I'm worth your time and we're still here." I heard the lilt in his voice; it was the same as when we were kids.

I looked out over the water. Black thick ripples bobbed toward the shoreline.

A server came to the table and asked for our drink order. "I don't drink alcohol," Steven said to me, "but if you . . ."

"No," I said. "Me either." I looked up at the server. "Sweet iced tea if you have it, please."

"We do," she said.

"Sounds good," Steven said. "Make it two."

128

Steven pulled the menus from a chrome holder at the end of the table, handed me one, and said, "The coconut shrimp is my favorite."

"With fries?" I asked.

I watched his eyes slide from his open menu to mine. "Yeah," he said, slow and sweet.

My feet tingled. "Coconut shrimp and fries, then."

After he placed our identical orders—which we soon learned came with coleslaw—he rested his elbows on the table, laced his fingers, and said, "So, did you see Rosa?"

I took a sip of tea. "I did."

"What was that look for?"

"What look?"

"You made a face. What happened with Rosa?"

I shrugged. "She's just different than I remember her."

This time, Steven made the face.

"What was *that* look for?"

He chuckled. "Never mind. Did she say if she could help you find someone?"

"She said she'd try. I don't know, Steven. I felt . . . it seemed like . . . well, like she really didn't *want* to help me. Like she was holding some kind of grudge or something. I expected her to at the very least be happy to see me."

"Sounds just like Rosa."

"Meaning?"

Steven leaned toward me as though he were about to tell me some grave secret. "Rosa has had some chip on her shoulder since we were teenagers."

"You're kidding."

"I wouldn't kid about those years."

I felt myself grow warm and prayed I wasn't blushing. "Oh, well . . . I guess I will continue to try on my own to find someone. In the meantime, I'm getting a little done around the place."

He smiled again. "Tell me about yourself, Kimberly-Boo."

Just then our dinner was served, so I waited to answer. After the server asked if we needed anything else and then walked away, Steven said, "Do you mind if I say a blessing over our food?"

I blinked. "No. No, of course not."

Steven's prayer was short, to the point. When he was done, he said, "Dig in."

I popped a hot, perfectly seasoned fry in my mouth. "Yum."

"Good, huh?"

"Very." I took another sip of tea and said, "I'm a teacher."

"What?"

I laughed. "You asked me to tell you about myself, remember?"

The dimple returned. "I did, didn't I? Okay, then. What do you teach?"

"Not what. Who. Second grade."

"Hmm . . ." Steven bit into a shrimp.

I nodded, felt my ponytail tickle my skin. "Second graders can be both a challenge and a lot of fun too. Their minds are like sponges."

"Hmm . . ." he repeated.

We both laughed. "What about you?" I asked.

Steven looked out over the water and then back to me. "Well, as you know, I'm tending Dad's business until . . . well, who knows how long. Before I moved here, I lived in Atlanta and worked as an executive manager of one of the malls."

"Really?"

"I couldn't make that up."

I also took a bite of shrimp. "You were right. These are fabulous."

"Not necessarily good for you, but hey . . . what is these days?"

"True."

He took a sip of his tea before asking, "You have sons, you said. Chase and Cody, was it?"

"Chase and Cody, yes." I could feel myself glowing. "I have photos, of course, if you'd like to see." Even as I suggested it, I was reaching for my purse.

Steven wiped his hands on his napkin and then reached across the table as I produced a small photo album. He flipped through it, made dutiful noises, then asked, "Did you take these?"

"No. Their father did, actually. And, of course, the school pictures . . ."

Steven looked hard at me as he handed the photo album back across the table. "You told me last night that you don't take pictures anymore. Why?"

I shrugged but I didn't answer.

"Your mother?"

I nodded as I felt tears sting the back of my eyes. "Change the subject," I said, nearly choking on the words.

He was quiet before he said, "All right then. What would you like to talk about?"

Part of me wanted him to explain to me what exactly had occurred the year after our summer romance. How he'd so casually tossed aside what we'd had for the girl he'd met at college. But, so far, we were having an okay evening and I didn't want to ruin it, so I said, "You said you have a daughter?"

"Eliza, yes. The apple of my eye." He winked as he wiped

his hands again on the napkin and reached for his back pocket. "Now it's your turn to look at photos."

There were four pictures of his daughter between the sides of a black soft leather wallet. The first showed Eliza standing on her grandfather's boat, another was of her high school graduation, and the last two were of her with her father, arms laced, both dressed in formal wear. The photos showed evidence of her being tall, fair in complexion, with long strawberry-blonde hair and dark blue eyes. I noticed that in each photograph she wore an apple-shaped necklace, which I pointed out to Steven.

"The apple of my eye," he said again. "Remember?"

"You said that, yes."

He took the wallet from me and turned the pictures toward himself. "I had that necklace specially made by one of the jewelers at the mall where I worked," he said. "Fourteen karat gold. Rubies and emeralds." He looked up at me. "Cost me a little, but she's worth it."

I found myself in an unlikely place. I didn't know the young woman, and she looked sweet enough. But I didn't want to talk about her anymore. I looked out over the water again, then toward the sky. It had turned dark blue; the clouds the color of pink cotton candy. "Do you think the tide will take the water way out tonight?"

"Might. Would you like to go out for a walk?"

I did. I didn't. I did . . . "No. Not tonight."

I felt Steven's hand brush against mine. "Kim?" I looked at him as I slid my hand to my lap. "What's wrong? Did I say something that's upset you?"

I shook my head. "No. I'm fine, really I am." I forced a smile.

Steven looked down at where his hand continued to rest

on the table and said, "I was thinking that maybe tomorrow morning we could watch the sunrise together."

"What does *that* mean?"

He laughed. "No . . . no, no, no. Nothing like that." He leaned back in his seat. "Man, that sounded like I wanted you to come up and see my etchings, didn't it?"

I nodded. "I should say."

"What I meant was that maybe I could pick you up early. I'll make a thermos of coffee. We can sit near the boat dock and wait for the sun to rise. Then, we can go have some breakfast at Kona Joe's."

It was so tempting. This whole thing . . . so tempting. And, for a moment, I felt as though I were some lovesick heroine in a romance novel, about to fall in love all over again. Maybe for the last time. I imagined the sun rising on the silhouettes of Steven and me, arms wrapped around each other, lips pressed together . . . like when we were young, before our parents even knew we'd snuck out of our respective homes . . .

I shook my head. "I don't think so, Steven."

Disappointment registered on his face. "Maybe another time, then."

"Maybe," I said, though my heart whispered, *No. Never.*

14

September 1987—May 1988

In the beginning the letters came often enough. At first, every two days or so but eventually only once a week.

College, Steven wrote, *takes up a lot more time than high school, Boo. And I'm not just talking about the frat parties either—ha ha*.

I didn't like the idea of Steven at frat parties, and I told him so in a return letter.

```
Maybe you should just concentrate on your
studies, Steven. And not frat parties. I
hear all kinds of loose girls go to them.
They get drunk and they let boys do things.
I don't want to think about you with any
loose girls.
```

Steven wasted no time; another letter was on the table lying askew in the pewter bread tray my parents used for incoming and outgoing mail only a few days later.

```
Oh, baby, don't think like that. I was just
horsing around with you. The studies keep
me plenty busy and then Dad and Mom want me
back in Cedar Key every weekend I don't have
something going on here. Believe me, between
studies and my folks, there's little time
for women.

Besides, with someone like you waiting on
me, why would I ever be interested in anyone
else?
```

"He's lying," Heather had said as we sat across from each other on the twin beds of our shared bedroom.

I reached over and snatched the pages from my sister's hands. A whiff of Steven's cologne struck me; he always dotted the pages with it so I wouldn't forget him, he told me. I did the same back. My Lady Stetson to his Stetson for Men.

I pressed the pages to my chest. "He is not. Why would you even think that?"

"Oh, please. Do you honestly believe that a guy as good looking as Steven Granger is sitting in his dorm room night after night, hunched over the books or writing you letters? I bet there are all kinds of girls checking him out."

I squared my shoulders. "Maybe that's true. But Steven is not the kind of guy to fall for their wiles."

Heather stretched out her legs and fell toward the thick pillow at the headboard. "Whatever you say, Kim."

I stood over my sister. "I say, Heather, because no matter what temptation I placed in front of him, he was always the gentleman."

Heather rose on her elbows. "You'd better not let Dad or Mom hear you say that. You'll never go out with him again and you know it."

I blew out my frustration toward my sister, then stomped over to her desk to write a return letter.

I miss you so much. I cannot wait until Christmas. Honestly, if Dad and Mom say we aren't going to CK for the holiday, I swear to you, I'll run away and meet up with you there. This letter writing is fine and dandy, but what I need, Steven, is to hear your voice and to feel your arms around me one more time.

And then Christmas came. I could hardly contain myself as we drove to our island home the Saturday before. I had already written to Steven and asked him to meet me that day at City Park.

Two o'clock, and don't be late.

His return letter had been more than a week in coming, but the words he'd written were all the Christmas wonder I needed.

I'll be there. I cannot wait to see you either. You'll be a breath of fresh air and a sight for sore eyes. (I know, totally cliché, but I never claimed to be a poet.)

When I told my parents I wanted to—*had to*—take the car to the park, they'd complied. "Why don't you take Ami with you?" Dad teased. He winked, but nearly five-year-old Ami had overheard and made her fussy demands.

"Dad," I said through clenched teeth.

But he only said with a chuckle, "Sorry, Boo."

And so Ami had tagged along, meaning that Steven and I couldn't really be alone. I couldn't lose myself in him as I'd daydreamed of doing. I would have to keep an eye on the toddling, always prancing around Ami.

In the end, it didn't matter. Steven was waiting for me—alone—by one of the children's play sets. I ran to him nearly as fast as Ami ran for the sliding board. He opened his arms, and I slammed into his chest with all the force of a lost lover. "Wow," he said. "Miss me much?"

I leaned my head back. "Don't you dare tease me." And then he kissed me, long and hard.

"What's with bringing Ami?" he asked, eyeing my kid sister.

"She was being a brat, so Dad said I had to."

Steven laughed. "She's our chaperone."

I allowed my voice to go low and smoky. "Do we need one?"

He kissed me again. "I'd say we do."

But for the week we were together, Steven remained the gentleman he'd always been. We didn't see each other nearly as much as I hoped; it seemed he always had something he had to do. "You know moms during Christmas," he said by way of excuse. I didn't like the restrictions on our time—hated them, in fact—but I had little choice but to go along with it.

The moments I wasn't with Steven, I hung out with Heather and once with Rosa. We went out on the family boat on a warm day, scouting for birds and dolphins. We docked at At-sena Otie and hiked—as Steven and I had done in the summer months—from the shell-scattered beach, under the crooked fat branches of the oaks, and between the thick fronds of the saw palmettos, until we reached the old graveyard, where I photographed the headstones and Rosa made up stories about the deceased.

"Look at this, chica," she said as she stood before one of the graves. "They practically put the life stories on these headstones."

I walked over to the time-yellowed, mossy tombstone. "J. R. Hudson," I read. "Born February 16, 1835. Died January 5, 1883."

"Over a hundred years ago."

I continued reading. "Leaving a wife and five children . . ." I squatted to take a photograph. "You're right," I said. "It is like reading their life stories."

"Wonder what they'll write on our tombstones," Rosa mused.

I stood then. "Kimberly Claybourne Granger," I said with a smile. "Wife of Steven. Mother of . . . hmm." I looked at the writing near my feet. "Five perfect children."

Rosa laughed lightly.

"What about you, Rosa? What will yours say?"

Rosa's eyes rose to where the blue sky peeked between the limbs and leaves of the gnarled trees. "Rosa . . . last name here . . . loving wife. No. *Passionate* wife of . . . first name here. Mother of . . . three. Lived to love. Loved to live."

I furrowed my brow. "Last name here?" My tongue slipped across dry lips. "Come on now, Rosa. You've been seeing someone, haven't you?" The look on Rosa's face confirmed what I had suspected since we'd returned for the holiday. "Aha! Does your mother know? She doesn't! I can tell. Ooooh, Rosa! Tell me, who. Tell me." I giggled at the thought of Rosa sneaking around with some boy on the island.

But Rosa shook her head. "No one you know."

I picked up a branch lying nearby and poked it at my friend. "Tell me, Gooney-bird."

Rosa laughed as she danced away. "Just some boy my cousin Luis introduced me to."

I was right behind her, holding tight to my camera lest it bam against me and leave me bruised. We ran along the winding trail leading back to the beach, giggling like schoolgirls, until we reached the boat. I held the key up and said, "No leaving this island until you spill the beans, chica."

"It's nothing big," Rosa said. "Only, I think I love him very much but . . ."

"But?"

Rosa shook her head and kicked at the remainder of an old horseshoe crab shell. "It's nothing."

"Does he live on the mainland?"

"Yes."

I crossed my arms. "You're being so mysterious," I said with a wink. Rosa looked up but didn't smile. A realization hit me, making me feel dizzy. "Is he . . . *married*?"

Rosa laughed then. "Yes, Boo-Boo. I'm fifteen and dating a married man on the mainland."

I waved away the sarcasm. "Okay, okay. Is he . . . older?"

"*Un poco*. A little."

I tapped my temple as if I were mentally filing away the clues. "Okay. He is a friend of your cousin. He lives on the mainland. He is a little older. And he does *not* know your mother."

"He knows Mama. *She* just doesn't know that we have seen each other a few times."

"A few times? And you think you're in love already?"

"I know I am."

139

"Rosa . . ."

"Don't make fun of me, chica." Rosa's eyes filled with tears. "You don't know what you are talking about."

I reached for Rosa's hand and held it. "Okay, okay. So, you don't want me to know anything more, I take it?"

"No. Best you don't. In case Mama gets suspicious and asks you questions, you can say that you don't know about anything."

We squeezed our hands in oath. "Okay. But promise me you'll tell me when you can."

Rosa kissed me on the cheek then. "I promise. You'll be the first to know."

In May, when the final letter came—and the letters came only once a week by then—I fell apart. I stayed in my bed and cried for days. I refused to go to school. I didn't care that these were the last days of senior year, supposedly one of the best years of my life.

Heather hovered close but not too close. Jayme-Leigh said she thought the whole thing was ridiculous. "Use your brain," she said. "Get a good education and forget about him." Ami cried with me, even though she didn't know why we were crying.

Mom and Dad both gave me the space I needed, and eventually I was able to add the letter to the top of the stack I kept in an ornate wooden box. The letter, which read:

You will always be special to me, Boo. Always. And don't think there was anything you did wrong. I promise there wasn't. It's complicated. Too complicated. I wish I could explain it all to you, though in time I know

140

you will understand all too well. And for
that, I am truly very, very sorry.

I allowed no one to read the letter. I said it was too personal, too private. I told them only that the relationship between Steven and me was officially over. That he had fallen for a girl he met in college. That he said he had never meant to hurt me, but that when he met Brigitte—and what kind of name was *that*?—he had found "the one."

It wasn't until later that year, when our family went to Cedar Key for our annual holiday vacation, that we learned the truth. The real truth.

Steven Granger was not just a young husband; he had become the father of a baby girl, born too soon.

A fighter from birth, we were told, whom he'd named Eliza.

15

Steven drove me home. We said an awkward good night at the door, then Steven bounded down the stairs as I slipped inside.

I pressed myself against the door, waiting until I heard the sound of his car driving back out to the road. "Max?" I called. A moment later, a sleepy Max met me at the door, sauntering toward me at a snail's pace. I slid down until I rested on the floor. "Hey, boy," I said as he nuzzled my neck, panting warm breath in my ear. I laughed. "Well, this isn't exactly how I thought my date would end . . . but it's better than nothing."

The next morning I walked over to Patsy's. She was sitting out on her deck, sipping on a glass of iced tea. I stood between our two houses, looking up at her, watching as she gazed out over the marshes. I wondered about the details of her life. What moments—good and bad—had brought her to this point. Inside her home were many framed photos . . . family members I'd yet to ask her about. I genuinely wanted to know who they were, who they'd been to her or were to her. How her life had been affected by theirs and vice versa.

"Hello, there!" I heard her call.

I jumped, startled. "Good morning. I thought I'd see what you are up to this morning."

"Just sitting out here talking to the Lord," she said.

"Mind if I join you?" I asked, already heading for the staircase. "Not to interrupt your prayer, but . . . I mean, to just chat?"

"Not at all."

When I reached the top I noticed her iced tea had watered down in the early morning heat. "Patsy, want me to get you some more tea?"

Patsy turned to look at me. She smiled. "Get yourself a glass too," she answered.

Minutes later I returned with a tray holding two glasses of iced tea and three photographs. "I picked these up too," I said. "I hope you don't mind."

She looked over to the tray, seemingly focusing on the photographs—old black and whites—and smiled. Try hard as I might, I couldn't tell if it was happy or sad or somewhere in between.

I sat next to her, took a sip of sweet tea, and said, "It's going to be so hot today."

"It's already hot," she answered. "Where I come from, we used to call it a 'scorcher.'"

"Where *do* you come from, Patsy?" I asked. "I know you moved here from South Carolina, but where did you grow up?"

Patsy reached for one of the photographs on the tray I'd placed on the small table between the Adirondacks. I crossed one leg over the other and settled back.

"This man right here," she began, "was my father. My real daddy, I guess you could say."

A familiar story. "He didn't rear you?"

143

She shook her head. Her eyes shimmered moist and sad. "He died when I was just a little thing. Four years old to be exact. Nearly five, though. My mother . . ." She reached for another photograph and held the two frames together. "What a beauty, huh?"

I took the photograph from her hand and studied it. It was a wedding photograph. Her mother had been a slender woman, with dark bobbed hair and thin brows. Her lips held a deep Cupid's bow and were painted what appeared in the sepia finish to be red. Her dress was elegant; the veil wrapped the crown of her head then spilled to the floor with her gown's train. A single strand of pearls dipped at the base of her swanlike throat, and a massive cluster of flowers was clasped in her hands. "She's nothing short of gorgeous," I said. "She could have been a model."

"You are actually right there," Patsy said. "But she chose instead to marry my father."

I looked at the photo Patsy continued to hold in her hand, the fingertips of the other lightly stroking the image. It appeared to have been taken while her father strolled along the sidewalk of a city. He wore a double-breasted suit and a derby hat and carried a tall umbrella. "Dapper, I believe is the word," I said.

"Handsome. So handsome. No wonder my mother chose to marry him." She smiled then as a giggle escaped her lips. "My mother." She reached for the photo I still held in my hands. "My mother was seven months along with my little brother when Daddy died." She looked at me fully. "Pneumonia," she said with a heavy sigh. "Not like today. Pneumonia in those days was the kiss of death, I suppose." Once again she held the two photographs side by side, gazing at them lovingly.

"What did your mother do?" I asked. "With a baby on the way and a four-year-old in tow?" I thought of Charlie then. He'd left the boys and me, yes, but he'd also made provisions for us to continue to live in our home and for the boys to have everything they could ever need. "Had your father left enough for you to live on?"

"Goodness, no. Those days were different, you know. My father did well enough, but he never dreamed of dying so young, I'm sure. There's always time, we think when we're young. But there isn't always."

Had Charlie died, I thought, rather than having had divorced me, his life insurance policy would have been more than sufficient. I could have quit my job, had I so desired. But had he died without that policy, I would have sold the house and perhaps had to move back in with my father and stepmother until I could get my bearings. "Did she return to live with your grandparents, then?"

"My mother told me once—only once—that her parents were quite up in age when they had her." She looked at me again. "She was the surprise, she said, after nine others." Patsy laughed. "Can you imagine? The baby before her was nearly ten when she was born. Yes, my grandparents were quite surprised when she came along. They doted on her, don't you know. Pinned a lot of dreams on her too, Mama said." Patsy's voice faded before she added, "She was only fourteen when she met my father. Only fifteen when they married."

"Fifteen?" I reached for the photo again. "She doesn't look fifteen. She looks . . . twenty, maybe."

"They worked very hard in those days to look older. Marlene Dietrich was a big influence. Actresses like her."

From what I could remember about Marlene Dietrich, I could see a faint impersonation of the classic actress in

Patsy's mother's photograph. "I see," I said. Then, "So, what did happen?"

"Mama told me that her parents didn't want her to marry Daddy, but she was determined. So, they threw a wedding unlike anything you've ever seen, then told her she and my father were on their own. Daddy, Mama said, made a good living for the times—he was older. Did I say that?"

"No. How much older?"

"By about twelve years."

"My goodness, Patsy. Today he'd be arrested."

Patsy laughed. "Times change. If you were living in their day, when you and your husband got divorced, he'd just more or less disappear from your life. And your sons'."

I took another sip of tea. "That kind of arrangement just might make my life easier. I admit to being torn . . ."

Patsy patted my hand. "Daddies are important, little one."

I nodded as I looked out over the marsh and the shimmering water. Several gulls played in the air—dipping, diving, soaring. I thought of Dad. He was demanding at times, clueless at others. But always with plenty of love to give to his family. "I can't imagine life without my father," I said.

"I not only can, I did."

I looked at the older woman. "Did your mother remarry?"

Now it was Patsy's turn to look out over the marsh. "Yes."

"Do you have any photos of him? Your stepfather?"

"No." She reached for the third photo I'd brought out with me. This one was of a younger Patsy—clearly seen in the shape of the eyes and her square chin—and a boy. "I was fourteen in this photograph." She held the photo of her mother and the one of herself side by side to show the difference. "I looked like my father," she said. "Nothing like my mother."

146

"But beautiful in your own right."

Patsy's face wrinkled with her smile. "You are too kind."

"I'm just calling it like I see it. Who's the boy? Your brother?"

"Yes. This was taken shortly after we came back together."

I shifted my weight and felt the sweat that had formed between my bare legs and the chair. "What do you mean?"

"After he was born, my mother gave my brother Lloyd to a couple who didn't have any children of their own. They raised Lloyd as their own son, and then when I was thirteen I moved away from my mother and lived with them too."

I blinked several times. "You're kidding. At thirteen your mother just let you go live with someone else?"

She took a long swallow of her tea before nodding.

"You mean you never saw her again?"

Patsy shook her head. "No. Shortly after I went to live in the Buchwald household, Mama and Mr. Liddle—her husband—moved away. They left no forwarding address. My adopted father—Mr. Buchwald, who I called 'Papa' like my brother did—took me to try to find them once. We talked with neighbors but . . . no one knew anything. And then . . ." Her voice trailed, as though there were nothing more to say about the subject.

I sat back in my chair. "Patsy, I just can't imagine . . . as a mother, I mean . . ."

Patsy sat up then, stretching her back as best she could. "I can't either. But that doesn't change what was." She patted the armrest of her chair. "I think I'll go inside now," she said. "What are you planning for the rest of your day?"

I shook my head to clear my thoughts, then said, "I'm going to the market in a few minutes. Need anything?"

She thought before speaking. "Oreos," she said. "I just love Oreos, and I haven't had any in weeks."

147

I smiled at the dear. "I'll bring you two packages, then," I said.

"Sounds like a good plan," she answered, then stood and shuffled into her home, leaving me alone for a moment to collect the glasses and three framed and telling photographs.

Moments later, I joined Patsy in the house. I placed the tray and glasses on the kitchen counter and returned the photographs to where I'd earlier found them. Patsy stepped out of her bedroom and into the living room, asking, "So, how did the date go last night?"

I shook my head. "It ended poorly."

Patsy pinked. "Oh, dear."

"No, no, no. Not like that!" I laughed. "It was my fault, really. Steven is a great guy and all, but . . ."

Patsy pointed to the sofa. "Sit," she said.

I did as I was told. Patsy went to a chair—I imagine her favorite from the looks of it—and sat. "Talk to me," she said, settling in.

My shoulders hunched as I brought my clasped fingers to rest on my knees. I smiled at the wiser, older woman as I said, "I haven't even talked to Heather yet."

"Heather?"

"My sister. She and I are pretty close." She'd called the night before, shortly after I'd returned home from Coconuts, but I hadn't answered. I didn't feel like explaining anything to her or hearing her make any derogatory comments about Steven, whom she apparently never forgave for hurting me when we were young.

"What's to talk about?"

"Patsy, Steven and I . . . well, I've known Steven my whole life practically. We grew up here on Cedar Key. Him, literally, and me during the summers and off and on during the year."

"I suspect someone had a summer romance, perhaps?" she said with a knowing smile.

I nodded. "He was eighteen and I was seventeen. I thought . . . well . . . that he was . . . that *we* were special."

"But . . ."

"But then he went off to college, met some girl, and got married."

Patsy appeared to study me for a moment. Uncomfortable, I peered around the room. Tapped my sandaled toes on the end of a throw rug. Pressed my lips together.

"There's more to that story," she said. "When did he marry the girl?"

I felt my cheeks grow warm. I shook my head and felt my ponytail brush the sloping of my shoulders. "Not too long after he met her." I took a deep breath. "The thing is, Patsy, is that Steven and I . . . we never . . . you know."

"Ah."

"I mean, it wasn't for lack of wanting to . . . or not wanting to."

"But you didn't."

"No."

"And then he went off to college and he did."

"Yes."

Patsy paused again. "What is it that Dr. Phil keeps on saying?"

Dr. Phil? "Oh. Um, I don't know, Patsy. I don't have time to watch television much."

"How is that working out for you? That's what he says."

Now it was my turn to pause. "So, is that what you're asking me now?"

She bobbed her head once. Her hands lay loose along the length of the armrests. I noticed her hands. Slender.

Thin-skinned. The wedding rings hanging onto her finger winked at me. "I am," she said. "Are you holding some sort of grudge because he made a decision that didn't include you?"

"I thought we were special, Patsy." I shook my head and chuckled. "My gosh, this is silly." I brought my hands together at my face, resting the tips of my index fingers at my nose. "It was a long time ago. Why should it bother me?" My hands returned to my lap.

"How does it bother you?"

I shook my head again. "I don't know, Patsy. Last night, we were having a good time, and I felt comfortable with Steven, like I did when we were teenagers. I showed him pictures of my boys and then he showed me a photo of his daughter—Eliza is her name. She's . . . she's in college. In college."

"And your sons are just young'uns."

"Yes. Looking at that picture, I was reminded of why I never heard from him again after . . ." I laughed again. "This is *so* silly."

"How come?"

"How come it's silly?" Patsy nodded at the question. "Because I'm just too old to be feeling these ridiculous feelings. Why am I jealous of a college student?"

"Jealous of a—jealous of a college student?" Patsy shook her head side to side as though she were watching a ping-pong tournament. "No, honey. You aren't jealous of that child. You're jealous of the reason she's walking on this earth. But that wasn't her fault, now was it? What her parents did to bring her to this life was no more in her power than when you brought your boys into the world."

I hung my head low. "Patsy, Patsy." I said. "You have such a way of looking at things."

"Good. Then you just go over to your house and call Steven

and tell him you'd love nothing more than to see him again. Have him take you out on that boat of his."

My head snapped to attention. I blinked. "No," I said. "Not quite yet. Granted, my attitudes and actions are a little juvenile, but I'm still a little touchy on the subject." I stood. "Thank you, Patsy."

She reached for my hand with hers, and I took it. We both squeezed. "Don't waste time, Kimberly. Time is something we all think we've got in abundance until suddenly the clock stops ticking. Don't waste a single minute of your life, you hear me?"

"I hear you."

"Especially not when it comes to matters of the heart."

"Yes, ma'am," I said. "I hear you."

16

I returned to the house, played with Max for a few minutes, then left for the market. Maddie looked up as I entered; she greeted me, and I waved back. My eyes automatically went to the bulletin board. A man stood before it, gently tearing away one of the strips with my phone number.

I looked at Maddie, who winked at me, and then back to the man. He was richly tanned, with hair so black it was nearly blue, and full lips that were naturally cherry. "Hi," I said, nearly skipping toward him. "I'm Kimberly Tucker."

He jumped at the sound of my voice, turning fully toward me. "I'm sorry?"

I laughed lightly. "No, no. I'm sorry." I extended my hand and steadied my breath. "I'm Kimberly Tucker. You just tore my phone number off that little poster there."

He looked at the poster and then to me again. A smile spread lazily across his face, showing straight white teeth and a deep dimple in his right cheek. The topaz in his eyes—almond shaped and deep brown—twinkled in the sunlight coming through the windows. "Well, then," he said. He waved the little piece of paper near his shoulder. "I guess you just saved me a phone call."

"Do you know someone who may be interested in the job?"

Another dimpled smile. "Me," he said. Then he shook his head, which caused his thick hair to shimmy. "Actually, my new company, of which there are two employees. Myself and my sister."

I thought for a moment. "Do you have a card?" I asked.

He reached into his back pocket, drew out a leather tri-fold wallet, removed and then extended a business card toward me. I took it between my fingers and read it. "Luis Muñoz."

"That's me."

I smiled up at him. "I like the name of your company. 'Keeping It Clean.' Cute."

"My sister," he said. "She is the one who came up with it."

"Well, tell her I like it." I paused, then added, "I've got to pick up a few things here, but if you have time and can follow me back to the house . . ."

"Be happy to."

Luis drove his car, following mine until we reached the house. I asked him to wait outside a minute while I ran the Oreos over to Patsy. He nodded in agreement. I didn't bother to tell Patsy that I might have found someone to take care of the house. I only knocked, then opened the unlocked door as I called her name.

"I'm in the bathroom," she called back.

"I'm putting the Oreos on your kitchen counter," I said.

"Okey-dokey!"

When I returned to the house I found Luis standing on the cement platform, his feet spread wide and his arms crossed over his muscular chest, looking out at the water. I'd run from

Patsy's, so I stopped long enough to catch my breath then approached him from behind. When he heard me he turned and smiled. "This is some view, chica."

My breath caught. "What did you call me?"

"*Lo siento*. I'm sorry. It was a slip of the tongue . . . something between my family and me . . . something we always do."

I shook my head as I took a few steps closer and finally reached the platform. "No, it's just that a friend of mine who lives here used to call me that when we were kids. Rosa Fuentes. Do you know her?"

A twinkle danced in his eyes. "Why do you ask that? Do you think every Latino knows every Latina?"

I blinked. "Goodness, no." I placed a hand on my chest. "That did sound a little racist, I guess."

He laughed then. "No worries. Actually, Rosa is my cousin. She told me about you needing some help. She said you gave her a piece of paper with your number on it but that she'd misplaced it. Then she remembered that you said you'd placed a notice at the market."

"Luis! I remember you! Well, I mean, we never met, but I remember Rosa talking about you . . . about visiting you at her grandmother's house on the mainland."

Luis's expression was that of old home week. "That's right. Small world, no?"

"I feel like I'm hiring a friend of the family. My father is going to be happy to hear this." I looked toward the house. "So, let's get started. I'll show you what needs to be done, and then you can give me a price. If it sounds good to Dad, then we're set to go."

And, I thought, I can get home where I'll be closer to my sons, sooner rather than later.

154

I ran up the outside z-shaped staircase to call Dad as soon as Luis's car was down the road and out of sight, heading toward Highway 24. "I think I've found someone," I told him. "He and his sister own a cleaning service; they can start on Monday. I'll stick around until Tuesday. I can be home by Tuesday afternoon, no later than evening—"

"Whoa there, Boo," Dad said. "What's got you so breathless?"

"The run up the stairs for one thing. And, Dad, I really think you'll be pleased with who I've got." I took in a few breaths, then exhaled. "I want to be at home, Dad. To be near the boys."

"You're as close to them there as you are here. Charlie isn't going to have you over for potluck, you know."

I was in the living room, leaning against the frame of the sliding glass doors, watching the sun dance on the water. I closed my eyes and sighed. "I know, Dad. But still . . ."

"Okay, Boo. Tell me about these people. How do you know you can trust them? Have you run a background check?"

I felt the air blowing out of my sails. "Well, no, but . . . it's Luis. Rosa's cousin."

"Rosa?"

"Yes. I remember her talking about him when we were kids."

"That means nothing to me, Kimberly. He could have been a straight-A student then and be a registered felon in the state of Florida now."

"Dad . . ."

"I'm serious, Kim. I want you to have a background check run on him."

155

I gritted my teeth and shook my head back and forth. When I was done with my version of a temper tantrum, I said, "And how am I supposed to do that?"

"You're a smart girl. Figure it out."

"Isn't it enough that Rosa recommended him?"

"No, Boo, it's not. This is my home. I own it. It's full of precious memories and things I have no desire to lose."

"I understand, Dad. I do. But, if you met Luis—"

"I don't need to meet Luis. I need for you to do the job I sent you down there to do and run a background check on him. Do you still have my credit card information?"

Some time ago Dad gave each of us his numbers and other vital information "in case of an emergency." I supposed in his mind now was one of those times. And not that Dad couldn't have done all this himself, I figured. But then, just as quickly, I reasoned this was another one of his ways of keeping me occupied. "Yes," I said. "I have it."

"Good. Order a background check. If he is supposed to come on Monday, I suggest you do it soon."

I sighed again. "All right, Dad. But you'll see. I'm right about this guy." Then I chided myself silently. *Well, you thought you were right about Steven Granger and Charlie Tucker too.*

With all the activity of the day, I'd hardly paid attention to Max. After I hung up the phone with Dad, I fed him, adding extra to his bowl to make up for the misery I might have caused him, and then went outside with him for a game of fetch.

The only problem with playing fetch with Max was that he had the retrieval part of the game down but not the return. In the end, I did more running around than Max, which left me soaked with perspiration.

"Okay, boy," I said, panting harder than he. "One more throw and one more time of me getting the ball out of your mouth and we're going inside. You are rank, and I'm not that far behind you."

Max yelped in anticipation, a bossy, *Stop talking, Mom, and just get on with it.*

I threw the ball, Max bounded for it, and then I took off after him. As I wrestled the slimy red orb from between his clenched teeth, tires crunched along the road from the highway. I looked up, horrified to see Steven's Jeep Wrangler Rubicon driving toward the house.

I looked at Max, who was looking at me with his long pink tongue hanging out and his eyes questioning. "Max," I implored. "Did you call him and tell him to come?"

And with that, Max ran for the automobile gliding to a stop. An obvious yes.

When Steven exited the car, Max bounced in welcome as I ran my fingertips over my sweaty face and moaned. My old flame looked remarkable in dark blue shorts and a tan shirt with the boat tour's logo etched across it. His hair was combed and in place with the light breeze from the water feathering the front, which only added to the boyish charm he still possessed.

And he smelled good too.

I, on the other hand, looked a mess and I said so.

"You look . . . fine," he said with a smile as he reached me. "Max been running you too hard?"

I placed my hands on my hips. "Actually, yes. He has." I looked toward the house and then back. "What brings you here, Steven?"

His eyes had followed where mine had gone, then back to rest on what I knew to be the pitiful sight I was. "Well, I was hoping maybe we could talk."

My heart hammered. "About?"

He looked out over the water. "About fifteen minutes, I'd say." Then he smiled. "I've got a two o'clock tour scheduled." He looked down at his watch. "I'm barely going to make it as it is . . . but I really wanted to talk to you about a few things and I didn't want to wait."

"Okay." I licked my parched lips. "I'm listening."

He chuckled. "Kim. It's hot as blazes out here and you look like you could use a glass of something wet and cold, so why don't you ask me inside."

"All right then." I started toward the stairs, and he followed. When we were inside I asked if he wanted anything to drink. He asked if I had sweet tea. I did. I had an entire gallon of it chilling in the refrigerator.

I prepared a couple of glasses. After handing him his, we sat at the kitchen table. He took a sip; I nearly gulped mine.

Again he chuckled. "Thirsty?"

I looked over at Max, who was slobbering all over his water bowl. "I'm afraid I've learned table manners from my dog."

"Don't worry about it." He took another sip, then placed the glass down on the table. When he had crossed one leg over the other, he came to the point. "Kim, did I do something or say something last night that upset you?"

If my face were not already neon red from the heat, I was sure it was now. I'd tried to end our date kindly. Apparently, I had not succeeded. And, like he'd always been able to do, he'd read my thoughts . . . or at least my actions. And he'd read them well.

Still, it wasn't a conversation I felt ready to have. I'd thought he would fade from my life again—as he had before. That I would go on with my life and he with his. "Steven . . ."

Before I could say anything more, he continued. "Because

if I did, Kim . . . if I did," he added, his voice lowering, "I'm sorry. It wasn't done on purpose. I've gone over it about a million times in my mind. Everything we said during dinner. Even everything our server said. I thought we were having fun. I thought . . ."

When he didn't finish I asked, "What, Steven? What did you think?"

He sighed as he ran his index fingertip down the side of his glass, taking the beaded sweat with it. "That maybe while you were here, we could . . . you know."

"No, I don't know."

"See each other a little. Kick back like old times." His eyes—passionate and royal blue and framed by tiny laugh lines made white by his tan—danced in sincerity. "I know you said you don't date much . . ."

"Don't date at all, Steven. And no. You didn't say or do anything," I lied. "It's just that, like you said, we'd only be seeing each other while I'm here, and that's going to be such a short time. I didn't want you to get the wrong idea that we would start something we couldn't finish."

Perplexity shot across his face. Like the glimpse of a dolphin leaping over water, had I blinked, I would have missed it. "What does that mean? Start something we can't finish? I'm just talking about dinner, maybe going to some of the local touristy kind of places, taking a boat ride or two. I'm not talking about . . . you know . . ." He took a nervous sip of his tea. I couldn't tell if he was uncomfortable with where the conversation was going or if he was just thirsty.

I stood to refill my glass, stepping over Max, who lay next to his bowl, snoring. As the topaz liquid fell over what was left of my ice, I heard Steven say, "This is about when we were kids, isn't it?"

I turned with my glass clenched between my fingers. "Look, Steven, I really don't want to get into this."

He stood. "I wish you would, Kim. I wish you'd just tell me like it is—tell me the truth—so I know."

"All right then." I took a breath, let it out slowly. "You hurt me, Steven. I know it sounds silly. I know it was a lot of years ago. But you hurt me."

"I know I—"

I held up my free hand to stop him. "Don't say anything. Just listen. It's silly that a woman my age can't just pick up and move forward, but the truth is—and you said you want the truth—the truth is that you hurt me. You were my first love. I'd had a crush on you since I was twelve, and then after five years of pining away for you and you just thinking I was some little kid—you finally noticed me. Really noticed me. And I thought you felt like I did . . . don't say anything, Charlie!"

He blinked. "I'm not Charlie."

I raked my teeth over my bottom lip, then said, "No, you aren't. But you may as well have been."

"Why do you say that?"

"Because, Steven, after you there was no one else until Charlie, and I thought I had met the man I really would spend the rest of my life with. And I thought he felt the same way too. We were *it* for each other. There had never been anyone else before . . . in that way . . . and I thought . . ." I swallowed. "Things were good between Charlie and me. We were both close to our families and had jobs we both loved, and we had kids any parent would be proud to have. We built a beautiful home and talked about what we would do when it was just the two of us again. Where we'd go. What we'd do. Life was idyllic, and while I rarely thought about you, I can honestly say that when I did, I still felt the pain of your dumping me the way you did—"

160

He opened his mouth, but again my hand shot up.

"But if I'm going to be honest, as time went on, the wound wasn't nearly as tender. Though I admit that when I heard you had gotten a divorce there may have been a little 'serves him right' in my heart. And yes, I am ashamed to admit that."

"I deserve that."

My shoulders fell. I set my tea on the countertop behind me and said, "Yes, you do." My voice was barely audible, even to me.

"So then what happened? Between Charlie and you, I mean."

I looked him in the eye. "Like you, Charlie found someone he loved better than me."

"He's remarried?"

I snorted. "Goodness, no. Since her, there's been a whole lot of somebodies, if what my sons tell me is true." I looked at my feet. "So here I am again. I've loved only two men in my life, and those two men have found me . . . not good enough." The words forced their way around the knot in my throat. My eyes now burned from holding back the tears. I stomped my foot lightly. "I swore I wasn't going to do this. I'm not going to cry." I blinked until the threat of a waterfall passed. "This is what I'm talking about, Steven. I can't . . . I can't do . . . *this*. You have your answer now. I'd rather live out my life single than hurt like that again."

Steven crossed the distance between us. His fingertips slipped to the back of my head, his thumbs forcing my face up to his. When his lips—tender and warm—came down on mine, my breath caught in my throat. The kiss was over the same moment it began. Had his hands not stayed where they were, I would have fallen in a heap at his feet. "I'm sorry," he whispered. "I'm sorry for my part in your hurt. But we were *kids*, Kimberly."

161

I slipped from his grip, taking several steps away from him . . . from that part I'd always found irresistible. I knew if I stayed too close, I still would. I kept my voice as kind as I knew how, even as I kept my eyes on his. "Maybe so. But we were still old enough to make babies."

He winced, then looked down at his watch before shoving his hands in the pockets of his shorts in a sign of resignation. "Look," he said. "I can't even finish talking about this. I have to get going. This has already taken longer than I should have allowed it to. But . . ." He sighed. "Look here. I know you said you weren't going to be here long. I'd at least like it that when you leave, we can call ourselves friends."

I nodded.

He took several steps toward the door, then turned. "One more thing. I don't have anything after this next tour. The kid we hired for the summer is taking the last one of the day so . . . there's something I'd like to show you, okay? Will you meet me at the dock? Around 6:00?" He waited. When I didn't answer, he added, "Just say yes, Kimberly."

I shook my head, but then I sighed and said, "Yes."

He gave a faint smile. "Will you do me one little favor though?"

"I don't know. Depends on what it is."

He winked. "Clean up a little, will you?"

17

November 1988

Steven Granger stood at the window of the third floor waiting area, peering out as though he were looking for someone in particular. His eyes shifted like the slow pendulum of a clock as he watched people walk along the sidewalk running horizontally in front of the hospital. Several were dressed in white lab coats and uniforms, but most were patient visitors, both coming and going. He chewed on the inside of his bottom lip, wondering if anyone from his family or Brigitte's would be among them anytime soon.

Or at all.

In the corner of the small box of a room sat a man using the telephone. Steven closed his eyes against the drone of information the guy passed along to what felt like the thirty-secondth person. At this point, Steven was quite positive that if the man came down with a sudden case of laryngitis, *he* could take over. Yes, his wife just had their third child. A boy.

Yes, a boy. Finally. Yeah, I know. Of course they were naming him after his daddy. And then the hearty laugh, followed by, "If we can just figure out who he is!"

More laughter.

Steven looked down at his watch, then back to the world outside and below.

It was then that the closed door to the waiting room opened. Steven whirled around as Proud Papa said a hasty good-bye and hung up the phone. A couple of prospective grandparents who sat on the faux-leather sofa across the room stopped in their idle time activities to greet the nurse who stood in the framed doorway.

"Mr. Dickerson?"

Proud Papa stood. "Yeah, that's me."

"Your wife said to tell you that she needs you pronto." Then she smiled. "Those were her words, not mine. And, she suggested this is where I might find you."

Steven couldn't help but snicker as the man quickly followed behind the nurse like a private behind a drill sergeant. He then looked at the prospective grandparents. The woman returned to her needlework. The man, who had been reading a year-old *Reader's Digest* he'd plucked off the scarred coffee table in front of him, winked at Steven.

Man code, Steven thought.

And he was a man now. No longer just a kid frolicking without a care in the world in Cedar Key. No longer just a college student trying to keep his grades above failing. Now, he was a husband and he was about to become a father.

The mouth chewing started again.

"Your first?" the man asked him.

Steven moved away from the window and to the chair previously occupied by Mrs. Dickerson's husband. "Yes, sir," he said, sitting. He ran his palms down the length of his jeans, hoping to remove some of the sweat pooling there.

"Boy or girl?"

"We don't know," Steven admitted. "Brigitte—my wife—and I are among the remaining few who really don't want to know until it's born."

The woman stopped in her needlework and said, "My husband and I are awaiting our first grandchild, so I suppose we're in the same boat as you. The forever 'wait and see' for the family members. Except that we know we're having a boy." The woman grinned.

"Our son's son," the man said, smiling just as broadly. "Our daughter-in-law didn't want to be surprised, and that settled that." He sighed. "I guess it makes *some* sense to find out beforehand."

"The nursery is all set up for a boy," the woman said. "We've had several baby showers, and, of course, all the gifts were for a boy."

Steven nodded. He and Brigitte had scraped up enough money to buy a secondhand crib. One evening while she read to him from a "what to expect during delivery" book, he'd put it together and then pushed it into one corner of their already cramped bedroom. Some of Brigitte's friends had put together a shower for her. About ten or twelve giggling near-adult women gathered in their joke of a living room, playing diaper pin games and asking way too many personal questions . . . all of which he could hear behind the closed bedroom door.

They had brought some pretty good gifts, though. Mostly disposable diapers and bottles and the kinds of things babies need and he couldn't afford. Not on the meager salary he earned in the kitchen at Pizza Hut.

Life sure had changed for Steven Granger . . .

"Do you mind if I ask you a question, son?"

Steven looked up, unaware that his mind had drifted off until that moment. "Yes, sir?"

"My wife and I had our first child when I was twenty-eight and she was twenty-one. You don't look like you could be a day over seventeen."

It wasn't really a question and it wasn't really a statement either. But Steven understood it. He nodded. "I'm nineteen, sir. And yes, I'm too young to be a father. If you want a second opinion on that, you can just ask mine." It wasn't said to be harsh; it was just the reality of the thing.

The wife placed her needlework in her lap. "Now you listen here. Many a nineteen-year-old boy has become a father in the course of the world's history and no doubt did a fine job of raising their children. Why, there was a time when most young people were parents multiple times over by the time they hit their twenties."

The man chuckled. "But honey . . . they were dead before they hit fifty."

Steven couldn't help but laugh with him.

The woman poked her husband in the side with an index finger, and he jumped before she asked, "So is there a reason why you aren't with your wife right now? Most young people today—both the husband and the wife are in the delivery room together."

Steven shook his head. "My wife's . . . um . . . there's some complications. They're taking the baby by caesarean."

"That's too bad," she said. "She'll have a longer recovery, you know. The next couple of weeks, you'll be nursemaid both to her and to your baby."

He hadn't thought of that. He brought his hands together

and cracked his knuckles, wondering how he was going to manage that, work, *and* school. At least the Thanksgiving and Christmas holidays were coming up and he'd have a break in his class schedule.

But there was also another complication, one he didn't bother to mention to the kind couple across the room. Brigitte was only eight months along in her pregnancy. Before they had scurried off to surgery with her, the doctor said not to worry. Still . . .

"Yes, ma'am," he said finally.

They smiled at each other then. The woman returned to her needlework and the husband to his magazine. Steven stood, walked over to the window again, and peered out. He wished, oh, how he wished, that his mother were here. He wasn't sure about his father—they'd hardly said two kind words to each other since he and Brigitte had married six months earlier. Since he'd told them what they'd done in the cold confines of a judge's office. He now winced at the memory. Even the news that they were going to be grandparents hadn't softened it. His dad was angry. Perhaps rightfully so. Like he'd said, he hadn't worked his fingers to the bone carting people all over the island for the last twenty years so that Steven could waste his college education on some two-bit—

"Mr. Granger?"

Steven's head jerked toward the door, his breath caught in his chest. "I'm Steven Granger," he said to the same nurse who had come to get Mr. Dickerson.

"Come with me," she said. "Dr. Lang would like to see you."

For a moment Steven felt dizzy. Something was wrong—he knew it. Instinctively, he knew it. He blinked, unable to move.

"Mr. Granger, are you all right?"

167

He blinked some more. "Yes," he said, his voice no more than a hoarse whisper.

He moved toward the door on legs made of quicksand. A quick glance over to the couple on the sofa—he'd not even asked their names—and what he knew was a weak smile. He scolded himself. He needed to be a man now. Not a little boy wishing he had his mommy nearby. A man.

"Good luck, son," the man called out to him.

Steven could only nod in response.

Then, as the door closed behind him, he heard the woman say to her husband, "That young man needs our prayers, Jack."

"Then let's pray," her husband answered.

Three weeks later and Steven had never known this kind of fatigue before in his life. Even summers working the tour boat with his father with the sun beating down on his body, draining it of every last drop of water, weren't this strenuous.

Dr. Lang had met with him in the hallway near the nurse's station immediately following the caesarean. He brought more than just the good news that he was now a father. His daughter, the doctor informed him, needed to stay in the neonatal wing for a while. "She weighed in at just a little under five pounds, which isn't the worst it could be, but still under where we'd like. And her lungs are weak," he said. "I don't expect you to remember all the details so I'll just keep it at that." The doctor peered over his glasses at Steven. "I can see the worry on your face, Mr. Granger. Don't worry. She'll get round-the-clock care from our specially trained medical staff." He gave Steven a weak smile as his brows peaked in the middle. "We'll take good care of her, I promise."

Steven squared his shoulders and stretched his back, hoping

to look older than the bare nineteen years he'd lived. "But she'll be okay. I mean, she'll make it." He spoke the words as though it were and not as though it may not be.

"I don't foresee any further complications," Dr. Lang answered. "But I'm not God either, Mr. Granger."

Steven understood. Clearly understood.

Dr. Lang tilted his head then. "Would you like to know how your wife is doing?"

Steven was startled by the question, knowing he should have asked that already. "Um . . . yes, sir. Of course."

"She's in recovery right now. And she's going to hurt like the dickens when the anesthesia wears off. But she's young and healthy, so she should do just fine. Before she leaves the hospital we'll have some paperwork for you."

"To sign?"

"No, Mr. Granger. To read. It will tell you everything you need to do for her." He cleared his throat. "And not do."

Even at nineteen, Steven understood.

Brigitte came home after a week. They were given a list of things to do and not to do. She wasn't to drive for the next couple of weeks. She could shower but not take a bath. Even then, she had to be extra careful washing around the incision. Afterward she was to pat dry, then rub Neosporin over the wound. She was to take Tylenol for pain unless it became too great; then she was to take the medication prescribed by the doctor.

Brigitte never took the Tylenol, instead opting for the narcotics. The one time Steven made a comment about not wanting her to become addicted to something she'd soon run out of, she yelled at him. Steven didn't understand what she was going through, she whined. If he ever had a scalpel cut him like a pig across his stomach, then he could say something.

169

Steven said nothing else about it after that.

Eliza stayed in the hospital five days longer than her mother. Every day, Steven was there to hold her and feed her. Not once did Brigitte go with him, even though the doctor had said she would be fine to do so. When Steven asked if she wanted to go, she shook her head, then turned her attention back to whatever she was watching on television.

For Steven, it was just as well.

On the third day of visiting his daughter alone, he was surprised to find his mother waiting for him at the entrance to the neonatal unit. She wrapped him in her thick arms, and in spite of his resolve to be ever the mature father, he cried. When he was done, he introduced his daughter to her grandmother.

Their bond was both instantaneous and unbreakable.

On the day he brought Eliza to the tiny apartment her mother and he called home, he found Brigitte lying on the sofa, watching her daily dose of *The Young and the Restless*. "We're home," he said in a near whisper.

"So I see," she replied, then stretched out her arms and cooed, "Bring her to me."

For a moment, Steven felt elated. Maybe, he thought, just maybe they would make it as a family. Maybe they'd one day find themselves out of this place and in a starter home. And years later, with a few more kids in tow, they'd build their dream house. Steven would be a successful businessman and Brigitte could stay at home . . . or continue working at the Estée Lauder counter at Dillard's.

And it wouldn't matter how old she got, either. For sure she would still be pretty enough. If there was one thing Steven couldn't deny, it was that his wife was and would always be incredible to look at. She exuded a beauty that—from the moment he met her—taunted him, drew him, and then sucked him in. Wrapped him in creamy skin, pouty lips, fire-green eyes, and long blonde hair that forever looked as though she'd just gotten out of bed. Not once had the sight of her not turned him on. Even at that moment, dressed only in one of his T-shirts and a pair of dingy white socks and without a stitch of makeup and her hair hastily scooped into a ponytail, she looked good to him.

Too good.

Thanksgiving was a non-holiday that year. He'd hardly known it came and went. But Christmas was another issue. Brigitte's family—who hailed from Maine—wanted them to come up and spend the holiday with them. Brigitte wanted to; Steven could see it in her eyes. But they couldn't afford the trip. He reminded her of their dire circumstances over a dinner consisting of bowls of tomato soup and grilled cheese sandwiches.

Brigitte nodded. She held her spoon vertically between her thumb and index finger. Every so often she touched the tip of it to the soup and watched the orange-red wake reach from the center to the sides. "What if they said they'd pay?" she finally asked.

"Will they pay for my days off from Pizza Hut? I've already arranged to get extra shifts, what with most of the guys who work there going away for winter break."

She made a pouty face. "I know. I was just hoping . . . I haven't seen them since before you and I started dating."

"Have you thought about asking them to come here? I mean, not here to the apartment but here to Tallahassee? To a hotel?"

Brigitte shook her head. At that moment she looked like

171

a china doll that some little girl had played with too hard. Forlorn. Forgotten. "No," she said finally. "They won't hear of anything outside of a white Christmas."

"Even to meet their granddaughter?"

Her eyes met his. "Let's not talk about it anymore," she said.

In the end, they'd spent Christmas Eve and Christmas Day in Cedar Key with Steven's parents. His father—who up until then had pretty much avoided them—had been swept away by Eliza's loveliness from the moment Steven brought her into the house. At nearly two months of age, she wrapped the leathery seadog around her curled pinky. He even managed to soften in his attitude toward his son and daughter-in-law.

Christmas evening, Steven drove his young family up Highway 24 toward the mainland. He had to work both shifts the next day, and he was tired just thinking about it. He took a sip of the coffee his mother had prepared for him, then glanced over to the truck's passenger seat, where Brigitte stared out her window at the passing tropical scene. Between them, their infant daughter slept soundly. Tiny milky bubbles from her last feeding formed on her lips.

He sighed in contentment. It had been a good day.

But when he passed the road leading to the Claybourne house, his eyes cut ever so slightly to where, he imagined, Kimberly was celebrating the holiday with her family.

And he wondered if she knew . . .

18

I took a shower after Steven left then went ahead and dressed for the evening, choosing a long spaghetti-strap dress of teal and espresso. I decided to wear my hair down but slipped a dark brown scrunchie around my wrist just in case. After stepping into a pair of dressy Bare Traps sandals and deeming myself presentable, I practically skipped to Patsy's.

She answered the door, coughing.

"Patsy? Are you all right?"

She waved a hand at me. "Nasty summer cold, is all." She paused and squinted. "What's got into you?"

"What do you mean?"

"Come on in," she said as she stepped back. "No need in letting the mosquitoes in."

I followed Patsy into the kitchen, where Lipton tea bags simmered on the front burner of the stove. I took a seat and watched as she added sugar, then clamped a lid on top and flipped the switch to "off."

"Sit," she said. "I've got some tea already in the fridge. Want some?"

I shook my head. "I'm fine."

She poured two glasses anyway, then walked them over to the table, where I had taken my usual place. "So, what's going on with you? And don't bother saying nothing. I saw that young man over there a little while ago. And now here you sit at my table looking all spiffy."

I sighed and smiled as I took a sip of the iced tea. It slipped down my throat like a perfect summer's night, cool and delicious. "I don't know, Patsy. I thought I didn't want to see him again . . . that the past had somehow settled things between us. But maybe he's right. Maybe we were just kids back then."

"You've lost me," she said. "Maybe you'd best fill me in?"

And so I did. I told her everything about the summer romance I thought would carry me through my whole life. I choked back tears when I got to the part about his getting married and how I'd gloated over his divorce. I told her how I'd felt like an utter failure when Charlie left and that I still didn't know why our marriage had ended. When there was nothing left to say, she blinked at me before commenting. "That's quite a story."

"And now Steven wants to show me something," I said. "But I have no idea what."

"Well you just be careful of a man who says he wants to show you something," she said, her eyes twinkling.

"Oh, Patsy." I laughed.

"So is that why you came over?"

I shook my head. "No. I need to borrow your computer."

"You ready to set up Facebook?"

"No . . . well, yes. Actually, I am. But right now I need to do a background check on someone."

"Ooooh," she said, sounding like a little girl. "I like detective work. Who are we investigating?"

"I've hired someone to take care of the house when no one is there. I thought he was perfect, but Dad wants a background check done." I shrugged a little. "I have to admit, he's right to have me do this . . . and I want to do this right. If there's one thing I don't need right now, it's to disappoint my father."

Patsy stood clutching the side of the table as she always did when rising. "Well, come on. Let's get started."

I pulled up a chair next to Patsy's at the desk, then watched as she booted up the computer. "Okay," she said. "Which background service do you want to use?"

I blinked. "There's more than one?"

"Oh, honey, there's tons of them." She typed "background check" into the search engine. Within seconds, dozens of choices were lined up before us. "I hope you have your credit card," she said.

"In my pocket," I said as I reached for the paper with Dad's credit card info.

"Okay, then. Pick one."

I went with the second one on the list. And $79.95 later, I had all the information on Luis Muñoz my father could ever hope to have. And not a line of it was bad. He didn't have so much as a traffic ticket.

I gave Patsy a hug before I left, told her to watch her cough—which had raised its head a few times during my visit—and promised her I'd return the next day so she could help me set up my Facebook account.

"And tell me all about your date," she said.

I nodded. "We're just friends," I said. "And that's all it will be."

"I was just friends with my husband," she stated matter-of-factly. "And then love took over."

175

I kissed her powdered cheek before closing the door on my way out.

I called Dad as soon as I got home and gave him the details of the background check. "Good job, huh?"

"I'm impressed."

I felt myself beam. "Thanks, Dad. So, you think it will be okay to have him start on Monday?"

"I don't see why not. Are you still planning to come home on Tuesday, then?"

"Sure, unless you have something else for me to do while I'm here?"

"I'll think on that," he said. Then he paused. "Have you spoken to Heather lately?"

Heather. All I needed right now was for Heather to hear that I was going somewhere with Steven Granger later on. I'd purposefully not called her since Wednesday. It had been only a couple of days, but sometimes Heather and I couldn't go two hours without talking.

"Not since Wednesday. Why?"

"You should give her a call," he said.

"That's it? You're not going to fill me in?"

"No, Boo, I'm not going to fill you in. Say good-bye, now."

"I love you, Dad," I said. When he told me he loved me too and the line went dead, I looked at my watch. The time was closing in for me to leave if I was going to meet Steven at 6:00. With a shake of my head, I dismissed Dad's request to call my sister. Within minutes I had Max fed, said, "Good-bye and be a good boy," and then made my way down the steps and to the car. Earlier I'd applied plenty of body lotion and regretted it now. I sighed an "oh, well." If I didn't look good to anyone else, the mosquitoes already loved me.

176

I parked near the marina, checked my lip gloss before shutting down the car, and then stepped out onto the scorching hot asphalt, ready to make my entrance. I was a little early, and it appeared that while a boat bobbed in the water at the dock, no one was in sight save the few tourists walking along the sidewalk and a couple of fishermen daring the heat. I looked across the street to the little shop I'd seen days before—Dilly Dally Gally—and decided to pass the time inside rather than out. The afternoon temperature still hung in the nineties.

I left the store having seen Maddie (who was buying a new hat) and also having made fast friends with the salesgirl—who said she knew and absolutely adored Anise—and with a silver paua shell and pearl double-strand bracelet. As soon as I walked down the dark lavender painted steps leading to the shop, I spotted Steven waiting at the edge of the dock near the sidewalk. He looked from my car to his watch. He then glanced around, finally spotting me as I walked toward him. He waved and I did likewise.

"What do you have there?" he asked, glancing toward the store's telltale bag. He pulled his polarized sunglasses from his face; they hung around his neck by a neon blue floating cord.

"I bought a bracelet," I answered.

"Really? Let me see." He was already reaching for the bag; I willingly handed it over.

He took the bracelet out of the white gift box, held it up in the sunlight, and said, "Why, Miss Boo, this is just gorgeous."

I smiled at the sentiment. "I thought so."

He looked back at me. "Swarovski crystals?"

"How'd you know?"

"I managed a mall. Remember?" He admired my purchase again. "And I have a daughter."

I nodded. "Swarovski. Yes." I took a breath, exhaled, and pointed. "And paua shells and pearls."

The bracelet slipped over his upturned fingers. "May I help you put it on?"

I shrugged. "Sure. I guess."

I should have known better. As soon as the warmth of his fingers touched the tender skin of my wrist, I felt myself go dizzy once again. And I wondered if he felt the same or if I was alone in my emotions.

"There you go," he said when he was done. "It's perfect with your dress."

I took a single step away from him. "I wasn't sure where we were going."

Sweat beaded along his brow, and his eyes drank me in. "Can I tell you something?" he asked, not answering my question.

"Sure."

"Promise you won't get mad?"

I narrowed my eyes. "I'll try not to."

He laughed then. "You look fantastic."

I smiled. "You can say that any day of the week, Steven Granger. So, where *are* you taking me?"

"This way," he said, motioning toward the water. It was then I noticed that two boats—one the company boat and one a white and green motor-driven skiff—were hitched to where only one had been before.

"Where's your teenaged worker bee?" I asked, walking the unpainted planks beside him.

"He'll be back in a few. We've got another tour going out in a little while. A sunset tour." We stopped at the end of the dock by the boats where three steps led to the water. "Do you want to get in first?"

"Um . . . maybe I'm not dressed . . ."

His hands slipped along the tops of my arms. "You're dressed just fine. Want me to get in first?"

"No," I said, slipping away from his touch. "I'll go first."

Steven waited until I had stepped into the skiff before joining me. The boat bobbed from side to side, and so I sat facing forward. "Good thinking," he said. He stepped to the back of the boat, picked up a paddle, then used it to push from the dock. He guided the boat out a few yards, past the barrier rope lined with birds, then started the engine. I turned fully to face him, watching him through the dark tint of my sunglasses as he worked with ease, doing what he'd done a million times or more. Instinctively, he slipped his sunglasses back to the bridge of his nose. I gathered the long folds of my dress and secured them between my ankles. He caught the movement and smiled, then turned his gaze outward to the western sky while I remained content with the view of where we'd been versus where we were going.

I wrapped my fingers along the edges of the wide fiberglass seat and tilted my head back, allowing the sun to drench me and the wind to cool me. I breathed in, intoxicated by the marshy smells of salt and fish, heat and the lingering scent of my body lotion.

I assumed we were heading to Atsena Otie. When enough time had passed and we'd yet to hit shore, I opened my eyes. Steven sat directly before me, watching me. I felt my blood turn to liquid sunshine. I blinked at him. He didn't bother to turn away, and I realized then he might have just as easily been looking past me, toward wherever it was we were heading.

But then he smiled. I returned his smile, then looked over my shoulder. I watched in delight as the sunlight skipped across the rippling water. Herons and gulls flew along the horizon like a giant brushstroke from God. Soon we neared a sandbar where hundreds of gulls, egrets, and a few dowitchers watched us. When we came close enough, they spread their wings in unison and lifted themselves upward. The sound, even over the motor, reminded me of linens flapping in a spring breeze.

Steven pointed just then, and I followed his direction until I spied dolphins dipping and curling over the water, their gray bodies sleek. I threw back my head and laughed out loud then waited for them to reappear. I was in love with the moment; if it never ended, it would be too soon.

I realized then where we were going. Shell Mound was up ahead; the long dock stretched its arm in welcome. Steven shut the motor down, and we glided toward the shore's pristine sand. When we slipped beside the dock, Steven grabbed hold of a line of blue synthetic rope, tied the boat to it, then climbed the old, unpainted makeshift ladder. I sat watching until he turned, extended his hand, and said, "Grab that cooler and backpack, will you?"

For the first time I noticed the small insulated cooler behind me, lying beside a couple of lifejackets I was glad not to be wearing. Propped next to the cooler was a small waterproof backpack. I picked both up and handed them to Steven, who promptly placed them on the dock at his feet. "Now you," he said, reaching.

I felt the heat rising inside me again, willed it to go away. He took my hand into his, guiding me as I took each rung of the ladder, one at a time. I felt his hand cup my elbow, his strength becoming my own. As soon as my feet were secure on the dock, I pulled my hand from his. He, in turn, squatted next to the backpack.

"Better put some of this on," he said, raising a can of

insect repellant. "Otherwise they'll be diagnosing you with malaria by Sunday."

I doused my arms and rubbed the repellant into my skin from my fingertips to my shoulders. I then sprayed my hands and rubbed them along my bare chest and up my throat, aware—all the while—that Steven was watching. When I was done, I handed him the can. "Your turn."

"Better put a little around your face too," he said. "The mosquitoes are thick as thieves."

I complied, then watched as he sprayed his legs and arms, then patted his face. "And to think I used my best aftershave this afternoon in hopes of impressing you," he said.

My laughter was light. Thinking ahead, I pulled the scrunchie from around my wrist and swiped my hair into a ponytail, asking, "So, what's in the cooler?"

"Just some water," he said. Then he took me by the hand and said, "Come on, Boo. Let's walk."

19

"What do you get," Steven spoke softly, "when you add a thousand years of Eastern Woodland Indian cultures and discarded oyster and clam shells?"

I looked across my right shoulder and smiled knowingly. "Shell Mound?"

"Ah," he mocked me. "You've been here before, I presume."

I looked straight ahead. The white sand road—lined with thick, prickly flora and canopied by the thick branches of the live oaks, their mossy veils dripping toward the earth—curved before us. We walked where the tourists and locals walked each year, and yet, remarkably, the land remained virginal. "About a million years ago."

"Before the Native Americans . . ."

I bumped his shoulder with my own. "Don't toy with me." I breathed in deeply. "I remember my mother telling me once that Shell Mound was, to her, a place where her soul could breathe."

"A lot of people feel that way." Steven swiped at a pesky insect that couldn't decide whether to light on him or escape the repellant he'd bathed in earlier. We'd walked now for ten minutes; only two of those included me wondering what we were doing here. At some point I'd let it go . . . and relaxed in the cool of the early evening shade.

"There's a place right here," Steven continued. "I can't wait to show you."

We veered right in the road then cut through an area where the vines tangled overhead and moss grew thick on the old oaks. Insects hummed in tune as the smell of the marsh wafted toward me. To keep from tripping on a low vine, I kept watch on my feet. Then, when the foliage cleared, I looked up.

"There you have it," Steven said.

I sucked my breath in. The water of the Gulf, remarkably blue, lay flat and serene. I could see the dock and Steven's boat rocking ever so slightly beyond. It reminded me of the way I used to rock my sons when they were babies and I thought them to finally be asleep. Beyond the dock and the boat a strip of land housed a few trees; one held an osprey's nest—complete with osprey—on top of it. The sky had begun its nightly show of colors.

I was only barely aware that Steven had set the backpack and cooler on the sandy ground. When I stopped staring at the scenery and returned my attention to him, it was to find that he had pulled a blue and white throw out of the backpack and was unrolling it onto the ground. "Here, let me help," I said. I bent down and grabbed two corners.

"Sit," Steven said when we were done.

I complied. I kept my knees bent and in front of me, my ankles together, and the skirt of my long dress over them all. I took in a breath and held it as I waited for him to sit behind me, close enough, and yet, not touching. "I've got something for you," he said. I felt his warm breath on my ear and forced myself not to quiver.

I wasn't sure if I could get the words past my dry throat, but I tried. "What's that?"

"Close your eyes and hold out your hand."

I cast my eyes over my right shoulder. "Steven . . ."

I heard him chuckle. "Just do it, Kimberly."

I closed my eyes and held out my hand. I listened as he unzipped a pocket of the backpack, removed something, then zipped the pocket closed. Something heavy and metal then rested in the palm of my upturned hand. "Can I open now?" I asked.

"Go ahead."

I looked. I was holding a mid-sized Olympus point-and-shoot camera. I wanted to drop it, but even I—who hadn't touched a camera in years—recognized its monetary worth. "Steven . . ."

"Just try it, Boo."

I shook my head. "You don't understand."

"I do . . . I know how much you used to love taking pictures with your mom . . . how much you loved your mother."

I felt tears burning the back of my eyes. "I can't . . ."

"Can't what? Take a picture? Or can't face the fact that your mother died?"

I raised my chin and looked straight ahead. Both hands now gripped the camera. "I faced that fact a long time ago. I faced it when Dad married Anise."

"So what keeps you from the camera?" As he spoke, his fingertips made trails up and down my arms, so light that at first I'd not even noticed it. But then my spine began to melt like butter in a hot pan and . . .

"I don't know," I finally whispered.

"I do."

The tears that I'd kept at bay slipped first down one cheek and then the other. "You think you're so smart."

The trailblazing on my arms ceased. I felt a thumb graze my cheek, catching the tear, preserving it. "You think if she isn't here to brag on you, to tell you how marvelous your work is, then it's for nothing."

"That's not . . ."

"I know you, Kimberly-Boo."

"You *knew* me."

His hands now cupped my shoulders. I licked my lips; they were so dry I feared they'd crack.

I felt myself slipping backward, the weakness of my spine curving into the strength of his chest. His arms circled me; I could feel the sweat of our bodies mingle. He reached down, took the camera from my hand, and deftly turned it on.

It sang to life; my heart skipped.

"You can either use the viewfinder or"—he pushed a small button on the right side—"you can use the monitor."

"Digital photography."

"Welcome to the new millennia, Kimberly Tucker."

I breathed out, then reached up and took the camera from his hands. It felt lighter than before. I played with the mode dial, found the right scene setting, adjusted the zoom and the angle, then raised a shaking finger to the smooth metal shutter button. I inhaled, then pushed. The scene on the monitor froze. Perfectly.

"You haven't lost it, Boo," Steven said.

I switched from monitor to viewfinder; it was where I was most comfortable. I shot several new shots, changing the zoom and the settings. I focused on the sun, the marsh, and the dock. And when I was done, I held onto the camera with my right hand, then buried my face in my left. The sobbing began slowly at first, then with an intensity I didn't know was inside me. The resolve not to cry escaped from where

I'd held it captive. Part of me wondered what Steven must be thinking and the other part didn't care. I felt his strong arms slip tighter around me, moving the camera out of my hand and then holding me, keeping me grounded. I sputtered a few times, groaned in travail, screamed out to my mother in such intense anger that she'd left me . . . left Dad . . . left us all. I cried for what I'd had with Charlie and what I'd lost. I wept as only a mother can for the mistakes we'd made and the price paid for them by our sons. And when there was nothing left inside me, I collapsed against the man I somehow knew had never stopped thinking of me. Never stopped caring. And had always known me as I'd known myself. Even in the short, sweet time we'd been together. It had always been there, this connection. First loves never really died, I thought. They only grew more memorable with time. His lips had been the first to ever press against mine . . . and his were the ones which now drew mine again. Tender at first until our passion grew hungry. His hands held my face; my body twisted somehow into his. For a moment, I thought I'd break in two. For a moment, all I could think was that it had been so long since a man—any man—had kissed me at all, much less with desire.

I became keenly aware of nature around me. The gritty sand between my sandals and feet, the gentle waves brushing against the green reeds and rushes, the birds overhead, calling to each other in the rustle made by the wind trembling in the palm fronds. My muscles burned. Just when I thought I could take it no longer, Steven pulled away and turned my body toward the beach again. His arms clasped me as though I were a life preserver; his head hung limp on my shoulder. I lay my head back and gasped for air, knowing full well that the short breaths coming from behind me were from a man trying to gain control of his emotions.

Finally, he spoke. "You're doing it again."

I shook my head and said, "I don't know what you mean."

"You know," he said. He straightened, reached for the cooler, and brought out two large icy bottles of water. He handed one to me. I drank as though I hadn't seen a drop for years. He did the same. When I'd drunk half, I poured a little into the cup of my hand and splashed my face. Rivulets ran down my throat and chest as I returned the bottle's cap and dug a place for it in the sand with its base. By now Steven had done the same. He slipped a few inches away from me. I heard him clear his throat. "I never meant to hurt you."

"Don't," I begged. "I've cried enough this afternoon. I'm sure I just look a mess."

He reached up and turned my chin toward him. "You look great," he said with a smile. Then he sobered. "If you want to know what happened, I'll tell you."

I kept my eyes on his for a moment, then nodded. "Okay."

"You nearly drove me crazy that summer, did you know that?"

I turned back toward the beach. Of course I knew it. I knew it now; I hadn't known it then. Teenage girls rarely know the depths of the power they have . . . or the damage that power can cause.

"I'm not blaming you," he went on, slipping close to me again. "I'm just telling you the way it was. Eighteen and all hormones and you looking like you did. Coming on to me like you did."

I started to say something, but he stopped me by speaking quickly. "I remember . . . I remember not wanting to do anything to hurt you. Not you. Not in that way. Sometimes I'd think, 'Man, would she? Nah, not Kim . . . she's too good.'"

I closed my eyes against the memory. "Teenagers and hormones should have never been put together," I spoke quietly. "I wonder what in the world God was thinking when he designed us that way."

Steven chuckled. "You and me and cold showers—that's the way it was that summer."

My eyes opened. Two egrets danced together in the marsh in front of us. Their own love ballet, I supposed. One seemingly much more playful than the other, much more determined. I wondered if it were the female of the two. Like me at seventeen. "But you never even so much as tried anything, Steven. Don't beat yourself up. You were a good kid. Now that I have sons, I can only hope that when they start dating . . . I can hardly wrap my mind around this, but . . . when they do, that they will treat their dates with the same respect you gave me."

"I met Brigitte about a month or so into school," he said, as though I'd not uttered a single word. "She was one of those girls who hung out at frat houses. I'm not going to tell you that she wasn't pretty because she was. She was beyond that, actually. She looked like one of those girls you see advertising underwear and blue jeans. The kind of girl I keep praying her daughter never becomes." His fingers brushed away a mosquito that had bravely lit on my arm. Somewhere in the distance, the sound of an airboat passing on the water grew loud and then faded. All the while, Steven remained silent.

"Go on," I finally said. "I can take it."

"She set her eyes on me. Only she was more persistent, more . . . cunning . . . than you'd ever thought to be. I figured . . . she and I . . . I figured what the heck? Go for it. Who's gonna know? Who's gonna get hurt?" He sighed so deeply I wondered if there could possibly be any air left in his lungs.

"But she got pregnant," I finished for him.

He sighed. "Yeah."

"And you married her."

"Because it was the right thing to do."

We sat silent again. I found the camera still lying next to me, picked it up, and shot a few photos of the sun as it made its scheduled descent. The sky was nothing short of brilliant, the sun as red and round as I'd ever seen it. When I was done, I braved the question. "Did you love her?"

"Goodness." He took the camera from my hands, pressed the playback button, and studied the shots for a moment before answering. "What does an eighteen-year-old know about love, Kim?"

I peered over my shoulder at him, wondering what kind of picture I made at that moment. A silly thought, but there it was. "I was seventeen and I thought I was in love."

His face—rosy from the sun's glow—grew pinker still. "I know you did. But now? Now do you think you were?"

I nodded. "Mmmhmm. As much as I knew how to be."

"That's fair."

I continued to study him, and his eyes never left my face either. I swallowed, then asked, "So what happened after the baby was born?"

A mosquito lit on his face, and he swiped it. He pulled his hand back, studied the smear of black insect and red blood on his fingertips. I grabbed my water bottle then used its contents to wash his hand.

"We'd best get going," he said. "Pretty soon it'll be too dark to see to get back to the boat."

Disappointment washed over me. "Sure, I guess you're right."

We packed up the few things we had with us, then walked hand in hand, silent, to the boat. "Want to get in first?" he asked me again.

I shook my head. "No," I said, then encircled my arms around his shoulders. His head tipped back; his eyes searched mine. "First," I said, "I want you to kiss me one more time."

20

When Steven lost his job at Pizza Hut, he slammed out the back door of the kitchen and stomped through the parking lot, right past his truck. The back alleyway—used mostly for deliveries and employees—stretched right to left like a road to nowhere. It was lined by squatty trees and oversized trash cans.

Steven shoved his hands in his jacket pockets and turned left. He kept his head down, focused on the pair of shoes in bad need of replacement, and wondered how he was going to tell Brigitte. Then he wondered what she would have to say, if she would be sympathetic and supportive, telling him that she still had her part-time job at Dillard's and they'd make do until he found something else. Or, if she would cry and curse and ask him what he'd done wrong to deserve being fired. He'd tell her then that he wasn't fired. He was let go. That a lot of people were being let go, but he'd find something else for sure. He wasn't being paid enough anyway, now that they had another mouth to feed.

191

Which brought him to another point. With every other mother out there getting back into breastfeeding, what was wrong with Brigitte that she never did? It would have saved them a fortune in formula. Not to mention it was good for Eliza. But all Brigitte could think about was what it would do to *her* physically. "You want me to look like my grandmother before I'm even in my twenties?"

He shook his head now at the thought. Steven didn't even know her grandmother. He hardly knew her parents. They'd spoken on the phone, that was it. And they promised to come soon to meet their first grandchild. Steven supposed they wanted to meet him too. One thing he knew for sure—if some kid in college ever got Eliza pregnant, he'd make sure he got to know him real fast. So fast the boy's head would spin.

He came to an intersection and turned left again. The chill in the air whipped around his face; he turned up the denim collar of his jacket and kept going. He walked until his shins ached and his calves burned. Eventually he hit a major intersection; the noise of traffic surprised him and he looked up. He blinked, completely unsure how long he'd been walking or where, exactly, he had managed to land.

A Shell station stood at his right. Across the six-lane highway, a Texaco station competed for business. Between the two of them, he'd say, they were doing all right. Not wanting to risk the traffic, he rounded the sidewalk in front of the Shell station and kept walking. Eventually, he figured, he'd either walk straight into the Gulf or return to the restaurant where he'd left his truck.

He continued past a vacant stretch of property scattered with overgrown shrubbery and discarded trash. Just past it, an oversized warehouse-type building dominated a lot. Letters spelling out "Jack's Boats" in red were displayed on the white aluminum siding over the double front doors. A massive parking lot was about half full of customer trucks and one—in Steven's mind—very nice Ranger bass boat.

His feet guided him into the store, which was more showroom than anything else.

"Can I help you?" a voice from his right called out.

Steven looked at the man walking toward him. He felt his brow furrow. "Hey, I know you," he said.

The man extended his hand, and Steven took it. "Jack Cason," he said.

"As in Jack's Boats?"

The man laughed. "One and the same." He pointed at Steven. "Son of a gun, I believe I know you too. You're the young man in the maternity waiting room."

Steven nodded. "My wife and I had a little girl." Even after several months, his chest swelled with pride just mentioning the baby. "We named her Eliza."

"Eliza. Now, that's a pretty name for a little girl."

Steven felt his face grow warm, and he turned to look at the showroom. "You've got some nice boats here. I don't think I've ever seen so many pontoons in one place."

"You know boats?" Jack asked. Together they stepped closer to the displays.

"I know boats," Steven said. "My dad owns a tour boat company in Cedar Key."

"No joke?" Jack stopped short. "My wife and I used to love to go there. We haven't been in years but . . . yeah. We used to enjoy Cedar Key."

"You should come back to visit sometime. One thing about Cedar Key—it never changes."

"My wife used to say that Cedar Key wasn't a town, it was a way of life."

Steven smiled and nodded in agreement. "Speaking of your family, sir, how is your new grandson?"

Jack threw back his head and laughed so hard it echoed throughout the warehouse. "Our grandson turned out to be a granddaughter. All that planning . . . all those little boy clothes and the nursery set for the next major league phenom . . . and the next thing you know Jack III is now Jacqueline the first."

Steven couldn't help but laugh along with the older man. When they'd both sobered, Jack put his hands on his hips and said, "So what brings you in to my place, son?"

Steven shook his head. "Nothing, actually. I . . . well, to be honest, I got laid off from my job today and I just started walking. Next thing I knew, I was here." He extended his hands. "It's boats! One thing I know a lot about."

Jack peered down at him for several moments before saying, "Enough to, say, sell them for a living?"

Steven blinked. "Are you serious?"

"Small base salary plus commission. I also have a pretty good insurance plan if you're interested. And with you supporting a small family, I'd say you should be."

Steven knew he looked taken aback and he didn't care. "I . . . well . . . you know I'm in school."

"We'll work around that."

"Are you kidding me? Just like that, you offer me a job?"

"No, not really just like that. One of my part-time salesmen just left; moved back to Alabama."

Steven smiled at the way Jack said the name of the state; emphasis on "bama." Jack Cason was what Steven's father called a good ole boy. Like himself. Like Steven had hoped to be. "How could I say no?"

"How indeed?" Jack slipped his arm around Steven's

194

shoulders and said, "Come on back to my office. Let's talk some business, shall we?"

―――――

It took five years for Steven to earn a four-year degree, but he did it. By then, he and Brigitte and Eliza had moved from their tiny apartment to a more spacious two-bedroom duplex, which had a fenced-in yard, small but perfect for a toddler and all her Fisher Price yard toys. By then, Steven worked nearly thirty hours a week and Brigitte had scaled down to no more than ten at the mall. Between the two of them and Mrs. Cason, they'd managed to keep Eliza out of daycare until it was time for her to attend pre-K.

On the morning of Steven's graduation night, Eliza graduated into kindergarten. Both sets of grandparents came, and Jack and Mrs. Cason as well. The whole clan also attended Steven's graduation.

For Steven, the most important accomplishment of the day was Eliza's. Somehow, this little girl he hadn't banked on just a few years back had managed to take center stage in his life. And he knew, above all else, she always would.

―――――

Steven's in-laws gifted him and Brigitte with a two-week, all-expenses-paid trip to Hawaii in honor of his accomplishments. Steven insisted he couldn't take that much time away from work; Jack insisted he could.

Eliza went with her paternal grandparents for the first of what would become many two-week visits to Cedar Key.

Hawaii was good for Steven and Brigitte. They were somehow able to leave life in Tallahassee behind and just *be*. Steven even found himself drawn to his wife again, which was something that hadn't happened in a while. He was either too tired physically or worn out emotionally from her constant demands to make their lives better. Nothing ever seemed to satisfy her. Not even Eliza.

But in Hawaii things changed. They touched. They held hands. They made love like they had their first year of marriage . . . like they meant it. Like it mattered.

The most amazing place they visited was the Seven Sacred Pools in Haleakala National Park. They'd hiked along trails and through the bamboo forest. When they reached the pools, they stopped to sit on the rocks by the water. Brigitte laid back and closed her eyes while Steven rested his elbows on his knees and focused on the beauty and the people around him.

This also gave him time to think about what he was going to do with himself now that his diploma had been earned, matted, and framed. Jack would let him work full-time, no doubt about that. But Steven wasn't sure that was what he wanted to do. He'd toyed with the idea of returning to Cedar Key, but he knew Brigitte would just as soon die first. She hated going even for short visits.

He heard a shriek of laughter coming from one of the bikini-clad girls splashing about in the water. He turned to gaze at her. Her long blonde hair dripped water, her face was alive with happiness. In front of her, a young Hawaiian of about seventeen cupped his hands, filling them with water, and then threw the water on her.

"Stop it, you fiend," the girl said with a laugh. "I'll tell your mother on you!"

The young man said something Steven couldn't make out, but it didn't stop him from splashing the girl again. This time, though, she returned the gesture, only he caught her by the hands, wrapped his arms around her, and kissed her fully on the mouth. When their lips parted, the girl laughed so fully it made Steven laugh too.

He shook his head then, remembering that summer so long ago when he and Kimberly had toyed with each other like that. She'd driven him nearly crazy looking like she did. Feeling the way she did in his arms.

What a summer that had been. He was all boy and all man in one package. He was ready to take on the world and about as ill-prepared as he'd ever been for the way Kim had made him feel.

And then, of course, there'd been Rosa . . .

"What are you thinking about?" Brigitte asked.

He turned his head and looked down at her. She used her right arm to shield her eyes from the sun. Steven couldn't help but notice how tan she'd become since they'd arrived on the island. That morning she'd put her hair up into a ponytail; it splayed across the rocks under her. She wore a pair of denim shorts and a neon pink bikini top. Her navel sported a new pink zircon heart-shaped belly-button ring. Steven reached over and touched it with his finger, allowed the sunlight to send fire from the stone. "You look hot, you know that?"

Brigitte laughed then. "That's not what you were thinking. I saw you looking at that girl over there."

He smiled at her. "Only because she and her boyfriend were laughing and playing with each other."

"And you were thinking about how we used to play around like that when we were dating?"

"Yeah," he lied. "And how I can't wait to get you back to our hotel room."

Jack didn't offer him the full-time position like Steven thought he would. Instead he sat him down over a $1.99 breakfast at Krystal and told him about his brother who lived in Atlanta. "There's a job he knows about," Jack said after taking a long sip of coffee. "And he thinks you'd be perfect for it."

"But he doesn't even know me," Steven said.

"He knows everything I've told him about you, and all that's been nothing but good."

Steven started to take a bite of his biscuit but instead put it back on the Styrofoam plate. "Thank you, Jack. I appreciate that."

"You've earned it." The older man shook his head. "In all honesty, I don't want to see you go . . . but I can get another salesman. You'll never find a job quite like this one."

"What is it?"

"How would you like to manage one of the new malls in the greater Atlanta area?"

"Are you kidding me?"

"My brother said he can help you and Brigitte find a place to live. The people at his church will help you get settled in. The job starts in a month."

"I don't even know what a mall manager does. The only time I even go into one is to pick up Brigitte or when she makes me go clothes shopping."

Jack pulled a folded piece of paper from his shirt's front pocket. "Well, let's see what we have here for a job description." He adjusted the reading glasses he perpetually wore near the tip of his nose and cleared his throat. "It says here: staff supervision, budgeting, office management, development of mall marketing programs, sales analysis, financial analysis, community relations, tenant relations, and leasing stores including the negotiation of contracts between the mall and the tenant."

Steven shook his head. "But, Jack. I don't have the experience for something like that."

"You'll be highly trained," Jack said, replacing the paper.

"By whom?"

"My brother."

"Your brother?"

"He owns the mall."

Simon Cason helped Steven and Brigitte find and rent a townhouse in Marietta. It had a spiral staircase Brigitte absolutely loved. She said it made her feel like a movie star when she went up and down it. It only served to make Steven nervous. His first purchase for the new place was the best child gate his money could afford to keep Eliza from climbing up and tumbling down it.

It took them two weeks to get settled in. Brigitte applied for a cosmetic job at one of the new mall's anchor stores and was hired immediately. Steven asked her to work only part-time; his salary would be enough, he said, and he wasn't sure about putting Eliza in daycare. But Brigitte would hear nothing of it. She was bored, she said. Bored silly with home life.

Simon and his wife, Abbie, took them to church and introduced them to their array of friends. They also told Brigitte about the daycare program that would be perfect for Eliza. While Brigitte wasn't fond of the "going to church" idea, she loved the idea of a church-affiliated daycare. She was also pretty thrilled to hear that Eliza could go directly from the daycare to the church's accredited private school, which began with kindergarten.

By August they both worked full-time. Eliza came home from daycare each day and, during dinner, sang whatever new song she'd learned at "school" that day. In September she began kindergarten. Every morning Steven got her dressed and ready, then drove her to school before heading in to the office. He told her it was their special time of day.

"Why doesn't Mommy drive me to school?" she asked from her car seat secured to the backseat of the silver Toyota Cressida he'd traded in his truck for.

"Mommy works at night," he said. He forced a smile. "Remember?"

"Why doesn't Mommy work in the daytime like you, Daddy?"

Eliza was nothing if not bright and inquisitive. "Because," he said, "somebody has to work during the daytime—that is called first shift—and somebody has to work second shift. Mommy works second."

He glanced into the rearview mirror. Eliza's strawberry blonde hair was scooped to the top of her head in a ponytail secured by a dark green bow. She played with one of the oversized ladybug buttons on the dress he'd put her in earlier. Her cupid lips were pursed, and her blonde brows were knitted together.

Steven's heart flipped.

"I don't like it that Mommy works at night," she said.

"Me either, baby girl," he told her.

———

It was true. He didn't like it that Brigitte worked second shift. It meant they rarely saw each other. It also meant that the bulk of caring for Eliza fell on his shoulders. Not that he minded, but with learning a new job, getting to know new people, trying to make his way in the world . . . it sometimes felt like too much.

Brigitte also managed to stay as unattached from their home during the day as possible. From what he could put together, she slept until nearly noon, vegged on the sofa in front of the television for an hour, then showered and got ready for work. Jason Morgan—a single man of about thirty-five who lived just a few doors down and worked the men's department of the same store—picked her up at 2:30, which gave them an hour to get to work.

Steven got off work—in theory—at five. He had until six to get to the church and pick up Eliza. Every evening, as he drove back to the townhouse, she regaled him with what she'd learned that day in school. New words. New books. New numbers. Jesus walked on water.

"Can you walk on water, Daddy?" she asked him.

"No, sweet pea. Daddy cannot walk on water. Daddy used to drive a boat on water every day though."

"At Grandpa and Grandma's?"

"Yep. In Cedar Key."

"I wish we lived with Grandpa and Grandma . . ." Her voice trailed.

"You don't like living in Atlanta?"

"It's fine, Daddy," she said with a tender sigh. "I just like having water all around." A glance in the rearview mirror showed him his daughter with her little fist pushed against her cheek, her elbow on the padded bar of her car seat.

She saw him looking at her, and she smiled. "Hey, Daddy," she cooed.

"Hey backatcha," he said.

One thing he could say for Brigitte—at least she waited until *after* the holidays to leave him and their daughter behind for what she declared would be a better life for herself.

"Jason is my soul mate," she wrote in the six-page letter left on the dining room table. "He gets me in a way you never could," it went on.

I'm leaving Eliza with you, Steven, because you are the one she is most connected to. I could never do that to my daughter. I could never rip her from her home and from her daddy. And you are a good daddy, Steven. You just aren't fulfilling <u>my</u> needs. Jason not only understands them, he fulfills them in a way you never could. I'm not saying that to hurt you, but just so you can understand that there is nothing you can do to change how I feel.

I'm sorry to say I don't think I ever loved you. I loved the idea of you. Now Jason has shown me what true love is. I tried to fight my feelings, but I know now that I have to have what he gives to me.

I'm sorry.

———

Brigitte and Jason were halfway to Nashville when he read the letter. They eventually settled in a small town just north of it. In the beginning she drove the three-hour difference about once a month on a Saturday. She took Eliza to places like the zoo, Chuck E. Cheese, and the mall. While it gave Steven a much-needed day to himself, those days were always followed by a night of his daughter crying hysterically for her mother.

Twelve months of once-a-month visits went by. Then, late one February afternoon when Steven had dropped his keys on the kitchen countertop and pushed play on the answering machine, he received the call he somehow knew would come.

"Hey, Steven." Brigitte's voice was whisper soft. "It's me.

Um . . . listen . . . I've left Jason and I'm moving to Dallas. Um . . . I met someone who . . . oh man, how do I say this?" Steven stopped the tape. Eliza stood at the kitchen door.

"Was that Mommy's voice?" his Einstein asked.

"Yeah. She was just calling to say hello."

"Who did she meet?"

Steven looked from his daughter to the answering machine and back to his daughter. "The Muffin Man. Now then . . . what do you say to you and me going out for some pizza tonight?"

Eliza jumped up and down. "Yes! Yes! Pizza! Pizza!"

"Then go upstairs—hold on to the handrail—put away your book bag and brush your teeth before we go, okay?"

Eliza was out of the room before he finished the command.

After supper and bedtime book reading and after Eliza's breathing told him she was sound asleep, he listened to the rest of the message.

"How do I say this? His name is Clarke. Clarke Biscoff. He's from Texas and . . . well, I don't have to tell you, do I? He's got money, which Jason never would, *and* he gets me. It's like the first time I met him I thought I had known him my whole life. Anyway, I've left Jason, and right now I'm on my way to Dallas with Clarke." She giggled. "Actually, right now I'm in the bedroom of a fancy suite in Atlanta's Ritz-Carlton. Clarke just went out for a minute and I thought this would be the best time to call. So . . . anyway . . . kiss my angel for me. Tell her she's my stars in the sky. Tell her I love her to the moon and back. And tell her I'll call her soon." She took a breath. "Oh, and Steven . . . I'll send some money to you soon for child support, okay? I mean, I'm going to be rich. I can afford it now, right? My father and mother are going to be thrilled at *this* news . . ."

But the calls rarely came. And the money never showed. Not that he needed it. He and Eliza got along just fine on what his salary provided.

Eventually they only heard from Brigitte twice a year, on Eliza's birthday and at Christmas. And every couple of years the calls or the gifts came from somewhere else, where she lived with somebody else who had more money than the last someone else.

And it was always someone who "got" her.

21

I woke Saturday morning feeling like a new woman. I felt loved, even though the "L word" hadn't been said. But we'd kissed good night like young lovers and we'd set a date for the following night, tonight.

I premade a pot of coffee the night before, had it scheduled to come on at 8:00. When I heard the last gurgle and its rich scent reached the bedroom, I got out of bed long enough to let Max out, get a cup, and then return. I propped up with a book I'd snagged from Dad's library on the way back from the kitchen. For the next two hours, I sipped coffee and read a musty, time-stained copy of Charles Mercer's *There Comes a Time*. It outdated me by more than a decade, but I found it riveting.

Around 10:00 I let Max in, got dressed, made both of us breakfast, then sat cross-legged on the sofa and called Chase. He answered right away; the sound of his voice let me know something was up.

"What's going on? And don't say nothing because I can hear it in your voice."

"Nothing, Mom."

"Chase." My words were met with silence. Finally I asked, "Where are you?"

"At work with Grandpa," he said. "I'm standing in the middle of the azaleas."

"And your father?"

More silence.

"Chase Joshua Tucker."

"He's at the beach."

"The beach."

"Don't make a big deal out of this, Mom."

"Why aren't you at the beach with him?" Silence. I didn't have to ask any other questions. I knew the answer. His second weekend with our sons and . . . "He's with a woman?"

"I assume."

"He never quits," I said under my breath.

"Mom. Seriously. If you make something out of it I'll be so mad at you and I'm not kidding."

I sat stunned. My son would be mad with me? As always, I tried to put myself in his skin . . . in Cody's skin too. They loved their father. They loved me. They hated when we fought. "All right, I won't say anything. When will he be back?"

"He said tomorrow."

"Sunday."

"Yeah."

"Okay. You and Cody staying with Grandpa and Grandma?"

"Yeah."

"Well, that's not the worst thing that could happen."

"You know how it is. They're cool. And Grandma said . . ."

"What did Grandma say?"

"Nothing."

"No, Chase. Don't do this to me. Don't do it to yourself."

"Just that even adults with nearly grown kids have a right

to try to find love." He sighed. "I think she just doesn't want us to think bad of Dad."

I shook my head. This conversation was getting more difficult. I wanted my son to think this through without my saying anything negative about his father. "But, do you think that's what Dad is doing? Finding love?"

"With Dad it's kinda hard to tell. I mean, how do you know if it's love anyway?"

I blinked before answering. His question was genuine. "Well," I began, settling back into the cushy softness of the sofa. "It starts with a nice, warm feeling when you're with someone. It's . . . it's like when you are with that person, you feel you've known that person forever. Like there never was a time when you weren't together. And when you aren't together, you count the minutes until you're with him again."

Chase chuckled on the other end of the line. "I don't think I'm going to want to be with a 'him,' Mom."

"Cute."

He didn't answer right away. "Is that what you and Dad had?"

I felt the knot form in my throat. "Chase . . ."

"Did you?"

"Of course." I closed my eyes and smiled. I had such memories . . . "We were just crazy mad in love with each other, Chase. And you and Cody came out of that love."

"So . . . then . . . what happened?"

I tried to swallow as I blinked. "Wow." Of all days for these questions to come. "I don't know, Chase. You'd have to ask your father that question. I didn't ask for the divorce." I took a deep breath, determined not to sound condemning. "I honestly don't know."

"He'd get mad if I asked."

I nodded. "He may. But you won't know unless you ask."
I tried swallowing again. "And I think you have a right to
know."

"He'll say it's adult stuff and kids don't need to be bothered
with adult stuff."

I pictured my son standing among multi-colored rows of
azaleas, none reaching higher than his knees. I imagined him
wearing a T-shirt with the nursery's logo displayed across
the front and a pair of long khaki shorts. I saw his dark hair
streaked with gold by the sunlight, windswept by the summer
breeze. "If you were five, I'd agree with him," I said.

"But I'm not." A moment of silence before he said, "Mom?"

"Yes, Chase."

"Do you think you'll ever fall in love again? I mean, *could*
you?"

I felt my heart take flight. "Yes. I could."

"I think I'd like that for you," he answered. "But can I tell
you something?"

"Sure."

"I don't think Dad would. I kinda think Dad wants to get
on with his life but he doesn't want the same for you."

I called Heather. It sounded to me as though she'd been
crying. "Are you okay?"

"I'll be fine."

"What's going on with you?"

Her voice rose. "Nothing. Seriously, nothing. Tell me about
you."

I shared with her about my date. I told her about being
in the boat with Steven for the first time in years. I told her
about going to Shell Mound, about the camera, and what
just may have been my last first kiss. I refrained from telling

her about how I'd cried and how Steven held me. I told her nothing about his admission of past sins.

When I was done, she said, "Well, isn't that all so very lovely for you."

The sarcasm hurt. "Heather, don't. Please. I'm happy for the first time in a long time. Can't you be happy with me?"

I heard it then. Ice clinking. I looked down at my watch. It was just a few minutes before noon. "Sure," she said, followed by a long swallow. "Sure."

"Heather," I said, keeping my voice even. "I need to ask you something."

"Advice for the lovelorn?"

I took a deep breath. I let my chest fall with an even exhale. "Heather, why are you drinking so early in the day?"

"Oh. My. Gosh. Ohmygosh. You think I'm drinking? You are so self-righteous, Kimberly. I cannot believe you're asking me that."

"I'm sorry, Heather. I'm sorry . . . it's just . . . I can hear the ice in the—"

"And you *assume* I'm drinking?"

"Heather . . ."

"No, Kimberly. You've gone too far. Who do you think you are, calling me with all your love talk and then accusing me of drinking? Who do you think I am, for that matter?"

"I—"

"You think that just because you've suddenly found your great love, you can call me—who is losing hers—and just grill me like a raw steak?"

"What?"

"Obviously I cannot talk with you anymore," she said.

The line went dead.

I stared at my cell phone with an open mouth. I started

209

to call my father, then changed my mind. Instead, I called Anise's floral shop, hoping she would answer.

She did.

"Oh, Kimberly," she said, almost breathless.

"Is this a bad time?"

"A little. We have—and don't laugh when I say this—three weddings and a funeral."

"Do you mean four? Four weddings and a funeral?"

"Oh heavens, no. I don't think I could survive if I had four."

"I can call you back . . ."

"Is it something important? Hold on . . . Melodie, I need more white roses . . . White . . . No, sweetie, not pink. White." She laughed lightly. "Those are pink, Melodie . . . well, sweetheart, turn on a light." She exhaled a slow sigh. "Okay, Kim."

"You asked if it was important. And it is . . . but you are clearly busy."

"What's it about?"

"I'm worried about Heather."

"Your father is nearly beside himself. He thinks Andre is having an affair; I guess he told you that."

"No. He won't tell me anything."

"But I think he's way off base. I think . . . hold on. Melodie, if that's all the baby's breath you can find, then we're in so much trouble. Please tell me otherwise . . . Oh, good. Fantastic, dear."

"Anise, I'll call you later. You're busy and I hear Max's nails on the floor near the door."

"I'm sorry, Kim."

"It's okay. Let's talk later."

When I opened the door to let Max out, he shot down the stairs as though he hadn't been outside all day. I stepped out on the landing and watched him dart next door. Apparently he hadn't needed a patch of grass; he wanted to play with his new best friend.

Which reminded me . . . Patsy.

I headed down the steps and crossed the lawns between our houses. I knocked on Patsy's door and ran my hands down my arms. In the short period of time I'd been outside, my skin had become clammy. I looked up at the sky; the sun was directly overhead and blazing hot.

The door cracked open. I peered between the frame and the door to see Patsy, clearly just out of bed.

"I'm not feeling so well this morning, honey."

"You don't look so well, either." I put my hand on the doorknob. "May I come in?"

She stepped back. "Oh, I hate for you to see me looking like this." She ran a gnarled yet delicate hand over the crown of her head. "I clearly do."

She wore a pair of checked cotton poplin pajamas that made her look all of eighty-five pounds. Her white hair was braided down both sides of her head, which made her look like an elderly Laura Ingalls Wilder. Her cheeks were flushed and her eyes swollen. She hacked as soon as I shut the door. My mothering instincts took over. "Oh, Patsy," I said. "You need a doctor."

Patsy turned and walked toward the back of the house. "Oh, pshaw. All I need is to rest, honey. It's not like this is my first summer cold. Good Lord willing, it won't be my last."

I followed Patsy into her bedroom—a room I'd never seen before, a room unlike the others in the house. The others were an eclectic blend of beachfront décor meets English country-side estate. This room was only the latter. The walls had been painted brick red. Cotton floral drapes of white, rose, and green matched the four-poster bed's comforter. The bed sat on the far side of the room. Overhead hung a large, matted black and white photograph of Patsy and her husband on their wedding day. Next to the bed, a matching nightstand was laden by an oversized lamp and a short stack of books.

My eyes took in the titles. *My Utmost for His Highest*, the current year's *Daily Guideposts Devotional*, and a thick, white-leather Bible with a tattered cover and pages dislodged from the spine. I couldn't help but think that God must find this the most beautiful book of all—his Word read so many times, it looked abused.

I had my own Bible, of course. Slim-lined. Pink. I read from it when I was studying the week's Sunday school lesson, when I needed guidance, and during church services. I rarely picked it up just to read. Something told me Patsy did. Something told me that, for her, this was more than just "another book." For a fleeting second the thought that I wanted to know more about her—that I wanted to emulate her even—swept over me.

The stooped-over woman inched her way toward the bed with its tousled bedcovers. I held them back, then straightened them over and around her after she'd gotten into the bed. Heat radiated from her tiny frame. "Oh, Patsy," I said, pressing my palm against her wrinkled forehead. "You are burning up with a fever."

"I'll be fine."

"Have you taken anything?"

"During the night. I took some of that Nyquil I have in the bathroom over there." She pointed toward the master bath. "Helps me to sleep."

I looked toward the bathroom and then back to Patsy. Her eyes were closed, the lids nearly transparent. Lying on her back had caused some of the wrinkles on her face to fall away, and I could see the young beauty she had once been. I glanced up at the photograph again and wondered briefly what I would look like when the totality of my youth had given way to the final years of my life.

Right now, I thought, I was vainly seeking the sunrise—those earlier years spent in Cedar Key when summers were carefree and filled with flirtatious love—while this woman was gazing toward sunset. I patted her hand.

"Just rest," I whispered.

I went into the living room, pulled my cell phone from the pocket of my Capri shorts, and called my father.

"Did you take her temp?" he asked me. "Any vitals?"

"No. But she's pretty hot, Dad. She says it's just a summer cold, but she's been coughing a lot and with her age . . ."

"The nearest doctor is going to be in Chiefland. Let me see if I can make some calls."

"I can get her there if necessary. I can have her there in no time."

"You're a good neighbor," he said. "And a good daughter."

My shoulders squared. I said good-bye, hung up the phone, set the ringtone to vibrate, and returned to Patsy, who slept. I noticed a small cushioned chair near a window and sat on the edge of it. Within seconds my cell vibrated in my hand. Without looking at the caller ID, I bound from the chair and exited the room.

"Dad?"

"No. Steven."

"Steven." I filled him in on Patsy's condition and told him Dad was making some calls to physicians in Chiefland.

"Hmm," he said. "It's Saturday, so medical offices won't be open. We could get her to one of the walk-in clinics there. They're open seven days a week."

213

"Just tell me where," I said.

"No, no. I'll drive you."

"Don't you have to work?"

"I'll figure it out."

I returned to the bedroom to observe Patsy, to watch the gentle rise and fall of her chest. Every so often she coughed as though her chest had been tickled, but she never stirred enough to wake. I noticed a few discarded tissues on the floor, picked them up, and dropped them into the wastebasket in the bathroom. While there, I picked up the Nyquil bottle on the vanity and studied the label.

The expiration date glared at me. It was over a year out of date.

I looked back at the tiny sleeping form on the bed before returning to the living room to call Dad again. Just as I pressed the speed dial number for him, I heard a light knock at the door. I placed the phone on an end table before answering the door.

Steven and a man I didn't know stood beyond the threshold. He was young and tanned and gripped the handle of a small black bag in his left hand. It seemed an extension of himself rather than an addition.

"Hey," I said, looking from one to the other, finally focusing on Steven.

"Kimberly, this is Dr. Willingham. After we hung up, I remembered that he and his family were here from south Florida." Dr. Willingham reminded me of a young Ryan O'Neal, an actor my mother had swooned over. I extended my hand in greeting, thanked him for coming, and then stepped aside. "The bedroom is this way," I said.

Patsy continued to sleep.

"I'm more concerned now than before," I said to Dr.

Willingham, who was dressed as casually as Steven: polo shirt and loose-fitting shorts. "I just noticed that the Nyquil she took has expired."

"By how long?" he asked as he reached for Patsy's right hand, presumably to take her pulse.

I went to the bathroom and came back with the bottle. "Over a year."

He shrugged. "A number of studies have determined that if medication has been stored in optimum conditions, there's little reason to worry. But, with it being a year over expiration, worst case scenario is that it just isn't working as well as if it were new."

"Her respirations are shallow but her lips and nails show no signs of cyanosis."

Dr. Willingham looked perplexed and impressed at the same time. "You sound knowledgeable."

"My father and sister are doctors. And I helped take care of my mother before she died. When it's important, you pay attention to details, right?"

Dr. Willingham placed his bag on the bed, opened it, and drew out a forehead thermometer. Without answering my question he swiped it across Patsy's forehead. I watched to see if she had any reaction, even the slightest movement. She didn't. I held my breath in wait before glancing over to the chair Steven now occupied. His elbows rested on his knees, and his hands were clasped together.

"One-o-two-point-six," the doctor said. He looked at me as he returned the thermometer to his bag. "Tell me what you know."

"Yesterday she was coughing. She said it was just a silly summer cold. Nothing to worry about. But with her age . . ."

"Do you know how old she is?"

I didn't. I shook my head.

"What's her name?" he asked.

"Patsy."

"Last name?"

I couldn't see that it mattered.

"Milstrap," Steven answered for me.

Dr. Willingham leaned over the bed, cupped Patsy's shoulder, and shook it. "Mrs. Milstrap!" he shouted. "Mrs. Milstrap! Can you hear me?"

Could she hear him? The dead could hear him.

Patsy's eyes fluttered as he called her name one more time. "Who in the land of the living are you?" she asked.

A breath escaped my lungs and I laughed, then glanced at Steven, who winked at me.

"I'm Dr. Willingham," he answered, his voice still elevated.

"Well, my goodness, why are you yelling at me?"

Dr. Willingham's smile was broad. "Mrs. Milstrap, can you tell me how old you are?"

"Of course I can," she said. She looked at me. "Do you know this man?"

I nodded. "Patsy, your fever is a little high. And you've taken cold medicine that is outdated. I called Steven," I said looking over at him, "who knows Dr. Willingham."

Patsy's lips formed an O. She looked at Dr. Willingham and said, "Well, I'm seventy-eight years old. And if the good Lord allows, on my next birthday I'll be seventy-nine." She sighed. "I do admit I don't feel so well."

I rubbed my hand along the comforter, where her legs stretched out like two short sticks. "We're going to get you better."

"Mrs. Milstrap, how long have you had this fever and your cough?"

"Just a couple of days. I thought it was just a summer cold. But I ache pretty bad, doctor. I clearly do."

Dr. Willingham smiled at her. "Well, I think you're probably right there. But at your age, a bad summer cold can turn into something more." He smiled again. "Don't you worry now. We're going to take care of that," he said. "In the meantime, no more expired Nyquil for you."

He straightened and turned to me. "Can you stay with her?"

"Of course."

He looked at Steven, now standing. "Steven, I'm going to write a prescription for Mrs. Milstrap. Not sure where you'll fill it," he muttered under his breath.

"I can handle it," Steven said.

"Kimberly, I'm going to leave my phone number with you. If her fever doesn't break or she gets worse, do not hesitate to call." He pulled a business card and pen out of his bag and jotted his number on the back of it. "This is my personal cell."

"Thank you," I said as he dipped his hand back into the bag and came up with a prescription pad. "I really appreciate this."

"Here you go," he said to Steven as he tore the top page from the prescription pad. "And I'll call you in the morning if I don't hear anything from you."

"Thanks, Doc," Steven said as though they were old friends. "I'll walk you out."

The doctor told Patsy he'd call in the morning, but she was sleeping again. I followed the men into the living room, where my phone glared, lit up, from the end table. "Oh," I said. "I'll bet Dad has been calling."

While Steven walked the doctor to his car, I called Dad, who was worried sick, he said. "I had all kinds of visions running around in my head."

"Don't worry, Dad. Steven came with a doctor who is vacationing here and took care of Patsy. I'm sorry I haven't called you back . . . the doctor is actually just leaving."

"Steven?"

My legs grew weak; I hadn't told Dad about Steven. About seeing him . . . dating him . . . feeling a little bit crazy when I was near him. I took a deep breath and tried to sound nonchalant. "Steven Granger. You remember him, don't you?"

"I remember him, yes. How is it that Steven Granger knew about Patsy?"

"I know what you're thinking, Dad. He just happened to call after I talked to you and—"

"Why was he calling you?"

I swallowed. "Because, Dad. We have a date tonight and—"

"You have a date tonight?"

"Dad, are you going to interrupt me every three words or are you going to let me finish?"

A moment of silence passed before he said, "I'm listening."

I turned toward the door to see Steven stick his head in and say, "I'll be right back."

I nodded. He closed the door behind him.

I walked briskly into the kitchen and sat in one of the chairs at the table. "Dad," I said, crossing my legs. "I don't understand the tone in your voice. Steven Granger is living here now. His father had a heart attack last year and he moved back down to help with the business."

"I know all of that, Boo."

"Okay. Well, then." I took a breath and spoke quickly through the exhale. "We ran into each other, he asked me out, I said yes, and that's that."

"Not a good idea and you know it."

"Dad—"

218

"Hear me out on this one, Kim."

My jaw flinched. "Okay."

"I've never seen you so hurt in my life as you were at the end of your senior year."

"You mean other than when Charlie left me and the boys?"

"Well, of course. But you were older then. Steven was your first love, and he ripped your heart out."

"You sound more like a mother than a father."

"A father doesn't forget that kind of heartache when it's his little girl who's crying."

I rubbed my forehead with my fingertips. I leaned over as though in pain. "That's sweet, Dad, but I'm not a little girl anymore."

"I know that. But you're still *my* little girl."

I smiled but remained silent.

I heard him sigh. "Well, then. Does it feel like it did twenty years ago?"

I straightened as I laughed. "Honestly? It's not as hormonally driven."

"I didn't need to hear that."

"I know you didn't. But . . . we had our second date last night. He got me to take pictures with his camera, Dad. And he made me laugh." *And cry.*

"I haven't seen Steven since you were kids."

"Well, he's not a kid anymore. Neither am I. And I don't know what all this means or where it will lead, but I have to tell you. I'm more than a little willing to find out."

"Just be careful, sweetheart."

"I will." I heard Patsy coughing from her bedroom. "Dad, I need to go check on Patsy. I'll call you later, okay?"

"Take it easy, Boo."

22

Summer 1946

With the war a lasting memory and the manufacturing of appliances back in full swing, thirty-year-old Bernice Liddle went to town and splurged on a new Maytag wringer washing machine. Not so much for herself, she told her husband, Ira—a man as tight with a penny as he was firm on her role as wife and mother—but to enable her to bring in other people's wash. It was for a good cause too, she'd told him, what with so many women still working outside of their homes.

"And goodness knows," she told her thirteen-year-old daughter Patsy, who rode with her to Gibson's Department Store on the day of purchasing, "we could use the extra money." She cut a sharp eye toward her daughter. "You tell Mr. Liddle I said that and I'll deny it, you hear me?"

"Yes, ma'am," Patsy replied. Not that her mother had to tell her. She was smart enough to know the rules of the house. No one demeaned Ira Liddle, not to his face, that is. Not to mention this was the first time her mother had said anything in confidence to Patsy, making Bernice's quiet firstborn feel all the more close to her mother.

"You're a good daughter," she said after several minutes.

Patsy knew her mother had been thinking. Thinking about what she'd just let slip. Thinking about what would surely happen if Mr. Liddle found out she'd said it, even to her own child. Her words of praise were no more than a line of insurance, but Patsy felt pleased to hear them anyway.

Patsy looked out the open passenger window of the oversized black 1936 Chevy coupe Mr. Liddle had purchased for his wife the year before. "To use when you have to do your shopping or if the kids get sick," he told her when he brought it home. "Not for any running around to visit with your friends."

As if Bernice Liddle had friends for visiting.

"Sure is hot out there," Patsy now said. "The beans are near about drying up before I can pick 'em."

"You just have to get out there earlier, is all."

Patsy's eyes scanned lazily from the side of the long dirt road they traveled to the woman behind the steering wheel. She was only seventeen years her senior, yet she looked and seemed so much older. Like a grandmother instead of a mother.

"Yes, ma'am."

They purchased the washer for $54.95 plus tax. As her mother counted out the last of the loose change, Patsy ran her fingertips along the wringers of the floor model. She listened when Mr. Gibson told Patsy's mother someone would deliver it to the house within the next few days. Then, Mrs. Liddle gave their address and phone number—931—and asked that someone call before they arrived. "To make sure we're home," she said, as though they had such a social schedule.

221

Patsy looked up, wondering where else they'd be when the washer came. She heard her mother whisper, "Will you let others know, Mr. Gibson, that I'm taking in wash now?"

Patsy walked away from the embarrassment of the moment. Not that she was ashamed of taking in wash; she merely felt the sting of her mother's humiliation. But a week later, that machine became her own cross to bear. While her friends from school met at Cassel Creek in the hot summer afternoons, Patsy stayed busy washing clothes for her family while her mother took care of what felt like the rest of Casselton, Georgia. Her days became endless hours of caring for her little brothers, five-year-old Harold and four-year-old Billy, picking and putting up vegetables, helping to keep their two-story bungalow clean, and washing clothes.

The washing was one thing. The ironing and the folding and the putting them away was another.

They kept the machine next to the door on the wide, screened back porch. Twice a week Patsy pulled the washer from the outside wall, ran the electric wire to a kitchen plug, added water and Duz detergent to the tub, allowed it to agitate for a few minutes, and then added the clothes. While they washed, she ran clean water into a wooden rinse tub, which she then dragged to the back side of the washer. After flipping the chrome switch of the machine to the off position, she pulled the soapy clothes into the rinse tub, added another load to the wash, and then began the back-breaking task of wringing the individual pieces.

When it was all done, she hung the clothes on the line, then set everything to rights on the back porch, including returning the Duz powder to its place under the skirted kitchen sink.

Oh, how her mother loved Duz. Their kitchen had been furnished by the goblets, dishes, dishrags, and drying cloths that came inside its box, which meant she didn't have to spend any extra of the allowance Mr. Liddle gave her, and she could still have nice things.

On the days she wasn't washing the laundry, Patsy ironed it. And on the days she didn't iron the laundry, she dusted the house and broom-swept the carpets. Living on a dirt road in a house that sat on a plot of land without a blade of grass meant the house always stayed dusty, and the rugs sometimes felt like a sandbox to bare feet. To keep from stirring the dust, she used the sprinkling bottle from laundry days and cast droplets of water on top of the worn wool before sweeping. She thought it a good idea, and her mother had even praised her for it.

One thing she was never allowed to do, though, was enter into her mother's bedroom, the one she shared with Mr. Liddle. Had it been up to Bernice Liddle, Patsy could have played in there all day. But it wasn't. Mr. Liddle said children didn't belong in the bedroom of their parents. Even though Patsy wasn't technically *their* child, she was forced to comply.

Until the day her mother was overwhelmed with other people's laundry and two little boys who'd eaten too much of the taffy they'd pulled the day before. "Patsy," she called out the back door as Patsy walked up from the vegetable garden; a bushel of peas rocked against her hip as she toted it in the late morning sunlight.

Patsy shielded her eyes against the sun and squinted to the back of the house. "I got enough peas to shell for a month of Sundays," she called back.

"Never mind that now," her mother hollered.

Patsy made her way to the unpainted wooden steps leading up to the porch before she set the bushel basket at her feet. "What's going on, Mama?"

"I need you to help me out here, clearly I do. I'm running back and forth with a chamber pot for your brothers and trying to stay on task with this wash here. Mr. Liddle will be home tonight from his sales route, and if he sees the dust that's built up in the house . . . well, you know how he gets. Go put on one of my aprons and get to work in the house, now."

Patsy ascended the steps and got right to it. Some time later she went to the kitchen in search of her mother, finding her there stooped over the sink, wearing her old house dress and a pair of Red Goose shoes in need of resoling, washing the peas from the earlier picking. "Mama, I dusted the whole house except for your room."

Her mother glanced over her shoulder. Her eyes went first to the kitchen wall clock and then to Patsy. She raised her hand to press against the brush rollers that held her hair in tight curls. "Lord-a-mercy, I gotta get my hair done too, so go ahead and dust in there too."

Patsy did as she was told before her mother could change her mind. Oh, how she wanted to be in that room . . . to touch the dainty items that rested atop her mother's vanity. She walked into the room as though entering a church— reverently, taking it all in. Every bit of furniture, every framed picture, every needlepoint pillow from her mother's hand. She started her work with the four-poster oak bed. She stuck a finger into the dust cloth, dropped lemon oil onto the finger so as not to spill it, and then meticulously cleaned the carved roses in the headboard.

She moved to the bedside tables, ever so careful to pick up the lamps, dust under them, and return them to the exact spot she'd found them. Patsy swallowed hard when she came to Mr. Liddle's chest of drawers. If he thought for a moment that Patsy—rather than his wife—had been the one to touch his things . . .

She drew in a deep breath, picked up each item one at a time—the brush and comb set, the matching lint roller, the small jewelry box placed perfectly in the middle. A library book—*Listen, Germany* by Thomas Mann—rested along one edge. Patsy picked it up to run the oily cloth over the wood. Thinking herself quite wise, she laid the book on the white crocheted bedspread her mother had made from a Star Book pattern so as not to get oil stains on the back cover of the book.

Her mother's vanity was neatly arranged. Her lotions, perfume, and dusting powder were to the left of the oval mirror. To the right, a faux gold filigree lipstick holder, with Cupid playing a guitar in the outside center, held four tubes of lipstick with the matching vanity set angled to the left in the center. Patsy glanced toward the opened door. With a captured breath, she removed each item and placed it on the padded stool at her knees. She oiled the wood until the patina all but reflected her image. Before replacing her mother's pretties, she pulled a dry cloth from the pocket of the apron and wiped each one as though she were drying a freshly bathed infant. She hummed in her efforts, imagining herself as the wife of some wonderful man—unlike Mr. Liddle—and caring for her own delicate things. When she came to the lipsticks, she took each short tube from its gold holder, slipped off the lid, and twisted the base. She watched with wonder as the cylinder of waxy color emerged, then quickly sent it back into its cave. When she got to the pink, she pretended to slide it across her bottom lip, pressed her lips together, then pursed them and peered into the mirror. *My, my, Miss Sweeney, but aren't you lovely this afternoon in your house frock and smelling like lemons?*

Before finishing the vanity, she inhaled from both the perfume bottle and the dusting powder tin and imagined herself getting ready for a fancy party, the likes she'd most probably never see. When everything was as it had been before she entered the room, she straightened and smiled. She'd done a good job, she thought. Maybe Mama would let her do it again.

"Patsy?" The voice came from behind her; it was neither harsh nor gentle.

"Oh, Mama," she said turning. "You startled me."

"Hurry, child, before Mr. Liddle comes home."

Patsy crossed the room to where her mother stood framed by the doorway. "I did a good job for you, Mama," she said.

"I know you did, now, come on. The boys need a bath and the dining room needs preparing, and then I want you to comb out my hair."

Her mother always put Mr. Liddle's traveling things up the minute he returned home from his sales trips, while her husband played with his sons first, then smoked a pipe and read the paper in wait for supper to be on the table.

He never said a word to Patsy other than, "Girl, you been helping your mama?"

"Yes, sir," Patsy always said. She tried not to look him in the eyes—they were steel gray and sharp as a shark's tooth—when she answered. She just replied and then went on her way.

It had always been like that between them. He only spoke to her—really spoke to her—when he was giving her a whipping. On those occasions—not as frequent since her twelfth birthday—his words came in staccato beats. "What. Did. I. Tell. You. About . . ." and then he'd finish with whatever he'd told her about that she'd not done. Or had done. It made no never mind. He'd hold her forearm by one sturdy hand and swat her with the other, most often on her rear end. One time he hit her across the back so hard she lost her breath. That night Mama tucked her into bed, which was unusual, asked if she was all right, then said, "Just don't make him mad, Patsy, and you'll be fine."

He never hit the boys. For that, at least, Patsy was grateful. But he'd hit Mama a few times—most often a slap across her face. Those times he called her names like "stupid" and "worthless" and said she was lucky he came along when he did and rescued her sorry self from "that pit five-and-dime and Mr. Harvey Jenkins."

Patsy didn't know what that meant, exactly, but she knew better than to ask.

That night—the night of the bedroom dusting and Mr. Liddle's return—was no different from the others. At least for the most part. While the boys sipped broth in their bedroom, Patsy and Mama listened while Mr. Liddle spoke of his travels and sales between bites and swallows. Afterward, Patsy cleared the table and cleaned the kitchen so Mama could tend first to the boys and then to her husband.

Patsy said good night to her mother—who sat knitting in her chair in the living room, the one she'd polished to a shine earlier in the day—and a quick, "Glad you're home safe, Mr. Liddle," to the man who chewed on his pipe and listened to *Abbott Mysteries* on the Philco console radio between him and his wife.

"Good night, Patsy," her mother said.

"See to it that you check on the boys before turning in," Mr. Liddle answered.

She did as she was told—the boys were both sleeping in their upstairs bedroom already, the one right across the hall from their parents'—and then returned downstairs to her own simple but comfortable room. She stripped out of the clothes she'd changed into for supper—they weren't fancy but they weren't ripe with the smell of field peas and lemon oil either—out of her under-things and into the pretty, thin cotton pink gown Mama had made for her.

It was some time later—she couldn't be sure how long since she'd slipped between the cool sheets of her bed—that she heard the racket coming from upstairs. Her mother's voice pleading. Mr. Liddle's voice demanding. On instinct she slipped out of bed and into her mother's cast-off slippers. Patsy was out the door and halfway up the stairs before she had time to think better of it.

"I've told you and told you," Mr. Liddle shouted. "Haven't I?" Patsy could hear the slap of flesh against flesh. "Haven't I?"

"Please, Ira," her mother whimpered. "The boys . . ."

Patsy took a few more steps up the stairs. She hardly breathed, but her eyes blinked rapidly. She'd never interfered in her mother's fights with Mr. Liddle before, but this time sounded . . . different.

"A man has to know," Patsy heard him say, as though spoken through clenched teeth, "that he can leave his home in proper order and come home to it the same way."

"And you have." Her mother's voice shook.

Patsy heard something—someone—stumbling across the room followed by the sound of something else dropping to the floor.

The book! She'd left it on the bed, had failed to return it to the chest of drawers. He would know her mother would never be so forgetful. Bernice Liddle kept everything in perfect order for her husband.

"I expect that when I leave this house, you and you alone come into this room. Haven't I made myself clear on that issue?"

Mama's answer came in sobs. "But . . . if you knew . . . how hard today . . . has been for me . . ."

"Stop your nagging." He swore the expletive Patsy's best friend Mitzy once told her saying was the unpardonable sin, then said it again and a third time. "I don't want that girl in my bedroom. And if I have to beat that into you, then so be it."

Patsy heard the sound of his belt buckle coming undone, the swish of it leaving the loops, the first smack of it against her mother. She fled up the remainder of the stairs, pushed open the nearly closed bedroom door, and screamed, "Stop it! Stop it! If you're going to hit someone, hit me! I left the stupid book on the bed!"

She reasoned later that it had been the shock of seeing her standing there and of hearing her shouting like a madwoman that stopped Mr. Liddle from hitting her mother that night. That it had been the sight of her nearly nude body silhouetted by the night's bright moonlight bursting through the gauzy drapes and open windows which caused him to stop seeing her as "the girl" and start seeing her as she soon was to be. A woman, fully budded. No longer did the gray of his eyes hold steel ready to rip her to shreds. Instead, they held something more monstrous than that. Something she'd never witnessed before but knew to stay away from.

And—she knew—no longer did his hands itch to hit her but to embrace her. To stroke her. To touch her in a way that would leave her permanently burned.

So it was that a few weeks later her mother had packed

her bags. Without so much as a day to say good-bye to her friends, Patsy found herself on a bus bound for a small town just outside of Charleston, South Carolina . . .

And the brother she'd always known of but had never gotten to hold.

23

"I can do it," I said to Steven after he returned from getting Patsy's prescription filled.

"I know you can," he said. His voice was kind but firm. "But the point is, Kim, you don't have to do it alone."

We stood in the middle of Patsy's doorway, me on one side of it, Steven on the other. Oreo's body slinked around my legs. His purr sounded more like an old truck's engine; no doubt he was hungry. I looked down at him, then back to Steven. "I'm not trying to do it alone."

"Then let me come in and help you." He extended the small white bag holding Patsy's meds toward me. "I can at least feed the cat for you."

I turned and walked toward the kitchen as he closed the door behind us. "I'll go ahead and give her the first dose," I said. I pulled a bottle of liquid medicine from the bag. "I guess the cat's food is in the pantry." I bobbed my head toward the narrow door at the opposite end of the room.

Steven stepped in the direction I'd given. "I'll find it."

I rattled around in the silverware drawer for a teaspoon. "His bowl is in the laundry room." I looked at Steven, who peered at me from around the open pantry door. "I know this because I started a load of clothes while you were gone."

"Ah," he said.

I took the medicine along with a small glass of juice to Patsy, woke her using the same technique Dr. Willingham used, and gave her the first dose. She made a face at me, said, "Awful. You'd think they could come up with something that tasted like fried chicken or at the very least chocolate cake."

I stifled a giggle before helping her to lie down again. "Do you need anything else?" I asked.

"Just sleep. Sleep is always the best medicine."

I put the medicine bottle in the bathroom before returning to the living room, where Steven had stretched out on the sofa. His shoes were off; they sat side by side on the floor near the end of the sofa where his legs crossed at the ankles. "Make yourself at home," I said. "Did you find the cat food?"

He shifted to upright. "Sorry," he said. "Yes, I did. In the laundry room." He waved me over to sit next to him and—in spite of thinking it not a good idea—I complied. He ran his fingertips along the side of my face, forcing me to look at him. "Hi."

I smiled. "Hi."

"You okay?"

I nodded. He leaned in for a kiss, sweet and quick. "I'm going to assume that our date is off for this evening."

"You assume correctly, sir." I leaned my face into his hand still resting against my cheek. "I can't leave her."

"Nor should you." He straightened fully before saying, "I've already got this thing figured out though."

"Oh, do you now?"

"Mmmhmm. I'm going to order us some pizza and we'll eat right here."

"Steven—"

"Because the way I see it," he continued before I could argue a word, "you're not leaving Patsy and I'm not leaving you. All gallantry aside, I'm hungry." He leaned toward me. "Are you hungry?"

I nodded. "Yeah, a little."

"Okay." He slapped his hands against his knees before holding up the index fingers on both hands. "Cedar Key has two—count them, two—great pizza places." He wiggled the fingers at me. "I'll tell you a little about them and then you can choose."

I ended up going with suggestion number one. Steven placed an order over the phone, hung up, and said, "It'll be ready when I get there." He gave me a swift kiss—the kind I used to imagine I'd get from him as he left for work each morning—mumbled, "See you in a minute," and left.

I made another trip to Patsy's bedroom to check on her— she continued to sleep and her fever already seemed to be breaking—then walked outside to the balcony to make the phone call I'd dreaded since earlier in the day.

My brother-in-law answered with, "Hey, Kimberly."

"Oh, the joy of caller ID." I pulled up my feet to rest them on the aqua-painted railing.

"That and I've half-expected your call."

I wondered what he meant but decided against asking. Andre—a brilliant mind if there ever was one—was too astute for someone like me to challenge. "Are you able to talk right now?"

"It's as good a time as any."

"Are you at work?"

"No. I just pulled up to the library, to tell you the truth." The library. It didn't seem like an Andre kind of thing to do on a Saturday. My stomach churned, half from hunger and the other half from concern. "Oh." I took a deep breath and plunged right in. "I talked with Heather this morning . . . more or less . . . and I'm very worried about her, Andre."

"Me too. I'm worried about her too." He paused. "I love her, Kimberly. I don't know what she's told you, but I want that much said before we go any further with this conversation."

I watched as a small flock of seagulls glided past me. They called to one another in screeches I was all too familiar with.

When I didn't say anything, he asked, "How's Cedar Key?"

"It's good. It's real good, actually."

"Heather told me she was surprised you'd gone. She told me about what happened when you were kids there. About Steven."

"Oh, did she now?"

He chuckled. "Anything to take the focus away from her and her problems."

I took another breath. "Well, since you've now brought it up, do you mind telling me what's going on with the two of you?"

"Did she indicate I'm having an affair?"

Right to the point. Wow. "She thinks you are."

"I'm not."

I closed my eyes at the revelation, praying he was telling me the truth. Charlie and I had been donned the perfect couple, but no more perfect than Andre and Heather.

"Can I be honest?" he asked.

"Of course."

"You and Charlie . . . Do you know how often Heather held our marriage up to the mirror of yours?"

"What? No."

"Yes. If Charlie so much as winked at you during a family

234

dinner, I caught it when we got home. 'Why don't you ever wink at me like that?' she'd ask. 'Why don't you love me like Charlie loves Kim?' It got to the point where, if I saw Charlie do anything for you, to you, whatever . . . I knew I had to one-up him." He coughed sarcasm. "I told Charlie one time, I said, 'Charlie, I'll pay you half my annual income if you'll just *not* be so loving toward your wife in front of Heather.'"

I pressed my hand against my forehead. I was sweating profusely in the afternoon heat but couldn't bring myself to go inside and disturb Patsy. "What did he say to that?"

"He just laughed. He actually said—and I don't say this to hurt you or bring back negative emotions—that if I loved Heather a quarter as much as he loved you, I'd be just fine."

I scoffed at the news. "Do tell."

"He was joking, of course."

"No kidding, Andre." I dropped my feet from the railing and leaned over, fighting a wave of nausea that threatened to turn violent.

"I'm sorry. But if we are going to be honest here—"

"And you're *not* having an affair?"

"Kim. I told you. No."

I pictured Andre—if he was where he said he was—sitting in his black Navigator, the one with all the bells and whistles—outside the public library. Handsome hardly described him. The closer he got to forty, the more appealing he became. While my sister worried over every little laugh line and gray hair, Andre's only served to change him from boyishly cute to dashing. If he were my husband, I'd worry too.

"Then Heather is just imagining all this?"

"It's more than that, Kim. It's . . ."

I stood and starting pacing the length of the balcony, hoping the action would bring enough of a breeze to cool me.

"Andre, just say it, okay? If I'm going to help Heather, I need to know."

"You already know, Boo. You just don't want to say the words."

I stopped pacing. The sun beat against my back in perfect rhythm with my heart. I forced myself to focus on something—anything—in front of me. The water had turned to gray. The scattering of islands in the Gulf were blurred by haze. Overhead, against the perfect blue of the sky, white wings fluttered as another flock of gulls headed toward the sunset. I blinked several times as I tried to force myself to find one thing . . . just one thing . . .

A *ping-ping* drew my attention to the oversized wind chimes hanging on the east side of Patsy's balcony. They echoed back the sun's light like a diamond under the display of Tiffany's lamps. I stared at the glint, widening my eyes, and told myself to not be weary. I knew this . . . I knew . . .

"I know."

"Then say it."

"I . . ." I couldn't.

"You want me to say it? Okay, I'll say it, Kim. Heather is an alcoholic. She's also addicted to prescription drugs. She's an alcoholic and an addict."

I sucked in my breath. "Andre . . ."

"And I'll tell you where I've been lately. I've been going to Al-Anon meetings after work. Not to a cheap motel with some floozy, like she's accused me of."

"Al-Anon?"

"Yeah. Al-Anon. Because I need help too, Kim. I've enabled her and I need help as much as she does."

"Enabled her? What do you mean? You've forced her to drink?"

"Don't be silly. You're too smart for that. Drinking is a coping skill she learned a long time ago. Long before we even met."

"I don't—"

"I'm the one, Kim, who has made sure she had whatever she needed from the pharmacy, which very well could cost me my job. But I'm not willing to sacrifice my *wife*. I won't lie and I won't enable her. Not anymore." His voice was strong, as if he'd rehearsed the words a thousand times so as not to get them wrong and in the repeating had come to believe what he said. Before I could reply, he added, "I won't treat this the way your dad did, Kim. I won't lose my wife to this disease."

The wind chimes moved, twirling round and round as though hurricane-force winds were upon the island. The screeching overhead reverberated in my inner ear. While the world turned upside down around me, I managed to find my chair. To sit. To remind myself to breathe. "What are you talking about?" I spoke through a clenched jaw.

"You know what I'm talking about. You've always known."

"No."

"Yes, Kimberly. Yes. Heather told me the way you used to play your mother. The way you used to get what you wanted by waiting until you knew she'd had enough to drink and you could mold the clay any way you wanted."

My breath came in ragged jerks. "No, no, no."

"Kim!"

I jumped, jolted back to the here and now and what my brother-in-law was saying to me. "Don't you talk to me like that, Charlie Tucker."

Andre groaned. "Oh, man. I'm not Charlie, Kim. I'm Andre. And I'm telling you the truth here."

I ended the call. One second later, I called him back. As soon as he said hello, I declared, "My mother died of liver cancer."

"Your mother died of cirrhosis of the liver. She was a functioning alcoholic, Kim. A *highly* functioning alcoholic, but an alcoholic nonetheless."

I raked my hand through my hair. My fingertips came back drenched in sweat. "No." I ended the call again.

And called him right back. "Andre, don't—"

"Don't what? Say it out loud? Determine that the cycle is going to stop here? I've got my own children to think about too."

I pressed my hand against my chest; my heart hammered beneath it. In spite of the news I'd just received, all I could think was that Steven was coming back with pizza and Patsy lay in bed with a fever. "I can't talk about this right now," I said.

"If you want to help your sister—"

"Of course I want to help my sister!" I clamped my hand over my mouth and looked in the direction of Patsy's bedroom. "Andre," I continued, my voice softer, "I'm caring for an elderly woman right now. I'm at her home. I just can't . . ."

"The timing is off then." I heard him exhale. "But the subject has got to be faced. You can keep hanging up on me and calling me back and you can put it off indefinitely, but it's not going to change the facts. Your sister is an alcoholic and a drug addict. She knows it. And she knows you know it but won't address it."

"Just this morning . . . I tried . . ." My words tumbled out like soiled clothes from a laundry hamper. "She only ended up yelling at me."

"I know. Believe me, I know the sting of her alcohol-induced fury."

238

Anger rose from inside me. I blew air from my lungs like a bull ready to stampede. "So what are you going to do about it, Andre?"

"I'm meeting someone here at the library. There are some archived articles he wants me to read. He's going to help me get Heather into a crisis center."

"And she's okay with that?"

"No, she's not okay with that," he said as though I were an idiot. "She insists every night that she can beat this on her own. But every morning she's pouring vodka into orange juice just to get by to lunch. At lunch she has a little something to tide her over, and at 5:00 it's cocktail hour."

I hiccupped to force my tears back.

"The kids and I have talked," he continued. "They know they'll be without their mother for the summer, and they're okay with that."

"But how will you manage? Heather takes care of them."

"No, she doesn't, Kimberly. She pretends to take care of them. They've been taking care of themselves for some time now. And it stops. Monday she either goes in on her own, or I'll force the issue."

"Andre . . ." I swallowed. "I'll be back on Tuesday, I think. If you can wait till then, the boys can stay with me."

I heard him chuckle before he said, "You don't have to fix this too, Kim."

If he had thrown cold water on me, it wouldn't have had any less effect. "What?"

"I'm sorry. It's just . . . you know how you are. You want to fix everything."

"No, I—"

"Yes, you do. And I love you for offering, but we'll be fine. It's not like they're babies."

"I see."

"And I'm sorry if I sounded cruel about your mother. I've tried to talk to your father, but he's still in denial. Not just about his wife but about his daughter too."

I wiped my face with my fingertips, grateful I wore no makeup. "Have you spoken to anyone else?"

"Just Jayme-Leigh."

"And?"

"She agrees with me."

"Even about Mom?"

"Yes."

I heard Steven's car tires crunching down the drive. I stood, turning in the sound's direction. "Oh. Oh, Andre, I have to go now."

"Kim—"

"No. I . . . my friend has come back with dinner. I have to go now."

"Just think about what I've said."

I stepped toward the sliding glass doors. "I will."

"I'd appreciate your support, Boo. And your prayers."

"Of course. Okay." I slid the door open, felt the cool of the air-conditioning pass over me.

"Call me back, will you?"

"I will." Steven's footsteps came bounding up the outside stairs. "Good-bye, Andre." I ended the call before pushing the door shut and locking it. Just then the front door opened, and I whirled around, wondering how in the world I was going to explain my condition to Steven.

24

Steven took one look at me and suggested I go home for a shower. "I'll take care of things here," he said. "The pizza and wings will be waiting for you when you get back."

He didn't have to suggest it twice. I ran out of Patsy's, crossed the yard as if I were running from a monster, and—with Max on my heels—entered the house and stripped off my clothes, leaving them piled on the floor. For the next half hour I stood in the shower, ice-cold water pelting my body. I pounded my fists against the slick tiles. I turned my face upward; the needle-like drops of water mingled with my tears, washing them down my body toward the drain. When I had expended all my energy, I slid down the wall and thought I was going to freeze to death. I wondered if, given enough time, someone would come looking for me. Maybe Steven. And he would find me drawn up like a baby, knees up to my chest, heels frozen like the ice sculptures on the party tables at Glenmuir Country Club. And he would never know what I now knew. What I'd known all along. What I'd been afraid to voice.

My mother had been an alcoholic.

241

I threw my head back, ran my fingers along my scalp. My hair was plastered there; it wrapped around my throat like a noose. I stared at the shower curtain—the one Anise had bought . . . had purchased and brought to my mother's home and hung in my mother's bathroom . . . the one that matched the comforter set in the bedroom. I focused on the lines in the designs; they looked like trails on a map. Hallways in a maze. A maze I may as well have been trapped in.

So Dad had known. And he had tried to make it all right. I thought of how Mom spent her mornings in bed here in Cedar Key. Dad took her a mug of coffee, then came back to drink his with me while I sipped on hot cocoa. "Be extra quiet this morning, Boo. Mom's not feeling well."

I tried to determine when I had figured it out. Had I been a teenager already? Surely by the time I was seventeen. I'd played Mom that year, knowing just when to ask her the questions that got me my way.

I shook my head. But no, no, no. I was too young to under-stand . . . I hadn't fully understood the disease. That it was a disease. I'd just seen it as Mom liking to drink too much. So when, then, had I *really* understood?

I twisted the faucets until the water shut off. I stood, pulled back the shower curtain, and stared at my reflection in the mirror on the opposite wall. I was nearly blue; with my thin frame, I looked emaciated. Poor and forgotten.

I hummed a song I remembered from long ago, then sang the one line I easily remembered: "Sometimes I feel like a motherless child . . ."

And right then, I did.

I returned to Patsy's with my hair still wet but combed straight back.

"Are you all right?" Steven asked as I sat in the kitchen chair across the table from him.

"Yes. No."

"Let me get you something to eat." He stood, walked over to the counter to the pizza box. It had already been opened; he'd eaten without me, not that I blamed him. "You said cheese only, right?"

I nodded.

He slapped the oversized slice of pizza onto a plate and placed it in the microwave. "Coke?"

I nodded again.

When he had brought my dinner to the table and sat opposite me, he said, "Do you want to talk about it?"

"I need to check on Patsy," I said, rising.

"Sit down, Kim. I've already checked on her and she's fine. Her fever has broken and she's sleeping."

I sat.

"Eat."

I took a bite.

"What's going on?"

After I'd swallowed and sipped the drink I asked, "What did you know about my mother?"

"Your mother? She was pretty," he answered with a smile. "She was always nice to me." Then he winked. "And she had the prettiest daughter of any mother I'd ever seen."

I smiled in spite of my heartache. "Did you ever think . . . did you ever know that . . . she maybe drank too much?"

"Drank too much? No. I mean . . . Kim, we were all kids. You know how it was in those days. We didn't really know or understand what was going on in our parents' lives. Besides, I knew her when she was here in Cedar Key, vacationing."

His eyes narrowed as though he were thinking my question through. "Why? What has someone told you?"

I told him about my call with Andre, about Mom and Heather. I couldn't eat more than a few bites of the pizza, so after a few minutes I allowed him to lead me to Patsy's living room, where we sat on the sofa—he at one end and me snuggled up against him like a little girl with her daddy. "In my heart, I always knew there was something different about Mom's drinking, something beyond 'social.' I even used it at times. But I refused to acknowledge it as *alcoholism*." I shook my head. "No wonder I was such an ogre with Charlie."

He kissed the crown of my head. "What do you mean?"

"Sometimes he would go out after work and meet some of his old high school buddies. They'd have a beer or whatever. When he came home I wouldn't speak to him for days. I never fully understood my actions, but at the same time I couldn't control *them* either." I breathed in the blend of Steven's cologne and the detergent he'd washed his shirt in and wistfully thought how good it felt, this inhaling of his scent. "Since the divorce, I've tried to continue to control them."

"Which 'them'? Charlie or your actions."

"Both." I released a tiny breath. "Ohhhhh, maybe that's it."

"Maybe that's what?"

"The reason why he left me."

Steven's hands gripped my shoulders, and he pushed me back just far enough so as to make eye contact. "Kimberly, a man doesn't leave his wife and kids because she doesn't like for him to drink occasionally. Not without a few fights to that end, anyway."

I lowered my eyes, completely unable to keep them focused on the tenderness of his. "Then what?"

He drew me back into his arms. "That's for Charlie to answer."

"But he won't. I've asked."

"Then there's nothing you can do about it. Sometimes people just leave. They think they have their reasons, but they're not really reasons at all. Brigitte left me and Eliza to 'find herself.' If she ever has, I don't know about it."

I lay my hand against his chest. "Do you ever hear from her?"

"She came to Eliza's high school graduation. I think Eliza hears from her on occasion, but I have no reason to."

A breath of relief passed over me. I turned my face up to his. "How was she? At the graduation, I mean?"

He kissed my nose before I rested my face against his chest. "She looked old. Much older than we are, anyway."

"Steven," I whispered. "What happened?"

I listened as he told me about their life in Tallahassee, about meeting a man named Jack Cason, and about moving to Atlanta. I heard him as he recalled the letter he'd gotten from Brigitte, telling him she had left him and their child. But his voice trailed down a long tunnel as he spoke of his life as a single father and of the fingerprints of God, which he felt marked the days of his life.

In the morning, when I woke on Patsy's sofa with a light-weight blanket tucked around me and a cool cotton pillow under my head, I realized I'd fallen asleep in the middle of his story. That I had missed the answer to my question. "Oh no," I said to no one but myself. Then I remembered what had exhausted me . . . the truth about my mother.

———

Patsy was awake, propped up in bed and reading her Bible.

"Good morning," I said. "You look like you're feeling much better."

"And you look like you could use a vacation."

I walked over to the mirrored vanity, leaned over, and groaned. "Kind of obvious I slept on wet hair, isn't it?"

"I'd say. Where's your young man?"

I turned to look at her. "Steven? I guess he went home. I fell asleep at some point . . ."

"He's a nice man, I think."

I smiled. "He is." I looked at my watch; it was a little after 7:00. "Enough of that. What can I make you for breakfast?"

Patsy waved a hand at me. "Don't fuss over me. It's Sunday. You're going to church, aren't you?"

I crossed my arms. "I haven't actually thought about it. But, Patsy, I don't really think I should leave you . . ."

Patsy closed her Bible and placed it on the bed next to her. "I'm fine. Besides, I have a favor to ask."

I sat at the foot of the bed. "What's that?"

"I want you to look in my purse and find my checkbook for me. I never miss paying my tithe, and I don't want the church to have to wait on it just because I've had a cold. So, if you will, bring me my purse, I'll write a check, and you can take it to the preacher for me. While you're at it, ask him to come see me this week. Tell him I think I'll just rest here until I know this thing has passed."

"I can do that," I said.

Nearly four hours later I parked near the church with my Bible on the front passenger seat and Patsy's check in my purse. I wore the only thing I'd brought which would be appropriate for services, a cotton and spandex green, black, and white floral skirt matched with a black summer sweater.

I crossed the street as others entered the church, blended with the small crowd, and entered the building. Inside the sanctuary—which smelled of old wood and an air-conditioning system that had just been turned on—I paused long enough to try to find a place to sit and spotted Rosa. Her eyes locked with mine. I smiled, waved, and quickly made my way to where she stood at the end of an aisle. "Rosa," I said. "I've been meaning to call and thank you for sending Luis my way."

She seemed ill at ease. I looked from her to the man sitting nearby and back to her again. "This is my husband," she said, though she gave no name.

The man—nearly too good looking for words—stood and extended his hand. "Good morning. I'm Manny."

"Manny," I said. "I'm Kimberly Tucker." I forced myself to smile broadly. "I was a childhood friend of Rosa's."

"Really?" he asked, looking from me to Rosa. "I don't remember you mentioning such a lovely friend, Rosa."

Rosa pursed her lips as her eyes softened. "Manny, you are always so charming. This is Kim Claybourne." Her brow arched. "Dr. Claybourne's daughter."

Manny's smile met mine. "Dr. Claybourne? Oh yes, of course." He turned toward the pew and said, "If you aren't sitting with anyone—"

"Kim?" Steven's voice came from behind me.

I turned. "Steven, I didn't know you'd be here."

"Cozy, cozy," Rosa purred.

"Rosa," Steven said. "How are you this fine Sunday morning?"

Rosa's chest rose. "I'm fine. You?"

"Good," he answered, then shook Manny's hand. "Good to see you, Manny." His other hand came to rest on the small of my back, sending chills along my spine and turning my arms to gooseflesh. "Honey, let's find a seat, shall we?"

Honey?

I felt heat rush to my cheeks before I stammered, "Sure."

We made our pleasantries with Rosa and Manny before Steven led me to a pew several seats back where Maddie sat. Upon seeing us, she slid over two spaces and patted the pew beside her.

"Hi, Maddie," I said. "I didn't know I'd see you here."

"Every Sunday of the world," she replied. "Didn't know I'd see you either." She smiled. "Or with who."

I returned the smile. "Excuse me," I said, then turned toward Steven, who had settled in next to me.

"What's going on, Steven?" I spoke quietly.

He shook his head. "What do you mean?"

"Oh, come on. It felt like an ice storm up there. What's going on with Rosa? Why does she act the way she does toward me?"

His eyes studied my face for long moments; a slow smile crept from the corners of his lips. "You sure look pretty this morning."

My shoulders sank. "I'm sorry I fell asleep on you last night."

He leaned toward my ear. "Literally."

"Steven," I whispered as though admonishing a naughty child.

He chuckled. "It's okay. I've bored better people than you to sleep, you know."

I gave him my best "I'm sorry" look before saying, "The last thing I heard, you were telling me how Eliza had gotten you to come to church with her . . . to see her in a little dramatic play."

"Oh, well, then. You missed the best part." He winked.

"Give me a second chance?"

He nodded. "Tell you what. After church, let's go to Tony's Restaurant, get some clam chowder—they have the best, you know—and we'll get enough for Patsy too. If she's doing all right, you and I will go out when it gets a tad cooler and I'll tell you the whole story. Again."

"Okay," I said. "But where will you take me this time?"

"The graveyard," he said. "Remember?"

Oh yes. I remembered.

25

After church and saying good-bye to Maddie, Steven suggested we walk up to Tony's Restaurant rather than drive. I thought it a splendid idea; after all, the small corner restaurant wasn't very far. As we strolled with my right hand clasped in his left, I couldn't help but reminisce about past summers spent in Cedar Key. It seemed to me that every crack in the sidewalk, every lean of one building and whitewash of another brought enough memories to fill the nearby Gulf.

In the heat my hand had started to sweat, but I squeezed Steven's anyway. Every few steps we slipped from shadow to sunlight and back to shadow again. The Gulf breeze skipped around us. It danced up my skirt—for which I was grateful—making me glad I hadn't worn pantyhose. I looked at Steven, memorizing every angle and line in his face as he cast it upward, toward the sky. He was studying the clouds, I knew, wondering about the possibility of rain.

"I didn't know you went to church," I said. "Regularly, I mean."

He stopped looking at the sky, turning his attention to

me instead. "If you'd stayed awake last night, you'd know," he answered. Behind the brown tint of his sunglasses, I saw him wink.

"Sorry."

"That's okay. Yes, I go to church. Regularly."

"I don't remember you going when we were kids, I guess I'm saying."

"No, we didn't. My parents never thought it necessary. I've tried to talk to Dad since he got sick, but . . . either he just doesn't care or he doesn't want to rock the boat with Mom."

"I'm sorry to hear that."

"Thanks. But Eliza's working on them too, so between us and Jesus, we've got it covered, I think."

"Okay, so you went to church to see Eliza in a play and . . ."

He smiled. "And I found something there that helped me out of the funk I was in since Brigitte left." He winced. "I didn't know how to say this last night, what with what you told me about your mom, but . . . I was drinking a lot back then."

"You were an alcoholic? I mean, are you? As in, recovery?"

"Yes, I am. And I go to meetings as often as I can. But I don't want you to picture me lying in a gutter somewhere before I hit my bottom. Being alcoholic is more than the bum on the street begging for money. Mine was more in the sense that I chose to drink at night to ease the pain. The loneliness. I chose not to bring another woman into my life, and I thought I was pretty admirable for that." His smile was painful. "Instead I brought in a bottle." He shrugged. "It became a cop-out. Even with Eliza there, not having a woman next to me, to share my life with, was difficult. When I realized that the obsession to drink had taken over, I made a commitment to Eliza, to myself, and most importantly to God that I wouldn't drink again . . . wouldn't fall into that cycle of trying to numb my pain . . . ever again."

I squeezed his hand again. "I'm proud of you. I'm also surprised you never brought another woman into your life."

He chuckled. "Not to sound egotistical, but believe me, there were plenty of women who lined themselves up. Especially, I'm sorry to say, after I got involved in the church. But . . ."

When his voice trailed and I was certain he wasn't going to finish, I put on my best smile and concluded, "But none of them were me?"

He laughed again, this time stopping in a patch of sunlight. He pulled me to him, kissed me without hesitation, and said, "Something like that."

I was burning up; the sun beating against my head and skin made me feel like I was standing in front of a hot oven. But I didn't care. I could have melted in a puddle of sweat or a pool of love right then and there and it would have been fine with me. "Steven Granger, what sort of spell have you cast on me this time?"

He kissed me again. "And what about the spell you've cast on me?" He smiled. "But let me say this: I can't say you were at the forefront of my mind back then—though I never really forgot you. It's just that raising Eliza was a full-time job, not to mention my other full-time job. And I didn't want to bring anyone into *her* life who might jeopardize *our* life in any sort of way." He smiled.

The knot formed in my throat again. When I couldn't think of anything to say, I coaxed him into walking again. Then, in a low voice, I said, "Rearing."

"What?"

"Rearing. You reared Eliza." I grimaced at my words but

figured I might as well finish them. "Sorry, the schoolteacher in me. We *raise* cattle, we *rear* children."

"Ah. I'll remember that the next time I'm *rearing* a child or *raising* a cow." He winked at me again and we both laughed. We walked past a short white picket fence dripping with roses. Their scent was sweet and—in the heat—intoxicating.

I rolled my eyes. "I can't believe I just said that. I guess old habits die hard."

"I hope not." He stopped me again, this time under the awning of Cedar Key's Historical Society building, a famous building in its own right. "Remember what we talked about last night? About how you try to control things?"

I nodded. "Yeah." We were only steps from the end of the sidewalk, across the street from Tony's and the large oblong sign announcing the award-winning clam chowder that simmered within. I could smell its spices, and my stomach rumbled. "Sorry," I said as I pressed my hand against my middle. "I've hardly eaten since yesterday."

"Smells good, doesn't it?"

"Yes." He led me onward with a tug of his hand, but I stopped him. "Steven, I just want you to know that I thought a lot—mostly in church, if I'm to be honest—about what we've talked about. And even what Andre said and Charlie has said. It seems to me that the majority rules on this one. I'm a control freak."

"I wouldn't call you a freak exactly."

"Thank you for that. But, you know what I mean. And I'm going to work on it. I whispered to God this morning that I'm going to trust him with my sons when they're at their father's. I'm going to trust him with Heather when she is in rehab. And I'm going to trust that Andre knows what he's doing with his own kids while she's there."

Steven touched the tip of my nose with his lips. "That's good to hear. Believe me, Kim, this is something I can attest to from personal experience. If you let go and let God, as the old saying goes, everything really will work out okay."

"I believe you." I sighed. "But it's not going to be easy."

"Nothing worthwhile ever is, Boo."

Patsy was at the computer in her living room when we returned. She wore her pajamas with a thin cotton robe and satin ballerina bedroom slippers. Her hair had been brushed and rebraided, and her face looked freshly washed. She told me she was "Facebooking" with her grandson.

She was delighted by the clam chowder. When we were done with lunch, Steven and I cleared everything away while Patsy went into the bathroom to brush her teeth. As I put away the last of the washed dishes, I told Steven I wanted to stay with Patsy for a while but that he could pick me up at my house at around 7:00, if that worked for him.

He grinned at me and said, "Tell you what. Why don't *you* let *me* tell you when I can pick you up? Then, if it doesn't work for you, we can negotiate."

I sighed. "Was I doing it again?"

"Only a little," he said, bringing his index finger close to his thumb.

I groaned, but he kissed me anyway, told me not to stress over it, and that he would, indeed, pick me up at 7:00. I rested my forehead against his shoulder. "Thank you."

His fingertips pushed my chin up until I was looking into his eyes. "Kim . . ." he said but didn't finish his thought.

"What?"

He blinked, shook his head as he lowered his hand, and said, "Nothing."

I placed my hands on his forearms and whispered, "What?"

He momentarily flushed, grabbed my hands with his, released one, and walked me to the door, holding the other. "I'll pick you up at 7:00. We'll go to the graveyard, then head over to the Island Room for something to eat."

I could only nod. Something was happening between us, something I couldn't quite verbalize, even if only in my head. He pressed his lips ever so briefly against my own, then walked out of the door.

I returned to Patsy.

I found her in her bedroom, standing before her mirrored vanity, pushing Jergens lotion from a pump bottle into the cupped palm of her hand. The pleasant scent of cherry-almond permeated the room, reminding me of my childhood. Oreo lay curled in the middle of her bed, his front paws tucked under his chest. "You two seem to be doing awfully well," she commented. She looked at the bottle of hand cream and said, "Want some?"

I pushed the pump once then rubbed the creamy lotion around my hands and between my fingers before bringing them to my nose and inhaling. "My mother always used Jergens. Funny, I haven't thought of it in years."

"My dressing table is never without it," Patsy said. "Wonderful for the face too."

I spied an antique gold filigree lipstick holder. A Cupid sat on the outside center, head turned to his left as though indifferent, silently strumming a guitar. Four small tubes—each of them noticeably old—stood like ladies of a bygone era in the center. I touched Cupid's head with my fingertip and said, "This is quite lovely."

"And quite old." Patsy reached for one of the tubes, pulled the top away from the base, then twisted until crimson red lipstick appeared. Whoever had used it previously had worn it flat. "These were my mother's," she added. She brought the tube to her nose and inhaled as I had done with the hand cream. "It smells like crayon wax to some, I suppose. But to me it smells like a woman who was once very beautiful."

She leaned the lipstick over for me to smell. She was correct; it smelled like crayon wax. As she returned the tube to its place, I asked, "Didn't you say your mother sent you to live with another couple when you were thirteen?"

"She did." She looked toward the door. "Let's go sit down, shall we? I'm clearly tired."

We walked into the living room; Patsy wrapped her arm around mine and leaned on me for support. When we were comfortable, she continued with her story. "My mother had packed my suitcase that day while I was at school. I remember thinking on the way home that I had field peas to shell when I got home and my friends—Mitzy and Jane were their names—wanted me to sneak away to Cassel Creek." Patsy's face held a faraway expression until she said, "Oh, my. We had so many white acre peas that summer. I remember thinking my fingers would fall off from the picking and the shelling." Patsy looked down at her hands—gnarled with age—then laid them in her lap. "But when I got home, Mama said for me to get in the car, that we had somewhere to go. So I did as I was told. I always did. Children in those days didn't argue with their parents like they do nowadays.

"Mama said my little brothers were at a neighbor's and that we had to go to a place called Slim's. Slim's was a service station and a bus stop. I remember Mama bought me a Nehi Peach before . . ." Patsy brought her hands up and back down to her lap again. She looked away from me, toward the sliding glass doors and the marsh beyond. "On the way there she started telling me about my little brother like I hadn't remembered him, and that he was living with these good people and that those good people were going to let me come and live with them too." She brought her fingertips to her lips and cut her eyes to me. "I cried, of course."

"Of course."

"But Mama said not to. She said she didn't have time for my tantrums. I knew she wouldn't whip me. She just couldn't bear to see me cry like that." She sighed. "I begged her to go get my little brothers and to go with me. We could leave Ira Liddle, all of us together. But she wouldn't do it. I can still see her standing outside the bus when it pulled away from the station . . . waving good-bye and blowing kisses."

I waited in the moment's silence until Patsy was ready to continue. "When I got to the Buchwalds' house, Mrs. Buchwald—who I called Mam—took me into the kitchen while Papa took my suitcase into their room." Patsy laughed lightly, though there was little humor in her tone. "Mam told me something that night I didn't even know before."

"What was that?"

"My brother's name." She sat quiet until she continued, "Mam unpacked my suitcase for me, what little bit I had in it. I found out later that the suitcase had been my mother's. That she had used it when she and my father had gone on their honeymoon."

"How'd you find out?" I kicked off my shoes and curled my legs up under me.

"Mam told me. When I married Gilbert she brought it down out of her closet. Still in pristine condition. She said, 'Patsy, I've been saving this for you.' Then she told me what Mama had told her. That it had been hers and that there was a gift wrapped up for me on the inside. Mama had told her to give the suitcase and the gift to me when I married." Tears pooled under her eyes, and, using those precious old fingers, she brushed them away, seemingly without thinking. "Inside were the lipstick holder and the lipstick. She'd seen me playing with it once, I guess. She knew I thought it to be the mark of a real lady."

She became silent again, then patted my hand and forced a weak smile. "Look at you. A young woman listening to the ramblings of an old woman."

"Patsy, I hardly think of you as *old*."

"I'm old enough."

"Never mind your age. How are you feeling today?"

"Much better. That doctor called while you were at church, by the way. He wants to come by to check on me later this afternoon, but I told him I was feeling so much better that he didn't really need to."

"So is he coming or not?" I asked.

She looked at her watch. "He said about 3:00 he'd come by anyway." She laughed. "He told me that he is the doctor so let him do his job."

"You gave in that easily?"

"Of course I did. Never mind my health. He's gentle on the eyes. Reminds me of my Gilbert."

I reached over and hugged her. "Oh, Patsy. You're so cute." When I drew back I said, "Now I need your help if you're up to it." I looked over to the computer and back to her.

Her eyes brightened. "You're ready for Facebook?"

"Not quite," I said. "But I could stand to use your computer to look up something."

She scooted to the end of the sofa. "What's that, hon?"

"Cirrhosis of the liver," I answered. "I need to do a little research."

26

After doing my research, helping Patsy to her bed for an afternoon nap, and sending Oreo outside, I went home to let Max out for playtime with his neighborhood friend. Inside the house, I went to my bedroom closet—the one my mother had kept her clothes in once upon a time—reached for a large vintage hatbox—the one decorated with tea roses and teacups—and pulled it toward me and off the shelf. I took it to my bed, slipped the top off, and then dumped the contents all over the comforter.

Hundreds of photographs.

I spent the next two hours shuffling through them all, sorting them until I'd found enough evidence. Subtle hints of a problem I'd denied for years. I then bounded off the bed, went to the framed photo of the glasses marked with lipstick, and ripped it off the wall. I returned to the bedroom and promptly called Anise. I asked first if she was with Dad.

"He's napping in the bedroom," she said. "I'm in the living room reading. But I can wake him if you need me to."

"No," I said, maybe a little too quickly. "Anise, I'd like to ask you a question. What can you tell me about how Mom died?"

She didn't answer at first, no doubt trying to determine how much I might know already. Then she said, "I know it was very painful for her. And for your father to watch . . . he loved her very much, you know that, don't you, Kimberly?"

I knew it. I still didn't understand why he'd married Anise so soon after Mom's death, but I knew for certain he had loved her. "And?" I asked. "What else?"

I heard her sigh. I made out the sounds of her sitting up, closing her book, and placing it on the coffee table. Buying time. "You've spoken with Andre."

"Yes. And I want to know the truth."

"It's too painful for your father."

"I'm looking at no less than fifty photographs presumably taken by my father, and one framed taken by my mother, that tell me my mother was an alcoholic. That she didn't die from liver cancer but that, instead, she died from cirrhosis."

"The picture of the glasses near the bar."

"Yes." I picked it up with my free hand and studied it again. Those were my mother's lips; I had no doubt about it.

"Your father took that photograph, Kimberly."

"My father?" I dropped the picture.

"He should be telling you this," she said. "But I know he won't. The . . . fights between the two of them about her constant drinking or her binge drinking are things he has shared with me. But he's never wanted you girls to know the full brunt of it."

I didn't know whether I should ask her to thank him for me or to shake him for not tearing away the veil sooner. "And the picture?"

"Those were the glasses from one night . . . a bad night, he told me . . . when she kept pouring drinks into new glasses, saying that as long as she wasn't drinking from the same glass, it didn't count."

My heart hurt. I looked at the picture again. "That's ludicrous."

"But it's true. You should know, Kimberly, that alcoholics need no real reason to drink, but they are masterminds at excusing their behavior."

I wanted to cry. The knot formed in my throat, threatening to overtake me, but I pushed it down and tried to force my words over and around it. "Why didn't Dad—"

"Tell you?"

"*Stop* her."

"Oh, Boo. You really must understand. Your father *enabled* her."

Enabled. There was that word again. "Then *he* killed her."

I heard a quick intake of breath. "Don't you dare. Don't you dare speak ill against your father. You obviously know nothing at all about the disease, about the people who are affected by those with it, you would never say such a thing."

"But if he had told me just how serious—he is a doctor, after all—maybe I—"

"No. Listen to me. This is one thing you could not fix. No one could fix it. Not your father, not you, and certainly not your sisters. Not even Joan's parents could stop her. Only your mother could have fixed this, and she chose not to."

This is one thing you could not fix. There it was again. "But maybe I could have . . . *maybe* she would have listened."

For a while, Anise said nothing. Then, "Kimberly, I want you to listen to me very carefully, and I'm not kidding when I say this. I don't want you to discuss this with your father if you are going to say anything to hurt him. He went through enough with Joan. He loved her, do you hear me? He *loved* her. In his mind, that love was not enough to stop her from drinking. He begged her . . . for his sake . . . for their sake . . . for the sake of you kids . . . but Joan wasn't able . . . wasn't willing to even try." She took a deep breath. "They say you have to hit bottom. Unfortunately, for Joan, the bottom was death."

"Anise . . ."

"Do you hear me, Kimberly? If you hurt your father any more than he has already been hurt, I won't forgive you."

I shook my head. Yes, she would forgive me. It was her Christian nature to forgive. But she wouldn't forget, and our lives together would be difficult. Forever different. "I won't say anything to him."

"Talk to him, yes. Discuss it. But don't accuse him of any such nonsense as killing Joan."

"You're right. Of course."

"Right now, you are shocked and hurt. I understand that. But think about it, read up on it, and you won't be."

"I promise, Anise. I won't say anything to hurt Dad."

"He loves you so much, Kimberly."

"I know. He loves us all." I thought of Heather. "Anise, what about Heather, then? If he knows the truth about Mom, why not Heather?"

"I honestly don't know. He just can't seem to bring himself to think about it. I think he believes if he ignores it, this time it will go away."

"But it won't."

"No. Andre called earlier. He's coming over later this afternoon to talk to your father."

"Do you think Dad will listen? Really listen?"

262

Again, Anise didn't answer right away. "Just pray that he does, okay? And I promise I'll call you later and let you know."

After I hung up with Anise, I called Chase and Cody and spoke to them both. Chase asked me again not to say anything to their father, and I told him, again, that I would not. "It's okay," I told Chase. "I'm turning over a new leaf where your dad is concerned. I may not like what he does, but I know now I can't stop him." I pressed my lips together. "As long as I know you're all right."

"I'm good, Mom."

"And that you know, son, that his behavior—going to the beach with women for the entire weekend and, I assume, staying in the same hotel room—is *not* what God ordains for a man and woman. Sex requires commitment, and that commitment is marriage."

"I know that too, Mom."

"I just don't want you to follow his example," I said. "Not in *that* way. He's a hard worker and he has always provided for us, but . . ."

"I know."

I laughed. "There's something else I want to talk to you about, but it'll wait. For now, let me talk with Cody."

Cody was a bundle of news. He told me about working with his grandfather, about his grandmother's cooking, about meeting a new friend in the neighborhood where they lived. "He just moved here and he's my age and he's really nice."

My heart smiled. "I'm glad, Code. I want you to enjoy yourself."

"Dad said he's going to take us to the beach next weekend." He lowered his voice then and said, "I suppose you know he went without us this weekend."

I couldn't help but laugh. "I know," I said. "But I'm not going to make it into something."

"Whew," I heard him say. "That's good to know."

I laughed again. "Code, I have to go now. Tell your brother and your grandparents that I love them all and I'll see you in a few weeks."

"One down, four to go," he expressed exuberantly.

"That's my little man," I said, and then told him again how much I loved him. "Oh, by the way. Tell Chase be on the lookout on Facebook for a new friend request."

"You?" his voice squealed. I listened as he repeated my statement to his brother between giggles.

Chase moaned. "If she feels she must . . ."

I thought it best we end the conversation there.

I was dressed in a floral, cotton scoop-neck summer dress and white flat sandals and ready to see the Cedar Key cemetery—a place I'd not been to or even thought of in years—and to dine at the Island Room.

Steven gave an appropriate wolf whistle when I opened the door and he'd sized me up a little. I grinned as I curtseyed. "I'd do the same to you," I told him, "if I knew how to whistle."

"How can you not know how to whistle?" he asked as I stepped past him and to the front porch. "And may I add how wonderful you smell?"

I rolled my eyes. "I bet you say that to all your dates."

Before I could take another step, he kissed me with such ardor I thought my knees would buckle.

"Wow," I said between deep breaths.

"Did I take your breath away?" he asked. I could have absolutely swooned at the lilt in his voice.

"I daresay."

"Good," he countered. "Because you've certainly taken away mine."

We stared at each other without blinking. I pressed my lips together to still my emotions. My yearning for Steven as a seventeen-year-old had been one thing; the desire for him now—both of us having been married—was something else. "Steven," I whispered.

"Me too," he said, reading my mind. "We'd better leave right now."

I wanted to check on Patsy one more time before we left and said so. He agreed. With a kiss to both our cheeks, she told us "children" to have a wonderful evening and not to worry one "iota" about her.

A few minutes later, we were driving between palms, live oaks shimmering with moss, and spiny century plants. A few of the palms had died, their fronds hung gray and still. The setting sun winked along the strings of silvery-gray moss and the wind played lightly with them all. Just ahead, the Cedar Key water tower—displaying pride in the Cedar Key Sharks—rose above the foliage and leaned to the right as though it had seen one too many storms. As we rounded the deep bend on Whiddon, Cedar Key School on our right, I leaned toward Steven. My seat belt held me in place and I asked, "Remember when we never wore these things and I sat practically under your armpit?" I pulled at the seat belt.

He smiled at me but jutted his chin to my side of the road. "There's the old day-in and day-out of my childhood," he said. "Lots of memories there."

"I bet."

We drove on in silence, past a bridge where young boys stood fishing alongside old pelicans, past small fishermen's houses with shady front porches sitting proud along a canal.

Behind them, well-tended boats tied to shanty-style docks rocked in the blue water. Across the narrow road, larger vacation homes, most left vacant for the hot summer months, stood regal and blocked the rays of the setting sun. I pulled my sunglasses down my nose an inch and kept my gaze toward the front driver's window, watching the colors of the sky as it appeared between them in the nearing sunset. It was like watching an old film, each frame flickering to the next. "We're near your home," I said as I pushed the shades back up. "Your mom and dad's, I mean."

"We are."

"Maybe we can go by to see them sometime."

He stared straight ahead. "They'd like that."

I pressed the folds of my dress with the palms of my hands. "Have you told them about me yet? About seeing me again?"

"Not yet." He glanced over at me. "What about you? Have you told your father?"

"Yes, I have."

He chuckled. "And what, may I inquire, was his reaction to that bit of good news?"

I shrugged. "Just to be careful."

"And will you? Be careful?"

"Will you?"

This time it was Steven who pulled his sunglasses down the length of his nose, stared at me, and said, "Touché."

He slowed the Jeep and turned the wheel right. We glided into the cemetery; he parked across from the long walkway leading into and along the water's edge. Perfect, I thought, for strolling on nights like these.

After Steven got out of the car and had rustled something out of the back floorboard, he opened the passenger's door for me. I slid out and breathed in deeply; the evening air was thick and humming with mosquitoes. I held out my right hand, palm up.

"What's that for?" he asked.

I looked to the case dangling from a strap held by his left hand. "What's *that* for?" I returned.

He pinked. "You know me too well." He raised the case, unzipped it, and pulled out a can of insect repellant.

I took three steps forward, stood with my feet a good twenty-four inches apart, and my arms extended. "Hit me with your best shot," I said.

He did.

"You have ruined the scent of my body lotion," I said with a pout.

"Yeah, well, that body lotion will draw those mosquitoes faster than the evening breeze brings the smell of clams and fish."

Done with soaking me in my chemical bath, he turned the can on himself. When he'd finished, I said, "Next?"

He cocked his head. "What does that mean?"

"The camera. Because I know it's in there."

He stared at me for a while, then swung the case toward me. I took out the camera and pressed the on button. The lens cap popped off; it dangled from the string holding it to the body.

"Let's walk down the walkway," I suggested.

Steven shook his head. "Not tonight. Come on . . ." He guided me through the cement gates of the cemetery.

"And to our left, ladies and gentlemen," I said, my voice sounding like that of a tour guide, "is a memorial to 'Miss Bessie' Gibbs—owner of the Island Hotel, city commissioner, city judge, mayor, and organizer of the Cedar Key Arts Festival."

Steven stopped. "Now how did you remember that?"

I turned to him. "Some boy I once knew took me on a tour of the cemetery, and that's what *he* said."

Steven's lips swept over mine. "Did he tell you the whole story?" he asked against them. "About how she brought new life to the hotel and to the town? About how some say her ghost still haunts the place? Hers and about a dozen more?"

"He did." My words danced between our lips.

"What else did he tell you?"

I blinked, raised my eyes to his as I said, "If I remember correctly, right over there by the broken headstones and the rickety fence, and under the shade of a pine tree, he told me he loved me."

Steven pulled his sunglasses from his face before pushing mine to the crown of my head. As he wrapped his arms around me and pulled me to himself, he whispered, "Then let me say it again. I love you, Kimberly-Boo."

27

Reality set in.

Somewhere after an incredible dinner beside the dark blue water at the Island Room (the fettuccini crab carbonara was to die for, and I said so with every bite) and a scrumptious dessert with coffee at the Island Hotel's romantic restaurant, my heart sank closer to a too-full stomach.

"A penny for your thoughts," Steven said in the Jeep's quiet darkness. We were halfway home. I'd spent the short trip staring out into the clear black night, gazing up at the stars, and thinking.

I looked across the seat. Steven—illuminated both by the moonlight and street lamps—looked straight ahead, concentrating on the narrow road of SR 24. "Steven." I spoke slowly. "Maybe all of this . . . maybe we're moving too fast."

Steven chuckled. "You're right. Twenty-four years is moving *way* too fast."

I smiled, but I knew if he could see my face it would register only sadness. "I mean . . . you know what I mean. I've not been here even a week."

He glanced my way then turned his attention back to the road. "A lot sure has happened in five short days."

I couldn't argue with that.

I looked out the windshield, saw the road leading to the house come into view, and sighed. We kept silent until Steven turned into the driveway and shut off the engine. Wordlessly, he opened his door, came around to my side, and opened mine. He offered his hand and I took it, and when my feet rested upon the gravel, he didn't let go.

"Let's go sit on the deck," he said. "I have some things to say."

I'd left the porch lights on; they shone dimly on the lawn. The lapping of water against the grasses and the song of cicadas drew us to the place where my father used to sit and wait for his girls to unpack and ready themselves for swimming. So much since then had changed . . . so much life had passed. Even still, if I tried, I could imagine the four of us squealing in delight, Mom's voice speaking her maternal orders, Dad's laughter . . . The Adirondacks had been repainted a few times, yet within them rested old memories waiting for new ones to be made.

Steven turned the chairs away from the water and facing each other. "Sit," he said.

I did and then he followed.

He reached over and took my hands. His thumbs traced a circle near the base of mine; with each round I felt a little of my resolve floating into the balmy air. His eyes were intent; they shimmered as he spoke. "You probably don't know this, but I called you once."

"What do you mean?" I kept my voice barely above a whisper. I had to. The knot had returned.

"After Brigitte. After I knew she wasn't coming back."

"Where? Where did you call me?"

270

"The only number I had. I called your mom and dad's house."

"And?"

"Your mom answered."

"And?"

"I told her who I was." He blew air between his lips. "She was sweet. Asked me how I was doing. How the baby was doing—not that Eliza was a baby anymore. I told her—in a roundabout way—that I was a single father. That I had custody of Eliza." Steven smiled. "She actually gave me some advice on raising a daughter."

I smiled too. "That was Mom. She always had a ready answer for any and all of life's problems and circumstances. After Charlie left I would sometimes drive to the cemetery and sit at her grave and pour my heart out. I didn't really expect her to rise up and answer or some great piece of wisdom to come floating through the trees, but . . . somehow . . . it made me feel better just talking to her there."

Steven released my hands, reached up, and swept the hair over my shoulders. His fingertips stroked the bare skin there, then trailed down the length of my arms. In the heat, I shivered. I straightened, forcing him to do the same. His elbows came to rest on his knees; his hands hung limp between them. "She was special."

"But . . . I don't understand. She never told me you called."

He shrugged and winced a little. "You weren't home. Not that home, anyway."

"But, still. I never got the message. If I had, I would have at least called you back."

"And then what?"

And then what? The possibilities ran wild inside my head. "Oh," I said.

He took my hands again. "Don't worry, Kimberly."

"But I didn't get the message, Steven."

"Kimberly, listen to me, because I'm only going to say this once." A mosquito hummed around his ear; he shooed it away, then reached for me again. "Apparently, my time is limited, anyway. Pretty soon these bugs will just carry me off and you'll never have to deal with me again." We both smiled before he continued. "When I met Brigitte, I was so passionately in lust, I couldn't think straight. A lot of things had led up to that—I won't get into all of it now—and, yes, you were a part of it. Not that I'm blaming you. It's just something teenagers go through when they're left to their own devices. Some successfully, some not so successfully. Eliza became both my consolation and my penitence. And, in the process, I lost one of the finest young ladies I've ever had the pleasure of calling my friend, not to mention a girlfriend."

"Me?"

"You."

"But I wasn't perfect in all that, Steven. I know now—as an adult and as a Christian mother—that I must have driven you completely crazy that summer."

He laughed easily. "You did that, sweetheart. You surely did. But . . . still." He swallowed. "So, here's what I want to say. Not to sound cliché, but we know what the Bible says in Romans."

I instinctively continued his thought along with him. "And we know that in all things God works for the good of those who love him, who have been called according to his purpose."

He blinked.

"Romans 8:28," I said.

"Our past is our past. And our future . . . it's up to us. I know what love feels like, Kim. And I know the difference between love and lust. I love you, Kimberly-Boo, and I don't need another twenty-four years to realize it."

I felt dizzy. Good, but dizzy. I squeezed his hands for support.

"So, let me propose this to you." He swallowed again. "Stay the summer. Stay here and spend the days getting to know me better. Getting to know us better. Meet my daughter when she comes next month for the big July 4th Clamerica celebration."

I grinned, perhaps a little too broadly. My cheeks actually ached.

He continued. "And when your sons are done with their visit with Charlie, bring them back here. We'll take them out in the boat. Every day and every night if that's what you want. We'll go fishing and clamming and walk all over Shell Mound and Atsena Otie." He swatted at the air again. "Unless these mosquitoes get any worse."

Reality set in again. "But come August . . . Teachers have to be back at school the second week."

Steven scooted to the end of his chair. Our knees touched; electricity shot through my body. "Maybe come August you won't want to return to teaching. Maybe come August, you'll be happy to be just a tour guide's wife."

"Steven . . ." I felt both breathless and full of life, all at once.

His hands released mine and took hold of my face. His fingertips splayed along the damp roots of my hair as he drew my lips to his. "Don't answer tonight," he spoke against them, then pressed mine with his.

When the kiss had broken but the magic had not, he said, "Think about it?"

I shook my head. "No."

He leaned away from me, but his hands remained locked around the base of my skull. "No? Kim . . ."

I shook my head again. "No need, I mean." Then I smiled. "I'm staying, Steven Granger. Wild dogs couldn't make me leave this island now. Not the island, not the house, and certainly not you."

As he kissed me again, I thought, *And maybe not ever.*

After I woke the next morning—after I'd had coffee and a shower and had applied insect bite ointment along my arms and legs—I went to see Patsy. Both to check on her and to fill her in on my evening the night before.

She was still tired, she said, but she was happy to know I'd found love again.

"It is love, isn't it?" she asked.

I nodded. "It sure feels like it." I looked at my watch. "I have to get back to the house. Luis is coming today for the first cleaning, and I really have to make some calls back to the family before he gets there."

"Any news from your brother-in-law? About . . . Heather, is it?"

I shook my head. "No. But . . . today is the day, I suppose. She'll be in rehab before the sun goes down."

Patsy patted my arm. "She'll be just fine, honey. Don't you worry. The good Lord has her in the palm of his hand."

"I know."

When I returned to the house I heard my cell phone ringing. I darted through the house to where I'd left it lying on the bed. It was Dad; he was more than a little upset about the chain of events with Heather and about Andre's accusations against Mom.

"Then, they're not true?" I asked, settling on the rumpled

sheets, which would soon be stripped, washed, and replaced so I hadn't bothered to make the bed. I looked at my watch again. In a half hour Luis and his sister would arrive. When Dad didn't answer, I said, "Dad?"

"Of course they're true, Kimberly. But these things are private. They should be handled just within the family and not discussed."

"But Dad, we *are* family. Andre is family. Heather is family."

"He's been going to those meetings. He shouldn't have . . ."

"Dad, how can you say that? You're a doctor, for heaven's sake."

"I was her husband!"

My right shoulder jerked. I was no longer talking about Mom, but Dad hadn't shifted. And he was angry; angrier than I'd seen him in some time. "I know that, Dad. And I know you loved her very much. But, if I'm to be totally honest with you, what I don't understand is why you didn't *do* something."

"Do something? What would you have had me do, Kimberly?"

I shrugged as though he could see me. "I don't know, Dad. Make her stop drinking."

"And how would you propose I do that? I could have removed all the alcohol from the house and she would have managed to smuggle it in there somehow. I could have forbidden it and she would have done it anyhow." I heard him sigh. "When Ami was a baby, she used to keep beer in that little baby pack thing because she knew I'd never see it there, did you know that?"

"Baby pack thing?" I had to think a moment. "You mean Ami's diaper bag?"

"Yeah."

275

I paused. Dad was clearly rattled, and I meant no pun in the thought. Finally, I said, "No, I didn't know that. I wouldn't . . ."

"I remember one time when we'd gone there, to Cedar Key. Ami was a baby—Joan had managed not to drink the whole time she was pregnant, not with any of you kids. But as soon as the umbilical cord was cut, she was asking me to sneak something into the hospital for her."

"And did you?"

"Never."

My back ached. "I'm glad to hear that."

"Not that I wouldn't have done anything to get her to stop begging. But my colleague, Dr. Terrance Mills—her OB/GYN—and I had a talk. He knew, of course. He told me in no uncertain terms that if I brought any alcohol to her in the hospital, he'd report me. That I'd lose my license to practice."

I could hear the pain in my father's voice, but I couldn't figure if he had been more afraid of losing his job or his wife. "Well, you couldn't have that . . ."

"Don't be insolent with me, Kimberly. If I had lost my job, how would I have taken care of my family? And your mother . . . she would have been exposed as an alcoholic. What do you think that would have done to her? Especially in those days?"

"Maybe she wouldn't have kept drinking, Dad!"

He laughed, but not like I'd said something funny. More that I'd said something foolish. "Kim, I gave that woman every reason not to drink. Every reason. But . . ."

"But, she wouldn't stop."

"No." He took a breath, exhaled. "It wasn't as bad after . . . there was this one summer. You were just a baby. She drank nonstop that summer. Kept calling herself a failure as a mother."

"Mom?"

"If it hadn't been for Eliana . . ." He continued as though I'd not said a word. "Eliana took care of you. Took care of all three of us, actually. She picked up after Joan and watched her constantly. I finally moved her and her husband into the house for the summer months because I . . . I couldn't trust what Joan would or wouldn't do when I wasn't there. Eliana became your mother that summer. I even talked her into leaving her family—her husband and her parents—long enough to come back to Orlando. Eliana talked Joan into going to a hospital to detox and—wonder of wonders—she went."

"How long was she gone?"

"About two months. Eliana stayed with us, took you to see her as often as she was allowed to have family visits, which wasn't often."

I had no memory of this, of course. I tried to picture it all. Mom in the hospital. Dad going to work during the day. Eliana taking care of me as a mother would. "I'm surprised Rosa's father allowed her to leave her baby and him."

"Rosa hadn't been born yet, of course."

"Oh, that's right. But, still. Mr. Rivera . . . I can't imagine he was too happy about that arrangement."

"Hector Rivera was a man driven by money, Boo. You wouldn't remember much about him . . ."

"Not really. I mean, he was gone before I turned six, I think."

"He was a burly man who loved to gamble and chase women. Eliana never said for certain, but I think he may have been physically abusive to her. I know he was verbally abusive. I had to call him down more than once."

"Dad. It's so hard for me to imagine all of this."

Dad chuckled. "It is hard, isn't it, Boo? To think that your parents had lives apart from you. To imagine your old man standing up to a brute like Hector Rivera."

My father wasn't exactly a squirt, so I didn't necessarily have any problem believing he wouldn't put up with a man—any man—being hurtful to a woman. "Maybe a little."

"All I had to do was wave money under that man's nose and Eliana was ours until your mother got home. I paid him—I paid them both—plenty well, let me tell you."

"Wow," I finally said. "I didn't know any of this."

"Of course you didn't."

"Was Mr. Rivera . . . do you think he was ever abusive to Rosa?"

"Hector Rivera wasn't *anything* to Rosa. Eliana used to say he hardly spoke to her much less touched her. Or hugged her. Or listened to her when she had something to say. Even as a little child."

I thought back to the days of our childhood . . . how Dad had always given Rosa hugs just as he had the rest of us. Kissed her. Laughed at her silly knock-knock jokes. Warned her about the dangers of boys and such at the same time as he lectured me. "Is that why? Is that why you were always so loving toward her? Toward Rosa?"

"I treated Rosa as I would treat any child. Children deserve to be loved whether they're your own or not. You're a teacher. You know that."

I smiled. "I do." My back ached enough that I had to lie back against the pillows. "So, when did Mom start to drink again?"

The conversation went still. "Somewhere between detox and getting pregnant with Jayme-Leigh," he finally said. This voice was laden with regret. "Like I said, she didn't drink during her pregnancies. She had started back about a month or so when she learned that Jayme was coming."

"So, Dad, what about Heather? What about now? You sent Mom to the hospital. Don't you think Andre should do the same for his wife?"

"Your mom volunteered to go . . . Heather is kicking and screaming. I am not completely sure this will work for her if she doesn't want to go."

"But you admit, Dad, that she *needs* to go."

Dad nodded. "My wife and I had a long talk . . . that woman makes a lot of sense sometimes." He paused. "And sometimes we just have to say the truth out loud, Boo."

I placed my arm over my forehead and tried to think. After several seconds I said, "Maybe I can get Andre to wait just a day. I promised myself I wasn't going to try to control this issue . . . and I told Steven I'd stay, but that doesn't mean I can't come back to Cedar Key later on, right?"

"Kimberly, what are you talking about? What do you mean, you told Steven you'd stay?"

I smiled. "Steven Granger asked me to stay the summer, and I told him I would." I spoke the words so quickly, they hardly sounded like English.

"I see. So it's serious then."

I wanted to tell my father that I loved Steven, but I knew it was too soon. Even for a man who married again so soon after my mother's death, I knew he wouldn't understand. After all, he was one thing; his daughter another. "I know this is going to sound corny, Dad, but it feels like . . ." I searched my heart for the right words. "Like the first time, again."

I heard Dad's light chuckle. "I guess maybe it would. Not too many folks get to find their first love and make all those feelings come back to life."

That much was true. And there really was nothing to add to it, except that I didn't want it to end as it had ended the first time. But I couldn't share that. Not with my father. "Dad, enough about Steven and me." I smiled. "At least for now. I want to talk about Heather."

"Boo . . ."

"I'll come tomorrow," I jumped in before he could finish. "I'll talk to Heather and then I'll go up to Atlanta to see Ami's performance. Then I'll come back here and . . . and we'll pick up where we left off."

Dad was quiet again before he answered. "First, I think you should talk to Andre before you go making any plans. Second, if you want to go see Ami's performance, Anise and I are going. You can ride up with us." He chuckled then. "And third, why don't you just stay and let Andre deal with his wife and you see if you can't find the happiness you deserve in Cedar Key, okay?"

"But, Dad, Heather needs—"

"No. Andre's right. Goodness knows between him and your stepmother . . . it's all I hear. Heather may go kicking and screaming—as I said—but Andre believes that once she gets there . . ."

"Maybe, Dad . . . maybe you should go and talk with her. Talk to her about Mom like you just talked to me. Be brutally honest. Maybe it will make a difference."

"Maybe so."

"Will you think about it? For me, Dad?"

He didn't answer right away but then said, "I will. I'll think about it."

I heard a knock at the door. I bolted upright and said, "Oh, Dad. There's someone at the door. Probably Luis and his sister . . ."

"Make sure they dust under the beds," he said.

"Oh, Dad." I laughed as I swung my feet to the floor. "What do you know about dust under the beds?"

"Nothing. But that's what your mother always said to Eliana so I figure it must be important."

I hung up, walked to the door in my bare feet, and opened it, expecting to see the handsome new business owner and his sister. Instead, Rosa stood on the other side of the threshold, finely dressed in a white linen Capri set, spiky high heels, her back arched and her shoulders straight.

28

April 1969

The day she met Joan Claybourne, Eliana Rivera wore white Grable shorts, a butterfly-sleeved whispery blouse, a pair of wide-strapped, clunky-heeled platform sandals, and sported a hand-shaped bruise around the richly tanned flesh of her left arm. They were standing at the same table during the annual Cedar Key Arts Festival, and they simultaneously reached for the same piece of jewelry.

Twenty-three-year-old Eliana quickly drew her hand away from the elaborate trinket crafted by one of the local artists. "I'm sorry," she said. She peered into the almond-shaped eyes of the woman who could have been no more than a few years older than she and yet looked so much more sophisticated. She wore her hair in a Gibson-girl puff; wayward ringlets framed her square face. She wore a long silk and chiffon empire-waist dress that grazed the tips of her pink-painted toenails and the leather of expensive white, flat sandals. Eliana thought she must be some sort of fashion model or movie star.

"No, no," the woman said. Her voice was as soft as a

melody, so different from her own, which was husky and still held traces of the island where she'd spent the first ten years of life. "I was only looking."

"Me too," Eliana said. She smiled. "I'm Eliana Rivera."

The woman extended her hand and smiled back. "Joan Claybourne." She shifted her weight and cocked her head. "Do you, by any chance, live here in Cedar Key?"

"Sort of. My husband—Hector—and I live in Gainesville during the week, but we come to Cedar Key on the weekends. My husband, he is a singer at one of the restaurants."

"A singer? Oh, how exciting for you to be a part of something so . . . artsy." She reached for the trinket again. This time Eliana noticed her hands; they were narrow, the fingers long and delicate, the nails polished a shimmery baby pink matching her toes. She looked up, her eyes searching for the artist. Spotting her at the other end of the linen-draped table, she said, "How much?"

"Five-fifty."

Eliana blinked as Joan Claybourne reached into a small, white patent shoulder purse hanging by a long gold chain she'd not noticed before. She pulled out a ten and handed it to the artist, who said, "Give me a second and I'll have your change for you."

"Will you wrap it in tissue paper, please?"

Eliana couldn't help but notice the way the woman spoke. As though all the class in all of society had found its place in her voice box. She smiled sweetly as the request left her lips, then turned back to Eliana. "I'm absolutely parched. Why don't I treat you to lemonade at the hotel? Maybe you can help me a little. My husband and I are looking at getting a little place here. You know, for weekends, holidays, the summer?" She smiled again.

283

CHASING SUNSETS

Eliana couldn't imagine having a place just for the week-ends. She and Hector rented a room from one of the locals every Friday and Saturday night . . . those make-believe two and a half days that became her reprieve from her husband's brutality. When others were around, like Mr. and Mrs. Trav-ers, the couple they rented from, Hector Rivera was a gentle-man. A Latin lover. But when they were alone . . .

"That would be nice," Eliana said, feeling hopeful. Perhaps, she thought, she and Joan Claybourne would become friends. Perhaps she would have someone other than her sister—one of the artists displaying her paintings at the festival—to talk with. Perhaps she would not be so lonely here in Cedar Key anymore.

When the wrapped trinket was placed in Joan's hand, she turned to Eliana and extended it. "For you," she said.

"Me?"

"You liked it, didn't you?"

"Yes, but . . . you don't even know me."

Joan shrugged. "So? I like giving gifts." She fanned herself with her hand. "It's getting wicked hot. So, how about that lemonade?"

———

Eliana soon discovered that Joan Claybourne and her hus-band Ross were in need of more than just a house. They'd actually already found it, Joan told her. They'd pretty much made up their minds to put a hefty down payment on a new piece of waterfront real estate. She'd even purchased furni-ture for it and had torn out pictures in magazines that were perfect for what she hoped to do.

Joan Claybourne was a nice enough lady, but as they spoke over two large pink lemonades, Eliana decided that perhaps she and the pretty lady would not be such friends after all.

284

They had little in common. Joan was a rich doctor's wife; she was a poor lounge singer's punching bag. Ross Claybourne had reached success even at a young age. He was able to buy his wife two houses already. It would take Hector two lifetimes to afford such a place as the waterfront property out on 24, much less to buy it as a vacation home.

"You have to come see the house sometime," Joan said. "When we get it all set up, I mean. Maybe give me some ideas for it."

Eliana fingered the trinket-gift she'd received earlier. "I'd like that," she said. "My sister, she is an artist. If you'd like to see some of her work, she's here at the festival. She can make your home here look very much like a beach house."

Joan smiled a half-smile. "I think that would be lovely," she said. "I'm a photographer myself and I was thinking . . . perhaps I could take some pictures around the island. Have them matted and framed. If I like your sister's work—what is her name, by the way?"

"Ariela."

"What an amazingly beautiful name." Joan Claybourne lifted her chin. Her eyes scanned the room's pale blue ceiling; her left hand fluttered around her face. "Like a whisper in the wind or a . . ." She looked back at Eliana. "A fairy."

Eliana swallowed hard as she eyed the jewelry gracing Joan's wedding finger. "Your rings are very beautiful."

"Hmm?" Joan Claybourne seemed truly taken aback by her expression. Then, as though her wedding set were an afterthought to her life, she flattened her left hand into the palm of her right and took notice of the cluster of diamonds resting there. "My Ross is quite adept at buying the perfect . . ." She looked up. "Everything." Then she laughed. To Eliana, it sounded like the tinkling of little bells.

Eliana thought to say something—anything to ease the oddity of the moment—but just then heard a cool baritone say, "So there you are."

Joan Claybourne's face lit up. Eliana peered over her shoulder to see a man—a handsome man with sandy brown hair swept toward his face, the sideburns fashionably long, and his eyes the color of a robin's eggs. His skin was bronzed by the sun, his smile white against it. "Ross! I want you to meet my new friend."

Eliana didn't know whether to stand or remain seated. She settled on the latter. "Eliana," she said, extending her hand. "Eliana Rivera."

Ross Claybourne took it. His hand was cool and smooth. "Ross Claybourne."

"Sit. Sit, darling," Joan coaxed. "I want you to join us. Eliana's husband is a singer here on the island, and her sister Ariela—have you ever heard such a lovely name?—is an artist. Her work is on display. Here, at the festival. I say we look at it, possibly for the house. What do you say?"

Ross Claybourne chuckled. "Slow down, silly girl," he said to the woman he clearly adored. Eliana felt a pang of jealousy pass through her. Ross and Joan Claybourne had such tenderness between them. There had never been much gentleness between her and Hector. Even their lovemaking was tinged with more aggression than passion. Ross Claybourne looked at his wife as though she were the most costly of assets. Precious and valuable. Hector only viewed Eliana as a possession he'd been stuck with since they were eighteen and sixteen years of age.

"I would be happy to show you where she has her paintings," Eliana said, more to stop her mind from rambling than anything else.

286

Ross Claybourne smiled at her. "That would be very nice of you, Eliana. And, may I say, that your name is just as lovely as your sister's."

Eliana couldn't believe the compliment. "Thank you. Gracias."

"De nada."

A waitress came to their table, pad in hand and pencil poised. "Can I get you anything?" she asked the late arrival.

Eliana watched how Ross moved with ease. He picked up his wife's glass, took a sip, and said, "Pink lemonade?"

It seemed to Eliana that Joan Claybourne turned as rosy as the drink. "Of course."

Ross looked up to the waitress. "I'll have some sweet iced tea if you have it." The waitress nodded and walked away. "Eliana," he continued, "where are you from? Originally, I mean."

"Puerto Rico. I moved here with my family when I was ten."

"Do you miss it? Puerto Rico?"

"Sometimes. Very much so."

The waitress returned with a tall glass of iced tea and asked if the "ladies need a refill." Joan nodded and Eliana did the same. "Be right back," she said as she swept the two near-empty glasses from the linen draped table.

"And your husband is a singer?" Ross continued.

"Yes. But only here on the weekends. He has another job during the week on the mainland."

"Children?"

Eliana shook her head. "Not yet." And, she thought, if Hector had his way about it, not ever. "You?"

Ross and Joan smiled at each other. Joan placed her hand against her flat stomach and said, "In about eight months. Right after the first of the year."

Eliana watched as Ross leaned over, took his wife's hand in his, and kissed her gently on her lips. "Congratulations," she said.

Joan Claybourne kept her eyes on her husband and smiled broadly. "Thank you, Eliana." She kissed her husband once again, then turned back in time to greet the returning waitress with a word of gratitude. She picked up her glass and took a sip. "As soon as we finish, let's go see your sister's paintings, shall we?"

Eliana nodded. Then again, she thought, maybe they could become friends.

––––––––

Eliana would never forget the night, just over a year later, when she told Hector she had decided to go to work for the Claybournes. That she would take care of their house after they'd left to return to Orlando and would ready it before they arrived. Her reason, she told him, was to help with their finances. Hector had gambled nearly every penny they had; they were barely getting by. Not that she mentioned that part to him. He would have slapped her to the moon and back, in spite of their being at the Traverses' at the time she broke the news.

He had taken her by the hand and dragged her out of the house by her wrist. It was two in the morning, so he'd been quiet in doing so. He towered over her small frame, told her through gritted teeth that if she put up a fuss she'd live to regret it. If she lived. She whimpered as he pulled her in her nightgown and bare feet across the rough gravel on the road, toward the Gulf, lying flat in the moonlight. With each sob he jerked her hand harder and squeezed her wrist tighter.

At first, she thought his plan was to drown her. For a moment, she didn't know whether to fight back or to simply let it happen. But it was soon clear that this was not his plan at all. He intended to discipline her, as he called it, outside of the earshot of the elderly Mr. and Mrs. Travers.

He pushed her to the wet sand along the water. Her palms pushed hard against the broken shells, and she felt the skin tear. Droplets of blood—rich and red—dotted the white of her cotton gown as she raised her hands to see the damage. She looked up. Hector blocked her view of the moon; his face was dark, he was nothing but a shadow of anger and fear. "Why would you embarrass me like this, Eliana?" he spat. "Why do you make me feel less of a man, making it look as if I cannot provide for you?"

"You provide just fine," she said. She had already planned her speech, and so she spoke it quickly. "But I thought this might help . . . you have been looking at the little house on 4th Street, no? Wouldn't you rather get there sooner than later? I am your wife, Hector. We're a team, aren't we? And no one in Chiefland has to know."

Even in the dark, Eliana could see her husband relax. He reached for her wrist and pulled her up. His eyes—which were now visible to her—shimmered. "You'd do that for me, Eliana?"

She had to appease him, to soothe the pride she'd wounded. "I love you, Hector," she said, wrapping her arms around his broad waist. "Of course I'd do that for you."

The truth was, of course, that she wasn't doing it for her husband. She was doing it for her friends, Ross and Joan Claybourne. Ross needed her. That sweet baby needed her too. And Joan . . . poor Joan. No wonder, she thought, Ross had wondered what drink had been in her glass all those months ago.

What she didn't know—wouldn't know for a little while

longer—was that she would save Joan Claybourne's life. "Joan," she whispered that day to her friend, who lay curled like a child on her bed in the middle of the afternoon, six days into a drunk that seemed would never end. "You have to go get help, now." Joan shook her head against the satin pillowcase. Her long blonde hair lay matted, the color had turned dull. "Don't shake your head at me, Joan Claybourne," she said. "These days, I know you better than you know yourself." She swallowed. "You're the strongest woman I know. And you have to be strong for your little girl, chica. Do you hear me?"

Joan's bloodshot eyes fluttered open. "I'm not brave. You are."

Eliana drew closer. The stench of stale alcohol assaulted her. "Not like you. I stay in my misery. But you . . . you are strong enough to go to the hospital and get well." This time Joan nodded at Eliana's words. "I'm going to get a bubble bath ready for you now, chica. I'll get you cleaned up and then Ross will drive us to the hospital. We'll have you all fixed up in no time."

Joan clutched her shoulder. "You'll take care of my baby while I'm gone?" Her voice cracked in a whisper.

"Of course."

"And Ross?" Joan quivered. "Ross can't do anything without me . . ."

"Yes, Joan."

"Do you promise? Promise you will stay? You won't go home to Hector? You'll stay and take care of things?"

"I promise."

Eliana started to pull away but Joan held tight. "He loves me very much, you know. He needs me. And I need him." She blinked, then repeated, "He loves me very much, you know."

Eliana smiled weakly. "Yes, chica," she said. "I know. He loves you very much."

––––––––

That night, while Joan began her detox in the hospital, Eliana rocked little Kimberly-Boo to sleep. She sang a lullaby her own mother had sung to her years ago in Puerto Rico. "*Contigo, sí. Contigo, no. Contigo, mi vida, me casaré yo . . .*" She hummed a little of the tune before returning to the lyrics, this time in English. "With you, yes. With you, no. With you, my love, I will marry." After she laid the sleeping child in her crib, she turned to see Ross standing at the door, watching her. She smiled at him, and in turn, he smiled back. But even in the dark, she could see the anguish and grief etched on his face, the tearstains along his cheeks. His shoulders slumped, weighed down with his life's burden. He released a long sigh and nodded once. "Good night, Ana," he said, then turned and walked away, his footsteps cushioned by the thick wool carpets running the length of the hall.

"Good night," Eliana returned, her voice inaudible to him now. As she stepped toward her bedroom, she returned quietly to the little tune she'd sung to the baby. "*Contigo, sí. Contigo, no. Contigo, mi vida, me casaré . . . yo . . .*"

29

"Rosa." I looked past her left shoulder to see if there were any others with her. There were not. "I was expecting—"

"Luis, yes, I know. I asked him to give me some time with you first." She peered into the house. "May I?"

I took a step back. "Of course."

As Rosa entered the house she'd practically called her second home during our childhood, I closed the door and then followed her into the living room. "It looks so different," she said. She dropped her purse—a real-deal Dooney and Bourke if I'd ever seen one—onto an end table, crossed her arms, and allowed her eyes to give the room the once-over.

"It does, doesn't it?"

She walked past me to take closer notice of a seashell wreath on the far side of the room. The scent of expensive perfume trailed behind her, making me suddenly aware of just how well-dressed she was in comparison to the JCPenney's shorts set and insect bite ointment I'd donned earlier. "The work of your stepmother?" she asked. She looked over her shoulder at me. "The whole makeover, I mean?"

"Yes."

"A get-rid-of-the-former-wife sweep?" She turned back to the wreath.

"I'm not sure I'd say it that way, but I do think Anise wanted a place that didn't have Mom written all over it."

Rosa turned fully to me then and jutted her thumb toward the wreath. "This is kind of tacky, though, isn't it?"

I couldn't help but laugh, even in my uneasiness about Rosa's visit. "Well, that was Heather's gift when Anise had finished redecorating."

"Heather?" Rosa strolled back to her purse and then, without another word, casually slipped one ankle behind the other and dropped into the chair beside the table. "How is Heather? I haven't seen her in . . . forever." She smiled at me, and her expression indicated I should feel free to sit as well.

I took a seat on my father's sofa. "Heather is . . . good."

Rosa's smile turned almost sardonic. "My mother told me that—some time ago—Dr. Claybourne had suggested she might be drinking too much." She cocked her head. "Is she?"

"Dad told Eliana about Heather?" I ran my fingertips through my hair, from the forehead back, and felt it as it instantly slipped back into place. "I would say I'm surprised, but with what Dad has told me about his and Mom's history with your mom, I guess it makes sense."

Rosa's lips pursed. "And what did Dr. Claybourne say, exactly, about my mother?"

I cupped my hands around my knees and allowed my eyes to focus on the action rather than the woman sitting so close to me, the one I'd happily grown up with and now felt to be only a menacing stranger. "That she was . . . instrumental in helping with *my* mother."

"You mean when Joan was drinking so much."

293

My head jerked up; my eyes locked with hers. "You know about that?"

"Mom told me all about it."

"When?"

"After Joan died." She shrugged. "Your father came by Mom's shortly afterward. They spent hours together, talking. I'm sure about everything that happened . . . back then."

I leaned over, replaced my hands with my elbows, and said, "What else did she say? Your mom?"

Rosa shook her head dismissively as her lashes fell and rose as though in slow motion. "No more than that, really. Any other questions I had were shooed away. But . . . Dr. Claybourne continued to . . . *employ* my mother, as you know. And I know, because of that, they talked from time to time . . . It was never just about the business of this house, you know. They were friends."

"I know."

"And Mom had some really nice things to say about your stepmother too."

I smiled. "Anise is hard not to like. She's been good for Dad." When Rosa had no response, I added, "Manny seems like a nice man."

"He's the best." The answer came almost too quickly.

Silence fell hard in the room. "So why are you here, then, Rosa?"

Rosa's chest rose as she inhaled. I scarcely noticed her releasing the breath. "I want to talk with you about Steven Granger."

I straightened. "What about him?"

"Just how serious are you, chica?"

Chica . . . I smiled. "He's asked me to stay the summer."

"And are you?"

294

"Yes. Dad and Anise will be here sometime next month. My sons too, so we'll all be here and, hopefully . . . Why do you ask?"

I watched as her tongue slipped from between her lips, ran along the lower to moisten it. The matte mahogany lipstick shimmered in the sunlight, and I couldn't help but think how different the girl—short and skinny and awkward—was from the sophisticated, voluptuous adult. "I think you should rethink your relationship with Steven."

I felt my brow furrow. "What? Why would you say such a thing?"

"Because there are things you don't know. Not only because of how wrapped up you were in him when we were children but also because you haven't been here . . . in Cedar Key . . . for some time."

My breathing became shallow. "Like what?"

She shrugged. "Where do you want me to start, chica?"

I felt white-hot anger pinging from one side of my brain to the other. "Just tell me what you came to tell me, Rosa."

"Very well, then. Steven Granger is known as a player on this island. Did you know that?"

I didn't answer.

"I see from your lack of response that you didn't. Because the Kimberly I knew wouldn't be so foolish as to share her man, at least not knowingly."

The knot in my throat had started to grow, but I managed to find my voice around it. "Define 'player'?"

She shrugged one shoulder. "I bet you can't name an un-married woman on this island who he hasn't dated and dis-carded once he's gotten what he's wanted from her. Oh, he's suave, all right. When he wants what he wants. But when he gets what he gets, he's . . ." Rosa flicked the fingers of her right hand as though she were pushing a nagging insect again. "Bye-bye, baby."

I shook my head. "That doesn't sound right," I whispered. "It doesn't sound like the man I've gotten to know since I've been here."

She shrugged the shoulder again. "And just how long have you been here? Never mind, don't answer that. We both know the answer." Her brows arched. "It's fine if you don't believe me, if you think you know him so well." She reached for her purse. "Go ahead. Keep seeing him. Find out for yourself."

I reached out a hand as though to stop her from leaving, or at least from appearing to leave. "Wait. How do I know you're telling the truth? Why, exactly, should I believe you over Steven?"

"I can answer that with one simple name. Brigitte Granger."

I raised my chin against the reminder. "He's explained all that to me," I said.

Rosa rolled her eyes. "All right then. Allow me to give you another name." She smiled. "Rosa Rivera."

I shifted until my back hit the sofa. "What are you talking about?"

She raised her perfectly manicured index finger. The nail looked like a claw. "Do you remember that time when we were on Atsena Otie, when you tried to get me to tell you who I was seeing?"

I shook my head. Of course I remembered, but I refused to believe what she was saying.

"It was Steven Granger I was seeing, chica." She crossed her arms. "And I would have married him too, had Brigitte not gotten pregnant." A half-smile returned to her lips. "Before I did."

I stood. "I don't believe you, Rosa."

296

Rosa raised herself ever so gracefully from the chair. She took her purse by the strap and draped it over one arm before lowering her eyes and saying, "Yes, you do, Kimberly. Right now, your heart is wrestling with your head because you *do* believe me." The eyes came back to rest on mine. "Take time to think about it. You and I were like sisters so long ago. We share so much. More than you know."

"And what does *that* mean?"

She didn't answer right away. Finally, her chest fell and she said, "It means, we both loved and we both lost the same man." Her fingertips grazed her chest, just below the strands of multi-colored crystal beads wrapped around her throat. "Now, I have married and moved on, so I have no reason to care about his present day antics. But you . . . Boo . . . you have a lot at stake. And now that I know your sons will be here, exposed to Steven Granger, a possible father figure . . . I have sons too, you know." She walked toward me, placed a gentle kiss on my cheek, and said, "*Lo siento mucho*, chica." As I stood unmoving, she glanced at her oversized watch and said, "I'll show myself out. Luis and Fe will be here any minute, I'm sure."

And with that, she walked out of my father's house.

I managed to collect myself long enough to greet Luis and his younger sister Fe and to show them where Anise kept the cleaning supplies, the vacuum, broom, and mop. "I won't stay underfoot," I said, my voice shakier than I desired. "I'm sure you know what you're doing."

"I'll start stripping sheets, Luis," Fe said. "Nice to meet you," she said to me before making her way down the hall.

Luis, however, lagged behind, looked on me with his piercing dark eyes, and said, "What's wrong, chica?"

I shook my head. "Nothing." But even to my own ears, it wasn't convincing.

He jutted his chin toward the door. "My cousin. Did she say something? Do something to upset you?"

"No." I cleared my throat. "Listen, I just need to run next door to check on the lady who lives there." I started to walk toward the door, then turned. "First, I need my purse."

Luis smiled, but his eyes remained somber. "If there is anything I can do . . ."

I had no reason to trust the man. After all, he was Rosa's cousin. Even though he had known her when she claimed to have dated Steven, I couldn't say for sure that he'd be honest with me. For all I knew, the two of them were in cahoots. She'd possibly planned all along to come here immediately before Luis was to arrive.

I smiled at him weakly as I passed him on the way to the front door. "I'll be back shortly. Before you're finished." I reached for the door handle, but my hand shook so, I struggled with opening it. I dropped my hand, squeezed it into a tight fist, then flexed it. I attempted to open the door a second time, this time successfully. "Oh," I said turning toward Luis. "If you hear scratching at the door, it's my dog, Max. He's allowed inside."

"Sure, chica," he said.

I closed the door behind me. My legs quivered as I took each step toward the shell-covered ground below. I clenched my purse's strap so tight I felt my fingernails digging into the pad of my palm. If I drew blood, I thought, I wouldn't care.

I walked across the lawn to Patsy's, climbed the stairs, and knocked on her door. I took in a ragged breath and blew it out ever so slowly before she answered. "Why, hon," she said with her first look at me. "Whatever is the matter?"

"Patsy," I said. "I'm sorry to bother you but . . . I need advice." I swallowed. "Godly advice from a woman who is wiser than I."

"Come on in," she said, stepping back. "And I'll see if I can't fill that order."

After making sure Patsy was feeling all right, I briefed her on what Rosa had told me. We sat at her kitchen table—a favorite place for her, it seemed to me. I gripped the sweating glass of iced tea she'd poured for me and stared at my fingers as I spoke. When I was done, she said, "Have you asked your young man about it?"

I looked up at her. "I don't know if I can, Patsy."

"I don't know if you *can't*." She pointed an age-marked finger at me. "Many an argument I would have saved myself from having with my beloved if I had just asked instead of presumed."

I shook my head. "I'm falling in love with him again." Tears burned the back of my eyes. "How could she have done this to me?"

"Done what, child? Lay down with a boy all those years ago or come now to tell you about it?"

I had to think before I answered. Finally, I said, "Both."

"Well, now," she said. "There's no accounting for the foolish things we do when we are young and impulsive."

"Did you, Patsy? Did you ever do anything impulsive when you were young?"

"Did you?" she countered.

I thought back to that summer when I'd done everything within my power to make Steven mine and about the times I'd worked so hard to trick Mom. "Of course."

"We all do. I did, you did." She smiled. "And I'd be willing to bet your sons will and your grandchildren will too. This is the time of life when we test the waters, so to speak. We push against the boundaries just to see if they'll budge."

I smiled at her. "I can hardly imagine you doing that, Patsy."

Then I shook my head. "And I surely don't want to think about my boys . . ." I sighed. "But I suppose they will."

"Well, now, I don't know what your boys may get into, but I can tell you that I got into plenty. I was angry and untrusting and—being that—I almost lost my Gilbert before I even had him good." She reached over and patted my hand. "But that's another story for another time. For now, you have to ask yourself why Rosa would want to hurt you so. Why does she want to pull the rug out from under your feet, so to speak, when she's already got a husband?" She pointed the finger at me again, this time with a wink. "And I'll tell you something else. Her sweet mother had a time with her, she clearly did."

"She did?" I felt myself sit up a little straighter.

"Oh yes. Now I don't mean to repeat what Eliana told me in private. That'd be gossip. But I'll tell you this, she used to come over here after she was done at your daddy's place. We'd sit right here and drink iced tea just like we're doing now and she'd tell me her worries and concerns. Eliana was a good woman, but she was awfully troubled."

"About what . . . or is that the part you can't talk about?"

Patsy shook her head. "Not in detail, no. But I can and will tell you that based on what she told me, I don't know if I'd trust anything Rosa had to say."

I took several breaths, aware of each one, as if, individually, they counted for something. "So, I should go talk to him."

"The sooner the better, I'd say."

I looked at my watch. "It's going to take Luis and Fe a while to finish up . . . Dad would kill me if I left the house for any real length of time with them in it." I sighed. "Not to mention Steven is working."

"Do you have a date tonight?"

I nodded. "But I don't know if I can wait that long."

"The Good Book says patience is a virtue, Kimberly."

She was right there. "Patsy, will you do something for me?"

She reached across the table and patted my hand. "If it's within my power."

"Will you pray with me? For me?"

"Right here, right now," she answered, then bowed her head and spoke to God on my behalf.

———

Luis and Fe did a good job on the house, and I couldn't wait to call Dad to tell him. Not only did I want the accolades I was sure to receive, it was a way to kill time. "Max approves of them too," I told him.

"When did you schedule their return?"

"I suggested they return just before you and Anise come . . . and the boys."

If I'm still here . . .

"Sounds good."

"I mean, it's just me and . . . how much of a mess can I make of things?"

Dad didn't answer the question. Instead, he said, "Andre called. Heather has been admitted into a rehab center."

"You're kidding . . . he did it."

"We can't see her, he said. No one can. Not for a while. And, they're going to want all of us in some kind of family counseling." Dad exhaled. "I dunno . . ."

It took a moment to realize where my father was heading with his thoughts. "Dad, we have to. *You* have to. For Heather. For her children, though children they hardly are anymore."

I heard Dad's deep sigh. "Well, let's just wait and see what God allows."

"All right, Dad. But if I'm asked to go, I'm going."

"Each of us has to do what we feel is best for the time.

When it happens, we'll see where things are. Until then, let's just keep her and Andre in our prayers, shall we?"

"Of course, Dad."

I hung up the phone and tried, for a moment, to take in all that had happened in less than three weeks. I walked out of a courtroom feeling defeated by my ex-husband and into the arms of a man I'd hardly thought of in years. I'd reluctantly left my home in Orlando to stay in Cedar Key to find a housekeeper and now, perhaps, would remain for the summer. I'd been forced to face my mother's alcoholism and I'd come to accept that my sister's fate, without intervention, could be similar. And I'd come to realize that not all of life was in my control, that some things happen seemingly for all the wrong reasons but, in reality, for all the right.

If only we let go and let God.

I looked at my watch. In just a few hours I'd know an all-important truth: either Steven was everything he appeared to be or Rosa was less a sister/friend than I'd known her to be. I bit my lip and blinked back tears.

In that moment, it was impossible to know which truth would hurt the least.

30

It was too hot outside to do anything but melt, so I decided to waste time with a little shopping in some of the local art galleries and specialty shops. Hours later, I returned home loaded down with a few new pieces of hand-blown glass jewelry, a sassy black halter dress, and a multi-colored Billabong floppy hat—all of which I planned to wear that evening—and a book about the island and its history. Somewhere between the car and the front door, while balancing to keep from falling over an anxious Max, my cell phone rang from a pocket inside my purse.

I couldn't search and answer without threat of an untimely death by falling; once I got inside and dropped my purchases on the sofa, I drew it out and checked to see who'd called.

Chase.

I called him right back.

"Is it true?" he asked without saying hello.

"Is what true?" I dropped to the sofa and started taking my purchases out, starting with the dress.

"That you have a boyfriend?"

I dropped the dress; it fell to my lap, slipped over my knees, and formed a puddle at my feet. "Who told you that?"

"Pop."

"When did you talk with Dad?"

"Just a little while ago."

"Did you call him or did he call you?" I frowned with the question. It was just like Dad to plow ahead with news before I had a chance to talk to my sons.

"Mom, does it matter? He told me that you have a boyfriend in Cedar Key and that we're all going there after we're done here at Dad's. Is it true?"

I picked up the dress and draped it over my lap. "Yes." When my oldest had nothing else to say, I added, "How do you feel about that?"

"I don't know. I mean, I guess I'm happy for you. Do you think it's serious?"

I blinked slowly. "Could be."

"Who is he?"

"Pop didn't tell you?"

"He only said he's some old boyfriend."

I laughed then. "Yes. His name is Steven Granger. I met him when I was just a little girl. He lived here on the island and . . . when we were teenagers we were an item, I guess you could say."

"Oh no. I don't wanna know about the goofy back-when-you-were-a-kid stuff . . . seriously, Mom."

"Okay, okay. I know it's hard to imagine your mother as a teenager and crazy in love."

"Repeat: do *not* want to hear this."

"Have you told Cody?"

"Not yet. Do you want me to?"

"Maybe I'd better. He's . . . I think Cody's heart still breeds hope that your father and I will somehow get back together."

"You're right there, Mom."

I raked my bottom lip with my teeth. "Oh, Chase . . . I don't want to hurt him. Either of you. I want . . . I hope you two will come here to Cedar Key and meet Steven and . . ."

"And maybe be like a family?"

If only I knew . . . "Maybe. Time will tell, huh."

"Dad is still our dad, though, Mom."

I closed my eyes. "I know that, son. And I don't want . . . wouldn't want to change that. Not for anything. With everything wrong that happened in our marriage—even the parts I'm not quite sure of—Charlie gave me the greatest gifts I could have ever hoped to receive."

After a pause, my oldest said, "Well, me . . . yeah. But Cody . . . that remains to be seen."

I smiled and raised my eyes heavenward. "I miss you so much, son."

"I miss you too, Mom. And on that note . . . I have to go. If Dad finds out I've been on the phone during work hours, he'll probably call off going to the beach for dinner tonight."

"Sounds like fun. Tell Code I'll call him tomorrow afternoon, okay? And tell him that I love him."

"Will do."

"I love you."

"You too. See ya, Mom."

I was as ready as a prosecuting attorney when Steven arrived. I resolved myself to keep an emotional distance until I had fully questioned the "suspect," but the accused had me completely undone the moment he walked in the front door.

"Wow," he said, blinking. "You. Look. Fantastic."

I didn't answer, though inside I'm sure I blushed.

"And when I say fantastic, what I mean is *fantastic*."

His arms slipped around my waist; the silk of the dress tickled my skin. He pressed his lips against mine and, help me, I didn't protest. "I've got something to tell you," he murmured against my mouth.

"Yeah, I've got something to tell you too."

His eyes searched mine. "Let's save it. Save them both. I've got something special planned for this evening so we can share our little secrets later." He tugged at the brim of my hat. "I'm glad you've got this on. It's cute."

When we got in Steven's car, he gave me a hint: we were going to Mill House Road on the east side of the island. "Okay," I said. Nothing more. Just "okay." In fact, I stayed silent pretty much the whole drive, but Steven talked non-stop. "There's a house over there I've been looking at for a while. The listing was a little pricier than I wanted to pay, but it recently dropped." He shot a quick look my way. "But before I do anything, I want your opinion, so you'll have to tell me what you think, okay? And be honest. Don't just say you like it because you think I do."

"Sure." I swallowed. "Is it listed with Rosa?"

"Rosa? No." He grinned. "There *are* other real estate offices on the island, you know."

I didn't know whether to be relieved or worried. What if Steven had avoided Rosa's office precisely because of what she'd said earlier about him? About them. Then again, hadn't he said that he rented from one of Rosa's places?

I asked the question pestering me. "Why did you rent from Rosa?"

He shrugged. "It was available, it was furnished, and it was in my price range," he said. "When Dad got sick, I had to move fast. You know what I mean?"

"I know." I forced a smile. "Tell me more about the house."

306

"It was built in the twenties, but it's in fine shape. Been renovated. Main thing for me is that it has a dock and a boathouse." He kept his focus on the road. "By the way, how do you feel about cleaning fish?"

"I think it's disgusting, why?"

Looking through the side of his sunglasses I could see him roll his eyes. "Some fishwife you'd make."

Fishwife. I wasn't ready to go there. "So what is this about cleaning fish?"

"There's a place for that."

"Well, I hope you and your fish are very happy."

He laughed. "All right then. I'll teach your sons."

"Cody will love it."

"Good." Traffic in front of us was building; Steven slowed the Jeep. "There are also four bedrooms."

I watched the familiar scenery on both sides of the road. The long straight sidewalks, the cottages, the church and the market. "Won't that be too much for one person?"

"I'm hoping it won't be just one person."

My breath caught in my throat. "Steven . . ."

Steven slowed the car to a stop at the crossroads of D and 2nd, right across from the bookstore I'd shopped in earlier that day. He rested his elbow along the back of the seat and shifted his weight before pulling off his sunglasses. His eyes met my reluctant glance with more passion than I dared try to focus on. "I know. I'm moving too fast. But the way I'm feeling . . . like I haven't felt in years . . . time can't possibly move fast enough."

"But still, Steven. Just so we're clear. I don't believe in . . . um . . . spending the night, let's say, before marriage."

He shifted back to face front and pulled onto 2nd. "Good," he said. "Because I don't either."

307

I returned to silent mode. Steven continued on 2nd, slowly cruising past the places that had started stirring my heart again. As familiar as my childhood, and just as precious. Steven pulled into Old Mill. We only had to drive a short distance before he parked, got out, and walked around the Jeep to open my door while I stared at the rambling blue and white Victorian with a wraparound balcony along the second floor. The passenger door opened, and Steven extended his hand. "Isn't she fantastic?"

I slipped out of the car. "Fantastic? Isn't that what you said about me not too long ago?"

"Ouch," he said with a laugh. "Sorry." He kissed my cheek near my ear; in the heat my flesh tingled. "You look fantastic. The house is . . ." He looked over his shoulder at it and laughed again. "I can't come up with another word."

"Sprawling."

He looked at me again. "It's over three thousand square feet."

I kept my eyes away from his and on the house. "Do you have a key?"

"Of course I do." He closed the passenger door. "What do you think so far?"

I was torn. I knew he wanted it not just for him, but for me. For us. But if what Rosa had said was true, there would be no "us." "What kind of kitchen does it have?" I asked, peering at him through the lenses of my sunglasses.

Steven grinned. "So I'll catch 'em, the boys will clean 'em, and you'll fry 'em up."

I wiggled my shoulder. "Maybe." Palm fronds danced around us in the light breeze. "It's getting pretty hot out here. Why don't you show me the inside?"

The house was beautiful and blessedly air-conditioned.

Every room was rich with glossy oak flooring, semi-gloss pure-white paint, and cypress wainscoting and trim. Each had ample natural light from the oversized windows. There wasn't a stick of furniture anywhere except in the sunroom; it offered a white wicker settee and two oversized chairs. "Comes with the house," Steven said, and I nodded.

When we reached the master bedroom, Steven leaned against the door frame and allowed me to wander around the expansive suite, complete with dressing room, large walk-in closets, and a his-and-her bathroom. When I rejoined him, I stopped halfway across the room. His look was so intense and he looked like a man at home, shoulder resting against the wood, one leg crossed over the other, hands in his shorts pockets. He wore khakis—as he nearly always did—and an island-inspired short-sleeved silk shirt. "So? What do you think?"

I crossed my arms and stood with my feet planted together. "What do *you* think? That's the real question."

"I like it. I like it a lot. I haven't even bothered to look at other places since I got here last year. I've got the money from the sale of my place in Atlanta and I really need to invest it this year before I get pulverized by Uncle Sam next year."

I nodded. "What do you like most about it?"

He grinned. "The outside."

"Inside, I mean."

His eyes turned smoky. "Seeing you standing in it."

"Don't get ahead of yourself. Room-wise?"

He straightened, pulled his hands from his pockets, and crossed his arms. "It's got a lot of space. I like the den and the bonus room, which I could use as an office. That's one thing Dad never had. He turned the third bedroom into his office and Mom always complained about never having anywhere for company to sleep."

"Well, this certainly has room for company."

He grinned at me again. "Hey," he said, long and slow. "I got special permission from the realty office to bring something for us to eat here. It's not much. We've got some croissants and crabmeat, raw vegetables and berries waiting for us down in the kitchen."

"Sounds perfect," I said. "We can eat in the Florida room."

"That's what I was thinking."

After we'd eaten and talked about all the things he hoped to do with the yard just beyond the windows, Steven and I drove to the beaches along G Street to watch the sun set. He pulled two folding chairs from the back of the Jeep and set them up on the side of the road. The breeze and sunlight felt balmy against my face and skin. I tugged my floppy hat a little lower on my forehead.

"So, now that we've got all that out of the way, tell me what you wanted to share with me," he said, reaching for my hand and linking his fingers with mine.

"Why don't you go first? Or was the house it?"

"No. The house wasn't it. The house was just the beginning of all my good news." He giggled like a schoolboy. "I've been talking to Eliza . . . about us—about how I feel about *you*, in particular—and about your sons coming after July 4th. And she told me she's planning to come here on the 3rd to spend the holiday with her grandparents and me. I've talked her into staying a few extra days before heading back, so she can meet Chase and Cody, and they can meet her." He paused. "What do you think?"

I closed my eyes then opened them again. Several gulls flew overhead; I watched until they were out of sight, their cawing barely audible, drowned out now by the slapping of water against the shoreline. I sat straight and turned to

Steven. "Can I ask you a question?" My voice came out lower than I'd expected.

"You don't seem happy about my news. I know; too much, too soon."

I turned fully to face him, to touch the side of his face with the fingertips of my free hand. It felt warm and smooth. "No, it sounds good. It sounds wonderful, in fact. But before I can allow myself to get too excited—about Eliza or the house—I need to tell you . . . to ask you a question."

Steven scooted back enough that my hand slipped from his face. He caught it with his free hand and held it. "Ask. Anything."

"You told me you haven't dated, really, since your divorce."

He blinked, but his eyes never left mine. "I haven't."

"Not even anyone here on the island?"

"No." His body shifted so that his elbows rested on his knees, which was awkward for me. I moved to accommodate him. "Why? Has someone . . ." His jaw flexed. "Rosa," he hissed as he looked out at the water. "That's why you asked about her earlier." He jerked his head toward me. "Right? I'm right, aren't I?"

My stomach lurched. I couldn't speak, I could only nod.

"What did she tell you?"

I decided to begin at the end. "That you've dated all the single women on this island."

Something like a growl came from deep within him. He stared at his feet. "That woman! Honestly, sometimes I don't know how Manny puts up with her."

The sky was turning dark red. I pulled my sunglasses away from my face and rested them along the brim of my hat. "It's not true, then?"

He turned his attention back to me. "Of course not. Look,

Kim, if I tell you I've never dated anyone since Brigitte, then you have to believe me. I'm not a man who's used to lying or even to having his word doubted."

Hope stirred inside me. If this part of Rosa's story wasn't true, then perhaps . . . "There's one other thing. Rosa stated that she and you . . ." I pressed my lips together. They were dry again, as parched as old bones. "That the two of you . . . when we were younger . . ."

Steven straightened. His hands released mine. He folded his arms over his chest and his eyes went cold. "Did she tell you that we were together? Like a man and woman, together?"

I nodded.

He threw his head back, then shook it before bringing his eyes back to mine. "My word, Kim, I've been with one woman my whole life and I *married* her." He ran his hands down his face. In one fluid movement he turned his chair to face mine, his left foot tucked under the bend in his right and his hands wrapped around my wrists. "Listen to me . . . I want you to believe what I'm about to tell you."

I looked down at my hands. "You're hurting me, Steven."

He released his grip. "I'm sorry." His voice cracked. "I'm just . . . I want to make sure you won't walk away from me."

I didn't like where this was going. Anxiety whirled inside me, and I shoved my hands under my legs to steady them. "I'm listening."

"Okay. So, yeah, when we were kids . . . Rosa used to come around. After you and I got together that summer, after we started dating, I guess you could say."

I tried to keep my voice steady. "While I was here? Before or after I left to go back home?" As if it mattered.

"Before." I watched his Adam's apple bob up and down in the warm glow of the sunset. "I don't mean to be crude, but

Rosa . . . she was like a girl on fire, if you know what I mean."
He made the growling sound again. A sudden wind came in
off the Gulf and lifted the hair resting along his forehead.
The dimming sunlight played with the natural soft-brown
highlights. I looked out at the water; it rippled to the south.
A storm was coming.

My own hair wrapped around my neck and my hat lifted
from my head. I pulled it off and held it between the fingertips
of my left hand. I ran the fingers of my right through the
damp roots of my hair. "Go on," I said.

"She tried her best to get me to . . . do things with her. She
said things that drive a man crazy. Especially a boy at eighteen."

"Like what?"

He shook his head. "Nah-ah. No way I'm repeating some
of the things she said to me. But trust me, Kim, in those days,
whatever *you* had, *she* wanted."

"But you and I never . . ."

"She thought we had." His eyes narrowed. "And it wasn't
just me. It was everything. Clothes, house, family dynam-
ics . . ."

I frowned. "Meaning?"

The lines along his face softened. "Sisters. Mother and father
under the same roof. She had a lot of respect for them. Especially
your father." His mouth twisted. "Listen, Kim, if I'd known she
was still up to her conniving ways, I would have never suggested
you go see her about the housekeeper position."

I turned to face the water. It was the deepest shade of
amethyst; the sun cast the thick line of its golden shadow
toward us. Thunderheads grew in the distance. "I don't know
what's worse. Learning that my childhood friend betrayed
me or that you did."

Steven scooted to the edge of his chair. I looked at him;

he looked desperate and a little angry. "Kim, you have to believe me. I promise you, I never once laid a hand on her. Not in *that* way."

"Did you kiss her?" I held my breath and waited for the answer.

"No," it finally came.

I exhaled.

"But she kissed me."

I inhaled again. "What's the difference, Steven?"

"I never once came on to her, Kim. Yes, she kissed me and yes I kissed her back. I'm human, you know . . . But I promise you . . ." He took my face in his hands. "I promise you, Kim." Steven pulled me toward him, pressed his forehead against mine. "Don't do this," he whispered. "Don't let *her* do this. Not now. Not to us."

I shook my head. "Let it go," I whispered back.

He pulled away, but his hands rested on my shoulders. "What?"

"I can't control this. Can't control the past, can I?"

Steven smiled weakly. "No," he sighed.

"What happened, happened."

"But not because I wanted it."

Afraid to speak, I could only look at him. If one word left my mouth or one movement shifted my body, I knew I would fall apart. The thought of Rosa kissing Steven when we were younger sickened me. I couldn't let my mind go there or I'd explode with a hurt born more than twenty years earlier.

I turned again toward the sunset. The sky now exploded in shades of gold; the sun had disappeared behind the tree line on the side of the island farthest west. Steven resumed his earlier position and I relaxed into my chair. I felt his hand brush mine, and I closed my eyes to wait for what I instinctively knew would come next.

"I love you, Kimberly-Boo," he said, once again linking our fingers. "Do you hear me? I love you."

I squeezed his fingers with mine. "I love you too, Steven Granger."

Another few gulls flew nearby, soaring near the pier running into the water to our left. My heart wanted to take flight with them, but it hurt too much right then. Even with our words of love, my heart hurt. Rosa had betrayed me, not just once, but twice.

Tomorrow, I decided, for the sake of my own sanity, I'd have to resume a semblance of control. For my sake. For Steven's and mine.

Tomorrow I'd find out *why*.

31

1990

Rosa Rivera had no plans for college, but her mother did.

"You're going. And that's final!" With one hand Eliana pushed the swinging door leading from their kitchen into the dining room. The other cradled two china plates and enough flatware for their dinner meal.

Rosa was right behind her. "But, Mom. Just listen to me for a minute. Hear me out, okay?"

Eliana gingerly placed the plates at the head of the table, and with both hands gripping the sides of the stack, she looked up and said, "I did *not* work my fingers to the bone all these years, Rosalita, for you to come to me and tell me you will not go to college. I gave you a year to work and to find yourself as you asked and now it is time. Besides, it's been decided already."

"By who? Because it certainly wasn't me who decided."

Rosa watched her mother as she straightened inch by inch as though in pain. She planted both fists on her lean hips. "It was decided long ago. That's all you need to know."

"By you and my father?"

"Get the glasses, Rosa."

Rosa went to the corner china cabinet, broug
pretty crystal glasses, and set them at the right of e
her mother had arranged. "So? Am I right? He got tc
what I would do with my life and then he just took off
dead to me but I have to live by his rules?"

Her mother slammed a fork beside one of the plat
"Respéteme!"

"I do respect you, Mom. But I don't want to live by the rules you and Hector somehow managed to conjure up for me, okay?"

"I will not argue this point with you," she said. "You are going to college and that is that. No more discussion on this tonight."

A month later, Ross Claybourne came into the little restaurant where Rosa worked three nights a week and on weekends. "Hey, Dr. Claybourne," she said. "What brings you here? And alone."

"Oh, I just thought I'd come in and have a cup of coffee. Maybe take in the scenery."

Rosa showed him to a table near the water. "So a cup of coffee? Black, right?"

Ross Claybourne smiled at her. "And how about a piece of key lime pie."

She smiled back. "You've got it, Dr. Claybourne."

When she'd placed his order before him he looked up at her and said, "Sit down for a minute, Rosa. Let's talk."

Rosa looked over her shoulder and back to the man who had been almost like a father to her, at least when he came to the island. "My mother sent you to talk to me, didn't she?"

He laughed but didn't answer. "Sit down," he said. "I'll cover for you if the boss gets upset."

Rosa sat. "Well, it's not too busy right now . . ."

Dr. Claybourne took a sip of his coffee and, placing the mug back on the table, said, "Yes, your mother did talk to me. She was out at the house today."

Rosa sighed. "It's all about getting her way, Dr. Claybourne. She doesn't even want to know what *I* want to do."

"What do you want to do?"

She shrugged. "I don't know."

"Ah. Now you sound like Boo. We had a hard time getting her off to college too, you know." He took a bite of pie. "This is good," he said, pointing to it with his fork. "So, let me make a suggestion. Go to a junior college just to get your feet wet. At least it will get you off the island for a while, and maybe you'll expand your ideas as to what you may like to do for the rest of your life."

"I'll think about it."

"Your mother is a good woman, Rosa, and she's worked hard. She wants the best for you, you know?"

"Yes, sir. I know." He smiled at her and she smiled back. "How do I even find out about what junior college to go to and all that?"

Ross Claybourne swallowed another bite of pie before answering. "You leave all that up to me, okay? I'll get everything in order."

"You'd do that for me?"

"Of course," he said. "It's the least I can do."

In the end, Rosa was glad she went to junior college, and she eventually, as Dr. Claybourne suspected, went on to college. She found she had a quick mind for higher learning and just the right sass for the frequent parties that came with it. During her second year at West Florida, at one such party, she met the rather straight-laced Emanuel Fuentes. "Manny," he insisted she call him. "It's what everyone calls me."

Their courtship had been whirlwind; within five months they were married. Only their closest friends in Pensacola knew; she didn't even tell her mother until they were close to their nine month anniversary and then only because she was five months pregnant. Eliana had been hurt by the news initially, and for the first time in her life, Rosa felt grief for a decision that brought her mother to tears. Early on the night after she and Manny had driven to Cedar Key to bear both pieces of news, Manny said good night and went on to bed in Rosa's old bedroom. Rosa was now alone with her mother. Alone to talk. Rosa took Eliana by the hand and led her outside, onto the front porch. The evening breeze was heavenly. The night insects called to one another. After some encouragement on Rosa's part, the two women nestled together on the hanging porch swing. "I'm sorry, Mom."

Eliana sniffled. "I want so much for you, Rosalita."

"I know, Mom. I know you want a lot for me. But I'm happy and you'll see . . . Manny is a good man. He works hard at the bank and has plans to advance in the world of finance."

Eliana didn't respond. She just sat and rocked.

"And I love him, Mom. I love him so much I hurt."

Eliana's head turned. Her dark eyes were washed in tears, which Rosa swept away with the pad of her thumbs, just as her mother had once done for her when she was a child. "Do you, chica? Do you love him that much?"

Rosa nodded. "I know you and my father didn't have a good relationship . . . that you had a violent marriage." Her mother's face returned to face front. "I know you don't even like to talk about Hector. But, Mama, Manny is different. I promise you."

"I can only pray this is so." Eliana looked at her daughter again. "Don't you ever let him hit you, Rosalita. Or yell or scream at you."

"He's not like that. He's a good man, Mom." She gave her mother the best grin she could muster. "And he's tamed me in so many ways."

Eliana's lips curled upward. "Then he's a saint."

Rosa rested her head on her mother's shoulder. "Sing to me, Mama. Like you used to when I was little."

"Nooooo . . ."

"Please? Sing to me."

"Okay." Her mother swallowed before taking a breath. *"Contigo, sí. Contigo, no. Contigo, mi vida, me casaré yo . . ."*

Rosa sang the lullaby to her own sons, all three of them. And, in time, after she'd finally finished earning her master's, she and Manny moved to Cedar Key. Manny worked as the branch manager of a bank on the mainland while she worked tirelessly to start her own real estate office on 2nd Street.

One night in 2001, when sleep eluded her, she crept into the home office she and Manny shared, booted up the computer, answered a few emails, and then mindlessly started searching the internet. She typed in the names of several old friends, including Kimberly's, then Steven Granger's; he now lived in the Atlanta area. She read an article telling about his receiving a Businessman of the Year award; his picture was there too. She studied it. He was still remarkably handsome. His teenaged daughter stood next to him. She was rail thin, in Rosa's opinion, but pretty. Rosa also noticed there was no Mrs. Granger. She'd heard rumors over the years, but didn't know for sure . . .

She x'd out of the screen, then typed *Hector Rivera.*

Hundreds of thousands of links and photos came up.

She went back to the search engine, added the words *musician* and *Florida*. That brought the number down to about fifteen thousand. But even that was more than she could hope to weed through. Especially in a single night and with her eyes growing heavy.

Manny found her the next morning, her head cradled in the crook of her arm, which lay on the desk. "Hey, baby," he said. He ran his fingertips through her hair. "What were you doing? Burning the midnight oil?"

Rosa wiped the sleep from her eyes. "Yeah. Let me make us some coffee," she said, standing.

Over breakfast, Rosa told Manny of her search for her father. "You're such a good dad," she said. "And I've been thinking how much I missed not having a father while I was growing up."

"Have you thought of asking your mother? Maybe she can give you some clues as to how to find him."

Rosa shook her head. "She won't. My whole life, whenever I brought up Hector's name—you know—asking her about him, she'd say, 'You don't need to play with trouble, Rosa.' So, I left it alone." Rosa picked up her coffee mug, wrapped her hands around it. "I know," she breathed out. "I know *exactly* who will help me." Rosa felt her spirits lifting. "Tía Ariela. She'll tell me."

Later that day, Rosa called her aunt and begged for information.

"What do you want to know about him for, Rosa?"

"Please, Tía. It's something missing inside of me."

"If I told you what a snake he was, can you not just take my word for it?"

"I know and yes, I believe you, but . . . I just want to see him face-to-face one time in my life now that I'm an adult."

"Eliana would fry me for breakfast if she knew I told you."

"I won't say anything. I promise."

"All right, then. The last I heard . . ."

Tía Ariela went on to tell her the name of the band she'd last heard he was playing in. Rosa went back to her computer. She found a mention of the band in a club in Orlando. She told Manny she'd be back as soon as she could, then threw a small suitcase in the back of her car and drove the three hours it took to get there.

The club was off of Orange Blossom Trail, in a large hotel near some of the tourist attractions. The skies were overcast that afternoon; threats of rain and hailstorms were given on the local radio station she'd been listening to. She entered the opulence of the hotel and headed straight for the concierge. "Hi," she said, giving the best smile she knew how.

"How can I help you?" a young woman asked from behind a desk.

Rosa sat in one of the two chairs provided. "I understand a band plays here. Northwind? I was wondering what time they'll be playing tonight?"

The petite woman shook her head. "I'm sorry. They haven't been here in . . . probably a couple of months."

Rosa's shoulders sank. "Nooooo . . . But I checked your website, and it said they were here."

"I'm sorry. We really need to update that thing."

Rosa arched her back. "Do you know . . . do you know if a man named Hector Rivera was in the band?"

"Absolutely. He's a very gifted musician." She leaned over as though to tell her something in secret. "But I wouldn't want to cross him, if you know what I mean."

"No." Rosa feigned ignorance. "What do you mean?"

The woman smiled then, as though she'd said too much.

"Oh, you know. He's a big guy. He has quite a commanding presence."

"Co-manding or de-manding?"

The woman pinked. "You obviously know Mr. Rivera."

"I used to. He's, um . . . he's my uncle. I heard he was here and I was hoping to hear him."

The woman pulled a piece of paper from a drawer, scribbled on it, and then handed it to Rosa. "He's in Colorado last I heard. With the band. Playing at this club." She handed the paper across the desk.

Rosa looked at the name of the club the woman gave her, went home, searched for it on the internet, and then made a call. Yes, the band was playing there, she was told. A week later, Rosa flew to Denver, checked into a hotel, and then took a cab to the club.

He didn't recognize her, of course. She sat alone at a table positioned as close to the bandstand as possible. He noticed her at once. Winked at her. It gave her the creeps at first, but then she realized his thinking she was a pickup would at least bring him to her table when he took a break. Sure enough, it did. He brought a glass filled with ice and Hennessey, if Rosa had to guess.

"Can I get you a refill of your drink?" he asked her.

Rosa looked down at the cola she'd been nursing. "No, thank you." Rosa blinked at the stranger who was her father. "How have you been, Hector?"

The man's handsomely etched face showed puzzlement. He sat in the chair next to hers. "Do I know you? Forgive me; I meet so many people . . ."

"I'm your daughter, Hector. I'm Rosa."

He deflated against the back of his seat. "Rosa . . ." Then he straightened. "What are you—here for your mother? Does she want money, is that it?" He leaned over the table. The smell of cognac was fierce on his breath. "Or does she want her old lover back?"

Rosa was repulsed, and she felt her composure spilling from her veins. "Of course not."

"Well, you can tell her for me that I'm married again. And this wife doesn't question my role as her husband like she did." He ran the L of his thumb and index finger from his thick moustache, over his mouth, and then cupped his chin. "But you are a pretty one. Pretty as she was . . ."

Rosa felt a frown sketch across her face, from her eyes to her lips. "I just wanted to meet you."

"Ah, well. Now you have. How long are you in town for? You have two brothers and a sister, you know."

Rosa blinked. "I do? I'd often wondered."

"Well, now you know. I'm off tomorrow night. If you'd like, you can come to the apartment. Meet my wife and the kids."

"How old are . . . how old are my brothers and sister?"

"Gabriel is fourteen. Mina is twelve. And Manny is eight."

"Manny . . . my husband's name is Manny."

He looked at her hands then. "So I see. And? Am I a grandfather?"

"Yes, you are. I have three sons."

They were quiet in the midst of the club patron's chatter until Hector said, "So, I suppose you'll want a relationship with me now, huh? After all these years?"

Rosa shook her head. "I never had a relationship with you before; why would I expect one now?"

He shrugged. "Now that you are an adult and your mother is out of the way, I think I would like to get to know you better."

There was something disgusting about the way he spoke

to her. "We'll see," she said. "I would, however, like to get to know my siblings."

"Where are you staying?" he asked. "I'll pick you up tomorrow afternoon."

Rosa shook her head. "That's okay. Give me your address and I'll take a cab."

Hector looked at his watch. "Suit yourself. I gotta get back to work. Stick around and I'll write it down for you."

Rosa nodded.

That night—and for weeks afterward—Rosa cried herself to sleep. What had she expected to find, she wondered. Tía Ariela was right; Hector Rivera was a snake.

And he was her father.

32

"I feel like I'm living in a bad Hallmark movie," I said to Patsy the following morning over coffee. I'd also joined her for a Bible study, a first for us.

"Pshaw," Patsy said, throwing her hand into the air from her place at the kitchen table. "I love Hallmark movies."

"I do too," I said, "but I said a *bad* Hallmark movie."

Patsy shook her delicate head. "I've yet to see one of those."

I laughed in spite of my desire to make a point. "All right. You win."

"So, what's on the agenda for today then, Miss Hallmark?"

"I'm going to see Rosa. I'm going to confront her."

"That's the biblical thing to do." The elderly woman rested her elbow on the table and the side of her face in the palm of her hand. The wrinkles there intensified. "But you have to pepper your words with salt."

I smiled at her. "Cute, Patsy."

She straightened. "I can be." She pointed her finger at me as she seemed so oft to do. "But I want you to listen to me, now. I'm older and I'm wiser and the Word of God tells us old wise women that we're supposed to help you young chicks out." Her Bible rested beside her coffee mug. She placed her hand on it and patted.

I didn't know whether to laugh or take notes. "I'm listening."

"No one—not even Rosa—acts the way she does, the way she has, for no reason. Rosa has a hurt. Maybe many hurts. Deep down." She pointed to her heart. "It goes to the core of her and makes her act in ways we find displeasing." She looked away from me for a moment, then returned her gentle eyes to mine. "Eliana said that Rosa was a handful when she was growing up. Not a bad kid, just a handful."

"I'd say that's an accurate statement."

"She said that when Rosa married Manny, she settled down. She was a good wife. A dedicated mother to her sons. She worked hard to build her business and to have a solid home for her family."

My heart frowned. This was the part of Rosa I didn't know. I'd been so hurt my senior year of high school; I'd drawn inward. I'd gone to college to escape my feelings and had met Charlie. Then I made him my world. Him and the boys. I'd not made time for old friendships, especially those here in Cedar Key. "But?"

"I won't repeat everything Eliana told me, only to say that, one time, Rosa went in search of her father." She shook her head. "He was not a very nice man, I don't think."

"Dad has told me a story or two. And, no, he wasn't."

A look I cannot describe swept across Patsy's face. Sadness. Empathy, perhaps. "All I know is, she found him. Eliana said after that, Rosa was never really the same. She allowed her heart to turn to stone, Kimberly. And that is never a good thing."

I sighed. "I know. Sometimes I think . . . maybe I've done

the same thing." I wrapped my hands around the coffee mug, leaned back in my chair, and crossed my legs. "It's easier than allowing the pain to take over."

Patsy shook her head. "It's only easier for a short while. Eventually, if love doesn't pierce through, the heart will die." She pointed to her heart again. "I know."

I took a sip of coffee. "So what do I do, Patsy?"

"See Rosa as God sees her. Reaching the goodness inside her may not come today, but it will come." She patted the Bible again. "Mark the words of an old woman and this book. It will come."

I arrived at Rosa's business a little before 11:00. Her secretary told me she wasn't there, that she was at a new house they were placing on the market.

I crossed my arms and tried to look sure of myself. "Where?"

"I don't think she'd like it very much if you just show up there."

"Oh," I said. I walked over to the sofa across the room, sat, and said, "Then I'll wait." I reached into my purse and pulled out the book of Dad's I'd started reading on Saturday. I'd brought it along just in case.

"It could be a while." The tone of Rosa's secretary— Lannie, according to her nameplate—told me she could be as stubborn as I. But if I were going to adopt a bad attitude this early in the game, I'd be on the wrong path for sure by the time Rosa returned.

I smiled. "That's fine," I said. "I'll just read while I wait."

Which is exactly what I did for several minutes. Lannie continued to work—doing whatever it is she does—until I heard her sigh. I looked up. She extended a piece of paper to me. "Here. This is the address where she's at. She's there to get the particulars and to take some photos for uploading into the website later on."

I closed the book, crossed the room, and took the offered paper. "Thank you," I said.

I recognized the general location of the house. And with the island being so small, it didn't take me long to drive there. Rosa's BMW was parked out front; she was walking on the short walkway from the front door to the street, a camera in her hand. I stopped and exited my car quickly. "Rosa," I called out.

It was then she noticed me. She stopped, planted bright yellow high-heeled sandals—a nice complement to her festive halter dress—firmly together. "Oh. It's you."

"I'd like to talk to you, if I may." I slipped the strap of my purse over my left shoulder and then tucked my hands into the pockets of my Bermuda shorts. I knew enough about body language to know not to cross my arms as though ready for battle.

"Are you here to buy a house?"

I looked at the white Cracker house. The tin roof reflected the sun's light; hanging baskets and birdhouses swung in the breeze from their chains along the wraparound porch. "It's a cute little thing."

"It's two hundred grand," she said, matter of fact. "How's that for 'cute'?"

I stopped short. "Wow," I said. "I guess business *is* good." I wondered how much Steven's new house was going to cost him. It was two and a half times the size of this small-framed house.

She half-turned toward the house. "Do you want to go inside? I just turned the air off and it's too hot out here to carry on a decent conversation. Not that I think you want to talk out in the open anyway."

I shook my head. "No, I don't. And, yes, I'd like to go inside."

Unlike the house Steven and I looked at the evening before, this was still furnished, a fact I made note of.

"It's for rent, fully furnished, or for sale, with or without," Rosa said. She dropped the camera and her briefcase on a small table just inside the front door while I sat in one of the worn armchairs across the room. "I take it we're sitting," she said before planting herself on the sofa.

"Rosa," I began, keeping my voice low and calm. My eyes met hers; they reminded me of shimmering black coal. "Why did you lie to me?"

She smirked. "So he told you it was all a lie, huh?"

"No." I tilted my chin. "He told me about the two of you back when we were in high school." I didn't reveal that he'd flatly denied having come on to her. There was no need. My desire wasn't to spur another round of fabrications and fantasies. Having spoken to Patsy and wanting to take her advice, it was simply to reach out to my old friend. To offer an olive branch and hope it was accepted.

Rosa crossed her legs. "Did he tell you how we used to make love on Atsena Otie where no one could see us?"

I took a deep breath through my nostrils, then released it the same way. "He told me."

She blinked several times, defused. "Oh," she said.

I decided to cross my legs too. My brown BareTraps shoe slipped nearly off my foot, and I wiggled it to get the shoe back on. "Rosa, I'm not here to swap stories or to talk details. I just want to know why you thought it necessary to destroy the relationship I have again with Steven." When she didn't answer, I said, "I mean, aren't you happy, Rosa? Happy with your husband? Your children? Your life?"

Her jaw flexed; perhaps I'd gone too far. "I'm very happy."

I uncrossed my legs, placed my feet side by side on the floor, and rested my elbows on my knees. "I know. But, Rosa . . . don't I deserve to be happy too?"

She threw her head back and crossed her arms. "You? You've had everything your whole life. If you couldn't find happiness, then you had a problem, not me."

"Rosa, you know nothing about me."

"I know about you." She turned her head to the right, seemed to study the table with her belongings. I wondered if she were about to bolt.

"What? Tell me what you know."

She faced me again. The shimmer in her eyes was gone, replaced by fire. "You had the best family. A home here to vacation, a home in Orlando—a fine home—unlike anything I'd ever have unless I worked myself to death to get it."

For a moment I wondered where she now lived. There were no homes quite like the one I'd grown up in—not in the same design, at least—here on the island. But there were plenty of fine homes, sprawling and with views unlike anything one could fine elsewhere in the world. "I grew up in a good home," I admitted. "But there were things . . . that made it not so perfect. Not as perfect as it seemed."

Rosa blinked. "I know, remember? Your mom's drinking."

I sat straight. "Oh, that's right."

"After your mother died, my mother told me. And then, when my mother was dying, she told me a lot more. Her fever was very high and she said things I supposed she wouldn't have otherwise said."

Whirring passed in and out of my ears. "Like?"

Rosa shook her head. "Nothing I want to talk about now."

My heart beat faster than it should. I had to gain control of the situation again, I told myself. I took several deep breaths, exhaling them slowly. "Then you know my life wasn't . . . but what you don't know is how I was affected by Steven, initially. Charlie, eventually."

Her face softened. "I don't know anything, really, about Charlie."

I looked at the floor. "Neither do I."

"But he gave you two good sons?"

I looked up. She'd lost the anger somehow. She was Rosa, my childhood friend. My old confidante.

Before life got in the way.

"He did do that much." I shook my head. "I'm just not 100 percent sure as to why he left us. Everything we'd built together."

"I guess I'm blessed," she said. "Manny thinks I hung the moon."

I felt my eyes burn with threatening tears. "That's all I ever wanted, you know. And I thought I had it . . . in Charlie, at least. Now . . ." I shook my head ever so slowly. "Now . . ."

"What?"

I shook my head, unsure as to whether or not to be real with Rosa, to be honest even with myself. But, in spite of my trepidations, I finished my thoughts with her. "I'm left with the feeling that I never really measured up as a woman to any man." I swept the tears from my cheeks with the fingertips of both hands.

"Until now," she said. "With Steven."

I nodded.

She remained quiet. Outside the wind whipped around

the house. I glanced past the front door windowpanes; it was going to rain again soon, as it had the night before. It was that time of year. The usual din of birds calling to one another had ceased; they were seeking shelter already.

"Kimberly." Rosa broke the near silence. "I never slept with Steven Granger."

"I know."

"Not that I didn't make things very difficult for him back then."

"I know that too."

The wind grew stronger.

"We'll be stuck here if we don't leave now," she said, standing. She turned to look out the same windows as I had a moment before and crossed her arms.

I smiled at her back. "Would that be so horrible?"

She looked over her shoulder and grinned. "I wonder what we could get into here?"

I stood. "We could pretend we were in college and this was our own house that my father rented for us to live in . . ."

Her smile faded. "I remember . . . that was one of our plans, wasn't it?"

I'd forgotten, but . . . "Yes, it was. One of many."

She turned to face me. "Do you remember those things we used to play with as kids? You'd draw on them and then shake them and everything would disappear?"

"An Etch A Sketch?"

"Yes. An Etch A Sketch." She picked up her briefcase and camera. "Sometimes I wish life were like one of those." Her fingers gripped the body of the Canon, one I recognized as being top of the line.

I reached for my purse. "Just shake and start over."

When I looked up, her hand was extended toward me.

"Shake and start over?" she asked. Her usually steady voice quivered.

I took her hand. It was warm and soft. "Shake and start over."

It wouldn't necessarily be easy, I thought as we ran toward our cars in the sprinkle of large raindrops. But it was, at least, doable.

33

I couldn't wait to tell Steven about my time with Rosa. On the way home, driving through the downpour, I wondered if he'd been out on the boat when the storm hit or if he'd been cautious and not gone out.

I also couldn't wait to tell Patsy.

But when I arrived home, I had a very wet dog to contend with. Even from the road, I could see Max's golden fur, slick and plastered to his body. I didn't know whether to laugh or grieve.

I pulled my umbrella from the side pocket of my car door, opened it as I stepped outside, and called out, "Oh, Maxie!"

Max ran in circles under the overhang at the door.

I slipped inside the door, forcing Max to stay outside for a little while longer. "Let me get some towels," I said to him.

He barked in reply.

I pulled old towels from the back of the linen closet just as my cell phone rang. I ignored it long enough to get Max dried off and then to let him come inside, smelling just rotten. "You, sir, get a bath today."

He looked at me as if to say, "I just had a shower." Either that or, "Feed me, woman."

I poured a large bowl of food for him, freshened the water in his bowl, and went in search of my purse to retrieve my phone. I found it in one of the living room chairs.

I missed a call from Charlie.

My heart fell. Why would Charlie call me when the boys were with him, unless there'd been an accident? I pressed my thumb pad against the send button. Charlie answered with his usual, "Hey, Kim."

"What's wrong?"

He sighed. "Is that the way you're going to begin every conversation we have from now until the boys are grown?"

I wasn't in the mood to quibble. "Why would you be calling me, Charlie, if something wasn't wrong?"

A light chuckle, followed by, "I got a phone call from your dad. He said that he and Anise are going to Atlanta this weekend for Ami's opening night and wanted to know if they could take the boys. It's fine with me, but I wanted to clear it with you."

I sat on the arm of the chair and closed my eyes. "Say that again."

Another chuckle. "You heard me."

"I heard you, yes, but I can't imagine you wanting to give up . . ." My words faltered. Of course. A weekend without the boys meant a weekend with the girl of his choice.

"I know what you're thinking. And, no, that has nothing to do with it. Not that I won't make the most of my time with them away—as I'm sure you are—but I'm just trying to be a nice guy here. After all, I divorced you, not your family."

My body slid into the chair. I hit my head against the buoy

336

lamp on the nearby end table. I felt it rock behind me. I turned just in time to watch it crash to the floor.

"What was that?" he asked.

I sighed. "Nothing a hundred dollars won't replace."

"Oh. So . . . okay with you, then?"

I righted myself in the chair. "What's this going to cost me, Charlie? Another week away from my sons? Three days?"

"Kim, I'm not in this for anything other than that the boys can spend time with their grandparents and their Aunt Ami. I know ballet isn't their thing, but they love going to Atlanta, and your dad has promised a lot of fun things while they're there."

"Well, okay then. If it's okay with you, it's certainly fine by me."

A final chuckle came through the line before he said, "See? We *can* get along when we want to."

"Good-bye, Charlie."

"Good-bye, Miss Boo."

I frowned as I ended the call, stood, and surveyed the damage behind me. The lamp was made from an authentic Maine lobster buoy hand-painted in blue, yellow, and white. Fortunately I'd been with Anise when she'd ordered it online and could remember the name of the website. After I'd picked up the pieces and dropped them into a garbage bag, I called Patsy to see how she was weathering the storm and to tell her about my two interesting encounters that day.

"Do you see," she said, "how when we begin our day at God's feet, he takes care of the rest?"

"I've begun a lot of days at God's feet, Patsy, but I've never experienced anything quite like this."

"Then his name be praised."

"Amen to that." I looked toward the front door where the

trash bag of broken pieces waited for the weather to clear. "Patsy, when the rain stops, do you mind if I come over? I need to order a lamp like I broke today."

"Of course you may," she said. "And while you are here, we'll have some hot tea to warm our bones."

"Sounds good, Patsy. Sounds real good."

Steven was as surprised as I over my conversations with Rosa and Charlie.

"Makes me wonder when the sky will fall," I said.

We stood just inside the front door of the house, his arms around my waist and mine around his shoulders. He laughed; the scent of his Doublemint gum reached my face, and I inhaled deeply. "I'll tell you when," he said. "It was about 1:00 this afternoon."

"Ohhh, did you get caught in it?"

"I'd say. There wasn't anything in the weather reports about it. It got pretty scary out there."

I drew closer to him, squeezing him as tightly as I dared. "I'm glad you're safe now," I said.

He nuzzled my neck. "It's nice to have someone who cares."

I drew back. "Where are you taking me this evening?" I asked.

"It's a surprise," he said.

I stepped back. "Am I dressed all right?" I wore linen sailor wide-leg slacks with anchor-shaped buttons and a ribbed red and white striped sleeveless top. "You're perfect," he said. "As always."

The rest of the week was uneventful. I spent my days relaxing at home or at Patsy's and with occasional shopping on the island. Patsy set up a Facebook page for me;

I "friended" my sons, Heather's kids, and Monica, my ex-sister-in-law.

On Friday midmorning I received a text from Chase telling me that his grandfather had asked them how they felt about my new "friend," meaning Steven.

I was folding clothes, fresh and warm from the dryer, when the message came. I dropped the towel I'd been folding into a heap on the dining room table to read the incoming message. I texted back.

WHAT DID CODY SAY?

A few seconds later:

HE'S UPSET. I GUESS POP DDNT KNOW U HVNT TOLD HM YET.

No, he didn't. And no, I hadn't. Of my two children, Cody would take the notion of his mother in another man's arms much harder.

TELL HM I'LL CALL L8R

I was practically nauseous by the time a call came from Dad. I cancelled my date with Steven, telling him I had a headache—and I did—and that I needed to rest. When Dad's call came, I was lying on my bed, Max at my side, snoring. At the ring, his head jerked up; he looked around and promptly went back to sleep.

My father's first words were those of apology; I told him not to worry about it. "He had to find out sooner or later."

He put Cody on the phone, who sniffled a lot and said, "Does this mean we're gonna move?"

"I don't know what it means, son," I told him as honestly and as calmly as I knew how. "I only know that I have feelings for someone who has feelings for me too."

"You mean love," he spat. "Ugh!"

I rolled over onto my side. "Cody? Don't you want me to be happy?"

"I want you and Dad to be happy. Together. Like you used to be."

"I know. I know you do. And if it were possible, I'd fight for it. You know that, right?"

"Then why don't you? All you have to do is go to the beach with him and spend some time alone together."

I rolled to my back and laid my arm over my forehead, which was throbbing. "Cody, don't you think if that would work, he and I would have tried it?"

"You never did. You never tried."

I heard Chase's voice from near his brother. "Shut up, Cody. You don't know what you're talking about."

"I do too know! I've been talking to Dad and I know stuff."

Then my dad's soothing voice said, "Cody, give your mother some credit."

"Oh, Code," I said. "Listen, sweetheart. After the 4th of July, you and Pop and Nana and Chase will join me here at the beach house. You'll meet Steven, and I hope you'll give him at least half a chance." When he said nothing, I added, "I think you'll like him. He's got a boat and . . ." I swallowed. "He's buying a big house that has a dock and a place for cleaning fish. You'd like to go out fishing, right?"

"Not with him."

I hadn't expected this. Not to this degree, at least. Just what *had* Charlie been talking to him about? I took a deep breath. "Okay, Cody."

340

"Does that mean you'll stop seeing this guy?" The brightness in his voice never sounded so dark.

"No," I said. "I don't know what you and Dad have been talking about, and now is not the time to discuss it. But, what I'm saying to you now is that I'm going to let you work your way through this. Without trying to convince you this early in the game. Deal?"

"I won't leave Orlando. I'll live with Dad!"

My heart . . . The air went out from me; I was grateful to be lying down. I pressed my lips together. "No, you won't," I said, trying not to grit my teeth. "You don't get that option, Cody."

"You wait and see. I will."

"Cody, I'm going to end this call now. I want you to have a good time this weekend and try not to think about all this, okay? It'll work itself out. I promise." When he didn't answer, I said, "Code?"

"I'm here. And I'll have a good time, but I won't enjoy it."

I almost laughed out loud. "You do that, son, and I'll talk to you tomorrow. Give Aunt Ami my love."

"Whatever," he said, and disconnected the call.

I should have called him back and scolded him. I should have laid out his punishment when he got home, but I couldn't bring myself to do it. My heartache was too great at that moment. For a few days I'd managed to live carefree and like a woman in love. But now, I stared into a glass darkly. For now, my dreams were on hold.

————

Saturday morning with Patsy was spent in lament over my phone call the night before. Patsy said exactly what I expected her to say. "Pray about it," she said, "and God will take care of it in his time and in his way."

341

"Patsy, didn't you ever worry about anything in life?" I asked.

She laughed. "Oh, dear. If you only knew my life story."

"But that's for another time," I concluded for her.

She looked at me with a twinkle in her eyes. "Yes, indeed, it shall be."

Steven had planned that on Saturday evening we'd spend a little time with his parents—whom I hadn't seen in years—before he took me out to dinner. My inclination was to postpone for another evening; I feared the worry on my face might concern his mother.

"How are you feeling this evening? Better than last night?" he asked when we were on the way.

I nodded. "I'm fine."

He reached for my hand and held it in his own. "You sure? You seem a little . . . preoccupied."

My smile was weak, I knew. "I'm okay. Really. Don't worry." I peered out to the narrow winding road, down which his parents' house nestled behind one of the many split-rail fences and between the foliage near the water's edge.

"If you're sure . . ."

"I'm sure."

After a few moments he asked, "Have I done something to upset you?" which only made me laugh.

"No," I said. I drew the hand holding mine to my lips and kissed the knuckles. "You've done not a thing wrong."

Steven's mother looked exactly as I remembered her, only much older. His father's face and body showed sure signs of his recent illness. It broke my heart to think of Dad ever being in that kind of shape one day.

Steven and I visited his parents for nearly an hour. Mrs. Granger spoke with excitement about seeing Eliza the following month, and when she did, Mr. Granger's expression became more jovial. Before we left, Mrs. Granger gave me several jars of her homemade preserves and home-canned vegetables. "You can't get food like this from a store-bought can," she said.

"You're exactly right there, Mrs. Granger," I said.

She kissed me on the cheek as Steven opened the old, rattling front door and said, "Thank you for bringing a little joy back into his life."

I smiled and hoped my angst didn't show.

From the house to that night's restaurant choice, I thought of all the things that could go wrong now that Cody had made his objections known. I could force things, I knew, but what kind of relationships would we all have then? I could make it happen and pray for some sort of breakthrough. But what if it never came? More than anything, I was torn between allowing my son to call the shots in my life and standing my ground as the adult in our relationship.

During dinner Steven told me his offer on the house had been accepted.

"Oh, Steven, that's wonderful," I said. I reached over the pink-linen tablecloth and took his hands. "When will you move in?"

"I sign the papers in a few days, and I'll start moving in on the first. My rent is paid up until then so . . ." He shrugged.

"Have you called Rosa already? To tell her?"

He nodded. "She was a little miffed that I didn't buy through her."

I winced. "I bet."

"But I explained that I started looking before you and she had your talk, that I was still a little unnerved around her."

Our fingers intertwined and danced with each other. "Dinner was delicious as always," I said.

"You can't beat Cedar Key for good food."

"What are we doing next?"

"First of all, no dessert for you. I want to take you back to the house," he said. I must have looked puzzled because he added, "There's something I want to show you."

I nodded an okay; ten minutes later, we left.

Steven had somehow—once again—managed to snag the key before the sale of the house was complete. "Dessert is being served in the Florida room," he said. "Go sit. I'll serve."

The wicker chairs were still there. I sat in one and waited until he came in, carrying a large silver tray with two champagne glasses half-filled with something bubbly and a crystal bowl of chocolate-dipped strawberries.

"What are we drinking, Steven Granger?" I asked.

"Mom made it for us. It's a nonalcoholic champagne punch." He lowered the tray; I took a glass with one hand and a berry with the other. He placed the tray on the wicker table between the chairs, then picked up the remaining glass. He raised it and said, "To the most beautiful woman I've ever had the chance to love, not once but twice in my life."

"Oh, Steven, that was beautiful," I whispered. We both took a sip. "Delicious," I said.

"Try it with the berry."

I did. It was even better. We nibbled on berries and sipped on punch and talked about what he hoped to do with the house. He asked for my thoughts and ideas on each room. "What about the bonus room?" he asked.

"I thought you wanted to use it as an office."

He placed his fluted glass on the tray and said, "I do, but . . ." He stood and extended a hand to me.

I took his hand; he led me to the bonus room. "Where would you suggest I put my desk?" he asked.

"I don't know. How big is it?"

"It's an executive desk—single pedestal—so, it's about five and a half feet in width and I'd say about two and a half feet in depth."

I pointed to the only windowless wall wide enough for such a piece of furniture. "Then I'd say over here."

"But what if I wanted to have it in front of the windows? You know, so I could look out over the marsh."

I looked at him. "And what if we have a blowing storm like we did the other day and the water leaked through and got everything wet?"

He moved around me until he was behind me. His arms slid around my waist and his lips whispered near my ear, "But what if I want to look at the marsh?"

My skin turned to gooseflesh. "Steven . . ."

"Come on," he said, slowly walking me over to the window, keeping step behind me. "Look at how beautiful it is."

The windows were covered in dark plantation shutters, four sets—two on top and two on bottom—over one wide window and then duplicated over the second window beside it. When we reached them, he reached around me and pulled open one of the top panels. "See?" he said. "Isn't this quite a view?"

"Steven . . ." I felt my legs turn to rubber. Placed on the sill, pointed directly at me, was an exquisite ring—a large radiant-cut yellow diamond flanked by two half-moon white diamonds.

The fingers of his right hand gingerly picked up the ring as his left hand brought mine toward the fading light from the window. I felt him slip it over my ring finger; it was cold and heavy. He turned me toward him, his hands cupped my face, and he kissed me ever so sweetly. "Kimberly Claybourne," he spoke against my lips. "I want you to marry me. Please say yes."

"Oh, Steven, I . . ."

His lips nuzzled my chin, my jaw line, my ear. "I know. It's so soon. But I've waited a very long time to find what I know in my heart is right. I'm not asking you to marry me tomorrow." He drew back; his eyes looked directly into mine. "I know we need to allow your boys to grow to love me as I know I'm going to love them. Time for us to be a family. I know we need time to work out all the details. I know."

"I know that too."

"And all that's fine. Until then, I just want to know that you'll marry me, one day, when you and they are ready."

Was Patsy right? I wondered. Was this the beginning of God taking care of my problems? Of me, without me at the helm? Could he possibly be at work so soon? "Well, why not?" I heard the elderly lady say, and I smiled at the notion. "He works in mysterious ways; he clearly does."

So I nodded. "Yes, Steven Granger." I nodded again. "Yes, I'll marry you . . . one day."

34

I told Steven that I wouldn't wear the ring until my sons had met him, and he agreed. Until then, it would stay with Steven.

I also had no choice but to wait to tell Heather. She was my best friend—not just my sister—and yet I couldn't share one of the most important moments in my life with her.

Jayme-Leigh and I had never been particularly close, but I decided to call and tell her, hoping perhaps it would bridge part of the gap. She mumbled "hello" into the phone followed quickly by, "Dr. Claybourne." Though Jayme-Leigh was married, she continued to practice by her maiden name.

"Jayme-Leigh, it's me, Kim."

"What's wrong? Is it Dad?" Her voice cleared remarkably fast.

"Dad? No, why would you ask that?"

"Oh. Wait." There were several moments of silence followed by mumbling and finally "Hey. I'm back."

"I'm sorry if I scared you. Or woke you."

"It's okay. I just . . . you never call unless something is wrong."

That wasn't true—exactly—but I didn't want to start my

news with an argument. "I have something to tell you, though. Something personal, and this time it's good news."

She cleared her throat. "Okay. I'm listening."

"Do you remember Steven Granger?"

"Yeah, of course I do. Dad already told me you're seeing him again."

"More than seeing him . . ."

"Don't tell me you're going steady or something equally as juvenile."

"Um, no. We are, however, engaged. Unofficially . . . but engaged."

I heard my sister's breath catch in her throat. "Wow. Let me see if I've got this straight. You've been gone, what? Not quite two weeks? And you're engaged?"

Though it was well past 8:00 on a Sunday morning, I lay in my bed still, flat on my back. I threw my arm over my eyes at the retort and sighed. "I know. It's fast. But we're not getting married right away. We know we need to wait a while, I want the boys to meet him and him the boys, I need to meet his daughter, and . . . Jayme-Leigh, I love him." I giggled like a schoolgirl. "I *love* him. And he loves me and . . . it just feels right."

"And there you have it, ladies and gentlemen. Fools rushing in. Where *is* Ricky Nelson when you need a theme song?"

My sweet, wonderful, intelligent, overanalytical sister. Mother of none, wife of Dr. Isaac Levy. I sat up, pushed the pillows against the headboard, and crossed my ankles. With my arms draped over my knees I said, "Shall I remind you of the stink you caused when you fell in love with Isaac and decided to get married under a *chuppah*?"

"I should have known you'd go there."

I hung my head. "I'm sorry. But, just remember that we

gave—*I* gave—the two of you a chance, and look how wonderful your relationship has turned out. You *are* happy, aren't
you? I mean, in your academic sort of way?" And in spite
of your lack of faith on both levels, I thought, but decided
not to go there.

"Yes. Very much so. In our academic sort of way."

"So then be happy for me."

She pondered the idea but eventually said, "Okay, Kimberly.
Just don't rush anything."

"We aren't. We know we've got a lot to take care of first."

"Will you come back here to teach school after the summer?"

"I haven't really decided that yet. Maybe for another year.
Then come here on the weekends to see Steven. I don't expect
we'll marry before next year anyway."

"It's going to be a long year, you know."

"I know. In more ways than one. But, we've waited this
long to find each other again, I'm sure we can make it another year."

"What do you think Charlie will have to say about all this?"

I shrugged. "What can he say? He divorced me. There's
nothing he can say or do to control my life."

———

Steven and I met at church—Patsy was there this week.
Both she and Maddie sat with us—and then Steven took the
four of us out to lunch at Anne's Other Place on Dock Street.
We sat at a table out on the deck and under an umbrella.
While Steven entertained me with his plans for our evening,
Patsy and Maddie watched the pelicans line up along the
long pier and the recreational boaters already heading out
into the Gulf. When I told him I'd made my decision and
please let's drop it, we ate in relative silence the remainder
of the meal.

Not ten minutes after I arrived back at the house, my phone rang.

Charlie.

"Hello, Charlie," I answered.

"I received some very interesting news from my youngest son this morning."

It couldn't have been that I was engaged; I'd not told Dad yet and I certainly didn't want the boys to know. Unless Jayme-Leigh . . . "What's that?"

"He tells me you're seeing someone in Cedar Key. That boy from high school you told me about one time."

I walked over to the sliding glass doors off from the living room, pushed them open, and stared out at the marsh. The day was unusually cool so far, and I planned to enjoy the low heat and humidity as long as I could. "First of all, Charlie, he's not a boy. He's a grown man now. And secondly, what's it to you if I'm dating someone? After all, you've been dating *a lot* of someones, have you not?"

"But I don't intend to get serious. I know you, Kim Tucker. You aren't the date-and-see kind of woman."

You don't know me . . .

"Again, I hardly see that this is any of your business."

"It most assuredly is my business. Do you plan to have him around my sons after they leave here?"

"Of course I do." I leaned against the door frame, crossed one leg over the other, and pointed my toe against the floor. The sweet smell of marsh and summer wafted toward me. Out in the distance, an airboat raced across the surface of the water.

"I want his name, social, anything and everything to do some background."

I nearly dropped the phone. "Don't be ridiculous, Charlie.

I'll give you no such thing. Whatever you need to know about Steven, I'll tell you, but you're not about to do a background check on him."

"Steven . . . what was his last name again?"

I stood straight. "Don't be idiotic, Charlie. I'm certainly not. You'll just have to trust that I'd never allow my sons around anyone who might hurt them."

"Let me make something very clear to you, Kim. *Very* clear. If you get the dim-witted notion of marrying this guy and moving my sons across the state, you've got another thing coming."

"What does that—"

"What that means is very simply that the state of Florida has a law against such things. It states that the custodial parent may not relocate more than fifty miles from the noncustodial parent after a divorce. So you just date all you want. But any thoughts of marriage and moving will have to be put off until *after* my sons are grown. Unless, of course, you send them to live with me. Then I don't care who you marry or where you go."

I could hardly find the sofa so I could sit. Tears stung my eyes; I refused to let them fall. My chest hurt and my mind whirled. "I don't understand . . . how . . . or why . . . you are so mean to me, Charlie. What did I ever do . . . to make you . . . hate me so?"

"I don't hate you, Kim. You're the mother of my children. I just couldn't live with you. But that doesn't mean I'm going to allow some other man to raise my sons."

Rear! Rear! You raise *cattle, Charlie Tucker!*

"I'd never, *ever* leave my sons," I cried instead, then threw the phone across the room. It hit the wall with a thud; the battery popped out of the back, slid out the door, across the balcony, and dropped over the edge to the grass below.

I had to pull the phone battery out of Max's mouth. Thankfully, he hadn't bitten down on it. I dried it on a towel in the kitchen, then set it on the table and prayed for full recovery of power. Otherwise, I'd find myself driving across the bridges to get a replacement.

While I waited to see what the damages would be, I walked over to Patsy's, thanking God for her along the way.

"I need to borrow your computer," I said.

"Oh? Want to Facebook a little?" She stepped back and I walked over the threshold.

"No. I need to look up a Florida law."

"Oh, dear." Patsy closed the door behind me. "Sounds ominous."

I nodded. "It is. Charlie says I can't move the boys here if . . . when . . . Steven and I marry."

Patsy tsk-tsked as we walked to the computer, which was booted up and displaying a game of online Scrabble. "I play with my great-granddaughter," she said. "Here, let me tell her I'll have to get back to her."

"Oh, I can wait."

"Don't be silly. You're obviously disturbed by this, and we're just having fun."

Patsy typed a few words then x'd out of the game. After she rose from the chair, I took her place. It felt warm beneath me.

"I'm going to go make a fresh pitcher of sweet iced tea, how does that sound?"

I looked over my shoulder at her. "Marvelous."

She gave my other shoulder a pat and said, "Just take your time."

I didn't know where to begin. Charlie had been specific when he'd said "relocation," so I started there by typing "relocation laws in Florida" into the search engine. Pages of links came up; I clicked on the one that seemed to have the information I needed.

Patsy came up behind me. Her arm rested against my shoulders. "How's it going?"

"It says here that under a new law in the state of Florida, a custodial parent cannot move more than fifty miles from the noncustodial without following strict procedures."

"So, it's not impossible?"

I shook my head. "But it is improbable. I'd have to get Charlie to agree in order to move our sons here."

Patsy leaned over and pointed to a paragraph on the page. "Or, file a Notice of Intent to Relocate with the court and hope a judge sees it your way."

I looked up at her wise face. "What are the chances of that happening? I won't even begin to go into what happened when I brought it to the G.M.'s attention that Charlie spends more of his visitation time with women and whiskey than his children."

Patsy patted my shoulder. "Come drink your tea. It's about ready."

I rose from the chair and followed her into the kitchen. Together we prepared the tea while I continued in my lament, telling her how hopeless I felt at that moment.

We went out to her balcony, sat on the Adirondacks, and together we gazed out over the marsh. "Tell you what I'd do if I were you . . ."

"What? Please tell me, Patsy. Advise me."

"Clearly, the first thing I'd do is I'd go talk to my sweetheart. In your case, Steven. Then, I'd either call or go see my attorney and see just what my options are. Legally, you know." She nodded once. "You don't really know what you're up against until you talk to someone with a little more knowledge about the law."

I sipped my tea slowly; the sugary nectar of it slid down my throat icy cold and delicious. "You're right," I said finally. "I'll talk to Steven tonight." I looked at Patsy. "He's cooking for me—grilling, I believe he said—at his place."

Patsy's eyes narrowed. "You behave over there, now."

I laughed out loud; it felt good. "Oh, Patsy. I promise you." I raised my right hand. "We're behaving."

"It's not easy."

"No, ma'am, it's not."

"But, it's doable."

"It is."

"I know." She gave me a firm look. "I was young and in love once, you know."

"I bet you and Gilbert were something else."

Patsy looked away toward the horizon. "Gilbert was. That man was something else."

I rested the tea glass on the arm of my chair. "Tell me all about him, Patsy. Tell me about this man you loved so much."

Her head lolled back and she closed her eyes as though in the sweetest of dreams. "I remember the day we met as if it were yesterday," she began. "It was the same day my mother put me on a bus headed for Trinity . . ."

For the remainder of the afternoon I listened as she told her story. It was one I would not soon forget.

———

I told Steven that evening as we sat in folding lawn chairs perched on his front porch, waiting for the sun to set and sipping on iced decaf hazelnut coffee. With Steven's camera resting in my lap, I told him—as kindly as I knew how—how Cody had reacted and how Charlie had behaved.

354

Or maybe it was the other way around.

I could see the pain etch its way across his face at the news about Cody but a resolve when I told him about Charlie. "I'm not nearly as worried about that," he said.

"But, Steven, don't you understand? There's a law. I won't be able to move here, and your job, your family, your ill father—your new house—is here. What will we do? See each other on weekends until Cody turns eighteen or Charlie decides to stop being a jerk?"

Steven took my left hand in his. "Look at that sunset," he said.

He diverted my attention from his handsome face, bathed in the afternoon colors, to the source.

"There is a song of Asaph in the Bible—Psalm 74 to be exact—and it says, 'But you, O God, are my king from of old; you bring salvation upon the earth. It was you who split open the sea by your power; you broke the heads of the monster in the waters. It was you who crushed the heads of Leviathan and gave him as food to the creatures of the desert. It was you who opened up springs and streams; you dried up the ever flowing rivers. The day is yours, and yours also the night; you established the sun and moon. It was you who set all the boundaries of the earth; you made both summer and winter.' I think about that psalm a lot, especially when I'm watching such a sunset as this one."

I had turned my view away from the horizon and back to him, and so I looked out again. The sun had set some time ago, but its orange and gold reflection hovered along the skyline. The water had turned gray-blue and had receded enough that locals and tourists walked along the rippled bed of the Gulf.

"See that blue heron over there, the one perched at the end of the pier?"

"Mmmhmm."

"What do you think he's thinking about right now?" When I didn't answer, he responded to his own question. "He's worried about his children . . . no. He's worried about tomorrow's food supply. Nooooo . . . He's thinking, 'Who are all these people and when will they leave my stomping grounds?'"

We laughed together.

"I get your point."

"He knows who is in control, Kimberly, and it's not him." He squeezed my hand again. "And it's not you and it's not me. If God can take care of the sun and the moon and the waters and the Leviathan, if he can bring about salvation to the earth . . . if this day is his and this night as well, then so is tomorrow and the next day and the next." His hand released mine, and I brought it back to my lap, pressing it flat. "I love you, Boo, and quite frankly, I cannot imagine what it's like to be in Charlie's shoes. I had the privilege of raising—*rearing*—my daughter." He looked at me.

"But you were a good father."

His hand cupped my chin. "I'd be willing to bet Charlie is too. For the most part. He's just scared, that's all. The good Lord knows I know what that feels like."

I pulled my chin from his fingertips. "I'm going to Orlando first thing in the morning, Steven. I'm going to try to see my attorney as quickly as I can. I have to know what I'm up against."

Steven's face returned to look out at the heron. About that time, the bird lifted his wings and, with a leap, took off and soared across the water. "Do what you feel you must."

"You're angry."

"No, I'm not."

"You sound angry."

His elbow came down on the arm of his chair as he leaned toward me. "What will you do, Boo, if the answers you seek don't fall in your favor?"

I said nothing. He knew the answer as well as I. I would fall back into an old pattern. I'd take the bull by the proverbial horns and I'd somehow make it work.

And if that didn't work . . . well, then we were doomed.

35

Long before the sun rose over Cedar Key the next morning, I loaded Max into the car, purposefully leaving everything but my toiletries at the house. I then drove the long road home.

The house felt cold, in spite of the fact that I'd set the air-conditioning system to eighty-one degrees before I left. As soon as I pulled into the garage, got out of the car with Max scrambling behind me, and opened the house door, I felt as alone as I'd ever felt before.

My footsteps echoed in the house. I realized they always had. The house was large by most standards, was tiled throughout, and I'd hung very few paintings to absorb the emptiness. To make matters worse, it stood without a single male—save Max—in it. I could open the windows and hear birds chirping to one another, but the marsh and its smells and sounds would not welcome me.

Worst of all, I missed Steven already. Perhaps too much.

I fed Max, then went through the mail my neighbor had daily left for me on the island in the kitchen. Most of it was trash. There were a few bills. No good old-fashioned letters.

When I'd cleared that away I trudged up the stairs with Max behind me. "Come on, boy," I said. "Let's take a shower and make ourselves presentable."

———

I called Andre at 8:45 to tell him I was in town and to see if there was any news on my sister. "We can't see or talk to her for the first two weeks," he told me. "So, no. The only thing I know with absolute certainty is that she hasn't escaped."

If he hadn't sounded so beat, I would have laughed. "Well, that at least sounds positive."

"Yeah. And I'm holding on to every ounce of positive I've got right now."

I honestly didn't know what else to say. "If you need me, you'll call?" I asked finally.

"Yeah."

I forced a lilt into my voice. "Promise?"

"Promise."

It was 9:00 when I placed the call to my attorney's office. I told his secretary who I was and that I needed to speak with Tom as soon as possible.

"I can put a note on his desk," she said. "But he won't be in until around 10:00."

"Tell him, please, that I need to speak with him right away. It's extremely important."

Tom never called back, but his clerk did. She told me who she was and wondered if there might be something she could do to help me.

Fear and panic set in. "I'd like to come in," I said, relying on my old methods when I felt I was losing control. "If I wanted to talk about this on the phone, I would have called from Cedar Key." I stomped my foot. No. No. I wouldn't take control. I'd trust God . . .

"Okay," she responded with a mild tone of trepidation. "I'm not altogether sure what that means . . ."

"I'm sorry," I said. "I'm operating on fear right now and trying very hard not to."

A pause and then, "Let me see if I can fit you in sometime this week."

"No," I said too quickly, then breathed in. Out. "Today. Please. This won't wait until sometime this week."

"Mrs. Tucker—"

"Call me Kimberly, please. If I hear myself being called Mrs. Tucker one more time, I may scream."

"Okay," she said again. "I have a very limited amount of time at 1:30 this afternoon. But you'll have to make it quick."

"I'll be there," I said. "Thank you, thank you so much."

In the fifteen minutes I was allotted, I learned that if I decided to go to court with my petition, the judge would look at a list of facts and circumstances.

"Which include," the law clerk—a young freckle-faced woman with long strawberry blonde hair—explained, "why you are moving, how much time your sons spend now with their father and how much they'll spend after your relocation, the relationship your sons have with their father, what trained professionals will determine to be the physical, educational, and emotional effects from the move and—most notably—upon not being close to their father and whether or not the move will improve the quality of life both for you as their mother and for the children."

"What does that last part mean?" I asked.

"If you are moving because of your job, will you have great financial gain . . . are you moving for the sake of your own emotional health . . ."

"Yes."

She smiled at me. "I suppose you could say that." She took a breath. "Also, if you are seeking an opportunity for higher education . . . ?"

"No. I just want to get married and be with the man I love. Plain and simple."

She shook her head. "I'm not sure that's going to sway the judge, Mrs. . . . Kimberly."

My shoulders sank. "What are my other options, then?"

She leaned her arms onto her desk. "If I were you—and mind you, I don't know your ex-husband—I would go see him. Talk to him. Make him an offer he can't refuse, as the old saying goes."

"Like?"

"A reduction in child support, perhaps? More visitation? That will usually sway a noncustodial."

I nodded, looked at my watch, and said, "My fifteen minutes are up." I stood, extended my hand. "You've been very helpful. Thank you for seeing me on such short notice."

She laughed and said, "I'm not sure I had a choice from the sound of your voice."

I winced. "I can be a bit of a control freak," I said. "I'm sorry. Believe me, I'm working on that."

I'd left my phone in the car so as not to be disturbed. In the brief time I'd been inside the law office, I'd received three fully spelled out texts from Steven.

The first one said:

DO YOU KNOW HOW MUCH I LOVE YOU?

The second one read:

DO YOU KNOW HOW MANY TIMES THE BIBLE

REMINDS US THAT ALL THINGS ARE POSSIBLE WITH
GOD? TRUST HIM, BOO.

And the third:

I AM PRAYING FOR YOU. I LOVE AND MISS YOU SO
MUCH IT HURTS.

"Oh, Steven," I whispered in the stifling heat of my car.
"I love you too."

I dialed Charlie's number.

"What?" he answered.

"I'm in Orlando," I began, "and I want . . . I'd like . . . to
see you."

"I'm not going to be talked into anything," he said.

"Charlie, please. If you ever loved me at all, please just see
me for a few minutes. I'm not asking to see the boys; I'm just
asking to see you."

"I'm working, Kim, you know that."

"Are you planning to work all night?"

"No, but the boys are coming home this afternoon from
Atlanta and I want to be here when they arrive."

"I know that, Charlie. I talked with Chase and Dad yesterday when I took a break driving home. For Max's sake."
Not that it mattered when or why. "They said they'd be back
by 3:00."

Charlie sighed. "I have to be in Baldwin Park for a meeting
later today. Meet me at La Bella Luna at 5:30."

"I'll be there," I said.

"Don't be late."

"I won't." I started to say good-bye, but instead, "And
Charlie?"

"Yeah."

"Thanks."

———

The restaurant where Charlie asked to meet is near Lake Baldwin, one of Orlando's many bodies of water. A nice breeze was kicking off the lake, making for a perfect afternoon. I decided to dress nicely for our meeting and chose a coral halter empire-waist dress that stopped just above my knees and flower thong sandals. Other than a large coral bangle, I wore no other jewelry.

Charlie—who looked as handsome as ever—greeted me by sliding out of the booth and standing when I walked into the pizzeria. "You look good. Island life obviously becomes you," he said.

As uncomfortable as I was with the compliment, I replied, "Thank you," before sliding into the seat opposite him.

A young server came over.

"What will you have?" Charlie asked.

A beer served in an ice-cold mug stood between us. I looked from him to it and then to the server. "Coke, please."

Charlie chuckled when the server walked away. "I took the liberty of ordering a small pizza bianca for us."

We'd dined here before—when there'd been an "us"—and he obviously remembered how much I adored the pizza bianca. "Thank you," I said again. And this time, I meant it.

Charlie took quick control of our eating together. Of my wanting to talk. So, while we ate, I listened as Charlie shared news about the business, from his family and some of our old friends. Not once did he bring up the boys, so I finally asked, "How did Chase and Cody enjoy Atlanta?"

Charlie beamed. "They had a blast. Your dad was pretty

worn out, and I don't think Anise had the energy to get out of the car. But the boys had a good time."

I couldn't help but laugh.

When nothing was left but crumbs to the pizza, Charlie ordered two cups of coffee, then leaned in and said, "All right." His face turned stoic. "Tell me what you've come to say."

I took a deep breath, whispered a prayer, and said, "I want to make you an offer."

"I'm listening."

I drew my shoulders back. "Charlie, I have no intention of doing anything anytime soon, but I think that, yes, I will marry Steven and I will move to Cedar Key. Permanently."

My ex-husband opened his mouth, but I raised my hand to stop him just in time for the server to return with our coffees and to ask if we wanted red velvet cake for dessert. Charlie said that we did and to bring two forks.

"Keep going," he said when the server had walked away.

"When I do," I continued, "I want to make an offer. I'll petition the court to take off a third of your child support payment. We'll continue with every other weekend visitation, you'll get half the summer versus four weeks, and every spring break. On weekends with Monday holidays, you can keep the kids the extra day. Nothing else changes. We'll alternate Thanksgiving and Easter as before and Christmas Eve and Christmas Day as before. I'll drive halfway for their visits. Unless, of course, you'd like to just come to the island for a visit." I took a deep breath, exhaled. "I'm not offering low and hoping you'll counter. I'm letting go of wanting it all and truly . . . truly . . . making a sacrifice so you'll meet me halfway."

The server brought the red velvet cake to the table. Charlie picked up his fork, but I left mine lying tong down on the edge of the plate.

"You seem to have thought this through fairly well."

"I have."

His eyes bore into mine as he returned his fork to the table without taking a bite. "Has he asked you to marry him?"

I didn't know whether to be honest or not, but I decided to go with what was right. "Yes."

He looked at my left hand, then back to my face.

"I'm not wearing a ring until after he's had a chance to meet my sons. *Our* sons."

Charlie squared his shoulders against the padding of the booth's seat back. "I see." He pressed his hands against his thighs.

"Charlie," I said. "I want you to know something. I'm sorry if I smothered you or tried to control you when we were married." A sound like the wind being let out rushed from between his lips. "I've come to realize that this is one of my downfalls."

He shook his head. "It wasn't just you, Kim."

I leaned forward. "Then what was it?"

His head fell back and then straight again. "Ahhhhh . . ." He laughed a little. "I *did* love you, you know that, right?"

I nodded.

"And life was pretty good until . . ."

"Until?"

"Some of the crewmen at work . . . they were young, single. They went out after work for drinks. Told exploits of the women they'd been with over the weekend." Charlie shook his head. "They didn't have a responsibility in this world, and it just all became so tempting. And then there you were . . . Miss Merry Homemaker. There wasn't anything you couldn't do and do right. Perfect, in fact."

"So, then why, Charlie? Why give all that up?"

He shook his head again. "The collar just got a little too tight. The leash too short."

I didn't say anything for a while. We sipped our lukewarm coffee and nibbled at the cake until I said, "Are you happy, Charlie?"

"I'm doing all right."

"I see."

He leaned toward me. "But I want you to know something, Kim. I love our sons. Yeah, I've used them a little like pawns a few times, but I do love them. With everything I've got."

"I know, Charlie . . . but you have to be there for them when they're with you. I know we both deserve to be happy again, however we choose to find that happiness. I'm not here to dictate that to you, I promise. And just because we're parents doesn't mean we've stopped being human. But . . . just put yourself in their shoes, okay? Chase wants to make you proud and Cody just wants us all to be together again. Like we were." I shrugged. "And if not like we were, at least getting along."

"I think I can work on that," he said, his grin impish.

I pulled a folded piece of paper from my purse. "Here," I said sliding it toward him. "It's the stipulations I just told you about. I want you to have them on paper. I've signed it and dated it and even took it to the bank and had it notarized. All I'm asking you to do is think about it and let me know as soon as you feel comfortable."

He unfolded the paper, studied it for a minute, then folded and slipped it into the left pocket of his slacks. "I guess we're done here," he said.

"I believe we are," I answered.

There are four bridges leading into Cedar Key, but there is only one road. On Tuesday morning, just a few minutes before

10:00, I turned my Honda off US 19 and onto State Road 24 at Otter Creek. Fifteen minutes later I passed through the infamous Rosewood, Florida, where a racially motivated massacre occurred during the first week of 1923. Little evidence of the horror remains; just a black and white historical highway marker and the home of John Wright. Another fifteen minutes later, I approached Bridge Number Four, ironically the first bridge one comes to when approaching the island. The sun was directly in front of me. On both sides of the road, the dark blue water—dotted with dark green islets and little pink spoonbills and white egrets—stretched toward the haze along the horizon. Nearing the end, to my left, I noticed several men and women standing on the public pier, casting their lines. Two women read their books in lawn chairs under brightly colored umbrellas. To my right a pole rose high from the water. On its top, an osprey stood watch over the world from her nest. The traffic was light; I pulled to the shoulder of the road, got out of the car, and took several snapshots with the camera I bought before having dinner with Charlie.

The road leading to my home and to Patsy's was just ahead, but I kept driving, past the long pier known as Wooden Bridge Road and the maroon and white sign welcoming me and those like me—wayward children returning home—to Cedar Key. The speed limit slowed to thirty-five; I applied my foot to the brake and allowed the island to come to me slowly. Reverently, the way she ought to. This place, I marveled, truly is the land time forgot. And I thanked God for it. It was secluded and unhurried and—right then—it felt like it was all mine.

In front of the market, Maddie swept sand from the door to the sidewalk. She looked up just as I passed, waved, and I waved back. I stopped at 2nd Street, turned left, then right again on A. I immediately caught sight of Steven standing under the awning on his dock, writing something on a clip-board. He looked up as if he sensed my presence, dropped the clipboard on the nearby wooden bench, and walked to where I parked my car. I jumped out, Max right behind me, and ran straight into his arms at the edge of City Park. I buried my face into the curve of his neck, smelled the heat and sweat, and said, "With him all things *are* possible."

He craned his neck to see me better. "Are they?"

I nodded.

"I love you, Kimberly-Boo."

"And I love you, Steven Granger."

His kiss held all the passion it should and none that it should not. And when we broke apart, I wept. We were stand-ing right where we'd stood so many years ago—two kids just hoping to watch the sunset together.

Seeking Sunrise

Spring 1964

Patsy Milstrap sat on the passenger's side of the jet black '63 Ford Falcon Futura. Her husband, Gilbert—whose face seemed transfixed on the road before them—rested an arm over the steering wheel as though they'd not a care in the world.

Earlier in the drive from their South Carolina home to Cedar Key, Florida, and as the sun grew warmer, Gilbert had lowered the convertible top. It was now midafternoon. In spite of the scarf tied around Patsy's head and secured under her chin, her long hair had been whipped to a frenzy. Her face felt sunburned. She would ask Gilbert to raise the roof, but she couldn't find the energy to do so.

Besides, she liked knowing her body could still feel . . . something. Lately, she'd only wanted to slip between the sheet and the coverlet of their bed—the one she'd shared with Gilbert for nearly fourteen years now—cover her head, and sleep. Not her devotion to her husband nor her love for their children—five, ranging from four years of age to thirteen—could penetrate the pain she'd been living with of late.

Or had it been forever?

Clearly, she was dying, she thought. Clearly no one could hurt this much and survive.

And the pain . . . so deep . . . maybe even Jesus couldn't reach it. So deep . . . like the blue-green water on both sides of the road leading into Cedar Key, where Gilbert had rented a cottage for them. They would stay a week, he'd said. Just the two of them. The children could stay with his sister Janice and her husband. And their children. It would be like going off to church camp, he said, while Patsy and he would come for the arts festival Gilbert had heard about.

She liked art, didn't she? he'd asked.

And they would go boating. Take bike rides. Relax in the sunshine. It had rained so much in Trinity lately. It would do them *both* good.

Okay, she'd said. Okay.

"And maybe," he'd hinted with a wink, "we can snuggle like we used to."

Patsy closed her eyes at the thought. If she came up pregnant again . . . it would be worse than the other times. Every time, a little worse. Every time . . .

"We're nearly there," Gilbert chimed from beside her.

She opened her eyes, turned her head slowly toward him, and forced her lips to curl upward into a smile. She could do that much, right?

"Was that a smile I just saw?" he said. The deep dimple of his cheek came into view. "See there? One minute in Cedar Key and you're getting better." He squared his shoulder. "I knew this was a good idea."

Patsy looked back to the front of the car. A town—a little harbor town—was coming into view. Fishermen on a dock. Weathered hands pulling crab baskets from the water and into a boat. The scent of the marsh washed over her.

In spite of its pungency, she liked it.

"Are you hungry, Patsy? I'm ravenous."

She looked at him again, nodded. "Yes. A little."

The dimple returned. "See there?" he repeated. "Another good sign." The car slowed as they entered the city limits. "Let's get to the cottage, settle in, clean up, and find this place Walter told me about."

"Sikes?"

"Sikes Seafood. I'll bet the food is about as fresh as anything you can get on the coastline."

Patsy inhaled deeply. She liked a good fried shrimp. And deviled crab. She hadn't had that in ages. That with a baked potato . . .

The cottage was everything it had been touted to be. The cottony-white walls, the dark, rich furniture, the white eyelet curtains and bed linens, and the polished hardwood floors helped Patsy begin to relax. To feel that maybe her life was going to be okay. Even if only for a week.

A week in Cedar Key.

Patsy unpacked their luggage while Gilbert showered. When he was done, she took a quick bath, worked the tangles out of her hair, then brushed it until it shone. She worked it into a long braid that snaked over her shoulder, before dressing in a knee-length mint green A-line skirt with matching sleeveless blouse. She wore no jewelry, no makeup. Only coral-colored lipstick.

The way Gilbert liked it.

371

"Will you put the top up on the car?" she asked as they stepped from the front porch of the cottage. "It took forever to get the rats out of my hair."

Her husband slipped an arm around her waist. "Anything for my lady."

She sighed as he opened the car door for her. Allowed her to get in gracefully. Closed it. She watched him sprint around the front to his side.

He is trying so hard.

A few minutes later they arrived at the seafood restaurant near the harbor they'd heard about from Walter, one of Gilbert's business associates. He'd also told them about the tropical healing balm of the island.

Already a line was forming at the front door of the establishment. Patsy glanced at her watch. It was only five o'clock. She thought they would have been early enough. Maybe the food really was that good.

She waited at the end of the line while Gilbert gave the restaurant's hostess their names. He returned a minute later. "Fifteen minutes. That's not bad."

Over the fifteen minutes, she found herself drinking in the sights and sounds of Cedar Key. Already she liked it here. It called to her, like an old friend, and made her feel as though she'd been here before.

Seagulls soared overhead. Patsy craned to watch them, then lowered her chin to view them through the glass walls of the restaurant as they dove into the rhythmic waves below.

Gilbert slapped his flat stomach as they inched closer to the inside of the restaurant, drawing Patsy's attention from the white birds to the pressed white of his button-down shirt. "I smell good ol' fried seafood. I think I'll have shrimp. What about you?"

"Deviled crab."

He wrapped his arm around her waist again and squeezed. "Somehow I knew you'd say that."

"You know me well."

"Since you were no more than a pup on a bus."

"Milstrap, party of two?" the hostess called over the heads of the few hopeful patrons left standing in front of them.

Gilbert raised his hand. "That's us."

They entered the restaurant, Patsy behind the hostess, Gilbert behind her. It was all wood and glass. The walls sported lifesavers and nets with shells caught between the yarn. Large mounted fish. Stuffed replicas of tropical birds perched on beachwood. It was typical tropical, and to add to the setting, the Beach Boys sang "Surfin' U.S.A." from a jukebox.

The hostess stopped short before turning toward a man in dress casual attire. "Oh, I'm sorry," she said to Patsy and Gilbert. "Just a minute, please, while I ask my boss a question." She returned her attention to the man. "Mr. Liddle?"

At hearing the name, Patsy felt the air suck into her lungs before feeling her intake of breath. Gilbert's hands gripped her forearms.

The man stopped. Turned toward them. Smiled briefly. "Yes, Brenda . . ."

How could it be, Patsy wondered. How was it that here, in Cedar Key, she stared into a face she hardly recognized. And into eyes she would never forget.

Eva Marie Everson is the author of over twenty-five titles and is the Southern fiction author for Revell. These titles include *Things Left Unspoken* and *This Fine Life*. She is the co-author of the multiple-award-winning *Reflections of God's Holy Land: A Personal Journey Through Israel* (with Miriam Feinberg Vamosh) and, of course, the Potluck Club and the Potluck Catering Club series with Linda Evans Shepherd.

Eva Marie taught Old Testament theology for six years at Life Training Center and continues to teach in a home group setting. She speaks to women's groups and at churches across the nation and internationally. In 2009 she joined forces with Israel Ministry of Tourism to help organize and lead a group of journalists on a unique travel experience through the Holy Land. She is a mentor with Christian Writers Guild and the first president of Word Weavers, a successful writers critique group that began in Orlando and has since become the Jerry B. Jenkins Christian Writers Guild Word Weavers. She serves on its national leadership team.

Eva Marie lives with her husband, Dennis, and their fourth (and final) child, Jordynn. Eva Marie and Dennis are parents to three incredible adult children and the grandparents of the five best grandkids in the world.

Eva Marie considers a trip to Cedar Key the perfect respite.

Meet Eva Marie Everson at

www.EvaMarieEverson.com

Read her blog and learn
interesting facts!

Follow her on Twitter
🅑 EvaMarieEverson

You will laugh, cry, and fall in love with this stunning southern novel!

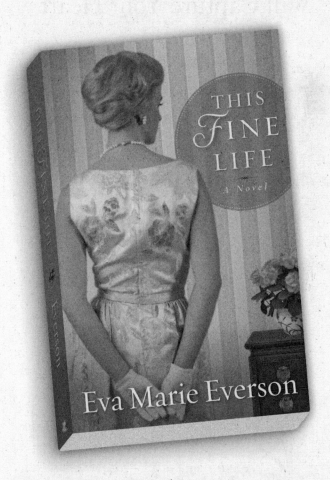

"*This Fine Life* proves that growing into love can rip one apart and quitting might be the easiest thing, but walking away is out of the question. I bled with these characters as they struggled to become who they were meant to be."—**Lauraine Snelling**, author of the Red River of the North and Daughters of Blessing series

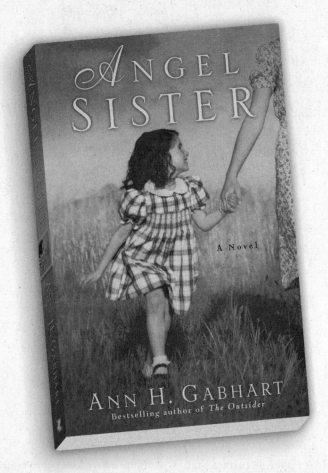

"Walsh demonstrates that, like Nicholas Sparks, men are capable of writing romantic fiction."
—*RT Book Reviews*

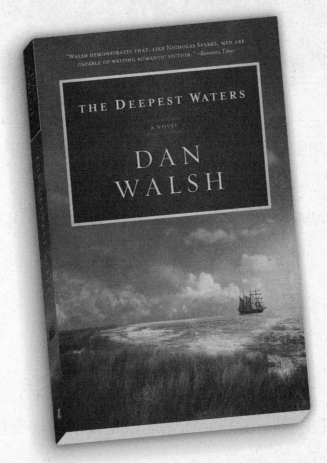

Talented author Dan Walsh skillfully tells an epic story through an intimate focus on two lost lovers. Inspired by real events, this moving novel will capture the hearts of all who dive into its pages.